One
woman

One
myth

Three
Goddesses

Love
& the
Goddess

Mary Elizabeth Coen

GoddessMECA

First published in 2013 by
GoddessMECA
www.goddessmeca.com

Paperback	ISBN: 978-1-909483-03-3
Ebook – mobi format	ISBN: 978-1-909483-04-0
Ebook – ePub format	ISBN: 978-1-909483-05-7

Produced by Kazoo Publishing Services
222 Beech Park, Lucan, Co. Dublin
www.kazoopublishing.com

Kazoo Publishing Services is not the publisher of this work. All rights and responsibilities pertaining to this work remain with GoddessMECA.

Kazoo offers independent authors a full range of publishing services. For further details visit www.kazoopublishing.com
Cover design by Andrew Brown
Printed and bound by CPI Group (UK) Ltd, Croydon, CR0 4YY

Contents

Foreword

*W*hen I sat down to write this book, I first considered doing a memoir covering a period in my life when dramatic events were an almost daily occurrence. Some were traumatic while others were inspirational, bringing healing along with renewed joy, hope and laughter. And so I wished to share some of the wisdom and systems of healing which helped me through a difficult time in my life – they are woven through the fabric of this story.

Ultimately I decided to respect the privacy of loved ones and acquaintances I met in Ireland and South America, including the wonderful Healer referred to herein. Instead I chose to write a work of fiction with as much authenticity and humour as possible. In the interest of the story having a realistic feel, I have, however, used authentic place settings, with the exception of the fictitious village referred to as Kiltilough in north Galway. No such place exists.

The Goddess theme is central to the story as Kate uses the names of each of the Goddesses in the myth of Persephone, Demeter and Hekate at various times on different internet dating sites. As she identifies with each Goddess, she attracts different men into her life who mirror some aspect of herself. Her voyage of self-discovery and healing takes her from Galway in the West of Ireland to an Ashram in rural

Brazil and on to the Andean highlands of Peru.

This is entirely a work of fiction and any similarity to people, living or dead, is purely coincidental.

Chapter One

*I*t was my dream home, the kind I'd always imagined living in as a child. There was something reassuring about old houses with meandering ivy wrapped around them like a lovingly hand-woven comfort blanket. Yet now I sighed as I took stock of the house where I had lived for the past twenty-three years. What was wrong with me? I should be glad to be home. It was the last day of term and three months of summer lay ahead of me. No more trekking into Galway in rush-hour traffic, no more teaching temperamental young cookery undergraduates all determined to be the next celebrity TV chef.

I turned off the car engine. A flock of swallows darted among the orderly row of evergreens which flanked the house like soldiers on sentry duty. The rigidity of the trees bothered me. I'd always thought that trees, shrubs and flowers should be planted in sinuous beds, curving languidly as nature intended. But there was no convincing a man who liked everything to conform to straight lines and neat geometric shapes. Being married to a perfectionist had its challenges and sometimes I felt that – unlike this house – I didn't quite live up to them.

Taking a quick peek in the rear-view mirror, I pulled out my make-up purse from my bag and applied a slick of red lipstick. Grabbing a brush, I attempted unsuccessfully to transform my flyaway copper red mane into well-defined layers. Still far from perfect. With dark shadows under my eyes, I looked as if I'd been plugged into an electric socket and left there to fry. Hardly surprising – today had been the most unpleasant ending to a college year I'd ever had, with my worst student threatening to challenge the mark I'd given him for his practical exam.

I grabbed two plastic bags of shopping from the back seat. Things had been more strained than normal between myself and Trevor, so tonight I'd planned his favourite meal. Struggling up the steps with my lecture notes and the shopping, I noticed that the front door stood ajar. My stomach fell. Trevor was home ahead of me. Why today, of all days? I'd hoped to have everything ready before he came in from the surgery.

Inside, after kicking off my court shoes in favour of indoor pumps, I slipped my files on to the hall table. Tucking my white cotton blouse into the waistband of my skirt, I anxiously tried to make myself look presentable. Part of my plan had been to change into something a bit more elegant than the navy work skirt Trevor was always scowling at. My black cocktail dress was hanging waiting in my dressing room, but there was no time to change now. I'd have to straighten myself up as best I could. "I'm home", I called out. The scent of disinfectant hit me and I guessed he was in the kitchen. Had I left a mess this morning? Anxiety fluttered in my chest. I was sure I hadn't – so what had he found to clean?

When I pushed open the kitchen door, he was standing with his back to the Aga. A shard of sunlight came through the French windows, hitting the arrangement of copper pots overhead, causing them to twinkle in all their polished glory.

The kitchen was spotless, exactly as I'd left it. I heaved an inward sigh of relief. "Trevor. You're home early?"

His brown eyes met mine and he made a half-hearted effort to smile, sweeping his hand through his wavy salt-and-pepper hair. Recently, he'd started to look older, the lines on his forehead deepening and crows' feet settling into more permanent folds around his eyes and mouth. Despite my being fourteen years younger than his fifty-eight years, I still found him more attractive than any other man. I dropped the shopping on the floor beside the island unit, and stood on tiptoes to kiss his lips. He turned away, a distant expression on his face, and pulled out one of the high-backed wooden chairs from the island. "Sit here."

"In a few minutes." Unnerved by his snub, I headed to the fridge to take out a bottle of wine. "I've had such a day. Ron Clarke claimed he'd overbaked the lobster because my notes were wrong. Imagine him blaming me. He'd completely botched the timing. And his Tarte Tatin was hopelessly undercooked. And then he said I'd better give him a distinction or he would challenge the result." My words rushed as I struggled to uncork the wine. "Dear old James had to give me a hug in the staff room. He said I should take a break from it all by joining him on some mad trip to Peru." Smiling, I turned to hand Trevor a glass of wine.

He didn't take it. "Kate, please sit. We need to talk." His tone was curt.

"Talk away." I forced another smile. I was determined to remain upbeat in the hope of diffusing his strange mood. I placed the wine on the counter and reached for the shopping, hauling out a bag of risotto rice, shiitake mushrooms, and a bag of prawns. "I'll have your favourite dish rustled up in jig time." Droplets of melted ice fell from the bag of prawns on to the granite work top. I could feel Trevor wince and imagined him doing mental arithmetic on the bacterial count. Sure enough, he grabbed a bottle of anti-bacterial spray and placed it in front of me with a thud.

"You talk too much and never listen," he said.

"Me, listen?" I threw down the bag of prawns, reached for a dish cloth and furiously squirted the spray around. "I'm trying to multi-task here."

His voice was low as he spoke: "I want a divorce."

I felt as though I'd just been slapped across the face. Did I hear right? "What do you mean?" I knew I was standing there like an imbecile with my mouth open, but I couldn't do anything about it.

"You heard me. Come on. It's no surprise. We've been strangers these past couple of years."

My head was reeling. I put my two hands up to my temples. "I thought we were going through a rough patch. I thought we'd be all right in the end."

"The rough patch has lasted too long. You've never been the same since he died."

His words twisted a knife in my heart. I drew a sharp breath. "Of course I've not been the same. How could I be? I can't just pretend it never happened. It's not my fault I couldn't just box it up and package it neatly the way you do with everything. Hardly a reason for divorce, is it?"

"Plenty of other reasons." He spat the words at me. "You always wanting me to go to therapy despite the fact I think it's a load of rubbish. I've a bell in my ear listening to you quoting that so-called 'therapist' of yours, yet he hasn't managed to get you off sleepers, has he?"

"That's rich coming from you, since you're the one who prescribed them in the first place, along with those awful anti-depressants – which I've only just managed to ditch, by the way."

"Yes, against my wishes. At least Prozac kept your mood even!"

"Turned me into a spaced-out Stepford wife, you mean. Do you realise how absurd your supposed logic is regarding pills?" I shook my head, confused by what he was saying. His increased eagerness to point out my every fault had certainly not helped my mood of late. But divorce? I couldn't fathom it. I blurted, surprising myself, "Is there someone else?"

"Yes." He lowered his head.

His confession hit me like a tsunami. "Who?"

"Martha."

"No. No!" I was conscious of myself shouting, and could hear the incredulity in my own voice as realisation hit. "Not… Martha?" I searched his face in the hope this was some sick joke but his expression remained stoic. Surely this could not have happened with *her* of all people, his dowdy secretary. My mind flew. I'd noticed she'd smartened herself up, had a new haircut… But, *Martha?* "How could you do this to me? I love you more than my own life!"

"Kate, I didn't plan this. I'm sorry."

"Does it mean anything that we are a family? What about Julie? Does she matter to you at all?" I gestured weakly to the family photograph on an overhead shelf. Julie's trusting smile now seemed out of place as she sat between us. Taller than me, with a full-toothed smile and effortlessly erect posture, she was strikingly like her father. I stared at him. "Does … Does everyone in the village … Do all your cronies at the golf club know about this?"

"Nobody knows. This has not been going on behind your back. It happened unexpectedly. I'm sorry, Kate."

His compassionate tone was more than I could bear. "Did you wait until I was old to dispose of me like I was a second-hand car to be thrown on the scrap heap?" Seized by a fiery gripe in my lower belly, I wrapped my arms around my abdomen in an effort to hold back the mounting pain. "You always loved getting new things and throwing away the old, didn't you? My child-bearing years are over so I'd fail the good old NCT test. Is that it?"

"Your age has nothing to do with it." He shook his head, his voice becoming practical, factual. "I constantly compliment you on your style and how well you look. You look better now than you did at twenty – you even laugh at yourself in that picture of the hippie dress with your hair all curly. You've come a long way since then."

"Well, despite me molding myself to suit you, it didn't work did it? I suppose I should have seen the signs when Martha lost weight and started dressing like me – or rather, the way you like me to dress." I placed my hands on my hips. "You're a veritable Professor Higgins in your ability to groom women. They should offer you a job on *Extreme Make-Overs*! You'd save them a fortune in plastic surgery."

Trevor gave me the kind of bored look I'd become accustomed to whenever he wished to dismiss me. The look that made me feel annihilated, like I no longer existed. "I'm not staying here tonight, Kate, when you're becoming hysterical." He strode towards the door but caught his foot on the bag of shopping, the contents spilling out on the floor. Muttering under his breath, he kicked a honeydew melon into the hallway where it hit the skirting board with a thud.

I followed him as he climbed the white painted staircase and marched down the corridor to our bedroom. There I stood, watching him from the doorway as he crossed the room to slide open the wardrobe doors. The room was perfect; all cream and gold, spotless mirrors, not a crease on the duvet cover. Why had I bothered? I had to get up half an hour earlier than I needed to, to get the house exactly as he liked it before I left for work each morning. Why had I bothered?

He hauled down a canvas overnight bag, reaching for a nearby alarm clock to throw in. It was only then I realised the bag was already packed – blue-striped pyjamas and socks sitting on the top. Registering how prepared he was, I wanted all hell to break loose. "Hysterical, am I? Your favourite word for describing women. Martha's welcome to you. She'll have her work cut out with you once she finds what a bloody perfectionist you are to live with."

He shot me his trademark smirk. "Don't pretend you haven't enjoyed the benefits of my high standards, Kate. Other women would kill for seven-star holidays in Dubai and Vegas."

"Everywhere we went was fake and sterile and shallow. I hated Dubai and the pretentious plastic people. And the only good thing about Vegas was the Indian reservation."

"Is that what you really thought? Well I hope you enjoy staying in a flea-infested hut on your next holiday to Bongo-Bongo land."

I recoiled, shuddering. "Martha really is welcome to you. She doesn't know how misogynistic you are. All she sees is the charming, caring doctor. Once she sees the extent of your God complex, she'll find out how big your ego is. And boy will she have to pander to it."

A moment later, he was down the stairs, and as the front door slammed behind him I collapsed on the bedroom floor sobbing, remaining there for what seemed an eternity, rocking to and fro like a baby as I cried my eyes out. Why me? I kept asking. And how had I not noticed anything? Trevor used to refer to Martha as "a frumpy country girl" so I'd presumed he was indifferent to her, found her boring even. Yet Martha, for all her fake smiles, had a disturbing way of narrowing her eyes when speaking to me. I had always felt she was too possessive of Trevor. Why hadn't I said anything? When she'd given herself a makeover, I'd wondered if it could be for the benefit of a man. Yet I'd dismissed any suspicions about her, reminding myself that she was a great organiser and an invaluable asset in Trevor's practice, convincing myself that any thoughts that she could have designs on him stemmed from my own insecurities. Or so I'd thought. Now it seemed that Trevor and Martha were not the only liars and cheats. I had placated myself with my own silly placebo of delusion.

Hauling myself off the floor, I wandered from room to room, mulling over the arguments we had had, the sulky repressed silences that could have resulted in either of us killing each other had we been so inclined. But no. We were too civilized for that. Instead we had stuffed down our growing resentment of each other, in the hope everything might work itself out. "Damn you, Trevor!" The walls and high ceilings echoed back my cry. I stared at those same walls in the vain hope they might offer me some consolation. After all, they had witnessed laughter more often than tears and shouting. In the first year of our marriage we had made love in so many different places, even on the stairs. It was funny to think of Trevor having been so enthusiastic as to tolerate the wooden edges digging into his back. Framed photographs down the stairs reminded me of family occasions like Julie's Holy Communion. I remembered the time, as a three-year-old, she had chanted out a verse from Roald Dahl's Revolting

Rhymes and we had fallen about the place whooping with glee, while the scent of muffins baking in the Aga filled the house. But what now? How was I going to tell Julie that there would be no more celebrations, that life could never again be the same?

I crawled into the living room shivering, despite it being a warm night. Wrapping a rug around my body, I curled up and sobbed until my nose became so stuffed I could no longer breathe. While I was daubing them with a sodden tissue, my swollen eyes caught sight of the hunting scene on the opposite wall. Scarlet-coated men sat on horses while a dog delivered a bleeding pheasant in its mouth. Trevor had bragged that it was an investment piece but I'd detested it from the minute it arrived into the house. There was my dishonesty again. I'd told him it was great, in an effort to please him.

Jumping up from the sofa, I strode across the hall to open the closet door and pushed a line of coats aside. I rummaged around until my fingers came upon a large flat package. Hauling it out, I tore aside brown paper, revealing a silver-framed picture. I hurried back into the living room and lifted down the wretched hunting scene. In its place I hung "The Triple Goddess", my cherished limited-edition print by Susan Seddon Boulet which I'd purchased from a Dublin art dealer.

I would never forget the look of utter disgust on Trevor's face when I'd excitedly showed him this print, holding it up in the hallway. He'd been about to leave the house for a game of golf. He'd scoffed, "God, Kate, it's about time you grew up. It's like some fantasy poster Julie had in her bedroom around the time she collected 'my little ponies'."

I'd been shocked. "It's by a very celebrated Brazilian

Shamanic artist. I'd thought about hanging it here in the hall. Do you really hate it that much?" I had hoped he would see how much it meant to me.

He stood sneering in the open front door. "Hippie stuff, no more than the silly dream catcher and carved wooden thing you bought at that Indian reservation outside Vegas. Return it to the gallery and get a piece of sculpture instead." The door slammed shut after him as tears pricked my eyes. I'd felt angry and hurt but I'd decided not to force my idea of art on Trevor, convincing myself that he was right – that the print would not be in keeping with the décor of our home. So instead I chose to hoard it with all my other secret treasures in the back of the closet.

Now, in defiance, my picture was hanging in pride of place. In shades of yellow, orange and green, the three faces of the Goddesses called to me – Virgin, Mother and Crone. I stood back and soaked it in. An eagle emerged from the central Goddess's head, along with a variety of symbols from lizards to a full moon and a lioness guarding a human baby in a lotus flower. A secret passageway and butterflies blended subtly into the fabric of the Goddess's clothing.

Everything in the painting symbolised transformation.

As I stood there entranced, I could almost imagine a mist enveloping me. Swept up in the picture's dream-like imagery, something stirred from deep within. Throwing my shoulders back, I straightened my spine as a tingling started in my toes and travelled all the way up my legs. This picture had been my secret guilty pleasure and now it was my first act of rebellion. It was the proverbial two fingers up to Trevor's stifling notion of convention. The feeling of a woman being one with nature was not something he would ever understand, never mind tolerate. In my defiance, I felt a spark of hope; a glimmer of the will to survive along with an urge to live life on my own terms from now on. Pleasing others had gotten me nowhere.

Chapter Two

*B*efore I could do anything, Julie had to be told. It was terrible timing. She was a second-year law student in Dublin, and about to head off to Boston for a three-month placement with a law firm. Our only opportunity to tell her that her family had fallen apart would be during the fleeting visit she planned to pay us on her way to Shannon airport.

Trevor collected her from the train station in Galway city. I stayed at home, busying myself in packing the clothes she had asked for from her wardrobe. As I was filling a plastic toilet bag with sun-block, sachets of shampoo and conditioner, I heard a key turn in the front door and hurried out on to the landing.

Julie came through the door first and I ran down the stairs to embrace her, stroking back her long dark hair. "What's going on, Mum?" Her tear-stained brown eyes studied me in disbelief. "He told me you two were breaking up!"

Trevor was walking in behind her. "Come and sit down," he said, steering us both into the living room and pointing to the sofa. I sat down, but Julie remained standing.

"I can't understand why you have to divorce at your stage in life," she screeched at me.

Taken aback, I jolted upright. Obviously, Trevor hadn't told her the full story. "You'd better ask your father."

Trevor was shifting uncomfortably in his armchair. "Like I said, your mother and I simply grew apart. Our relationship has become a battleground. It must have been difficult for you to witness during the past few years."

"Oh cut the crap, Trevor, and have the guts to tell her," I snapped.

"Julie." His eyes searched hers. His voice was pleading. "I've fallen in love with Martha. I'm not proud of the fact, but we can't choose who we fall in love with …"

Julie interrupted, her voice raised. "Martha? Your pathetic little secretary?" She moved to stand over him and he also stood up and tried to embrace her, but she crossed her arms like two swords to fend him off. A glimmer of satisfaction almost caused a smile to escape my lips. But I suppressed it. Right now, Julie's feelings were more important than revenge.

Trevor drew a shaky breath. "You have every right to be angry, Julie, but a part of me will always love your mother. I think she is the most wonderful woman I ever met. You were born out of love and nothing will ever change that."

"You love me …?" I was on the point of blurting out more, but thankfully stopped. A voice inside my head was telling me to hold still. Getting over-emotional could cause me to lose control and make a fool of myself. I wanted to be calm for my daughter's sake. Julie didn't seem to notice my tone; her eyes remained fixed on her father. "Well, don't expect me to give you a blessing. For an intelligent man you're a self-centred idiot. Now if you don't mind I'm going to finish packing." She moved away abruptly.

I said, "I have the big black case laid out for you, Julie. I've added everything you put on the list. All you have to do is finish up. The kettle's on for tea and there are sandwiches and scones in the fridge."

"Thanks, Mum." She closed the door firmly behind her. Her footsteps faded down the marble tiles of the hall to the kitchen.

I turned on him. "Why didn't you tell her about Martha?"

He avoided my eyes. "The words just wouldn't come out. I knew this would be deeply upsetting for her." He paused nervously. "I want to thank you for not labouring the fact that I am the one to blame. I appreciate that you didn't point the finger at me, Kate."

"Good. I'm delighted you can appreciate something about me after twenty-three years together." As I spoke, his head was turning in the direction of the Goddess picture. His face assumed a look of incredulity before filling with grave concern. He was obviously worried about the whereabouts of the hunting scene. For a moment, I wondered what he'd say if I told him I'd slashed it and thrown it out with the rubbish. I waited. He could choose to ask me directly or sweat it out until he came across it at the back of the wardrobe in the spare room.

"Kate?"

"Yes? What?"

"I don't want you to think I'm suggesting anything to you, but should you ever wish to live in Galway city, I'd have no hesitation giving you the apartment. You've always loved it."

Live in the apartment? It took me a moment to register what he was saying – he was expecting me to leave the house? I took a deep breath. "Well, thank you, Trevor. That may come in handy for the odd weekend. Yes, I think I could avail of that." Judging by his expression, his offer hadn't been received in the manner which he'd intended. I wasn't going to give up my home that easily.

There wasn't much time to spare before Julie had to leave. Trevor waited in the car while we said our goodbyes. Julie threw her arms around me and kissed me. "Look after yourself, Mum. I can't believe he fell for her when you are so much better in every way."

"I know Julie. Don't worry about me. I love you. Be gentle with yourself and eat well, won't you?" She'd always seemed so capable, but I knew she could be hard on herself. I worried about her going it alone in a strange city after finding out her parents had separated, but the decision had been made months ago.

"Yes, Mum." She was smiling. "Don't worry. I'll be fine. Look after yourself."

But as she sat into the car beside Trevor, she was obviously struggling to hold back the tears. Trevor was fussing over her, checking the seat was in the right position, that she was comfortable. It reminded me of the early days of our dating, when he used to call me 'Princess'. I felt a strange tinge of jealousy that he would never again regard me as special.

I knew it was only a matter of time before the whole village would be talking about the doctor ditching his wife for a younger model. Rumours must be spreading like wildfire with, I was sure, bits and bobs embellished as they went from person to person.

I tried to live like a hermit by parking my car around the back of the house and avoiding people as best I could. But eventually, I knew I had to venture out. I needed bread and milk and I couldn't drive into Galway again or call Tesco's to deliver the basics. It was a case of visiting the local supermarket or living like a hostage for the rest of my life.

I knew if Ella had been here she'd have come to my rescue with the essentials, but she was in Greece running a conference and I still hadn't been able to speak to her. I'd left her all manner of messages but usually turned my own phone off, so when she did manage to get free from team building and marshalling two hundred executives from breakfast to dinner, all she'd been able to do was to leave voicemails: "Hang in there, Kate. I'm back next week. Just hold on." She was my best friend, and I knew from her voice that she felt terrible about not being able to be with me.

I drew in a deep breath, as I parked my car in the supermarket car park. I had to do this or I might starve. Heading for the back entrance, I passed the local bank manager's wife, who I knew well. She had her head stuck in her car boot as she meticulously rearranged her bags of shopping. I glanced back as I passed her, to find her staring at me. "Hello, Sandra. How are you?" I summoned as cheery a voice as I could manage.

"I'm fine. In a terrible hurry." She blushed as she scurried around to the driver's door. I felt my stomach turn over. Was this how it would be? People I'd met and chatted to every day until now, suddenly avoiding me, too embarrassed to speak to me? Grabbing a shopping trolley, I braved it and headed into the supermarket. It was early in the morning and members of staff were stacking the shelves. I lingered by the vegetables. Orange baby carrots gleamed through their clay coating, smelling of freshly turned earth. Cauliflowers plump like cabbage patch dolls winked at me, suggesting a killer soup, bursting with vitality. Beside them sat velvety aubergines and crinkly celery in pale green corrugated sticks. Focusing on what I could do with all these lovely ingredients distracted me for a moment. Food had always been my thing. Family celebrations had seen me spend days preparing gargantuan amounts of food to thrill everyone, from my gourmet father to my sister Liz, who qualified as the crankiest dieter on the planet. The role of nurturer sat well with me and I'd developed all sorts of tricks for making food irresistible. Nothing pleased me more than to see guests stagger out my door, not from drink but from a belly weighed down with overeating.

Now there would no more celebrations to cook for. I found myself thinking it would seem like too much trouble to cook for myself. A shiver ran through me as I registered how lonely I felt as a single woman. Then a voice in my head scolded me with: *So, are you going to abandon yourself and let yourself become a waif? A pathetic victim? And what about always warning Julie to eat well? You hypocrite!* No. I wasn't going to let Trevor take away my enjoyment of food and cooking. As I was filling my trolley, a voice cut through my thoughts: "So, how are you?"

I spun around. An old woman was peering at me. Her face was familiar but I didn't know her name. I said, "I'm well and how are you?"

"I heard about your break-up."

I opened my mouth to reply but nothing came out.

It didn't stop her. "You're lucky to be breaking free at your age. Men get very bossy as they get older. Set in their ways. Your fellah was too old for you anyway. I had to wait for my auld fellah to die before I could get a bit of peace."

How could I answer that? "Well, thanks for telling me." I smiled and turned away. I understood the veracity of her words. But advice, no matter how wise or kindly the intention, now seemed overly intrusive. I somehow numbed out and began hurling whatever came to hand into the trolley. In my search for tinned tuna, I stumbled into the pet food aisle, looking at food for a pet I didn't own. Instead of kitchen paper, I mistakenly pulled down a bag of disposable nappies. My heart sank as I registered this mocking reminder of my passing years. I suppressed an urge to scream and hurl them down the aisle before a cheeky thought intervened to cheer me up. Maybe I should bring them to the checkout counter. That would really give the locals something to talk about.

It was clearly well known that Trevor had moved out, yet it didn't stop some of his patients calling to my door "looking for the doctor" after hours. That was the problem with being married to the only doctor in a small village, especially one held in such high esteem. Later that evening an old man arrived, puffing pipe smoke into my face as he spoke. "As you know yourself, this house has been in Doctor Canavan's family for three generations. I'm not taking no sides but I have to tell you the doctor's family wouldn't be too pleased to have you staying on here."

His words rattled me. I closed the door as politely as I could without slamming it shut and collapsed against it, my back to the cool wood. I felt the tears pricking. I knew it would be foolish of me to uproot my life in response to an old man's ramblings, yet it felt like he was right. The house belonged to Trevor and I'd always felt it was only on loan to me. His family might descend on me at any time, like praying mantises. He had offered me the Galway apartment, an investment property he had purchased in the Celtic Tiger years. Clearly he didn't think he had any chance of selling it for a profit now. And so why shouldn't I live in it? I was beginning to think that it might be in my best interests to make a clean break from the small world of the village and start my new life elsewhere.

Chapter Three

Ten days later, after a morning spent shopping for household essentials, I drove out along the coast road to Salthill, taking a right up Taylor's Hill. My apartment was in a restored former convent, elegant and stone-faced; set back off the road, it overlooked the promenade like an elderly aunt.

Pulling into the hidden car park behind the building, I found James, my friend and colleague, had got there before me. He was leaning against his ancient blue Aston Martin, the back window of which was piled high with last year's lecture notes and tattered cookery books. As I got out, he came towards me, put his arms around me and hugged me close. I reached up on my tip toes into his reassuring embrace. At least I still had one man in my life. Gulls squawked overhead and the westerly breeze carried the scent of seaweed from the beach.

"How are you?" He relieved me of my shopping bag.

"So-so." I balanced my right hand like a weighing scales. "It's still a bit of a muddle."

"Of course it is, but I have every faith in you building a wonderful new life for yourself." He sounded very British. His eyes scanned the house with its tiered terraces and domed Mansard roof. "I have to hand it to you, this is some building."

"It was an old convent, developed during the boom." I squeezed his arm. "Thanks for coming over."

"Delighted, my dear. But you do realise now you're living so close, you may never get rid of me?" He paused to exclaim over the fanlight and ornate stonework, as I turned the key in the double glass doors. On the far side of the hexagonal atrium, floored in mosaic tiles, was another door of heavy mahogany which led into the entrance hall. James opened it for me, with a flourish. His nose twitched as the scent of cooking greeted us. "Cloves. Someone's baking apple tart. How delightful – you live in a communal kitchen."

I laughed. "That's apartment living for you. Somebody on the first floor cooked a powerful curry last night." I glanced up at the ornate glass roof, shielding my eyes from the sunshine flooding down. Rows of heavy dark-stained doors surrounded by bevelled wooden architraves formed part of a continuous curved wall, cleverly devoid of sharp corners. I led the way down the blue-carpeted stairway to the lower ground floor. James followed, stroking the polished mahogany balustrade of the staircase which snaked around all four floors like one huge serpent. "The Church didn't spare any expense."

"Seems not. We bought the apartment from a developer before prices went sky high in the boom years, but we've had problems renting it lately – a sign of the times." I turned the key in number two. The entire apartment was drenched in light, pouring in through the large casement windows, their shutters opened wide. I stepped over a CD player on my way into the living room. "Mind you don't trip over any of the crates."

He wasn't listening – oohing and aahing, he was taking

in the high ceilings, wooden floors and original wainscoting. The day before I had scoured the local Oxfam shop for a patterned floor rug and two throws to cover the sorry-looking sofa. In shades of sapphire, amethyst and jade, they co-coordinated well with a curved Tibetan wall unit and the teardrop central light which tinkled like an earring in the breeze. I'd stumbled over the cabinet in an auction room and fallen in love with it immediately.

"This is a good move for you, Kate. I feel like I'm in Ali Baba's den." James threw himself down on the sofa, his camouflage jacket clashing wildly with the throw.

"I've always loved tales of the Arabian Knights," I said.

He pushed back a length of light brown hair as he looked approvingly around the room. His green eyes were set wide on either side of a slightly crooked nose, broken during his binge-drinking years. It was eleven years since he'd quit and entered a twelve-step program. He raised one quizzical eyebrow at the wooden figure sitting on one of two deep window sills. "Is that the carving from that Indian reservation you're always on about? Who is he?"

"Kokopelli. He plays his magic flute, which stands for creativity. Maybe he'll inspire me to finally write the cookery book I've always been promising to start. God knows, I've invented enough recipes to fill ten books. You have too. We could do one together."

"I should have known who he was – I'm the one heading off on a Shamanic trip. I could do with some inspiration to get my creative mojo back, but I'll leave the writing side of things to you. Here…" He pulled a book out of his jacket and handed it to me.

I studied the well-worn cover, stifled a half laugh. "*When Things Fall Apart* … a depressing yet appropriate title."

"It got me through some tough times, Kate. The woman who wrote it got her life together after her husband left her. Do you know the Chinese word for crisis also means opportunity?"

"I could have done without this opportunity, thank you very much."

"Don't be cynical, Kate. It's a positive way of looking at your situation. Think of it as an opportunity for self discovery. Speaking of which, I see you've finally found the guts to bring out that picture you like so much." He nodded at the Goddess propped against the wall. He had been with me on the day that I'd bought it.

"I know. Who'd have thought it would spend five years hiding in the back of a cupboard? I'll have to get you to hang it up for me."

"I won't do a single thing for you until you promise me you'll join me in Peru. You were full of excuses before. Now your time is your own."

I smiled a wry, sad smile, "You're right. For the first time in my life I can do whatever I want. When will you be there?"

"I'll have finished my three-week stint cheffing in Club Med Mexico by the end of July. We could meet up in Cusco early August."

I nodded slowly. *Cusco.* It sounded fabulous. But it was a big step heading off on my own – even if I was meeting James. "I know there's nothing to stop me. Just give me some more time." A grin twitched at the sides of my mouth. "Do you think I could possibly meet a straight version of you?"

James rolled his eyes, then turned serious. "Kate, don't make the mistake of thinking you need a man right now. Learn to love yourself first. When you're vulnerable you'll attract the wrong type. I know you're feeling rejected and wounded. But a man won't fix you."

"God, you'd certainly know you were into 'working through your crap' as you call it. Why do I bother paying a shrink for advice when I can get the same spiel from you for free?"

"Because he's a professional and I'm not. I just work my own process. Anyway someone close to you doesn't always offer the best advice." He struggled forwards on the soft sofa. "I've got to head off, but now I know where you are I'll come back to help with the rest of the unpacking. Are you all right for groceries?"

"I can manage with beans on toast for now. I'm pretty exhausted. I think I'll chill out in front of the television." And I hugged him goodbye.

Yet "chilling out" proved impossible. Anxiety was something I'd never been able to conquer. After a sleepless night in the grip of a demon, the first thing I did was book an appointment with my psychotherapist – the one Trevor insisted spouted a load of rubbish.

"At long last." Aidan Whyte made an exaggerated gesture of joining his hands together as though going into prayer, bowing his head. What was he suggesting? I wasn't in the mood for complex mind games. Without meaning to, I lashed out.

"I'm here to be consoled! Not mocked!"

He ushered me inside his consulting room before he replied, nodding to the receptionist who sat filing her nails. "Kate, you've been coming for counselling on and off for many years. Trying to put sticking plaster on a marriage problem way bigger than the sum of its wounds. This may seem …"

"What are you talking about?" I leaned forward to stare at his round face, his thin spectacles sliding down his upturned nose. Judging by the amount of laughter lines on his thirty-something face, it struck me that he must find the business of other people's problems quite amusing. I'd have thought it would depress the life out of most people, yet here he was dressed in a cheerful blue chambray shirt, cream trousers and matching sneakers, looking like he existed on a diet of positive thinking.

"Kate, you've been in denial. You never wanted to look at the state of your marriage. You wanted to believe you would wake up one day and everything would be hunky dory. Trevor would never agree to join you for counselling, yet you thought you could fix it all by yourself."

I couldn't keep the amazement out of my voice. "You really thought that and never told me? What was I paying you for?"

"I tried to get you to see it. He never wanted you to be a woman in your own power. He always had to be in control. This may seem like a crisis to you now, but believe me when I say it is your greatest opportunity for personal growth."

"Yeah, right. James gave me that line too. He even gave me that book by Pema Chodron." I rolled my eyes heavenwards.

"Great book, that. I was going to recommend it to you. And yes, your friend can see that you're a woman capable of grasping life – in a way you never felt free to do within the confines of your marriage."

"That's easy for you to say. I certainly don't feel that way. I'm forty-four, I've got a twenty-year-old daughter, and my husband's run off with another woman." I wrapped my multicoloured cardigan tight around me. "My marriage meant everything to me. I don't know how I'll survive without Trevor. I married him when I was twenty-one."

"And you've never had time to find out who you are. Now's your time." He held his hands out, beaming as though he were handing me Aladdin's magic lamp. If only he could have done.

"But I'm nobody without him. I thought I was, but these last couple of weeks have been horrendous. People I thought were friends avoiding me, like rats leaving a sinking ship. Trevor's friends and their wives have passed me by in their cars, pretending I'm invisible."

"So what's your problem? Most of those women never had an independent career. They rely on their husband for whatever status they think society affords them. Some may be clinging on to the last vestiges of a dying relationship. If that's the case they don't need you to remind them of that. Anyway, you've always been well able to put social climbers in their box. Am I right?"

"Suppose." I shrugged my shoulders.

"There are others, like the old woman you mentioned, who think well of you. If you constantly seek the good opinion of others you give away your personal power. Now you are starting a new life in the city, so leave the past where it belongs."

He was right. I knew deep down he was absolutely right. I looked at the emerald on my left ring finger and began frantically polishing it with the edge of my cardigan. It was all so much to take in. It wasn't just the end of a relationship, it was the end of my whole life as it had been. I was realising that now, and I needed to move on.

"It's just such a shock to be suddenly shunned after having socialised with these people all my life. People I had thought were friends. I feel like I've become my worst nightmare – the shunned single mother, all alone with nobody to love me."

"Start by loving yourself, Kate. Essentially we're all alone and it's good if you can learn to live with that for a while and get to enjoy your own company. What you had with Trevor was a co-dependent relationship." He leaned forward, slightly bridging the divide between us. Feeling uncomfortable I crossed my legs and in the process swivelled my chair towards the door. "Neither of you knew where one began and the other finished. Eventually that becomes claustrophobic. You told me so yourself. He constantly told you what to do and where to go. When he could no longer do that he found someone else he could control. Am I right?"

"I don't know," I said, biting my lip. Whatever the reality might be, I wasn't ready to accept it. My gaze once again dropped to my ring, as I found myself fidgeting with it. I couldn't forget the good times, they lingered in my head like a soothing nostalgic scent – and they had been good. Once. "In all my years with Trevor I never met anyone as gentlemanly as him."

"A self-individuated woman does not need a man to validate her. Why are you so hung up on having a knight in shining armour?"

"I don't know." I frowned and looked sideways, avoiding his eyes, still fidgeting.

"Maybe I've always believed in a happily-ever-after. I didn't date many men before Trevor. In fact the only lasting relationship I had was with the boy next door, and that's because Billy was the nearest thing I had to a brother. Trevor was my first real romance and I thought we were perfect for each other." I paused. "It's so hard to accept that it couldn't last forever."

"I know, Kate. But nothing in life lasts forever. And remember bad things fall apart so that better things can be created. Learn to embrace being on your own and start by being gentle and loving with yourself. And as I've said already, start approving of yourself and forget about seeking external validation from a man or anyone else." He raised one eyebrow, before asking, "Do you intend wearing the emerald ring going forward?"

"Of course," I said defensively. "You know how important this is to me. I've taken off my engagement and wedding rings, though I feel quite exposed without them. But I'll never part with this one."

"Oh, I wasn't suggesting anything of the sort, Kate." He placed his palms together in his prayer-like manner and raised them to his lips. After what seemed like a considerable time lapse, he asked, "How's Julie?"

"She's in bits. I'm worried about her and worried that I will try to poison her against her father."

"At least you're aware of that. The most important thing is to reassure her that it's not her fault. Children regularly blame themselves when their parents split up. And try for her sake to hold back on criticizing her dad. After all, he is half of her."

I nodded. He was right. I wasn't sure if it helped to hear it out loud or not, but he'd given me a lot to think about.

He said, "Call me if you feel you are getting worse, but between now and our next session I want you to think of all the things you wish you had done in life but haven't been able to because of your marriage."

Chapter Four

After four consecutive attempts to brown my toast, I turned the switch on the toaster up to maximum and went off to the bathroom. One of the problems with a new kitchen was getting the hang of everything. I felt a pang for my Aga and my copper pans, for the huge granite work surfaces. I'd designed it to be a real cook's kitchen. As I was washing my hands, I was suddenly shaken by the sound of a deafening *bleep … bleep … bleep.*

Heart thumping in my chest, I raced into the kitchen where I was enveloped by a cloud of thick black smoke. Wading through, I hastily unplugged the toaster. Flames were leaping from the slot where my toast had been. I grabbed a fire blanket and threw it over the choking appliance. Then, like a maniac, I searched for the fire alarm, scanning up and down walls through the thick fog only to discover it embedded in the high ceiling. No chair or counter high enough to reach it, I opened a window in the hope it would stop bleeping of its own accord. Just as the smoke was dying down and the alarm stopped, the doorbell rang. I looked at the intercom screen. Surely it wasn't the fire brigade? Relief flooded over me at the sight of Ella's face peering into the camera. I pressed the button, opening the front door, flapping my hands madly to clear the smoke as I ran down the hall to meet her.

"God, Kate, have you set the place on fire already?" Ella was fighting a smile as she handed me a bottle of wine, her mane of dark hair framing her heart-shaped face and swinging about her shoulders.

"No, just burned some toast. How was your trip?" I hugged her close. "I've missed you."

"Good, conference was mad, did you get my messages? I must have tried to phone a hundred times, the reception is terrible out there and I kept missing you. How are you?"

"Much better than I was – I can't get used to living alone, and I think I might have ADHD, but I'm alive."

She hugged me hard. "I'm so sorry I wasn't here when you needed me. I should have come."

I stepped back and looked at her aghast. "Ella, this is your biggest client, your biggest gig yet. You couldn't just up and leave in the middle. You've spent too long building your business."

"But…" A concerned look came over her face as she studied me up and down. She put her two hands on my upper arms, kind blue eyes focusing intently on mine. "Kate, love, I know what you're going through. I've been there and it's terrible. I should have been here."

"Ssh, and let's get this bottle open. I want to hear all about the conference and Greece."

She followed me into the living room. "Have you been eating? You're no more than skin and bone."

"You know me. I always eat, but if I'm anxious my metabolism races and I lose weight. I spend most of the night tossing and turning, so that fairly burns the calories."

"Yes, divorce is a sure fire way to lose weight. Calories going up in smoke! But you need to mind yourself, Kate. Promise me you'll mind yourself, lovey?"

"I promise," I said, smiling at her concern. "Wine?"

"Would you mind if I had some tea? I know the wine will go straight to my head – how about some of that Lapsang Souchong you always have?"

"Coming right up." I headed into the kitchen and put the kettle on to boil.

Ella followed me. Leaning over the white Formica worktop she reached across to pick up the box of tea, inhaling the scent. "What's your fascination with this stuff?"

"It reminds me of childhood. There was a storage shed at the back of our house where I used to go to read. It was filled with my father's old furniture from his parents' house, piled up in a sort of kamikaze mountain. As I climbed to the top, everything would slide and slip threatening to disintegrate beneath me. I could have killed myself.

But I always felt elated when I finally got to sit up there." I pulled down the teapot, warming it with water from the boiling kettle. "I used to curl up beside an old tea chest – it smelled of Lapsang and was full of old books, Greek mythology, anthropology, books on ancient civilizations and fairy tales. Sometimes I'd find tea leaves stuck between the pages. The scent of Lapsang brings me back to those magical worlds I read about." I poured Ella her tea.

"No wonder you're such a romantic, Kate. When I was a kid I read nothing but the Beano."

"My father loved those books. He used to read to us at bedtime. I think he would have liked to be an anthropologist but he was afraid to follow his dream and did law instead."

"Following the dream isn't always easy. Look at me – with this recession, everyone is organizing their own parties and launches."

"But you have a great client base built up."

"Thank goodness, and as long as they need conferences

organized in far-off places with sunshine and beaches, I'm there!"

We laughed.

"Here, come and sit down inside – are you shattered?"

In the living room, Ella eased her shapely legs into the velveteen tub chair as I took the sofa. She tapped manicured nails against her mug as she spoke. "You need a bit of fun in your life, Kate. Trevor's crushed your spirit. Why don't you have a look at one of the Irish dating sites and see what the talent's like? A lot of people are using them now. You need to be careful though, you're in a vulnerable place and men can take advantage, but you need to start getting out again."

"God, Ella, aren't those dating sites just the same as the personal ads in newspapers? I thought only people with no personality used them?"

Ella grinned at my surprised face. "Not at all. That thing of meeting someone in a pub or a club doesn't work when you're over forty. Everyone's on the internet now. In fact, I'm thinking of putting up a new profile."

"I never knew you did that. You never told me."

She smiled mysteriously. "It never arose because you weren't in the market for a man. Have you got the computer set up?"

"Yes. It's in my bedroom."

"Ooh, come on then, let's have a look. Listen, I'll open that wine while you do a search. We'll need a glass or two to get us in the mood – go on ahead in and Google dating sites. I'll be there in three minutes." Seeing my worried expression, she continued, "Ah come on, you need a bit of fun in your life. What harm can it do?" Ella's advice ran contrary to everything James and my shrink had said, but then Ella never went for safe and sensible if there was a fun alternative. Her enthusiasm reminded me of the good old days at boarding school when she was always up for a laugh. Seconds after I'd logged onto the site, Ella sashayed in with two glasses of wine. "How are you getting on?"

"I have to use a username. What'll I call myself? I mean I'm not really going to use this, but I can't use my own name."

"Use some name you like from the myths you're always talking about. How about the Goddess of Love?"

I smiled, glancing at her nervously. "I can't use something obvious like Aphrodite. That could be misconstrued as slutty. How about Athena? She's the goddess of justice, war and industry." I bit my lip, thinking hard. "No. She's too serious. Oh, I've got it. Persephone. I feel like Persephone right now – I spent a long time in the underworld, living under Trevor's obsessive compulsive regime of constant cleaning."

"Nice name," nodded Ella. "Who is she?"

"She's the daughter of Demeter, goddess of the harvest, and Zeus, king of the gods. When she was playing in a meadow, Persephone was seized by Hades and carried off to the underworld to be his bride. Her mother was so distraught, she searched for her throughout the world with help from the crone goddess, Hekate. Demeter refused to attend the earth until her daughter was returned. In the end, Hades gave in but because the girl had tasted of the food of the underworld she was forced forever to spend half the year there. She comes back to the world in spring each year, bringing new life and new growth with her."

"Hmm … Sounds rather depressing."

"But the story ends with the spring arriving." I was convinced it was the right name for me. "She was a victim and as vulnerable as I am. But it's a tale of hope, with her growing into her role as queen of the underworld. Persephone's return each spring shows her becoming a powerful woman as she helps her mother in nurturing the earth. The fact that she can walk between both worlds signifies her ability to balance her emotions – sorrow, loss and anger, set against joy, peace and serenity."

Ella's brow creased in a thoughtful frown. "Okay, I get it now. I took psychology in my first year at university. I think Carl Jung was into that stuff."

"That's right. I have his biography there." I cocked my head in the direction of the book shelf.

"Type in Persephone, then. See if the site accepts it." Ella took a sip of her wine.

I clicked. "It's accepted. Oh, no ... There's a questionnaire before you can continue."

"Crap, I forgot that bit. We'll do that later when I've convinced you this is the way to go. Click 'answer later' to all questions. Same on the next two pages." I did as Ella said and came to a page with the words "find your match". "Now you can start a search." Ella sidled in closer to have a full view of the screen. "Fill in the age group. What ages are you interested in?"

"Hmm ... Trevor was fourteen years older than me, so maybe go younger this time. How about 'twenty-five to thirty-five'?" I laughed at Ella's horrified expression. "I'm joking!" I typed in forty-four to fifty. Photographs appeared down the side of the page, with age and occupation stated opposite. The usernames and captions were listed on the right. It was quite a range.

"Click on him – he's a fine thing!" said Ella, enthusiastically pulling my clothes off the bedroom chair and pulling it over beside me. "It's quite addictive you know."

We looked through nineteen profiles, which included

photographs along with a list of what each man was looking for in a woman. Age, profession, marital status and whether someone drank or smoked were filled in along with what kind of relationship they were seeking: friendship, a date or a casual fling. Many of them sounded a bit overly serious and quite off-puttingly needy. I looked wide-eyed at Ella. "I can't believe the number of men on this. And some are better-looking than you'd see around. Is it really that difficult for them to find the right girl?"

"Too busy to socialise. But we haven't looked at what's available in Dublin yet. Go on, do a search for men in Dublin. The choice is bound to be miles better. Then we'll have a look at the women." She reached for my empty glass. "I'll top you up. Have you any nibbles?"

"Peanuts in the cupboard beside the fridge." I started a new search. "You're right, they are *much* better in Dublin!"

She was back moments later, grinning, the bottle under her arm and a bowl in her hand. "Move over! I'm dying to have a look."

"There's still some strange looking yokes but I've saved six of the best in a favourites option. What'd you think?"

"God yer man with the dark hair is gorgeous. Oh, he's a doctor." She nudged my elbow. "Imagine if you nabbed him! You could swan back into the village with a younger, better-looking version of Trevor. Give him a taste of his own medicine." She giggled at the pun.

"That sounds totally corny … But you know something, it would be such fun!" I was laughing. "But you know, I won't. I mean, you said yourself it's not the right time."

Her face fell as the prospect of mischief seemed to disappear. "Let's look at the women, age thirty-five to forty-five."

I clicked on the next section. "God, Ella. Some of these women are fabulous. What are they doing here?"

"Kate, if you ask that one more time, I'll punch you. I'm telling you, this is the way it's done now. Everyone wants to be online in case they miss out on their perfect match. After all, you're really widening your net here – anyone could end up contacting you. My sister's friend Jennie is gorgeous and she's doing internet dating. Do you know who she met?" She lowered her voice to a whisper.

"Who?"

"The owner of *Blaze* magazine."

"You're joking me. What was he doing on line? Doesn't he date models?"

"There you go again, spouting prejudice. These sites are affiliated to all the main publications, so you never know who you might meet. Now before I leave I want you to fill out your profile because I know you will chicken out if I don't make you."

"Look, both James and my therapist told me to give men a rest while I tried to heal and even you yourself have said I'm vulnerable."

"Avoid men? Are you mad? What you need is an ego boost and a bit of fun. I wonder how eagerly the pair of them would embrace celibacy. Now click on the profile page and I'll help you fill it out."

I did as she suggested and brought up the questionnaire, filling in answers to specific questions like what height, age, weight, star sign, marital status and occupation I had. When it came to the more general questions suggesting I write a paragraph about who I was and what I expected, my shoulders tightened. " '*I would describe myself as ...*' What do I answer to that since I don't really know who I am

– 45 –

anymore?" I searched Ella's face.

"Attractive, sociable and good fun, then list your hobbies," she said, with a wave of her hand.

"No, that sounds presumptuous. How would I know if a man could possibly find me attractive or good fun for that matter? I mean some of those women on the site have a lot more *va-va-voom* than I could ever have." I made a curvy gesture with my hands to indicate the female form. "As well as that, I've forgotten who I am. No, it has to be light-hearted or I can't do it." I paused and then began typing as inspiration came:

"Hi there, I'm an intelligent and creative yet slightly off-beat red-head with an adventurous spirit. I gave up my career as a Bollywood Star to pursue my real passion for ancient civilizations (I love mythology along with Incan and Mayan legends) but while I study that by night I work as a TEACHER by day to pay the bills. My friends tell me I'm attractive, sociable, a good dancer and great fun so they'll remain on my Christmas list for at least another year. Have recently taken up Taekwondo and scuba diving in preparation for my future career as a Tomb Raider."

"Great!" Ella's eyebrows arched in amusement. "But it will confuse a lot of them –they'll think you're serious!"

"Sod them if it does. Under career, I've written 'teacher' so if they don't get the humour, they can go elsewhere. Now, what's the next part?" I peered at the screen. "My ideal man? Haven't a clue. Let me think. Okay, got it." I typed:

"The man I'm hoping to meet has a laid-back attitude. He is active and fit enough to give me a run for my money,

yet will always treat me as an equal. He will not only put up with my messy creative pursuits, perhaps he will join me in cooking for large gatherings of friends and family. I'd like him to dance with me, rather than march through the rest of our lives. An adventurous spirit along with a positive outlook would complement me and in the process provide us with endless laughs and opportunities to broaden our horizons. If this sound like you, then feel free to get in touch."

"Right, next you have to put up a couple of photos… Yikes, listen lovey, I'd better run. I wanted to make sure you were okay but I haven't even unpacked yet. This was great craic and at least I got you set up. Will you take me internet shopping some time, since you know all the sites for discount designer gear?"

"That's more my usual thing – instead of shopping for men!"

Chapter five

*P*arking in front of the sprawling red-brick college building, I hauled out my big black folder from the passenger seat, tucking it under my arm as I crossed the tarmac. Despite my current crisis, I had had to face reality and return to college to enter my students' exam results.

The double doors opened automatically as I approached, revealing blue- and white-walled corridors. As I strode towards the staffroom an increasingly loud whirring merged with the fog of depression in my brain until, rounding the corner, I bumped smack into a large industrial floor polisher. My results folder flew out of my arms, shooting A4 pages into the air. As they fell in a heap, the cleaning woman fussing and apologising, Mike Darcey, head of my department, emerged from the nearby staffroom. His left eyebrow shot up at the sight of me gathering up my notes; a smirk escaped the corner of his mouth. "In a spot of bother are we now?"

"I'm fine, thanks. Just on my way to log in results."

"Call to my office when you're finished, will you?"

Two days previously, I had rung him to explain why I was running slightly late with my results. I'd given him the potted sanitised version of the Trevor situation. He'd been strangely conciliatory, given that I'd always had a difficult relationship with him since I'd started working here ten years ago. Reassuring him that I would call, I opened the door of the large common room. The place was deserted apart from the endless files and mountains of books piled high on every available surface including the chairs. The grey linoleum floor was equally hazardous, littered with more books and plastic bags. I often wondered about teachers having this strange ability to function among orderly chaos – it had to be a hangover from their student days. Maybe it's because they had never had an in-between period of not belonging to this particular system.

I spent the next two hours filling in results and typing in comments on each student's progress before making my way to Darcey's office.

"Take a seat, Kate." Mike Darcey pointed to the chair in front of his desk as he jumped into his black swivel chair. The seat was pumped up, giving him the appearance of being taller than his five feet six inches. He had a cringe-worthy habit of tossing a long lock of hair over his bald spot, drawing further attention to it. From across the desk, his eyes narrowing to slits, he seemed to be assessing me. With his flat nose and tiny mouth set in pale freckled skin, he reminded me of an albino corn snake swamped in a brass-buttoned navy blazer. "So you and the doc are really finished?" He always tried to use language in a "cool" way, but as usual it came across as painfully inappropriate.

"Yes. Trevor and I have broken up."

"Well, don't be stuck for someone to talk to. You can phone me anytime, you know. You and I haven't always seen eye to eye on department procedures but I think that was partly because of a certain chemistry between us. Now that you're single, our relationship should be much easier. My own marriage has been over a long time. I'm just sticking it out for the kids and will be leaving as soon as my youngest daughter finishes school."

I looked at him, baffled. "I'm sorry to hear about your marriage."

Standing up, he walked around to sit on the edge of his desk in front of me. My stomach turned. His breath stank, especially when he came so close as to invade my personal space. Feeling decidedly uneasy, I peered at my watch. "Gosh, look at the time. I'm so sorry, I really have to go." I stood up, fumbling with the buttons of my jacket.

"Oh." He appeared taken aback, as if he was reassessing his position. "Just one last thing before you leave. Did you resolve that dispute with Ron Clarke – his grades – something to do with lobster?"

"Yes, it's resolved." What the devil did he mean? I'd resolved it by not allowing myself to be bullied by a student. End of story. I turned to go. I felt his hand on my arm.

"Kate, don't be nervous. Remember you can call me anytime. I'm your friend."

"Okay, right." I pulled my arm away and headed out of the door as fast as was humanly possible without making it *really* obvious that I was about to throw up. God, this was absolutely the last thing in the world I needed right now. I'd always thought he was an insidious creep but I'd never thought he would try to assert his power over me like that. It felt strangely vulnerable to be a single woman. I'd forgotten what it felt like to be hit on out of the blue by a married man of all people. While I craved some form of admiration after having been rejected by Trevor, I definitely didn't want it from Darcey – of all people!

Ella was about to leave for a week-long conference in Kerry two days after James departed for a visit to his parents in the UK. I called over to see her as she was finishing her packing.

"I'd ask you to come with me if I thought there'd be any fun, Kate, but this crowd are so boring I'll need intravenous caffeine shots to keep me from falling asleep." Her eyes shot heavenwards. "Will you be all right for the week?" She pressed an elbow on top of her case as she pulled the zip shut with the other hand.

"Don't worry, Ella. I'll go for long walks, do a spot of reading and spend some time sorting out recipes. I'll be fine."

"Why don't you go to Dublin? Stay with your parents?"

"Like everyone else, they're on holidays right now. Gone to Spain with Liz and her family. Don't worry about me. I'm not a child."

"I am worried about you, because all of a sudden you will have nothing to do. You could go round the twist thinking about old times with Trevor. What about your Taekwondo class – are you still going to it? You made a few friends there."

"It's finished for the summer. Please stop worrying, Ella." Then, sheepishly, "Look – I've been thinking I might try a spot of internet dating."

She was delighted. "Good idea. Get yourself online and start dusting off your long-forgotten dating skills." I must have looked startled because she nodded her head vigorously: "Believe me, yours are well and truly in need of updating. And for that reason, I need to give you certain pointers."

"Pointers? Am I that green?"

"Believe me – you are."

"So, what do I need to know exactly?"

"Listen carefully, for I shall say this only once." This was one of Ella's favourite sayings, always delivered with hands on her hips and spoken with a French accent *á la* the 1980s television comedy *'Allo 'Allo*. I'd often sat down with her to watch a DVD from her box-set collection. I enjoyed the humour, but I was never riveted to the extent she was. "Number one: People may not be who they say they are or even the person in the photograph. Anyone can hide behind a profile. Do not give anyone your real phone number. Which leads me to number two. Buy another mobile phone in case you wish to speak to someone. Do you get me, Kate?"

"Yes, Ella." I saluted and smirked. "It all seems so covert. I'm beginning to feel like Mata Hari."

"You don't want a potential stalker having easy access, now do you?"

I nodded, finding it hard to keep a straight face.

"Number three: Rather than specify Galway as your place of residence, insert 'Ireland', thus widening your net. If a man is really into you he'll travel to meet you or you can meet him in Dublin. Number four: If you get on well with someone, that's your time to tell him you live in Galway. Otherwise you may appear shady or disingenuous. But – and this is a big BUT – do not tell him your address until you feel you can trust him. Promise?"

"I promise, Ella," I said, in a little girl voice.

"By the way, how's Julie getting on?"

"Great. She's good with emails. She's made a few friends and is planning a trip to New York. I think the break away came at the right time for her."

I'd advertised myself as "being on the singles market" and now pictures of men were scrolling across the top of the screen like battery chickens on a conveyor belt. Ella was on the other side of the country, and emails were pouring into my inbox. With my over-vivid imagination, I felt as though I was being stared at by hundreds of men, here in my room, and felt literally hot and bothered, not knowing whether it was from embarrassment, excitement or the dreaded onset of hot flushes. From time to time, as I worked through my emails, I had to grab my mouse mat to fan myself.

Some of the pictures were downright creepy. One guy with the username "Reginald" looked just like Norman Bates in Psycho: his face half in shadow, eyes staring out of a grainy black and white photograph. To cap that, he appeared to be cyber-stalking me, firing copious emails every time I logged on. I could have used the blocking facility, but I hadn't because he had been kind, sympathising with me about my recent break up. I knew I had a tendency to jump to harsh judgements which were really just silly prejudices. If my recent predicament was anything to go by, I wasn't a great judge of character.

I had sent an email to "Serotonin" aka "the doctor", but the site indicated he hadn't logged on during the last week. Maybe he had found someone else while I dilly-dallied deciding whether I would get involved in this or not. My indecision may have cost me. "But," as Ella had said, "you never know who might crop up at any given time."

There was one I thought of as "the auld fellah". Looking ancient enough to be my father, he was pictured sitting in a big brown armchair dressed in his Sunday best, grey hair parted to the side. He called himself "sexyboy". A message from him said, "Hi sexy, would you like to meet up?" "No thanks," I felt like saying. "Not on a desert island, even if I hadn't met anybody else for ten years." I decided not to answer that one and made a mental note that if he cropped up again I'd have to block him because seeing him would make me rush to take the vow of celibacy and exchange my lodgings for a real convent.

Someone else was using a picture of Ben Stiller, which I did not immediately recognize as I didn't consider him to be the archetypical heart-throb actor. Set among this lot, however, he stood out as drop-dead gorgeous. Another picture featured a man wearing a dinner-suit, seated at an outdoor garden table looking like a 1970s advertisement for Mateus Rosé. I hadn't contacted anyone apart from the doctor, but I'd trawled through countless profiles in the age group forty-five to fifty. I was the new kid on the block and the site highlighted new users. Some contacts, noticing that I'd checked their profile, messaged back, "Thanks for checking me out. I hope you like what you saw lol." (What on earth did 'lol' mean?) Some didn't seem to bother reading about me while others read my profile too literally, failing to see the joke – just as Ella had predicted.

A message from *"Bobdbuilder"* was similar to several others asking about my Bollywood career:

Inbox:
From:Bobdbuilder
Subject: famous
I was thinking you looked like someone famous. Which Bollywood film were you in?
Fancy meeting up for a drink?
Bob

Reply:
From: Persephone
Subject: It's a joke

Sorry to confuse you, but if you read my profile carefully you'll see it's a joke. I am a teacher.
Kate

The next one made me laugh so I answered it:

Inbox:
From: iwanttofly
Subject: pretty
Hi sweetie. Youre lookin so pretty in your dress. Youre lookin jus like a butterfly comin out a flower.

Reply: From: Persephone
Subject: re. pretty
Thanks for your compliment. I wouldn't mind having a pair of wings.
Kate

This was absurd. I hadn't spoken to anyone in such a babyish manner since Julie was six years old. *Iwanttofly* sent me three more emails about me looking like a butterfly, possibly on account of my picture showing me wearing a silver and pink lace dress, which I'd worn as a guest at a wedding. I saw he was Greek, so that explained his poor spelling. Others had no such excuse. As I scanned through my mail, my inner teacher kicked in, spotting bad grammar and spelling along with a general level of immaturity usually associated with pre-adolescents. The usernames were by and large uninspired and some of them were an absolute turn-off. Take *"spudsgalore"*. I wondered if he grew potatoes or gave a bag of spuds to the love of his life rather than a bouquet of flowers? Hmm

– maybe that was romantic if it was given with love?

Someone with no picture mistook "adventurous" for a willingness to be "up for it sexually" and asked me was I interested in a threesome. As I blocked him, I wondered what on earth I was exposing myself to.

Yesterday I'd bought a cheap pay-as-you-go phone registered under a fake name and address. I'd also set up a separate email for the dating business. I really was beginning to feel like a Russian spy. And I had a strange feeling of guilt – given that I was a mother, this did not seem quite proper. Also, I was a teacher responsible for sending students out into the world and this dating business felt juvenile. But perhaps it was my time to be silly and throw a certain amount of caution to the wind. I'd always followed the rules and been a sensible girl and look where that had got me.

One of the few men to understand my profile without my having to send several explanatory emails was a man called "*Wordsmith*", aka Alan. After exchanging a few friendly emails, I agreed to speak with him on the phone. And since we chatted like old friends, I agreed to meet him when his work brought him to Galway later that week. He told me he was an agricultural consultant with a passion for writing, and seemed well grounded with a good sense of humour. Also, he was very sympathetic about my break-up and offered me advice about how best to handle my divorce. The only problem was that afterwards I felt that I had shared too many personal details, despite Ella's repeated warnings whenever she rang to find out how I was getting on with the site. Quite simply, he had the kind of manner and voice that seemed to inspire the sharing of confidences – rather like a priest in a confessional.

A few days later, as I scanned through my mail on the

site, a new message came in from *"Wordsmith"* asking me would this evening suit to meet up, and if so where?

I messaged him back, suggesting the nearby Ardilaun hotel would be ideal.

I hadn't anticipated being so nervous. After all, this was not a guy I expected to fancy – although I knew I couldn't be sure of that until I'd met him. Arriving into the hotel bar ten minutes late, I did a quick scan of the room. I immediately thought he must not have shown up, and was oddly comforted by that thought. A man and woman in their thirties sat at one of the low tables. Several men sat in the extreme right corner drinking beer, their bodies tense with excitement as they watched a replay of the day's rugby match. Then I spotted an elderly man dressed in a crumpled jacket worn over a grey round-neck sweatshirt. He nodded in my direction as he descended from a bar stool. I turned around to see if there was someone behind me whom he had recognised… then froze as it dawned on me that this stooped grey-haired man could be *"Wordsmith"*. But he had named salsa dancing and Tai Chi as his hobbies! And his photo had projected such a vibrant, youthful image!

"Hey, Kate. How are you?" He extended his hand to me, while bending to kiss me on the right cheek. A whiff of something musty immediately assailed my nostrils. I glanced distractedly at the bar, wondering if it had been wiped with a dirty dishcloth. God, after spending so many years living with Trevor, had I become as cantankerous as him?

"I'm good. Sorry for being late. I hope you weren't waiting long?"

"No. Just enough time to get a gin and tonic." He led me in the direction of the bar where his glass stood almost empty, and I climbed on to the stool beside him. "What would you like to drink?"

"A glass of water, please."

"Oh, come on. That's not a drink. You should be celebrating your freedom. You're free of your husband now, Kate. It's the start of your new, exciting life."

"All right then, one gin and tonic. After that, just water."

Alan turned out to be pleasant to chat with and quite forthcoming about his own experience of marriage breakdown, having been divorced ten years with three grown-up boys. But when I looked at his grey face with its loose jowls, wide nose and bulging eyes, I was reminded of a toad. He looked considerably older than his photograph and he soon confessed to having lied online about his age – he was fifty-two, not forty-five, and looked even older than that. Despite my initial eagerness to meet any man who could possibly fancy me, it had turned out to be quite different in reality. On most profiles, the men talked about the need for chemistry. I'd had loads of chemistry with Trevor – before Martha, at any rate – so I'd begun to wonder if it was that important after all. Now looking at this guy, I figured out that when chemistry was lacking, I'd have more fun playing bingo with OAPs.

Alan regaled me with his dating stories. "Lots of women are just online purely for sex. Seriously! I've had loads of women contact me asking to meet up. Some of them married women. Once I tell them my job brings me round the country, the offers come flying in."

I studiously sipped my drink in an effort to hide my face, which had surely turned pink from embarrassment. Recovering myself, I pitched a bold question and made direct eye contact. I was not going to let him intimidate me. "And do they say they're only interested in sex?"

"Oh, yeah. Definitely." He briefly touched my knee. "And some of the women have told me about strange men they met on the sites. You need to be careful, Kate. An attractive woman like you. There are a lot of very weird people out there. It's not so easy to meet someone right."

"I can well imagine. I don't really know what I'm doing online, to be quite honest with you – I'm still traumatised by my marriage ending. I probably wouldn't be able to form a relationship just yet."

"Well, don't rule it out because you can never predict when you'll meet the right person. Life doesn't work that way. So stay open." He touched my arm reassuringly. "You need someone to talk to, Kate. It's good to talk to someone like me who has been through the same thing because the early stage is very raw."

"Thanks, Alan. That's kind of you. Your phone calls have been a support." Suddenly aware that I'd had two gins and tonics to Alan's four, I asked the waiter for a glass of water. Never one to tolerate much alcohol, I was now feeling somewhat disorientated.

"You are such an incredible woman. Your husband must be a very foolish man to let you go."

These words brought tears of self pity to my eyes and I found myself telling Alan about Martha stealing Trevor from under my nose. What had come over me? "I don't know why I told you that." I anxiously squeezed my hands together on my lap. Cupping his hands over mine, Alan gazed at me reassuringly,

"It's good to get it off your chest. It'll help you heal. You can trust me." He moved so close I felt my personal space being invaded. Now I realised where the moldy smell came from. Alan's clothes smelt musty, like he'd slept in them for the past five months without washing. I was sure I could also detect sour milk and silage. I knew he acted as a consultant to dairy farmers, but surely the least he could do was wash before meeting a woman for the first time? On top of that, it seemed like Alan felt my confidences allowed him to presume I was easy prey.

As he finished his fourth gin, he again touched my knee. Then he grabbed my wrist tightly and – locking my eyes with a narrow gaze – blurted, "Now that I've met you, Kate, I'm never going to let you go."

Aagh! Yuch! Alarm bells were going off left, right and centre as my stomach heaved. *I'm not going to be a bird in a cage for you or anyone.* It was difficult not to show my horror, yet I didn't feel I could go just yet. Wishing to change the mood and give his hands the slip, I asked him about his love of reading and creative writing. "I love Oscar Wilde's wit and use of language." I freed my hands from under his, and sipped at my water.

"Oscar Wilde was not a great writer. His language is overly descriptive – too flowery. He's not in James Joyce's league. I'm presently doing an evening course in creative writing and everyone says my writing style is similar to Joyce's. You need to forget about Wilde." He patted my knee.

I covered my mouth to stifle a yawn. I had trusted this man and now he thought I was so naïve that he could completely dominate me by overruling every opinion I held. His clothes were not the only things stinking up the atmosphere – his arrogant attitude had a pong all of its own. I disliked him more with each passing minute spent in his company. Now a flurry of yawns were emerging from behind my hand. I glanced at the clock on the wall. "God, I never realised it was so late. I should go now."

"You look exhausted, Kate. What you need is a good massage to liven you up and help get rid of all that tension. I did a course in sports massage." He looked at me in the way a priest would when offering spiritual advice, his tone mellifluous as he continued. "I'd love to see the new apartment you told me about. Do you want me to come back with you?"

"No thanks. I really have to go." I hopped off the barstool, grabbing my bag. "I have an appointment in the morning."

"Hey! Hang on a minute! Kate!" he called to my fast disappearing back.

Freedom had suddenly become a much cherished commodity as I escaped to what now seemed like the bliss of solitude.

Chapter Six

mails on the dating website were mostly ridiculous but for the first time in my life I was placated by empty flattery, partly due to the fact I didn't necessarily have to deal with the person behind it. Strangers telling me I sounded interesting or looked great was the ego boost I craved, irrespective of whether it carried less substance than a sickly-sweet giant lollipop. It had become increasingly compulsive to log on and see if anyone interesting had contacted me. Although from now on, I would be more careful about baring my inner thoughts. I had learnt my lesson.

After entering my password, the site highlighted that I had five emails in my inbox. I opened the first one to find *"Iwanttofly"* now telling me I looked like a flower and asking if I would meet him for coffee. I really didn't see that as a runner.

The next few were all inane small talk. I opened the final one: *"How about you and I meet to explore the hidden world beneath the sheets?"* I flushed hotly. Who did this man think he was to address me as though I was a hooker for hire? A look at his profile told me he was a hypnotist from Bulgaria living in Dublin. With a curly moustache, he looked like a circus ringmaster – a right control freak with glinty eyes under thick dark brows. I was in the middle of blocking him when a new email popped up. To my utter astonishment it was a reply from *"Serotonin"*, aka the doctor Ella and I had spotted on the first night.

Inbox:
Hi Kate,

Delighted to hear from you. I would love to take you out to dinner the next time you are in Dublin. Just let me know. I attach my contact details. Maybe you could text me yours and we can arrange to meet up.

Eddie

Reply:
Hi Eddie,

Great to hear from you. I will be in Dublin next Friday night if that suits. What part of Dublin do you live in? Maybe we could chat on the phone beforehand? I will text you my number.

Kate

Since Ella had warned me about men not being who they said they were, I decided to conduct an internet search for the doctor. Up came three pages on a cosmetic surgeon in Dublin. My initial reaction was to think this could not possibly be him, as nobody in that position would ever go on a dating site. Then Ella's voice rang in my head, telling me to stop being so prejudicial.

I checked his details and clicked on his clinic's website, *cosmosclinic.com*. Scrolling down their list of specialists, I found him listed with a photograph – undeniably the same person with whom I was in correspondence. A press release issued by the clinic cited it as one of the top centres for cosmetic surgery in Ireland, with Dr Commins's speciality being facial reconstruction after accidents. *How noble*, I thought, *but it probably means he's totally out of my league*. I was sure he must have an endless supply of young women running after him. But there was no harm in trying. At least I could find out if I could possibly be a contender at my age.

Late Friday afternoon, I arrived at my parents' house in Dublin with my hair freshly blow-dried in loose curls. I'd done my make-up before leaving and was wearing a deceptively simple silk dress with an overall print in subtle shades of smokey brown and tan. With leggings underneath it looked quite casual teamed with brown ballerina pumps. It would be easy to swap the flats for higher heels before heading out on my date. The fabric made me feel feminine and flirty and it felt good to make an effort to dress up. I would get my mojo back and prove to myself that Trevor had been wrong to turf me out.

It was oddly consoling to be back among the familiar walls of my parents' simple four-storey house, with the comforting scent of lavender, geranium and lemon pervading every room – my mother had a penchant for making her own pot-pourri.

"Kate, you're looking very glamorous," my mother said, taking me in from head to toe before kissing me on the cheek. She looked well after her holiday. The sun had faded her auburn highlights somewhat and her skin was turning from sunburned to lightly tanned. Judging by the fit of her floral blouse, she had recently gained a little weight around her once-slim waist.

"This is the new me, Mam," I said, twirling. "I've changed my style since the break- up. They say looking well is the best revenge and I feel freer dressing like this rather than in the suits Trevor liked me wearing."

"Hello, Kate," my father said, as I walked through the kitchen door. "You look very pretty. Is there a new man on the scene?"

"Don't be silly – what on earth are you asking her that for?" My mother still hoped I would get back with Trevor. I was the dreamer she had constantly worried about. The day I'd announced my engagement to Trevor, she'd felt all her prayers were answered in one fell swoop. At long last, her youngest daughter had someone to take care of her and save her from herself. She'd always worried about me ending up with an out-of-work artist or musician.

"No-one apart from you, Daddy." I pecked him on the cheek. Flattery always worked with my father, although, more rebellious than my older sister Liz, I had almost always resisted pandering to him. Maybe it wouldn't hurt to start now, as a means of deflecting attention away from myself and at the same time making an old man happy. Slightly taken aback by my change in attitude, he smiled bashfully before beaming his trademark megawatt smile. Though my father was reserved he had a natural charm which came forth whenever he felt relaxed. For a handsome man, I could never understand his innate lack of confidence. Taking a tin foil container from my shopping bag, I placed it on the table in front of him. "I made you a Bailey's cheesecake, Dad. Forgive the tin foil, but it travels best this way. Tastes the same as always." I'd learned at fourteen that the way to his heart was definitely via his taste buds. He'd started praising me for the first time in my life, when I cooked for him during the week my mother was in hospital with pneumonia. His words had stuck in my head until now: *"You're an alchemist, capable of transforming base ingredients into ambrosia, food of the Gods."* This was proof that finally I had come to exist as a viable person in my father's world.

Now his face lit up like a little boy's as he inhaled the aroma of the liqueur. "Nobody in the world makes it like you do, Liz. Thank you."

"Kate. It's Kate, Dad."

"I know you're Kate," he said, looking at me oddly. His short-sleeved white shirt showed off his holiday tan, yet he looked more than usually tired. His grey hair was receding further back at the temples, and his once-blue eyes were now pale grey in hollow sockets.

I was about to ask him if he was all right, when my mother burst in, "D'ya hear him going on about your cooking? I gave up after two attempts using your recipe for that cheesecake. He kept asking me was it shop-bought. Liz has tried and failed – what are we doing wrong?"

"Haven't a clue, Mam," I said vaguely, still concerned about my father's calling me by my sister's name. Anyway, I wasn't about to reveal that I threw in way more Baileys than the recipe specified and then added a large dollop of old fashioned Irel coffee essence. Liz would turn up her nose at the notion of so much booze and condemn the Irel as silly. No, I would retain the element of mystery, for the sake of gaining an innocent advantage.

"You'll never guess who's back in Ireland and asking for you?" My mother had a self-conscious snigger in her voice. "Billy. And like you his marriage is gone wrong. It seems to be catching. Almost all our neighbours have at least one child with a broken marriage."

Well, that was good to know, I thought (and was half inclined to say it, but decided to keep it to myself). Instead, I smiled brightly, "I must meet up with him. Do you know I was only thinking about him recently? We used to be so close. I don't know how we lost contact."

"He's wealthy, he's been very successful. But he's not your type, Kate." That was my mother's way of telling me to put on my chastity belt now that I was no longer a respectable married woman. Time to change the subject.

"Home-made brown bread and scones for you in the other bag, Mam," I said, cheerily pointing to the pink-striped plastic shopper I had left on the stained-pine table along with my shoulder bag.

"You're too good, Kate. Thanks, love. Do you know, I might just get some soup from the freezer and have it with that brown bread and some baked ham? How does that and a salad sound, instead of cooking a hot dinner? There aren't that many warm evenings, we should make the most of them." My father nodded his agreement. As he approached retirement, my mother had been taking charge more and more, with him seemingly happy to have her make all the decisions. It seemed my parents had come to fit together like the left and right of a comfortable pair of old slippers, toes turning in to meet.

"Sorry, Mam. I'm meeting some old college friends in town this evening. We're going for a meal." I knew the truth would invite endless debate and concerns for my safety. I didn't want that.

"Oh, that's nice. Have you got back in contact with them lately? That's good for you. They were a lovely crowd."

I left them both to excitedly fawn over the bag of goodies. They were like two children who'd managed to amass the contents of the local sweet shop. It was amazing what made people happy as they got older – once a Michelin-starred restaurant would have failed to come up to my father's exacting standards. Smiling, I left them sampling the brown bread as I went to freshen up before going on my date.

Before setting out to meet Doctor Edward Commins, I gave him a quick call on his mobile. I've always been partial to a man with a nice speaking voice, so I was disappointed when he proved to be an incoherent mumbler on the phone, forcing me to continuously ask him to speak up. I hoped it was just a bad line.

When I arrived into the packed bar of the Shelbourne Hotel, I couldn't locate him in the crowd. As I made my way through the well-dressed throng, I was conscious of being a woman on my own. In desperation I sent him a text, and he replied saying he was sitting in the rear left corner. When I found him, he was slumped there looking rather grouchy. As I approached, he half stood up, flicking the back of his navy blazer to the sides before sitting back down again. Why did men imagine brass-buttoned navy blazers were classy? I registered that he was a lot shorter than the six foot he had claimed in his profile. I greeted him with a warm smile. "Hi Eddie. How are you?"

"Fine," he grunted. He gave me a slippery wet-fish handshake.

I was immediately aware this was not going to be easy. "Have you been here long?"

"No. Just arrived." His voice was barely audible. The skin on his face was as smooth as a baby's and his forehead bulged in parts as if it had suffered an overload of fillers. It might photograph well, but in reality it looked plain weird.

"Oh, that's good! So tell me about your job?" I tilted my head to the side, the way I would if I were coaxing a child to tell me something.

"Just a job like any other. My neighbours are causing me terrible hassle at the moment. I built a clinic for private cosmetic clients on to my house. The stupid neighbours are objecting and want to put a stop to it. Jesus – nothing but problems! Then my stupid ex-wife wants to hang me out to dry in the divorce courts. Stupid bitch!" He gulped the remainder of his drink, banging the glass back down on the table in front of him.

How did I answer that? "You definitely have a lot on your plate," I heard myself say – and off I was again, pandering to another man I didn't agree with.

"And that's not all. Wait until you hear about my ex-girlfriend. Denying me custody of my daughter. She's looking for a fortune too. Bloody women! Do you want a drink? Or look…" He stood up, pulling his blazer together as he closed one of three brass buttons. "Why don't we just cut the bullshit and head back to my place?"

I said, amazed, "I thought we were going for dinner to Shanahans?"

"Not hungry any more." He took his mobile phone from his pocket. "I'll cancel."

I tried to calm myself down before I spoke: "Look. To be brutally honest, you are not what I expected. I could never have anything in common with you." I stood up as well. "I'm leaving on my own."

As I turned on my heel, I could hear him spluttering behind me: "Wha… What the hell? Bloody women!"

On the drive back to my parents' house, I felt exasperated by the amount of effort I had gone to for such a silly date. No wonder I had loved Trevor's gentlemanly ways, if I had just encountered the alternative. For all his airs and graces, the man I had just met was no more civilized than a Neanderthal. My good opinion of men was being rapidly flushed down the toilet to the extent I wondered was evolution going backwards. My mother had been right when she used to say, "Manners maketh the man."

As I drove in the gate, I was startled to see my sister Liz's car already there. Damn! I knew she'd guess by the way I was dressed that I had been out on a date and would assume I was back so early because I'd been stood up. I parked my own car around the side. Grabbing a packet of tissues, I wiped off most of my makeup and shoved my hair into a ponytail with a scrunchie that I found in the central console. Ditching the heels, I rooted around for the ballerina flats, then I pulled on a sloppy grey cardigan I kept on the seat beside me for chilly days. The result was more casual chic and should not arouse Liz's suspicions.

Just as I turned my key in the door, it opened from the other side. Liz was standing there holding the door open, dressed in immaculately well-cut camel slacks and a white shirt, her blonde hair pulled into a neat chignon at the base of her neck. An effortless preppy style which made most women look drab. "I heard your car arrive. Mam thought you wouldn't be back till later. She said you'd glammed up and gone out for a meal." She frowned, checking out my appearance.

"Good to see you, Liz. I met an old college pal and we decided to go to a bistro for a quick bite. She had to go home as her babysitter couldn't stay long." I pecked her on the cheek before heading for the living area adjoining the kitchen. I became aware of an overall quietness to the house. "Where are Mam and Dad?"

"Gone next door for a couple of drinks. How's Trevor?" Liz was smiling benignly.

"How would I know?" I answered, flopping into an armchair.

"All my friends said you were such a lovely couple. Don't give up hope." She joined her hands together and looked at me with her head tilted, lips pursed.

I'd half expected this since she had lectured me on the phone after we split up. She made me feel I was the one to blame and I hadn't bothered defending myself to her. But I was in no mood for her crap this evening. "What are you talking about? Get real! I wouldn't take him back at this stage if he crawled in on his belly."

"Oh Kate, that was always your problem. You never could compromise."

"Just because everything runs according to plan for you, it doesn't make the rest of us wrong!" I stood up to face her. "You seem to have been born with an inbuilt manual of how to live a successful life. You stage-manage your husband and your kids, just like you always do with Dad. You wrap him around your little finger. Life doesn't work that way for me. I've tried but it seems we're all different…"

Liz butted in, "You've nobody but yourself to blame for your marriage break-up, Kate. You've always hankered after some mad bohemian life that really you know nothing about. You were never grateful for what you had."

What was irking her? I had been through too much to let her away with this. "And we're all supposed to tell you how wonderful you are, aren't we, and what a failure I

– 71 –

am? My marriage break-up doesn't tie in with your family values, does it?" It all came blurting out. "You push your kids into studying what you choose for them and try to arrange suitable marriages for them, and you call that success? More like intimidation!"

"You're just jealous of me! Just because I was always Daddy's favourite!"

"And you had to tell me Daddy was disappointed that I wasn't a boy, since mam could have no more children after me. You told me my birth ruptured her womb and she had to have an emergency hysterectomy! Did you really have to tell me that at eleven years of age on the day of Gran's funeral?"

She paused for a moment, then said quietly, "Look, if I did say that I was only fourteen and I didn't really mean it. You seem to have carried that grudge for a long time."

Tears stung my eyes. "But you did mean it. And you knew I was upset over Gran's death! You pretend to be sophisticated but you like to get down and dirty, and you just love sticking the knife in whenever I'm at a low ebb!"

Her face turning red, Liz grabbed her coat from the back of a chair and stormed out, banging the front door. I couldn't believe it. We had clashed before but this was totally off the Richter scale. At least I'd finally stood up to her. And maybe that was the problem. I used to be a mouse but all this conflict had lit a fire in my belly. Knowing I was on my own was certainly making me tougher. And maybe it would make me a lot more honest. I'd felt foolish, having to make up a cover story for myself, sneaking around like a teenager, I didn't want to have to do that again.

After heading upstairs and getting ready for bed, I turned on my laptop. Once again, I entered the doctor's name in a search engine and scrolled down through the various pages

I had not bothered to read. On one site, a blog was devoted to complaints about the quality of his work, some people calling him a "botox-crazed brute". Why hadn't I checked more thoroughly before?

I'd had a lucky escape. I should have trusted my earlier gut instinct, when I'd spoken to him on the phone, but I hadn't been able to let go of the fantasy I had constructed earlier. From now on, I definitely needed to avoid doctors.

Chapter Seven

etween the ridiculous date and the unpleasantness with Liz, I was relieved to leave Dublin and arrive back in the west. There had always been an element of sibling rivalry from as far back as I could remember. But what had happened this time? A niggling voice in my head told me I'd been wrong to resurrect an old grudge against my only sister. Later that night, as I tossed and turned in bed, I felt ashamed – forgiveness was obviously something I needed to work on. The lack of it could cause embitterment and poison a person along with all their relationships. I had to contact Liz and set things straight. She had been there for me many times in the past, when I most needed her. No grovelling apologies – I didn't want her taking over my life. Just clear the air and silently wish her well.

In the morning, I found one missed call from Liz and three missed texts on my phone – two advertising sales, the third from Ella. I hit the playback button on my message minder: "I'm sorry, Kate. You were right when you said I was out of order. I felt sad that you and Trevor had split up. The following day I realised I had not been there for you during the past weeks. Hope you forgive me? Liz."

"It's fine, Liz. Everything's forgiven. Please forgive me for carrying a grudge." In many respects, I was more taken aback by her humble apology than I had been by her attack. Liz had never been one to back down before. Maybe she was becoming more enlightened, or maybe I was finally learning to stand up for myself. Either way I was glad to be on better terms with her. Just as I was about to put down the phone, a text came in.

"Of course. Would u like me to visit u? We could go for a meal and a nice walk? Liz x."

Relief flooded over me:"Thanks Liz. Sounds lovely but lots of unpacking to do. Let's have a night out soon tho. Kate x"

Next, I rang Ella who was back in town. She sounded exhausted. "Hi, lovey. How are you?"

"Not so bad. How was the conference?"

"Dreadful – the worst ever. There's got to be an easier way to make a living. The managing director's PA was a nightmare. She's a jealous cow who resented me doing my job – she set out to sabotage everything I had organised, right down to changing menus and cancelling the bottled water."

"That's just one bad experience. You'll get over it. The Vienna conference worked like a dream for you."

"Competition for that type of event is cut-throat and the business just isn't out there any more. Whenever it is, it's going to younger hotshots in Dublin. I have no bookings for the whole of July and August." She sighed. "Anyway, enough of my ranting. Have you gone on any dates?"

"I have. Not wonderful experiences. The doctor was terrible. I won't go into the story now, I'll tell you about it when I see you."

"I went online last night. I'd forgotten how addictive it can be. I'm determined to squeeze in a couple of dates this week. Have you any set up?"

"I was just about to log on when I noticed your text."

"Go on then, and call me if anyone interesting appears."

Despite my hitherto disastrous dating experiences, I seemed to be magnetically drawn back to the site in the hope a gallant knight might gallop into my world. There were five new emails. I opened them and looked at the accompanying profiles. Two were one-liners from men with no photographs, so I did not reply. The third was from an artist calling himself "luvpicasso", a bit dishevelled but cute, a bit like the Australian actor Simon Baker. Well, maybe I was stretching that a bit but there was definitely some similarity to the quirky grin, blue eyes and fair curly hair. At forty, he was too young for me though, and sounded a bit immature. I'd always been attracted to creative types, finding they had a dangerous type of sex appeal. Or maybe the sense of danger came from my mother having warned me as a teenager that I'd end up with a hippie poet or a penniless artist, if I wasn't careful. It conjured up images of living in a garret with barefoot screaming children. To please my mother I'd shooed the romantic chilled-out dreamers away, fearful that I might fall in love with any of them and so ruin my future.

"Luvpicasso" wrote:

Hi Persephone,

U sound interesting and intelligent! Maybe too intelligent for me, lol! I see ur creative so I was wondering do you paint? I'm an artist, currently working in oils. I'm planning an exhibition with a few other artists – in this economy… yeah lol! I'm an optimist lol! Anyway most of the women on this site are not too bright so I thought it would be nice to touch base with someone like u! Like you, I love mythology.

Geoff x

I definitely needed to ask someone what lol meant. I had assumed it meant lots of love, but now I wasn't so sure. He used it a lot. He seemed a bit "fly by night" (another of my mother's sayings for dreamers) but I decided there was no harm in contacting him. Maybe I finally needed to stop thinking I needed a dependable professional man.

Hi Geoff,

Thanks for your mail. I'm presently in Galway enjoying a bit of sunshine. Not sure how creative I am; I like craft work and have attended art classes. Really enjoy writing and cooking. Good luck with the exhibition.

Kate

The next one was from a forty-five-year old man, "Elmtree", who simply stated he was in business. Since he was very well-dressed, I immediately wondered if he owned a menswear shop. Tall, with dark wavy hair and hazel eyes, he was exactly the type I'd always gone for. This type seemed somewhat safer than the raw sexuality of creative men, which made me scared I could lose myself completely. A terrifying thought that would make it easy for me to run in the opposite direction. The business man had written a paragraph about himself:

"I would love to meet someone special; a woman to hold hands with and go for long walks by the sea. I like to consider myself a gentleman and believe in treating a woman as a lady. I swim, play tennis and go hill walking. I love art, theatre and literature. I believe in taking care of my body, mind and soul in equal measure."

I took another look at his picture and wondered was he too good to be true. At least he didn't play golf. I read his email to me complimenting me on my hair and my dress sense. He asked what subject I taught and was my username related to my interest in mythology. He signed himself "Ray". I wrote back thanking him for his compliments.

The final email was from "the diver", another businessman. He didn't have a photograph but his message captured my interest and aroused my curiosity.

Hi Persephone,

Toot… toot! Hoot… hoot! What a foxy red head you are and you sound like a gal who knows what she wants out of life! Fair play, I'm all for a gal who knows her mind and seduces me with her brain as well as … oh you know! Why call yourself Persephone, when you've got the body and tresses of Botticelli's Venus lol? With your Taekwondo, scuba diving and interest in Incan and Mayan civilizations, I can picture you as a female Indiana Jones. Better than tomb raider any day, I say! Definitely with that red hair, you'd put me in my place … quaking in my boots while hot under the collar lol! No seriously … you demand respect, even from a messer like me! If you want to get in touch send me your phone number and we can arrange to chat.

Steve

I wrote back to Steve asking him had he a photograph. I was more interested in "Elmtree" aka Ray, yet decided not to invest too much hope in him after my previous two experiences. If everything worked out, I could meet him the coming Friday. Meanwhile I was in a mood for experimenting, so two days later I agreed to meet "the diver", Steve. We had spoken on the phone and he told me he was a representative for a company fitting aluminium windows. I asked for a photograph, and he sent one right back. He was rugged looking with heavy facial furniture, a rather large nose, heavy jowls and a thin line for a mouth. Not exactly my type, but I was sure a lot of women would find him attractive. I found his humour hilarious, even if his hooting and tooting sounded more like a siren call for Jessica Rabbit. No matter, I needed a good laugh. Emails went to and fro and I agreed to a lunch date rather than risk another evening fiasco.

I was beginning to see this as Ella had suggested, "an exercise in dusting off my disused dating skills." Smirking to myself, I decided to call her and fill her in on my progress.

"Same as you, lovey. I'm in need of a laugh and an ego boost so I've two dates arranged for today. First a lunch date and then meeting another guy for coffee at four." We agreed to keep in touch throughout the day and meet up later to discuss the dates. I felt like a woman on a mission, preparing to take note of all the details to report back to HQ afterwards. It added to the excitement, that feeling of being an intrepid reporter working undercover.

In the Meyrick Hotel foyer, at a table to the right of the central table, which was adorned with a huge floral arrangement, Steve sat folding papers into a briefcase. I recognised him immediately. Hmm, not bad looking, although a little older than his photograph (I was beginning to think that was par for the course) and somewhat untidy, with shirt buttons straining over his mid-section.

He looked up. "Kate?" His eyes took me in. "Hey, you look great! Know something? I'm not very hungry. How about you?"

"I could eat the legs from under the table. I'll get weak if I don't eat something soon." The aroma of garlic, tomatoes and peanut soy sauce wafted past him and my stomach grumbled.

"Yeah?" He looked disappointed. "I suppose you can get some bar food." He ushered me towards the bar, where the barman came over and handed each of us a menu. I searched for the choice most resembling the aroma that had greeted me.

"Just a glass of wine, please," Steve said to the barman.

"I'll have the chicken satay and a bottle of still water, please."

When the barman left, Steve turned to me asking: "Is there a problem with the drinking water in Galway at the moment?"

"No. Why do you ask?"

"I always drink tap water." His face changed from concerned to animated as he launched into the conversation with: "Well, Kate, we've certainly had great chemistry with the banter in our emails! It's been fun! You have to have a sense of humour otherwise life could really get you down!"

"Yes, you're very humorous …"

"Now, I want to be open and honest with you from the start, so I need to tell you a few things. How are you with that?"

"Absolutely. I agree one hundred per cent. Honesty all the way." I put on a chirpy voice to deflect from my sudden sinking feeling.

"First, I have to tell you a bit about me. My wife and I didn't have sex for the last eight years of our marriage. Now I'm not going to crib about her because she's a lovely woman, but that's very hard for any man to put up with. And

I remained faithful to her while some of my buddies were off having affairs. But I respect women and I didn't do that to her, even though she often came to bed with her hair in rollers and would turn her back on me for fear I'd suggest anything." Too much information and this from the person I'd expected to entertain me with his mad-cap humour. I was embarrassed and confused. Nothing seemed to add up.

"I can understand that was difficult for you." Was that what I was supposed to say?

The waiter arrived with drinks and lunch. The chicken satay came on four skewers and was served with french fries. I was ravenous. "Would you like some?" I pushed my plate towards Steve. Without any hesitation he helped himself to a skewer of chicken, continuing to talk as he did so.

"Now, I was good to my wife in every way and in fact I still do more than my share of parenting, though the kids are fairly independent at eighteen, nineteen and twenty-one years old." He fiddled with the skewer, his eyes transfixed on the remaining two cubes of chicken as though he were forensically examining them. Why was he prattling on in such a defensive manner, unable to make eye contact?

"How long are you divorced?"

He launched back into chewing the chicken from the skewer. "Just separated six months." His mouth was full as he spoke. "Now the point is, I'm very attracted to you but I could never enter into another relationship like the one with my wife. Do you understand?" He grabbed a handful of French fries and tossed them in his open mouth. What a barbarian! What had happened to his inimitable sense of humour? I was beginning to find him common and coarse. Was he unaware he was wolfing down my lunch? The lunch he didn't want? I was annoyed that he presumed I would consider a relationship with him. His other hand sneaked towards a second skewer of chicken. I moved my plate away from him.

"It seems a bit early to be thinking about you and I starting a relationship – you live quite a distance away and we've only just met."

"Yeah …" He stuffed down another handful of my French fries. "But I would need to know right from the beginning that the relationship would include sex. Do you understand?"

"Yes, I understand – but it's a bit early. We don't know if we even like each other yet." I signalled to the waiter. "Could you please bring me another portion of chicken satay?"

"Certainly, madam. Will there be anything else?"

"Not just now, thank you …"

"Do you eat this much all the time?" Steve asked. Before I could answer, his phone rang. He pulled it out of his shirt pocket and looked at the screen. "Excuse me. I need to answer this." He got up to walk out of the bar.

While he was gone, I checked my phone. A message from Ella read: "Just met Mr Loves Himself."

"Eejit here just ate my lunch," I texted back.

"Make him pay. This guy runs 5 miles & cycles 8 miles a day!"

I acknowledged the waiter as he delivered a second plate of satay, then resumed texting: "Forget him. No time for a woman!"

"Yep. haf 2 go."

Steve arrived back and slid in beside me, nonchalantly helping himself to another full skewer. "Kate. Of course we'd get on great," he said, again with his mouth full. "I just have to have this issue out in the open before I get involved with you. I'm a very giving person and I wouldn't like to be taken for a fool."

I looked at him, stuck for words. Then cleared my throat. "To be honest, I find this line of conversation a bit over the top. You have no guarantees with any relationship that you will get every aspect right. I'm sure some women have similar complaints about men."

"Exactly my point." Glancing at his mobile phone, Steve assumed a harried expression: "I need to leave for a meeting. Phone me when you've thought all this through. Maybe next time we could meet in the evening?"

Stealing the final skewer of chicken, he vanished before I had a chance to comment. Flabbergasted, I sank back into my seat, feeling the wind had been knocked right out of me. Calling over the waiter I asked for the bill along with a stiff brandy. I felt I needed it.

Ella arrived to my apartment at six, as planned. Her effortless glamour, in shades of eau de nil and cream, contrasted with the grey leggings and long printed t-shirt I'd changed into for lounging around. Ella had a knack of co-ordinating outfits in soft jersey layers, always in cool toning colours. The end result looked thrown together but I knew a lot of thought went into getting it just right to best compliment her figure. She often said style was more about posture and the balance of clothing shapes than it was about someone's figure or budget. Yet this evening, I could see there was something wrong the moment she stepped through the door – she looked somehow ruffled despite her chic outfit.

"Are you ok?" I asked as she headed for the living room.

"No, I'm livid. Absolutely livid. I've just been stood up by a fellah from that website."

"Didn't he text or call you?"

"Only after me waiting forty minutes for him in a café. He sent a text to say he was sorry he couldn't make it."

"What's his username? Does he have a photo?"

"He calls himself "movielover". And no, no photo. You know, I'm sick of blind dates."

"Ah look, I don't know why we bother with the no-photo guys." Then I laughed. "Maybe he went to the movies instead."

Ella relaxed and began to smile: "You could be right. I'm only in foul humour because of the Mr Loves Himself guy this afternoon. What are the guys like that you've been in touch with? Maybe you're doing better than me."

"Come on, I'll show you, I've got the computer on." I led her through to my bedroom.

"First I'll show you the artist, Geoff." I clicked on his username, "luvpicasso".

"Oh he's gorgeous. Very sexy!" She almost salivated as she sat back in my office chair against the background of white-painted walls and lavender bedroom furnishings.

"Hmm … dangerously so. The funny thing is we've been emailing each other and it feels like I've know him for ages. He told me some of the women on the site were crazy. Bunny boilers, he called them. He seems very busy and content that we have a friendship, neither of us has hinted at meeting up. I like the fact that I have made a platonic friend. At least I have something real after the other eejits I've met."

Ella shook her head at me, blue eyes incredulous.

"What?" I aked.

"He doesn't look like the platonic type. I know I'd certainly like more from him than that. But each to their own, I suppose," Ella said.

I laughed, moving the mouse to the next picture. "And this is the flute I met today. Calls himself 'the diver'. Knows how to dive in on a plate of food after saying he wasn't hungry and didn't order anything."

"Did he pay or go dutch?"

"Neither. Disappeared before the bill arrived."

Ella read through his email and studied the accompanying profile, grimacing at the photo. "He's a messer all right. I should have realised when you rang – I met him two years ago, when I first started dating. He was on another site, calling himself something different, but the photo's the same. I just met him for coffee but he had a big sob story about not having had sex with his wife for so many years and how faithful he was. I saw through him immediately, just got up and walked out."

"Well, I endured him for a bit longer than you."

"You did well. After I met him, I was chatting to a nice guy on the site and he told me his sister dated him for two months. By the time she broke it off, she felt he had used her for sex. Worse than that, he sent her invoices for every meal he had ever paid for along with a receipt for the flowers he had sent her on Valentine's Day."

I was incredulous. "No! The cheek of him."

"Worse again – the poor girl paid him." Ella rolled her eyes. "He seems to think he can use women like prostitutes."

"Unpaid prostitutes, at that."

"Anyway, enough about him. Another one bites the dust," Ella said, as I blocked him from further contact.

"What happened with the exercise guy then – Mr Loves Himself? The one who exercised so much he couldn't possibly have time for a woman?"

"Another eejit. He had a great body but he was so

conceited about it. I've developed a questioning technique where I get information out of them – I pretend to prattle on about myself, disclosing loads of useless information, give the impression I'm real chilled out and anything goes. Then when I know they've fallen for it, I'll say something like: 'You know I'm a bit psychic?' 'Really?' they say, wondering if I'm bats or for real. It confuses them and that's where I'll slide in something about it being obvious they're married, but I'm cool with that."

"Did you say that today?" I raised my eyebrows. Ella was so much cleverer than most of these men. Her mouth twitched in a grin.

"Yes, and I immediately got a red-faced confession – he told me the marriage was over but they were living together for the sake of the kids and he just wanted to test the waters before leaving. They have such sympathy for themselves, especially if they think you'll buy it."

"That's unreal, Ella. I need to try that out."

"You'd have no problem doing it Kate. You initially have to be as honest as possible, without revealing too much and you need to constantly rely on what your gut is telling you. I kept up the sympathy act right until the end when I told him he wasn't for me."

"What was his reaction?"

"Devastated I'd say, after believing I was so bohemian about it. He gave me a sad puppy-dog look which said, 'How could I reject him with his beautiful body?' It's good to get one-up on a messer like that. Now show me who else you're in contact with, Kate."

" 'Elmtree' coming up."

"Hmm. I'd prefer the artist."

"Oh, but I'm getting on really well with Ray. We've spoken

on the phone and I love his voice. He is quite sensitive and spiritual. Seems to have good emotional intelligence. I'm meeting him on Friday night."

"They can all put on an act. He reminds me of Trevor. I don't want to be a killjoy, Kate. But make sure you don't find yourself falling for the same type again. You're still vulnerable."

"No, he's different to Trevor," I insisted, determined he would be since I was very taken with his picture and profile. Ella looked at me and frowned. I ignored her look, asking instead, "Tell me what does lol mean?"

"Oh I hate that lol thing. It means 'laugh out loud'. Most of the men on that site have no sense of humour so they're laughing at their own jokes. Honestly, they think they're hilarious. And since you would not get the joke they have to point it out and write lol at the end of the sentence."

"I thought 'lol' meant 'lots of love' but I couldn't understand how it was being used in the context. These abbreviations are a bit juvenile, aren't they?"

"Promise me you'll be careful with that 'Elmtree' guy, will you lovey? I can see you've already started imagining life coming up roses with him. It's dangerous when you start thinking like that."

"I promise I'll be careful, Ella. Now will you stay for lamb tagine and couscous?"

Chapter Eight

*M*y relationship with *"Elmtree"* aka Ray had really begun when his name popped up on msn instant messenger. I had never used this facility before and had decided it was not for me. That is, until I saw Ray's handsome photograph appear with the line: *"Hi, Kate. Do you have time for a chat?"*

Immediately, I answered, *"Yeah, sure. How are you?"* and we began our chat.

Ray: I'm great thanks. Just back from a long walk in the Wicklow mountains.

Me: Lovely. I had a long walk on the prom in Salthill today. Glorious day in Galway.

Ray: Are you in Galway for the weekend then?

Me: I live here. My parents live in Dublin so I visit regularly. Would that be a problem for you?

Ray: Not at all. I love Galway so you would provide the perfect excuse for visiting.

Me: I see you're single. Never been married then?

Ray: Well I was married and am now separated awaiting a divorce. But I see myself as single. I see you're separated. Any kids?

Me: Yes one twenty-year-old daughter, a law student. She's spending the summer in Boston. How about you?

Ray: Two sons and a daughter. I have them every second weekend. Do you live alone?

Me: Yes for the moment. I have the honour of being able to say I live in a convent. A renovated Dominican convent! I know I'd promised myself to hold back information. Maybe I had a bad case of low impulse control, me blurting everything out... but I was interested in this guy and felt I could trust him. Anyway he lived in Dublin and didn't look like the stalker types Ella warned me about.

Ray: Whoa Sister or is it Mother superior? I was a favourite of the nuns when I was an altar boy.

I was on a roll now. I loved this kind of teasing. It made me feel young and carefree.

Me: You still have that innocent altar boy look about you. Must work well for you in business... that trustworthy look! Do you work in the rag trade?

Ray: No, Sister Katie. You're not the first one to ask me that. I'm a financial adviser. And yes I like to think I'm trustworthy. Sometimes I'm way too trusting. My wife ran circles round me. How're you coping?

Me: Good days and bad days, since the split. I never thought it would happen to me and it's early days yet. I think I'm just on this site for diversion.

Ray: I'm separated over a year and it's still very raw ... coping with betrayal and lies. But I'm learning to trust again.

Me: You sound like you're in tune with your feelings. I like a man who's in touch with his feminine side.

Ray: That's unbelievable. My wife told me I was overly in touch with my feminine side. I'd love to meet you Kate. Will you be in Dublin any time soon?

Me: Yes it so happens I'll be visiting my parents next Friday.

Ray: Well then. We have to meet Friday night if you're free.

Ray booked a table in a fancy restaurant called Le Chevre D'or. I arrived by taxi, having left my car at my parents' house. He was standing outside the restaurant when I arrived, immaculately dressed in a cream linen jacket over navy trousers. I felt excited as our eyes met. Standing at six foot two, with brown hair in well-cut layers brushed back behind a generous quiff, hazel eyes and lightly-tanned skin, he had the clean cut good looks of a matinee idol from the fifties.

As I got out of the taxi, he took my hand and pecked me on the cheek. "Hi. You look well," he said in the clipped business-like tone I recognised from having spoken to him on the phone. He had a posh accent and I knew this was the way guys like him spoke, especially when they worked in the city finance. After exchanging pleasantries he waved his hand in the direction of the door. "Shall we go inside?" He signalled for me to walk in front of him.

Delicious aromas of garlic, olives, fish bouillon, wild game, tomatoes and roasted herbs wafted past me. The clientele were chic yet relaxed, ranging from early thirties to couples in their seventies. The waiter welcomed Ray like an old friend, leading us straight to our table, at a window overlooking an atrium. Pre-dusk light flooded into the restaurant, warming the yellow ochre walls with a golden hue, as the last sunbeams danced to the strains of Debussy's Clair de Lune. I was impressed – the polished mahogany floor gleamed in contrast to the starched white

table cloths, glistening with highly polished silver cutlery
and ornate candelabras. High standards for people in high
places. Yes, this was the part I had enjoyed about Trevor's
love of standards, if only he hadn't carried it to extremes. I
smiled at Ray, appreciating this as a treat and a well-earned
rest from my own cooking. The waiter asked us if we would
like anything to drink. Ray ordered a bottle of premier cru
Chablis Fourchaume. After we were given our menus, Ray
leaned across the table, holding his aqua blue silk tie flat
against his cream shirt and asked, "So, how are you finding
internet dating?"

"I haven't been doing it for long."

"Aah," he said, smiling and shaking his head. "I've been
on and off it since I split with my wife."

"And how have you found it?"

"Not much different to meeting people in pubs or clubs.
You meet some good and some bad." I noticed he had a
strange habit of curling his lip, before the odd smirk escaped.
I found it a little disconcerting without knowing why.

"Have you had any successes?" After I said it, I thought
I'd worded my question in a peculiar way.

"Ah yeah, I've met a couple of women, I've ended up
dating for a while."

"Excuse me, sir." The waiter turned to Ray, then to me:
"Madam." And then to both of us, "Are you ready to order
yet?"

"What's the fish of the day?"

"Seabass, sir. Served with tomato concasse, puy lentils
and gratinated potatoes. It is sup-perb!" He joined his thumb
and index finger, touched his lips, blew a kiss into the air.

In response to the flamboyant gesture, Ray inclined his
head towards the waiter and winked at me. "Great. I'll have

that please, Pierre."

I smiled as I relaxed into the rarefied atmosphere of the place. "Me too."

"Starters, *Monsieur, Madame*?"

"Not for me," Ray answered.

"Me neither," I said automatically.

After the waiter left, I reminded Ray he had been telling me about his dating experiences. Dating gossip was fast becoming the most enjoyable aspect of the entire dating game. Everyone seemed to love sharing stories and judging by Ella's gossip about *"the diver"*, the Irish world of internet dating was very small.

"Oh, yes. I met a very attractive actress on the site and went out with her for a while. Then she told me she was still living in the same house as her husband though they were legally separated." He shook his head and pursed his lips. "I just couldn't be part of a set-up like that. A woman is either with her husband or she's not. In my book there's no in between."

"I agree," I said, as I raised my glass to my lips. His eye rested on my emerald ring, and I blushed, worrying he might think I was like the actress, only semi-detached. That was probably why he'd asked me early on did I live alone. I decided I liked the fact that he was very ethical about standards. In between eating, our eyes met and we smiled. With his olive skin, smouldering hazel eyes and aquiline nose, I thought him very attractive apart from his chin. Yes, the chin bothered me. It looked like an implant, something almost separate from the rest of his face that jutted out awkwardly, lending him the appearance of an evil cartoon character when he turned sideways. I rubbed my temples as that last thought registered. Maybe the wine was hitting whatever part of my brain processed images? But there was something else too that I couldn't quite put my finger on. I scolded myself that perhaps I'd become impossible to please – some sort of a defence mechanism from getting hurt. I shouldn't allow such thoughts to impede me moving forward.

"The good thing about internet dating is that every now and again a little gem crops up," Ray teased.

"Really? And who is your latest gem?" I asked.

"You are," he said.

All of a sudden I was immensely pleased as if I had passed some kind of test. "No more wine for me," I told the waiter as he was about to refill my glass. I'd had one glass and did not wish to drink anymore.

"I was going out with a French girl for a while. Like you she was into different cultures and interested in spirituality. You're somewhat like her. She was highly intelligent but a bit boho." A smile flickered at the corners of his mouth.

"Boho? Is that bad?"

"No, honestly. Boho is good in my book. I just mean a little alternative – different."

Ping! There was that feeling again, as if I'd passed a test. I seemed to be chalking up points and felt mad eager to please. I was very attracted to him, although I didn't feel aroused in my body. Maybe I was too old to feel wet and gooey over someone? Maybe I was pre-menopausal and all my oestrogen had dried up? To cover my angst, I smiled and loosened my stiff posture by swaying my shoulders.

"The French girl – she went to Nepal for three months to meditate with the Dalai Lama."

"Really? How did she get on?" I was genuinely interested.

"I don't know. I haven't heard from her since." The waiter arrived and removed our plates. Ray announced he was too full for dessert, and I concurred, although the food was exquisite. Ray asked for a brandy and I asked for a camomile tea. "So tell me about your plans to go to South America."

"I've always been interested in myths and legends, ever since I was a kid. At one point I thought I would have loved to study anthropology since I'm fascinated by ancient civilizations. I'm thinking of going to Peru to do the Inca trail. I feel I need to expand my horizons after endless summers holed up in pretentious golfing hotels."

"I think you're great." He poured the reminder of the wine into his own glass and threw it back. "I admire the way you're following your heart. You have a very adventurous spirit."

I smiled. "Do I live up to my photo? You seemed to be very worried about that." He had asked me to send on extra photographs before he'd finally asked me on a date.

"That's because so many women use ancient photos. Actually I think you're better-looking than your pictures. Your eyes are more expressive in reality."

Ping! Something went off in my brain again. Why was I keeping score on myself?

I wasn't usually so easily flattered, but I was enjoying the affirmation that someone like him found me attractive. "What about you, Ray? Any holidays planned?"

"Not this year, I'm afraid. I need to work harder than ever to overcome a few obstacles. Owned a beautiful holiday home in Provence but in the interest of peace I handed it over to my ex. That's one thing I'd advise you – don't drag property issues through the courts if you can avoid it."

"Thanks for the advice. No, Trevor's fine that way. We haven't sorted anything yet but I don't intend to challenge anything."

"Divorce is stressful and expensive enough. If you can agree terms with your ex you save a lot of money. I've given in for the sake of peace. It's important where there are children involved. Though Judy was still determined to battle it out for as much as she could get her hands on. But I'm determined to work hard to get back up to where I was pre-recession and pre-divorce." As we finished our meal, the conversation turned to children and how hard the whole business of marriage breakdown was for them to cope with. "They are innocent victims in a mess made by their parents," Ray said. I admired the way he constantly put his children first. Like me, he obviously would have stuck the marriage out for the sake of keeping family together. We seemed to have similar values, unlike most of the other men I'd met. When the bill arrived I offered to go Dutch, but Ray wouldn't hear of it and insisted on paying in full. Ella was right about him being like Trevor in certain respects. He was well groomed, a gentleman to his fingertips and he certainly knew how to treat a woman. I felt very secure in his company, feeling fate had a hand in bringing us together.

Afterwards we headed to the bar in La Stampa hotel for a drink before going our separate ways. As I was getting into a taxi, Ray asked me would I like to call over to his house the following day for a casual lunch. "The kids will be with my ex."

I hesitated. "I'd love to but I don't know if my mother has planned something, and I don't know if I'll have time."

"I'll text you my address and directions. I'm not too far away. We've got on so well, I'd love to see you again."

After he kissed me on the cheek, I climbed into the taxi. I was on a high, feeling as though every cell in my body was tingling from the thrill of meeting someone who seemed to be resonating on the same wave length.

Chapter Nine

The following morning, I awoke to the smell and sound of rashers sizzling. As I arrived downstairs, my mother was standing at the cooker, metal tongs in hand, tea-towel slung over her arm. "I thought Dad was supposed to be watching his cholesterol." I regretted saying it as soon as the words were out of my mouth.

My mother shot me a look. "I cook everything on the grill for him, Kate. Give me some credit."

"Good morning, Liz." My father pushed his empty plate away and stood up to put on his jacket. "It's my Saturday morning treat and your mother is careful to poach the eggs rather than fry them. Don't forget who you got your talent for cooking from in the first place."

"Kate … It's Kate. And I'm not questioning mam's ability as a cook."

"Ah yes, Kate. Well, good to see you. I must rush to work now." He paused. "How's Julie? I would have given her a job for the summer. No need for her to go all the way to Boston." He bent to touch my arm as he passed by. It felt like a grip for support as he appeared to falter, his back stooped as he carried on.

"Next year, Dad," I called after him, as he headed out the

kitchen door. "Why's he going to work on Saturday morning?" I asked my mother.

"The recession hit the practice hard. He had to let a lot of staff go in the last few months, so he's had to make a lot of court appearances himself now even in minor cases where the junior partner would have stood in before."

The door burst open. It was my father again. "Now where did I leave my car keys?" He rummaged around the worktops, looking very flustered.

My mother sighed. "They're hanging in your usual spot." "Where's that?"

"In front of your eyes, where they've been for the past forty years." She handed them to him. As the front door banged shut, she said to me, "He's always forgetting things."

I sat down at the kitchen table. "I thought he was planning to retire soon? His working harder than ever is crazy at his age."

"Ah, look Kate, it's good for him. If he was around here all day he'd be bored stiff and he'd be like a child under my feet. He's better off having something to keep him occupied."

"Is he still on the anti-depressants he was put on when Uncle Harry died?" His brother had passed away six months previously and Dad had taken it badly.

"Yes, they seem to suit him. They've made him more mellow."

"Is he talking to anyone? A psychologist?"

"Not at all. What would he need to see one of those for?"

"I thought his doctor wanted him to go to a therapist? The Prozac will only treat the symptoms not the cause." I poured a glass of orange juice from the carton on the table.

"Kate, will you stop fussing. There's not a thing wrong with your father. He's in a better state than I am." She rubbed her back with her left hand. That was my mother's way of drawing attention to her own troubles as a long-suffering wife and mother.

"How's your back, Mam?"

"I'd say it's riddled with arthritis. What with my father's history, it's not like I didn't see it coming. Well thank God I have my faith in the man above. " She tossed her head towards the teak crucifix hanging on the wall above the cooker, then continued to moan as she filled a plate for me, piled high with rashers, black pudding, half a beef tomato and two poached eggs.

"Did you ever make an appointment with the osteopath, Mam?"

"I don't believe in any of that nonsense," she snapped.

I knew she was in a mood and there was no point trying to convince her of anything at this stage. Since my teenage years I'd been trying to persuade her it was possible to have a wider view of the world than the one from the narrow window she looked through. As I dug my fork into the food in front of me, I decided to take up Ray's invitation to visit.

Brooklawn turned out to be a new up-market housing estate, not far from my parents' house. Ray had texted me his address as soon as the taxi had left last night. I had slept soundly and felt very relaxed after our date the night before. That was surely a good sign, after how anxious I'd felt in Trevor's company for many years before we split. I allowed a delay of thirty minutes between Ray texting me his address and replying to say I would call for lunch.

I loved the way Ray looked, I thought, as I followed him

through the sparsely furnished contemporary house. The chin thing seemed to have been a trick of the light. I found myself thinking we could be great together and pictures of a romantic family life started to surface from the recesses of my imagination. I simply couldn't stop soft-focus pictures from forming in my head. I loved his easy going manner, and he seemed trustworthy and safe. Judging by the décor and his clothes, he had impeccable taste. His profile had said he had a degree in law as well as economics; he had to be highly intelligent. We sat at the kitchen island on bar stools, eating triangles of pizza between chatting and gazing at each other. He entertained me with funny stories about dating.

"I met one woman, lovely girl – but we knew straight away there was no spark between us. She had been on a date the previous week. Had arranged to meet a guy from the internet site in a large bar in Ranelagh. You know the kind of place, with nooks and corners and crannies where couples can sit, in relative privacy. Anyway, she liked this guy and they were getting on great to the point of arranging a second date. Next thing yer man says to her, as he stands up, 'Just wait there one minute. I need you to meet someone else.' So he leaves her sitting there, and she's suddenly wishing the ground would open up and swallow her whole. Next thing he arrives back with another woman, both of them grinning from ear to ear."

"Oh no!"

"Yer man says, 'I need to introduce you to my wife.' This woman thought she has him all figured out, until he explains that his wife is dying of cancer and he needs her blessing on his new relationship. Apparently the wife encouraged him to go online and she picked out a selection of possibilities for him."

"What a control freak! I mean I feel sorry for her but she obviously wanted control beyond the grave. God, there are nutters online all right."

"You're telling me. You and I don't need to be online. The only reason why we are is we couldn't be bothered trawling the club scene. But some people have a strange attitude."

I nodded, then I decided to broach an issue that had been niggling at me since meeting him last night. "Ray, I've just noticed you never use my name when you speak. Not on the phone or in person. Why's that?"

At this, he blushed from the top of his lemon polo shirt to his hairline. "I ... I wasn't aware of it. They say people use someone else's name a lot when they want to establish intimacy quickly. I'm not like that. I'm shy in lots of ways and I'm not contrived enough to effect intimacy." Then, brightening, he launched into jesting with: "Katey ... Kitty-Kate ... Hey Katie ... Isn't that a song? Hey Katie?" Jumping off his stool, he went to an iPod on a facing counter and scrolled through until he found what he was looking for. After replacing the iPod in the docking system, he extended his hand towards me. I put mine in his, and he pulled me gently off my bar stool and pirouetted me around before drawing me close to dance. In tune with the rhythm of Josh Kelley's "Hey Katie", we twirled and jived, albeit a little awkwardly, until the song had finished and he began gently caressing my neck with his fingers, before kissing my cheek sensuously. As the next track set a slower pace, I felt myself being swept away by a throbbing and an aching in my pelvis. His mouth searched mine and I responded eagerly, arching my back as my breasts thrust forward, moulding into his body. Taking my hand he led me to a downstairs bedroom, all the while keeping his smouldering eyes hypnotically locked on mine.

Hold on a minute – what was I about to do?

"Ray, I can't do this. I've never just jumped into bed with a man."

He sat with me on the side of the bed, kissing me. "Of course you're not. And I wouldn't dream of pressurising you into something. I'm besotted by you, Kate. I know you feel the same way. I feel as if I've suddenly met the soul mate I've been aching to meet all my life."

"We do have a connection …" I gazed into his earnest eyes.

"Exactly. We can talk about anything and we share the same values. I want you to be part of my life, Kate. I'm sorry there was a misunderstanding about this." He waved his hand around the bedroom. "It's just some women play a game based on 'the rules' and I respect people who are spontaneous and don't follow that stuff."

"What rules are they exactly?"

"Apparently it's based on some dating book. Women are told not to sleep with a man until after the third date – you know, play a game of being hard to get. If you ask me, it's very disingenuous because when two people want to be together they're going to have sex some time. Look forget about it. You and I are different. I know you're not playing games." He smiled and pecked me gently on the cheek. "You smell good."

Maybe he was right. After all I'd been out of the loop for so long, I couldn't possibly know the code of behaviour anymore. And it's not as if I could ever reclaim my virginity. I'd lived by rules all my life and maybe now was the time to break them. Facing me, he rubbed my shoulders reassuringly. My earlier resolve melted as he smiled gently, his dark eyes caressing my face in a seductive yet apparently sincere manner. I reached up to unbutton his shirt, thinking it was good to feel desired ... adored, even.

"It happened," I told Ella when I met her for coffee the day after in the little café on the seafront. It wasn't busy, but we kept our voices low. She threw me a worried look. I protested, "Why are you being such a prude? I didn't mean for it to happen. After all Trevor was the only man I ever had sex with. And oh, I'll go into a Catholic flashback... so please stop or you'll have me riddled with guilt."

"Kate." She looked at me softly. "You're misreading me. I'm just concerned. This guy seems like a smooth operator. I don't want to see you getting hurt. But there again, maybe he's what you need to get Trevor out of your system." Then, whispering, she asked: "Tell me, was it good?"

"No, that's the strange thing." I also dropped my voice to a whisper. "He was hopeless in comparison to Trevor. He had no idea of foreplay whatsoever and for someone so posh he smelled bad. He could do with an anti-perspirant. He thinks women are attracted to men's pheromones." I watched Ella's eyes widen with incredulity, and I felt the need to stick up for Ray. "In one way that's a good sign – probably it means he's a bit naïve? Not very experienced, right? I think I can probably teach him."

"Aagh, Kate!" Ella crinkled her nose and shook back her lustrous brown mane. "A lot of men are just pathetic lovers and unfortunately they're not for learning anything. Some women put up with crap sex and just pretend to come, groaning and squealing at the right moment, so their men never learn. And some men just want quick rocks-off sex and don't care if a woman is satisfied. Mind you, a lot of women seem to tire of sex too and just want it to be over as fast as possible. One woman I know says she'd like to be married to a paraplegic because sex wouldn't be an issue anymore."

"Gosh, I never thought it could be so complicated between a man and a woman. But what's all the big ta- do about everyone having great sex? Was Trevor exceptional?"

"He probably was. You remember what a certain Hollywood star said in an interview recently?"

I leaned closer to her. "No. What?"

Ella shook her head. "She said she had an awful lot of lovers and a lot of awful lovers." Two women at the next table looked over smiling, and one nodded before looking away. "A good lover is hard to find and the only one you will succeed in coaching is a young one, no older than thirty," Ella said. "In many ways we're at a grave disadvantage at our age. That is unless we go the cougar route and somehow that seems like cradle snatching."

Alone, later that evening, I felt as though nobody had ever properly explained the facts of life to me. I refused to accept Ella's scepticism. After all every man wanted to experience good love making and would take pride in becoming an accomplished lover. In France and Italy, young men are almost schooled in the art – and come to think of it, Ray had talked about a previous French girlfriend. He must have some potential or she wouldn't have put up with him behaving like a flat fish flapping around. I planned to unleash my inner courtesan the next time I met Ray.

Chapter Ten

"What on earth are you doing?" Ray had a puzzled, disapproving look on his face.

What did he mean, what was I doing? There I was standing in a sumptuously decorated hotel bedroom looking like Madame Bovary in Elle Macpherson's peaches and cream push-up bra and panties, all pretty bows and chantilly lace, wriggling out of my slip in the most provocative way I could. Aiming to create a romantic ambience, I'd booked a hotel room overlooking a pretty courtyard, so that we could come back here after dinner and relax in pleasant surroundings. He'd told me he had left his kids with a babysitter and "like Cinderella would have to leave before midnight". I'd set the place up like a spa with candles and essential oils and even ordered strawberries with two Kir Royals. Earlier, I'd gone to the trouble of applying discreet all-over body tan, the kind that merely adds translucence to my bleached-out skin. My hair had been pin-curled, crimped and coiled into a messy up-do that suited my Titian colouring … and he was asking what I was doing? The champagne-coloured silk slip obviously hadn't worked in my effort to get him a bit more playful. He was sitting on the bed with a look of horror on his face, as though he were in the presence of a lunatic.

I began to blush and felt like running into the wardrobe.

Did he think I looked ridiculous? Too old? Sad or pathetic? No hold on … Trevor was a man of taste and he thought I never looked more desirable than in my lingerie. Standing there in front of Ray, I refused to allow any negative thoughts to enter my head. Real men love their woman no matter what shape or age she is. "I thought you'd like a bit of erotica?" His face told me a different story. "Look, turn over and relax there, I've got a wonderful massage technique." I knew I was good at this – Trevor had always loved it. It was a talent I'd developed early in life from rubbing Sloan's liniment into my mother's back. Add a summer of working my Uncle Jim's pottery wheel, and a love of kneading yeast bread, and I'd developed magic hands. But no. He lay there like an inanimate warm corpse with not even an "Ooh" or an "Aah" of appreciation. Even an "Ouch … you're hurting me!" would have been better than this. "A reaction please!" I felt like screaming.

Deflated and confused, it was my turn to become the inanimate zombie as he turned over from his massage and peeled off my smalls, firing them to the floor as if they were army regulation supplies. He hauled my bra off so roughly, I almost screamed. My breasts were fuller than usual because of fluid retention, but they were damn sore. Then he pulled me on top of him and started his lacklustre routine. I tried establishing a rhythm, but my gyrating only seemed to puzzle him. "Have you an itch?"

I gave up. I desperately wanted to yawn. He put his arms behind his head, and that smirk appeared at the side of his mouth. I suddenly had to resist a mad urge to slap him wide across the face. The words: *"Ray is the name of a fish"* entered my head. And then: *"Not even a very exciting fish."* A few moments later and the terrible act had ended without a groan or a grunt. Then he rolled out from under me.

"Okay if I take a shower?"

"Sure. No problem," I said drily, as I wrapped the duvet around me. He'd need hourly showers if he was going to adhere to his no-deodorant policy. How were men so misinformed? I knew reeking of cologne or cheap anti-perspirant sprays was terrible but who told them this stuff about sweat and fabulous pheromones? Oh me and my pesky nose. I wished my sense of smell wasn't quite so acute. It could be such a drag at times. But the real issue here was how I had ended up in such a compromised position, unfulfilled and deflated while trying so hard to please. Was this what James and my shrink had warned me about when they suggested I would attract the wrong type of man? A selfish lover who understood nothing about the beauty of giving and receiving love and was instead content with a mere caveman's "bang, bang, bang" rocks-off sex?

Aha – maybe that's exactly where I'd gone wrong. I had mistaken instant attraction for the illusion of love, because that's what I'd desperately hoped to find. In my desperation to hold on to Ray, I had given myself too quickly, thereby diminishing my personal value. And perhaps I was equally to blame for expecting him to conform to my idea of a dream man. When I was younger I would not have jumped into bed so quickly with someone I barely knew. But I was a God-fearing Catholic back then, believing premarital sex to be a mortal sin. The very idea could still make me feel uneasy because I was still capable of falling into old patterns of thinking and worrying about a vengeful God totting up my sins.

My head was awhirl with contradictory thoughts as I stumbled out of bed and pulled the white robe from the back of the nearby chair. I wrapped it sari-like around my waist and walked across the room to the tea-making facilities. "Fancy a coffee, Ray?" I called, as I flicked the kettle on.

"No, thanks." He appeared round the bathroom door and started getting dressed. "Are you going back to Galway in the morning?"

"Yes, quite early." I poured out hot water.

"Well, I've got to rush now. I'm afraid I'm a bit like the panda. You know what that means?" Was he finally about to confess to knowing how God damn awful he was in the sack?

I said, feigning innocence, "No, I don't know the one about the panda."

"The grammar book?" He was smirking.

I said, confused, "Eats shoots and leaves?"

"Exactly. I've eaten, shot and now I have to leave. Thanks for dinner." He planted an affectionate but rushed kiss on my lips. I didn't know what to say as I watched him make his exit. His flippant joke left me feeling unsettled. If love in the twenty-first century was a game then I certainly had no notion how to play it. One thing struck me clearly: I chose correctly when I picked Persephone's name. I seemed to have spent the last twenty-three years asleep in the underworld.

After showering, I rubbed cream into my hands as I checked over my naked body in the large bathroom mirror. Rather lacking in the curves department, I was certainly no Aphrodite and never had been. But thanks to Trevor's insistence that I use old fashioned silcock's base cream all over my body during pregnancy, my skin was in great condition. Trevor had fancied himself as a bit of an expert on dermatology so he was always giving me tips on skincare. My eye travelled to my fuller than usual breasts as I took another splodge of the complimentary cream into my hand. I applied cream and began massaging my left breast. "Ouch!" My face contorted in agony from an acute throbbing. I had a bad case of pre-menstrual tension. Emptying the remainder of the cream onto my right breast, I began massaging it in. Also tender. I was more careful this time. Then I felt something akin to a hard little nugget under the flesh. *What on earth was that?*

I felt around, attempting to isolate the gravely shape as it slid left and right, making it difficult to grasp. It was unmistakably a lump – but it couldn't possibly be malignant, could it? No, it had to be a cyst. Life couldn't possibly deal me another blow at this stage. It was probably nothing. I'd had a mammogram done two weeks before breaking up with Trevor and I hadn't heard anything back from the hospital so I was sure that augured well. I'd previously been told that I was prone to benign fluid-filled lumps and I'd had them drained by means of a quick procedure. I really wasn't in the mood for such bother right now. Maybe it would disappear if I just ignored it?

Two days later, I was sitting with Ella in the conservatory overlooking her tiny garden, the doors open wide allowing in the fragrance of roses, lilies and begonias.

I knew I was a bit quiet – the lump I'd found in my breast had been niggling at the back of my mind.

"Are you annoyed with me because I wasn't keen on Ray?" Ella asked. "It's just you seem more aloof with me than usual."

I shook my head. "No Ella, I've just been a bit pre-occupied. I'm not the greatest judge of men, am I?" I curled my feet underneath me, as I cosied into a creaking wicker chair with its comfy floral cushions.

"None of us are, but we try to help each other whenever we can and sometimes it's easier to see a situation from the outside, rather than when you're directly involved." She raised her eyebrows, stretching her nose in the process as she locked eyes with me.

"I agree." I saw a worried expression cross her face as she turned to pick up her coffee. "What's up with you, Ella? Are you all right?"

"Aah, I've my own troubles with the business lately. I bust my ass on the Geneva conference and yet the company has gone back to using an organiser in Dublin. I've always battled being in the wrong location but when times were good it didn't matter much."

"Oh God, I'm sorry to hear that, Ella. You were getting on great. What are you going to do?"

"Nothing for the moment. But I have something else to tell you." She placed her hand under her chin and sucked in her cheeks.

"Go on," I said.

"I mentioned my sister's friend Jennie to you before – the girl who's been internet dating on and off for the past three years?" When I nodded, she continued, "Now you know I'm wary of Lorna because she's lethal for chat and gossip ..." It was true, I had only met her sister Lorna a few times but she'd been full of news on every occasion. She gossiped so much, she'd been in court for slander yet she had a wide circle of friends who found her highly entertaining. Ella was continuing, "She knows what every person in the city has for breakfast, yet people confide in her like she's the soul of honour and discretion. I tell her nothing, absolutely nothing, of my business or anyone else's, least of all that of my close friends."

"What are you trying to tell me, Ella?" Had Lorna some information about Trevor? A shiver coursed up my spine.

"Well, I know Lorna loves Jennie's dating gossip, so I asked her yesterday had Jennie ever dated Ray." Taking in my shocked expression, she said hastily, "No, hold on, Kate. Your name was never mentioned. Anyway she told me 'Jennie said he was a bollocks'. Excuse the French."

"Ah look!" I began, as I hurriedly uncurled my feet from underneath me. I really didn't want to hear anything against Ray.

"No. Let me finish please, Kate." Ella spoke in an authoritative tone. "Apparently Jennie was dating him and he started coming on to a friend of hers who was also on the site. Now he didn't know this other woman was a friend of Jennie's. Anyway they decided to set him up and her friend went along to meet him the morning after he'd been with Jennie the night before. When Jennie tackled him on it he said, 'So? We'd never agreed we were in an exclusive relationship. What's your problem?' Like you, she said he was pathetic in the sack. I don't like telling you this Kate, lovey. Are you okay?"

"Yes," I said. But my voice jarred as I felt a lump in my throat. I reached for the glass of water in front of me. I thought for a moment. "Ella, I didn't want to hear that, but in some strange way it makes sense. Yesterday, I had a strange phone call with him where I suspected he was with another woman. He was in a mad rush and sounded like he was trying to brush me off. It's as if I've been refusing to listen to my gut once again. I've been pumping up my ego with flights of fantasy instead. I haven't looked at that site for the last ten days because I thought I'd found Mr Perfect. Do you mind if we check online right now?"

"Of course not. I'll be right back."

Ella returned with her laptop, placing it on the coffee table in front of me. Kneeling down on the floor, I logged onto the site and went straight to "*Elmtree*". He was online. I checked through the rest of his profile, sensing something had changed. "Oh, Ella. I've never used the word before in my life but it's a *bollocks* he is!"

"What's wrong?"

"He was only a standard member before! But look at the date on his profile! Since he started dating me, he's upgraded to premium membership! Now he can be contacted by any girl just on for a quick internet browse! And I assumed he was so into me he would deactivate his profile! Instead, he upgrades." I stood up, hands on hips. "Bollocks… Bollocks… *Bollocks*. Ray is a *bollocks!* All men are the same and I need to avoid them like the plague." Then, calmed by the sight of the shrubs in the garden dancing in the late afternoon breeze, I inhaled deeply and turned to face a bemused Ella. "D'you know something? I've just made the connection between the name Ray and '*elmtree*'. Slippery elm tree. That's what he is. And he's also a slimy ray fish. He's a slippery slimy bollocks. Now, I'm glad I got that off my chest." And I grabbed a handful of cashew nuts from the tray in front of me and collapsed back into the wicker chair. It creaked and sighed beneath me.

"Kate, men like him usually hate women and they make a mission out of driving us crazy. I bet he has problems with his mammy and his ex. That's why he's a selfish lover. Though he doesn't merit being called a lover, judging by the reports and it seems he hasn't the ability to ever be any better. As for you, stop being so hard on yourself. You're still vulnerable, lovey."

"Yeah, Ella. Dunno anything about the mammy, but I do know he hates his ex with a passion. Do you know I'm kind of relieved in some strange way. I was losing the run of myself. I was trying to force something to happen because in some strange way I found being with him consoling. It reminded me of being with Trevor. It's about time I gave this dating business a rest. I'll just keep my little on-line friendship with the artist, and ditch the rest. I need a holiday. I might join James in August."

"Good girl. But I'm concerned about you. You look so thin and drawn."

"I'm still not sleeping well. I've lost weight from anxiety. But I'm surviving." I smiled at her, but it was window-dressing – deep inside me a worm of worry was uncurling itself. I continued brightly, "On top of that I just discovered a breast lump which has gotten bigger."

"Christ almighty, Kate, get that checked out."

"It's probably nothing. I had one before and the doctor just removed it with a syringe. I had a mammogram done before Trevor and I split up. I'm sure the hospital would have notified me if anything was askew." Yet I knew my oncologist had recently emigrated to Australia and it was Trevor's clinic which would have arranged any follow-up appointment for me – which was why I hadn't checked.

Ella shook her head disapprovingly. "What you're going through is very stressful. It can have disastrous effects on your health. Collect your mammogram and get an appointment arranged as soon as possible."

Chapter Eleven

I squirmed at the sight of pale yellow fluid filling the syringe. But this was a routine procedure. Routine. Lots of people had breast lumps. Despite my best efforts to push away fear, my heart galloped like a horse's hooves and I gulped deep breaths. *Calm down,* I told myself, in an effort at positive thinking. After all, I'd had this done by my former consultant, two years previously. "Fibrous breasts" he'd called them, saying they were "more prone to benign lumps". Benign was fine. Not a problem.

I suppressed a yelp as the doctor's short doughy fingers prodded at my naked left breast. My embarrassment was heightened by the harsh glare of the spotlight – I felt I was no glamour model, with my emaciated frame and slumped shoulders. The overhead light caused the consultant's wheat-coloured hair to glisten and the thought flashed across my mind that he could be sporting a toupé. He looked like one of the Munchkins in the *Wizard of Oz* . Wouldn't it be such fun to upset his thatch? I had a childish urge to let my raised arm fall awkwardly and give it a deliberate knock. "Ouch!" My thoughts had been rudely interrupted by the life being wrung out of my breast. He raised his head and scrunched up his face, little piggy grey eyes sinking into fat-rimmed sockets. I said through clenched teeth, "Is the lump gone now?"

"Get dressed and we can discuss your scan." He turned to disappear through the gap in the curtains. Why not just offer me some reassurance, I thought indignantly, hauling on my bra. Evading questions must be a skill taught in medical school. Trevor was an expert at it. Dressed, I slipped out of the curtained changing area and approached the large mahogany desk. He gestured towards the chair opposite him and I sat down. Holding up an iPad, he turned it sideways to show me a black and white scan. "I'm very concerned about your right breast. This is your mammogram, Mrs Canavan. Do you see this cloudy area here?" He indicated an area with the top of his pen. I peered at it, trying to interpret the unintelligible image.

"Yes?" It came out as a squeak. I cleared my throat.

He smiled a schoolboy smile. "You appear to have an area of calcification, which is not a problem at the moment, but could be down the road."

My heart beat faster, and my mouth grew dry. I slipped my hand to the edge of the hard plastic chair I was sitting on and held on tight. "What do you mean?"

"It can be a precursor to breast cancer which could develop within the next five years." He delivered this terrifying news as though he were commenting on the weather. I was rigid in my chair – barely breathing, never mind digesting the information thrown at me. "I need to do a biopsy under anaesthetic to thoroughly investigate this. I'm looking at a large section here. If it is calcification, it could necessitate removal of your right breast."

"But there's no history of breast cancer in my family ..." This couldn't be happening. My heart was deafening me. *How dare he look so composed?*

"I just want to prepare you. It could be better to have

a mastectomy than have to battle cancer in a few years, time. I can work with Doctor Reynolds, the plastic surgeon, and perform an immediate breast reconstruction. They're extremely successful."

"You mean, an implant?" I didn't want silicone inside my body. I'd read about implants and knew they could leak. I couldn't live with the thought of having some kind of active volcano slowly creating havoc inside me. No. No matter how much they would try to reassure me, my mind would work overtime on strange imaginings …

"In some cases, yes. Though I like to also combine natural tissue. For example I could use a length of muscle from your inner thigh for building and reshaping a new breast. If we can save the nipple, we will. If not, the nipple shape can be later tattooed on. We can talk about this after the results from your biopsy."

As he said goodbye, he offered me his small soft hand, which I shook, despite thinking of it as a potential weapon of destruction. At that moment I hated him, but – on automatic – I politely thanked him and left the room with his eerie words reverberating throughout my skull.

After paying the receptionist, I walked towards my car, all the while feeling like I was in some drug-induced haze. Gory images came flooding in, of me lying on the table with not only my breast slashed open but my thigh oozing guts and gristle as they hauled the muscle out. In all of this, the only word I liked the sound of was "tattoo". It was odd for me to think like that. I used to assume anyone sporting a tattoo was a renegade, someone not to be trusted. Now for some strange reason, colourful images of tattoo art presented in front of my bleary eyes. If my breast was going to go, I would end up being some kind of freak. I'd prefer to embrace that and become an authentic freak than have a fake breast. If I was to lose a part of myself then I needed to replace it with something better. An idea began to form – an idea I knew Trevor would hate, but which lifted my mood slightly. I could get a colourful Celtic swirl representing infinity tattooed over my breast scar, or an exotic bird of paradise about to take flight. I could research the Book of Kells before designing my own breast and seek out the best tattoo artist in the land. I laughed to myself. I could just imagine Ray's face, if I'd slipped out of my camisole to reveal such a tattoo!

I'd never been hung up on wanting big breasts, believing they interfered with dressing well. Since my weight loss, my breasts had shrunk to a B cup, what my sister Liz called "two poached eggs, sunny side up". I could style myself like a modern day flapper girl, but with longer hair, curls tumbling over my chest like the Goddess types Alphonse Mucha painted. An androgynous bob would not work, but a kick-ass attitude would. After all, I'd need attitude if I found myself a lover, someone who really desired me. As I'd undress seductively, I'd whisper: "Keats said 'Beauty is truth, truth beauty.' I say: beauty is art and life. What life took away I have replaced with a work of art. Prepare to be amazed." I grinned to myself. Yes, attitude was everything – and it would certainly separate the men from the boys.

I decided the news was too personal to share with anyone but my closest friends. I couldn't tell my mother or sister, as they'd probably whip up unnecessary drama and contact Trevor. That, I knew I couldn't bear. After getting into my car, I phoned Ella. Unable to get through, I rang James instead and told him what had just happened.

"Where are you now?"

"Leaving the hospital."

"How about we meet in Café Medina?"

Fifteen minutes later, I was sitting opposite him in the café nursing a large soya latte. "Why are you grinning?"

He fought laughter. "Sorry, Kate. I just can't get the idea of you reclining topless in the tattoo artist's studio out of my head..."

"It *is* funny, isn't it? I've always been condescending about tattoos but I think I must deep-down have envied women brave enough to get one." I took a sip of my coffee. There was something I needed to ask him. "Tell me about your cousin who recovered from ..." I had a problem getting the C-word out. Fear was gripping me, throwing everything else that had happened to me into the shade. "... cancer. What did she do?"

James became serious. "She's a great believer in alternative medicine. Does everything from acupuncture to meditation. First she went on a trip to a healer in Brazil who performs psychic surgery. There was a documentary about him and other spiritual healers on the television last month. Did you see it?"

I shuddered. "The one who cuts tumours out of people without sterilising equipment or anaesthetic?" My voice said it all.

"That's him. Maria found him great. Now she attends an Irish shaman who lives just west of Galway city. I went to a sweat lodge he organised. He's passionate about his work. Would you give him a go?"

"James, I'll try anything, but not black magic."

"Kate, he's not a witch doctor. He's an ordinary country

man who spent time as a Buddhist monk in France in his twenties. Later he worked as an addiction counsellor before studying shamanism. He survived cancer himself and makes regular trips to that healer in Brazil."

"He definitely sounds out of the ordinary – if you trust him, I'll give him a try. Can you get me his phone number?" I tried to keep the tremor from my voice.

"Of course. He's very busy, but tell him I sent you and he might squeeze you in fairly quickly."

I was apprehensive about my visit to the shaman. Despite myself, I'd absorbed old superstitious beliefs from my mother and even more so from her crazy sister who kept in regular contact with me by phone. Aunt Marge believed any kind of alternative practice was the work of Satan. To her, even yoga was a dark art. She regularly sent me emails about the evils of "inhaling Prana", which, as I'd tried to explain to her, was no more than concentrating on the breath during meditation or yoga. If anything, her warning emails seemed to lend more credence to the fact that perhaps these practices really worked on some level. And if they were forbidden fruits, then I found the idea of them all the sweeter.

Sean the Shaman had a long grey beard and a ponytail. The rest of his head was bald, apart from a few wisps around his pointy ears. He was wearing a purple robe and had nothing on his feet. He'd told me when I arrived that he'd gone to Peru to study shamanism and that he loved being able to really help people. "It's a form of energy healing that works on the body, mind an' spirit. It's very powerful. Take a seat." He ushered me to a chair in a small room painted a tranquil green. A sickly scent of burning sage wafted through the air.

Later, lying on the floor as Sean the Shaman danced around me making a succession of animal sounds – hooting, whistling, chirping, howling, elephant-trumpeting – while beating a drum and shaking a rattle, I have to confess that I did think of Aunt Marge. I could just imagine her face. Sneaking a peek, I found the shaman waving a huge eagle's feather over me before starting up something akin to a rain dance as he drummed and hooted. Even I wondered if he'd completely lost his marbles. Yet unexpectedly, I slipped into a trance-like state, where tranquillity and perfect bliss seemed to last for hours. A gong struck – once, twice, three times. I opened my eyes. He said, "That was to bring you back to the room. Your spirit was journeying."

As I came more into consciousness, I pulled myself into a sitting position, took in my surroundings. The ring of the drum still echoed through my head. I'd been lying there for only forty minutes.

"How do you feel now, Kate?"

I considered. I wasn't sure. "Relaxed."

"The message I've received for you is that you're fighting with reality, saying 'this is not the way my life should be'. Right?" Sean looked at me intently, his right eye larger than his left, recessed in folds of saggy skin.

"Of course I'm saying that. My dreams have been shattered."

"You've suffered a great loss."

"Yes. I wanted marriage to be until death do us part. It is a loss."

"I'm talking about the greater loss you had many years back."

What? My stomach dropped like a lift with a broken cable. How did he know? "I don't want to go there. I can't discuss that right now." I stared at my ring. I said, my voice low, "All my dreams have been shattered."

Handing me a tissue, Sean bent his head to look directly into my downcast face. "Kate." He waited for me to look up. "Not many people live the dream ... *'tis just an outer show.* It's all poppycock, my dear girl."

I sniffed back tears. "What do you mean, poppycock? Of course people have happy families."

"Yes. And happiness comes from living in the now. Accepting what is and handing over control to a higher power. When you do that you'll relax into the flow of life, girl. The way you are now, you're fighting everything."

"I was coping until this damn breast thing happened! And I was beginning to accept things, but this is just the last straw. Why me?"

"Why not you? Terrible things happen to people every single day. Many people are born incapacitated. Do you think you should be immune?" He peered at me like I was a strange laboratory specimen.

"I know terrible things happen to people, but I've always worked hard and dotted all my 'I's and crossed my 'T's."

He sat down, pulling his robe around him. "You have and you still think you can control everything. None of us can, girl. You need to surrender and begin believing in an all-loving God. If you don't like the word 'God' then a higher power or universal intelligence. The source of infinite love is available to you when you begin accepting what is. Now the other thing I'm picking up about you is that you're rejecting your body."

"What do you mean?"

"You referred to your breast as 'this damn breast'."

"Did I?" I was shocked.

"Indeed you did. Your breasts are connected to your femininity. You're fighting with your body. Now I want you to sit up straight in that chair with your two feet on the ground and get into a comfortable position."

I hauled myself up off the floor and did what he asked, pulling my spine up straight and settling myself into the support of the chair.

"Now place your two hands gently over your breasts and tell them how much you love them."

At this, I burst out laughing. "Love my breasts? That sounds so egotistical." I wondered was it also a little perverse.

"No I'm talking 'bout a love that's got nothin' to do with the ego. It's a love that's nurturing and full of compassion. And you need to start connecting with that infinite source. First I need you to visualise yourself bringing in a divine light as you breathe in to your belly. Close your eyes and see a loving white light coming from the top of your head … and as you breath in, feel the light travellin' round your body, bringing love everywhere … right into your breasts." He paused for me to follow his instructions, encouraging me to breathe in deeply through my nose, hold the breath for the count of five and then exhale slowly. "Now I want you to silently say 'I love you, my wonderful breast'. First to your left breast, while holdin' the emotion of tenderness and love."

I fought the idea, wondering was he trying to make a fool of me. Perhaps he'd burst out laughing like a crazy circus clown if I went along with him. I flicked my eyes open for a brief second but he was sitting there with his own eyes closed and a serene expression on his face like he was concentrating. He seemed serious. I did what he suggested. And it felt strangely good. I continued to follow his instructions for visualisation and meditation, until he finally counted backwards from ten to one and told me to open my eyes.

"Do you think you could do that morning and night for the next while, Kate?"

I thought about it, realised I could. "I'll do my best." It all sounded daft but I was determined to try anything that had even the vaguest chance of working.

Chapter Twelve

Twice daily, I followed what he told me. I meditated as best I could, though in truth I found it hard to still my mind. Emotions I was uncomfortable with started to surface and it took great effort to accept the feelings rather than resist and suppress my fears, anxiety and sadness. The shaman had told me: "Whatever you resist will persist, remaining locked in your body until you accept it." I didn't really understand this language in relation to accepting emotions but I was determined to stop denying what I was feeling. And after a few days the meditation helped calm me and allowed me to see my feelings as transitory. For the first time in my life I began to feel I was no longer at the mercy of every thought that entered my mind. I was becoming the observer of my mind rather than a slave to it. This realisation helped me to ease into meditation rather than fight it.

The shaman had also given me essential oil of geranium mixed with a base of almond oil to massage into my breast twice daily, along with a homeopathic remedy called Byronia. The mix of aromatherapy and homeopathy was purported to work on bringing down the lumpiness. A leaflet he handed me on holistic breast care warned that deodorants and underwire bras could be contributory factors in breast cancer. Ironically, after my disgust at Ray's aversion to antiperspirants, I was now considering abandoning them. I read that they contained aluminium which blocked the sweat ducts close to the breasts and could possibly encourage the growth of lumps. The advice was to use only an eco-friendly deodorant and to forego tight under wire bras in favour of the softer sports version.

A dilemma occurred as vanity battled with common sense over the latter. How could I swap my lace-trimmed push-ups for a black nylon over-the-shoulder-boulder-holder? That would be an admission that I was finally willing to let myself slide into middle-aged decay. But I supposed it wouldn't kill me to wear the shapeless sports thing under loose t-shirts and save the under wires for special occasions... would it? The advice I was following was what Trevor called "hippie stuff with no scientific data for back-up". Never mind him, I was willing to try anything and even believe in miracles.

There was one other issue I needed to resolve and for that reason my psychologist Aidan Whyte agreed to fit me in for an emergency appointment. After exchanging the initial pleasantries and filling him in on what had happened since my last appointment, he leaned forward to peer at me from over his spectacles.

"Kate, you have always battled with the 'God dilemma'. You are by nature a seeker and you crave a deep spiritual connection, but most of your life you've suffered from what is known as 'Catholic hyper-vigilance'. You're so afraid of a judgemental God, you've trained yourself to be ever watchful of yourself for fear you could even slightly transgress or sin unbeknown to yourself."

"I know and it's worse now I've started to think I could die." Shivering, I pulled the blue pashmina from my lap to wrap tight around my shoulders. "I've been writing in my feelings journal in an effort to make some sense of the emotions I'm going through because I have this terrible guilt around divorce being a mortal sin. Can I read what I wrote to you?"

"Of course."

I pulled my black hard-backed copy book from my handbag. "If I die, will I meet the loving presence Sean the Shaman talked about or will I meet the devil Aunt Marge warns of? The judgemental God my mother and her sister refer to seems just as bad as his arch enemy Satan in his desire to punish me. I am equally afraid of both. I prefer to connect with a loving spirit – the Holy Spirit or the angels."

"Hmm ... it's good that you've touched on that. Good that you can relate to a more friendly aspect of the divine, Kate. Because at an early age, something or someone convinced you that God was the scary old codger depicted in the Old Testament, mad to condemn us all to hellfire and brimstone. It's one of the reasons you live with anxiety as your constant companion. And it can take a long time to get rid of old beliefs established when you were a vulnerable child."

"I don't really believe that stuff on a logical level, yet it haunts me during sleepless nights." I shifted uncomfortably in my seat in an effort to relax my sudden tension. "My mother's family constantly talked about people and things in terms of good and evil. Thanks be to sweet Jesus, her sister Marge lives in Chicago because she talks about nothing else and still sends packages of leaflets and books on biblical prophecies, Armageddon and Satan. Until recently my mother used to rant on about some of that stuff too."

"And what do you think all that is about?"

Biting my lower lip, I chewed on his question before answering. "A projection of her own fears and a way to control other people?"

"Absolutely. And it's a habit she is unaware of and unable to break. She's probably just repeating stuff told to her as a child. The church and indeed society has always sought to instill fear into people as a way of making them conform. Your mother never worked on her own self-awareness as you are doing. Did anything else come up for you around the subject of your own mortality?"

"Yes. It hasn't been all bad. I've been thinking about all the things I want to do before I die and that has given me a new zest for life. Isn't that strange?" I was suddenly aware I was twiddling my ring.

"No. In our culture, we usually shy away from thinking about death. It's different in the east. In Tibet the symbol of a skull is a sacred reminder to live every day as if it were your last." Whyte slanted his head in a perky manner. "It sounds like you're beginning to value life and find your own answers. You may be doing me out of a job, Kate."

Buoyed by my enthusiastic therapy session, I went for a brisk walk on the windswept prom and thought about the many things I wanted to do. I'd been pleased that Whyte considered I was making progress. I hadn't told him that I was still taking sleeping tablets. First on my list of things was to try and wean myself off them. They did me no good, and I was worried about being addicted.

As I took in the view of the sea, darkly rugged against the silvery blue mountains, I thought about the cookery book I had always dreamt of writing. I'd spent a lifetime collecting and inventing recipes. I promised myself I would stop

Love & the Goddess

procrastinating and make a start on it soon.

My thoughts were interrupted by a small boy running smack into me, while his mother battled with another child screaming in a pushchair. I set the boy on his feet, and he ran back to his exhausted-looking mother. It made me think – something else I'd always wanted to do was to help people less fortunate. If my book garnered success, I wanted to use some of the profits to help other women, especially single mothers battling the recession. I'd only recently begun to realise how lonely it must be for some women raising kids without a partner.

Squawking gulls overhead flew in a V-shape, signalling the imminent arrival of rain. I ran for my car. Parked beside me was a red station wagon, and a dalmation dog had its head stuck out the window. I paused to pat it. I hadn't owned a dog since my beloved labrador had died, leaving me heartbroken at fifteen years of age. Maybe I could get a dog now. But how I would manage it, I had no idea. Whatever about anything else, I was going to travel to exciting places – and the sooner the better. In many ways, my present predicament was opening my eyes. I was beginning to see life as an adventure with me in the driving seat.

When the day for my biopsy arrived, I was feeling healthy and my breasts were considerably lighter, less engorged. I felt that I had begun to bring about very positive change, not alone in my body but also in my over-anxious mind. The act of meditation had reminded me to breathe deeply and helped slow the racing thoughts. I still wasn't sleeping soundly, but rather than toss and turn I'd been getting up to write in my journal as a way of getting in touch with my feelings, hopes and wishes. I'd made a list of all the things I wanted to do, and I held this list in my head like a light.

I was sitting up in the iron-framed hospital bed after my biopsy surgery when Ella and James arrived in to see me. "I wouldn't take one doctor's advice on it, Kate. It sounds radical to whip out your breast just because of some calcium deposits," Ella said firmly.

James chimed in, "I know he's got a good reputation, Kate, but doctors have been known to whip out wombs in the past for no good reason. Now every second woman your age is having her breasts removed."

Listening to them, I was glad I'd told so few friends. They meant well, but I found it hard to listen to the endless debate and fussing which went on. Ella was propping my pillows up behind me. "You need to take a holiday some time soon, after all you've been through ..."

And James was nodding his agreement. "I keep asking her to meet me in Peru, after my month's Club Med cooking stint in Mexico ... I'm off there tomorrow." He was rubbing his hands together and smiling at the thought of it. "Come on, Kate, say you'll join me ..."

"Ah, I'll miss you. But I'll have to wait and learn what the outcome of this is before I make plans. I was watching that Brazilian healer on YouTube. If I'm desperate enough I might just be game for trying him. I could meet you in Peru afterwards."

"I thought you were too much of a doubting Thomas for psychic surgery?" James said.

"I know – but if other people can have blind faith and receive a miracle why not me? Oh, and remember to photograph the food when you're away."

A week after the biopsy, I was home and insisted on cooking for Ella. At four o'clock that afternoon, as I was unearthing fresh crabmeat from its shell, my phone rang.

"Munchkin man," I thought, as I heard the voice of the consultant. My heart leapt into my mouth and a throbbing started in my left temple.

"Mrs Canavan, it's good news. You're totally clear. I can't understand it to be quite honest with you, given how your mammogram looked. I need you to follow up with annual visits to me, along with regular mammograms."

Was that all he could say after putting me through hell? What a fool ... he shouldn't be let loose on the world until he gets a bit more experience! Suddenly that thought was replaced with intense relief. I couldn't stop myself as I danced around my kitchen in ecstasy singing The Beatles: *"All you need is love"*. Then screaming, "Whoopee!" as I jumped into the air. As soon as I calmed down, I rang Ella and told her we would be celebrating with shellfish, Kir royals and strawberries. While I'd been recuperating I'd developed a new recipe for smoked salmon timbales. Definitely a substitute for sex: the sauce set with a little gelatine was rich in cream and homemade mayonnaise, flavoured with brandy, garlic, thinly diced shallots and ginger – all these wonderful ingredients held the crabmeat together within the salmon mould.

"Kate, it's divine but there must be ten thousand calories in it. It's all right for you. You need to pile on a few pounds, but look!" She moved her chair back from the table to pull up her double-layered aqua-coloured jersey tunic. Then she sat back in her chair, laughing. "You know I looked that healer up on YouTube. Are you still on to go?"

"Yes, I emailed James right after I got the all clear,

and told him I was going there for the first fortnight and afterwards I'd join him in Peru."

"I'd love to go to Brazil with you."

"Really?" I couldn't keep the surprise out of my voice. I would have loved her to join me but I knew it wasn't the type of holiday she was used to. "I'm not sure if you'd like it, Ella. It will be very basic. You don't have any reason to go to a healer."

"I do! I suffer from gastritis and my back has been acting up. And I don't always need five star accommodation, you know. I just feel as if I'm being called to go on this trip with you. I don't know what it is. Business has dried up and I'm stressed. Maybe a bit of spirituality will bring me luck." Then suddenly, she added, "My grandmother always said what you do for charity comes back to you ten-fold. I could help out over there, couldn't I?"

"I suppose with the people in wheelchairs …"

"There'll be people there who are that sick?" Ella scrunched up her nose in horror. "But will there be a spa, you know, for massages and pedicures?"

"Oh God, Ella! This doesn't seem remotely like your idea of a trip."

"Kate, I'm serious. I want to go. And look, lovey, you won't be lonely with me around." She jumped up to hug me.

I certainly wouldn't be lonely, but I wondered would Ella be bored out of her tree. On the other hand, she was endlessly gregarious and never had problems making friends wherever she went, so perhaps I didn't need to worry. She was only interested in the first leg of my journey, to Brazil, and she had been very good to me during the past few weeks with all her advice about online dating.

Although, how could I have believed I could start a new relationship with a man without first healing myself?

Chapter Thirteen

"Ella don't buy a ticket – you're on the wrong bus. We need to take the 45."

"But the bus driver says we can get a connection from this bus to Rio ..."

"We're not going anywhere *near* Rio. Come on, quick. The other bus is nearly full." I was jumping up and down in frustration at the sight of other passengers from the airport pouring on to the bus we needed to take.

"Ah Kate, lovey, let's forget about the healer. Ten days on Copacabana beach will do a lot more for you. I'll treat you to the ticket." Ella tilted her head and smiled like a little girl lost.

"Don't be ridiculous! Come on, I have our suitcases! The 45's about to leave."

"Have you never heard of serendipity? It's a very spiritual concept. When something happens by accident you should go with it. Hey, I'll even buy you a new bikini."

I'd begun to wonder if I was dealing with an adult. It was just like when Julie was six years old and going through her stubborn stage. I'd had enough. "Ella, I'm off, with or without you." I marched off across the airport tarmac, pulling my bag behind me.

"Wait." Ella came hurrying after me. "Stop. You could

visit that spiritual author you like so much. What's his name? Pablo Coelho. He lives in Copacabana."

"Copacabana is not like Salthill in Galway! It covers *miles*. And he's Paulo, *Paulo* Coelho, and he's a celebrity author who probably has a bodyguard to keep people like us away." Why was I wasting energy entering into this nonsensical argument? "Come on, quick!" We made it to the right bus, out of breath, just as the driver was about to close the doors. Disgruntled, he descended, perspiring and muttering what were clearly expletives in Portuguese. He opened the baggage compartment and roughly hurled in our luggage. After buying our tickets I was lucky enough to get a window seat directly behind the driver, sitting next to a young Brazilian girl. Ella secured a seat three rows behind, a handsome businessman beside her.

The two-hour journey began, the bus vibrating like a pneumatic drill and leaping Evil Knievil-style over every bump. Potholes the size of baby baths threatened to explode the tyres and the driver revved the engine furiously to escape getting stuck, careering wildly all over the road. No wonder many of the older passengers, mostly women in headscarves, busied themselves with the frantic clicking of rosary beads. The test of faith had begun and I felt vulnerable. Shivering with hunger and cold, I rummaged around in my bag for a quick carb fix of homemade flapjacks. I'd been told it could be chilly in the mornings and evenings at the end of July so thankfully I had packed my blue merino sweater. I pulled it on over my long t-shirt and jeans.

We climbed rolling hills and descended into valleys teeming with giant broccoli-like vegetation. Gazing out at meadows awash with wild dancing flowers, I recalled the mixed reactions I'd received from people when I told them

I was heading off to see a healer in Brazil. Aunt Marge believed I was moving over to the dark side. My mother had said, "Halfway round the world to visit a quack. My only consolation is that I know you won't stick it. It'll be like the time you bawled your eyes out to get home after a few days in Irish college. Maybe it will finally cure you of all that hippie stuff." Julie had seemed annoyed that I would choose to visit a Brazilian healer rather than join her in Boston. A sceptic like her father, she'd always needed scientific proof before she could accept something as real. Trevor used to tell her from when she was little, "You know your mother can be a bit of a ditz!" She had heard it so often, I feared she partly believed it. Between the lot of them, the questioning and explanations had been exhausting. I agitatedly twisted my emerald ring. What business was it of anyone's, what I did? I was fast approaching forty-five and it was high time I stopped trying to be a people pleaser.

Only Liz hadn't passed any judgement. I was deeply concerned about my father, who seemed increasingly infirm, but my sister had assured me she would keep an eye on him. At least I would be able to pray and leave special petitions for him with the healer. I desperately wanted to concentrate on prayer and meditation away from the obligations of organised religion. It would hopefully help me release my own worries and relax into the feeling that I could hand everything over to a higher power. I looked down at my ring, and felt the old familiar ache in my heart for what had been. I blew on the large emerald surrounded by twelve small diamonds and polished it with the end of my sweater. A gleam of sunlight caused it to twinkle as though Tinkerbell had sprinkled fairy dust on it, and my mood instantly lifted. I reminded myself I'd survived – and had survived very well without Trevor for the past six weeks, to the point of working positive thinking and the law of attraction in healing my health problem. If I remained upbeat, my life could only get better from now on.

I must have dozed off, because suddenly I was jolted into wakefulness by the bus hitting a bump so enormous that my head ricocheted violently, sunglasses shooting off my nose. "Christ Almighty – what is he at?"

The girl beside me stifled a giggle, and asked in English if I was all right.

"Yes, sorry. I just got a shock. Are we here?"

"If you're going to see the Medium, then you are here."

"Do you know him?" I knew that the Healer was sometimes referred to as 'the Medium'.

"My grandmother lives near him." She pursed her lips. "I'm sorry, I don't believe in this man."

I looked into her eyes. "But he has healed lots of people …"

"I know peoples come from all over the world to him but I would not go to him. I just do not believe in any of that. I only believe in God. But I hope you enjoy your time here."

"Thank you …"

She stood up to leave, and I began gathering up my belongings. Ella appeared at my shoulder. "I heard what she said – do you think she's right?"

"Everyone's entitled to their own opinion, Ella. We've all seen him on YouTube and we've read the testimonials. Come on, let's get going."

We were just in time to save our suitcases from being tossed into a nearby sandpit by the sweaty bus driver. After recovering them, I asked him where we could get a taxi. "Where you go?" he grunted.

"Poussada Agnelo," I answered, showing him the address

and printed google map.

He threw his arms out. "No taxi here." He jabbed his finger at the map. "You walk dat way, you find one." Dragging our bulging bags behind us, Ella and I set off. Before long, we found ourselves on a narrow dirt road, puffing and panting as the smell of farm manure filled our nostrils. The sun appeared like an orange satellite dish, its rays belting down on top of our heads.

"How come no taxis have passed us yet?" asked Ella.

"Because no vehicle of any description has passed us." I snapped. "It looks like we've ended up on some back road."

"Look at the chickens." Ella pointed to five gangly fowl wandering over and back, quaking and flurrying as we passed. "It reminds me of my granny's farm in Connemara, back in the seventies – all the fields with weeds growing wild and the old stone cottages with their tin roofs. Though I don't think her farm ever smelt this bad." We burst into a fit of giggles at the sight of three black pigs, their snouts in a trough, happily munching potato skins and slops behind a barbed wire fence. It reminded me of that old Ireland too – my mother grew up on a farm in the midlands. But I'd never experienced anything as sticky as the red clay on this road. My black trainers and Ella's sandals were covered in it. "Just imagine if we were back home right now –we would be at the Galway races dressed in all our finery," said Ella.

"That's one reason I'm delighted to be away. Trevor and I used to attend every year with Liz and her husband. This year he'll be swanning around with Martha instead."

"I never thought of that. It's good you came away at this time, so," Ella said, rubbing my back in a reassuring manner.

No taxi passed us, but we weren't on the wrong

road after all, and we finally arrived sweaty and grimy at our accommodation. It was called a *poussada*, which in Portuguese means an inn. It was a very plain long one-storey building with small windows and a corrugated roof. A rotund Brazilian woman greeted us and briskly led us down a long corridor to our adjoining rooms, sparsely furnished yet spacious, with two beds each and stacks of fluffy towels in the plain but immaculate en-suite bathrooms.

"Not much hanging space, but much better than you predicted, Kate," said Ella brightly.

Yes, much better than I'd expected after listening to Trevor constantly warning me about "the flea-infested kip I'd find in lieu of a five-star hotel" if ever I visited a "third-world country". "You can leave some of your clothes in the suitcase and use it like a drawer on top of your spare bed," I suggested.

To which she merely replied, "Hmm ... I'll see."

Leaving Ella to unpack, I returned to my room for a shower. I sighed contentedly as warm water ran down my back, helping unwind tight knots in my aching muscles from the long flight and bumpy bus ride. A glance in the mirror startled me – a ghostly face framed by a mass of fiery candy floss stared back. My skin had taken on a deadly pallor, due to exhaustion. Thankfully I'd brought some tinted moisturiser, otherwise I was sure I'd end up being mistaken for one of the spirit entities that allegedly floated around the Healer's ashram. I rubbed serum into the mess that had become my hair in an effort to combat the effects of humidity.

Afterwards, I unpacked the excess of clothing I'd brought, from waterproof fisherman's trousers, in case of monsoon rains, to t-shirts, dresses and tunics for over leggings and skinny jeans. I laughed at the idea of having a choice of clothing sufficient to dress for dates with a variety of men from "spiritual" to "outdoor" types. I could probably glam up to satisfy a "sophisticate" in the sticks if it came to that. But no, I reminded myself, I'd left dating behind and was here for the good of my soul. After pulling on a blue tunic over navy cotton chinos, I sat on the edge of the white-covered bed to check if my mobile phone was working. I had three text messages. The first was a "Welcome to Brazil" greeting from a regional network. The second from Liz made me sigh as I read her warning, "Kate, have a great time. Mum said don't let that healer near u with a knife!" My mother had obviously forced her to write that to me, since she never ever sends texts herself. I scrolled open the next one, "Enjoy Brazil. Be safe Mum, Julie x". My heart warmed at the thought of good wishes from my daughter and I immediately sent her back a text telling her I loved her. Then I jumped up, grabbed my shoulder bag and left the room.

"Come in, door's open," Ella called as I knocked. I entered to find her fixing a bandana around her head. It matched her azure-blue embroidered kaftan worn over flared white trousers. Smiling at me, she twirled a triple row of beads dangling from her neck. "What do you think? Do I look the part?"

"If you mean 'hippie tourist on the spiritual trail' ... then yes. But you know we have to wear all white to the ashram whenever the Healer is present? Apparently it's easier for the spirits to work on us when we're dressed in white." I rolled my eyes heavenwards.

"I know, you told me. I picked up some great chain store bargains before I left. When I'm finished accessorising, they'll look couture. What are we doing this evening?"

"After dinner, we've to go to the ashram for an

introductory talk."

There was a knock on the door, and Ella rushed to open it. I stood out of the way as a Brazilian man wheeled in an empty clothes rack. We had passed it earlier on the corridor and obviously Ella had noted its potential. I'd forgotten how resourceful she could be. "Obrigado!" she cried, squeezing a five dollar bill into his hand. Then, "Oh look at these!" scrunching her nose in disgust, examining the distorted metal hangers dangling from the rail. "Not to worry, I'll work on getting a few proper ones from him later." She clapped her hands happily. "See how quickly I can turn any place into a home!"

As we entered the dining room, we were met with a clatter of conversation, at first difficult to decipher as four or five different languages vied for ear space. A group at the top table spoke German, while an elderly couple to their left spoke French. After passing a Japanese family, my ear tuned into English spoken in several different dialects: American, Cockney and Irish were somewhere in the mix. My nose twitched to aromas of garlic, lamb stew and roast chicken mingled with zingy citrus scents and wild herbs. Excitedly, I took in the mouth-watering display of vegetable and nut salads vying for space on the buffet table with a sunburst-yellow display of star fruits, melons and mangoes. "Oh Ella, I'd definitely run my own cookery school or restaurant if only I could buy fresh sun-ripened produce like this back home," I said wistfully, running my hand over the soft hides of papayas, apricots and nectarines sitting together like satin pompoms in a bowl.

"Stop romancing the papayas and get your meal," said Ella laughing, as she thrust a plate under my nose.

We travelled to the ashram by taxi, a black cab similar to London cabs but with two rows of seats facing the driver's back. There seemed to be no shortage of taxis in this area – several others arrived just as ours pulled up inside the high-walled enclave surrounding the blue and white building. Following the crowd, we made our way to a small room at the side of the building. There we took our seats on one of the middle row of benches among other new arrivals of all nationalities. Looking around me I observed smiling faces and noted that none of the people present looked obviously in need of healing.

"Who are the paintings of?" Ella asked, pointing to the row of pictures on the azure blue wall.

"Saints and ascended masters from different spiritual traditions," I answered. Since my breast scare, I had been in contact with James's cousin Maria who had mailed me a book and some photocopies on the Healer, so I understood what I was looking at. One of the Healer's main attendants stood up at the front of the room to explain how the Healer worked. "The Healer is an incorporate medium, meaning he allows one of up to three hundred benevolent spirits or entities to take over his body and work through him," she told us.

I shivered at the word "entity" – what had I come to? What if this was some strange cult? Would I end up frothing at the mouth and writhing on the floor spouting obscenities in a cloud of sulphur? A lifetime of Aunt Marge mailing evangelical leaflets from the States warning of Satan's rule had definitely got to me. The leaflets often told of how clever Lucifer was at disguising himself as an angel, a saint … even Jesus himself. Beads of perspiration clung to my brow. Christ almighty! I was here to get help with my anxiety and insomnia, and already I was a nervous wreck worrying about ghouls, demons and things that go bump in the night. Would I ever rest easy again? I grabbed Ella's arm. "Maybe we shouldn't have come."

"A bit late for that – you missed the opportunity of going to Rio."

A woman sitting in front of us turned around with her finger over her lips. "Ssh! Silence please."

I fell silent, still nervous – yet a scan around the sixty-odd smiling pilgrims in the room told me everyone else was happy and relaxed, as if this was nothing out of the ordinary. As soon as the introduction ended, we were joined by a tall American girl called Naomi who had spotted us arrive earlier at the *poussada*. "Believe me, people have amazing stories here." Her amber eyes widened as she swept chestnut waist-length hair over one shoulder of her gypsy-style top. "Earlier today I met an Italian lady who was back to give thanks. Last year she was here with three requests. She wanted to find love, financial security and healing. A year later – and I'm seriously not kidding you – she has met the love of her life, landed a great job and she is healed."

Ella pulled herself up to her full height, in an effort to hear the tall girl better. "I didn't think you could ask for material things when you put in your requests?"

"Why not? Material things are not bad in themselves, unless they are used for gratifying your ego. We live in an abundant universe and there is nothing wrong with working with the law of attraction. You just open yourself to receiving from the Divine." She held her upturned palms softly in front of her. "Receiving is a different principle to 'taking' which is like grabbing as if you were a greedy thief, jealous of what others have. We all need to count our own blessings and never compare ourselves to another. I used to constantly do that." Naomi sighed as though her previous attitude brought a recollection of pain. Then, visibly brightening, she continued: "Now I thank the universe every day for all the blessings I have and say I am willing to receive whatever else will enrich my life and so assist me in helping others." She gazed intently at each of us in turn. "In this way I have manifested greater health and doors have opened to me in my career as a dancer and a teacher of healing dance. At the moment I am leaving my heart open to the right man coming along for me."

"What you're talking about is like that book on the law of attraction, isn't it? The Secret? Tell me how you work it." Ella leant in closer to Naomi. I could see she was determined to get some new business venture going and if a philosophical way of thinking helped, she would work on it. I excused myself and wandered off through the crowd of chattering pilgrims, hoping to hear something that might assuage my fears. Many were discussing what a great honour it would be if the entities appeared to them. An elderly Irish man there for the third time told me, "This place is like a spiritual hospital. You get healing on every level of your being – physical, emotional and spiritual. This is my third visit and I will keep coming back. Last time I was here I actually saw the entities floating around as orbs of light." He must have noticed the blood drain from my face as I fidgeted with my ring, because he added softly, "Don't worry. Everyone has a different experience and the entities are very gentle. You won't experience anything you can't handle. Healing happens in strange ways. Just be open to it."

As we got a taxi back, I prayed silently that I wouldn't get cold feet and want to leave the place. My mother was right. It reminded me of going to Irish college when I was thirteen – after five depressing days in the remote wilderness of Achill Island I rang home begging to leave the place. I didn't want to be a quitter but I was having serious reservations.

Chapter Fourteen

"Doesn't everyone look gorgeous!" said Ella, as we turned the corner on to the main street and joined hundreds of white-clad pilgrims walking purposefully towards the ashram. It was certainly uplifting and my insecurities from the night before had dissipated as soon as the cock crowed at dawn and a ray of orange light streamed through the gap in my faded floral curtains.

"Hmm…" I looked the two of us over. "Even if we both happen to be dressed like twins in embroidered tunics and leggings. Looks better on you though, with your sallow skin. That lace wrap is to die for. I used to make lace as a hobby, you know?"

"Ha! Knew you'd appreciate it." Ella twiddled the ends of the delicate scarf, wrapped cowl-like around her neck. "It's vintage all right – a bit of altar linen, would you believe? I got it for a song at an auction. But what are you on about – me look better than you? You've a better figure for white. And look, all those women are wearing identical kaftans, probably from that stall across the street." Seeing us noticing his heaps of white clothing, the stall vendor winked and beckoned. "Need a hat, ladies?" But we kept on going.

"Look at the jewellery – isn't it fab?" I said excitedly, after noticing a short plump woman arranging a display of crystal and silver jewellery on a table outside her shop. They looked like something Julie might like. Rows of magnificent cave-like amethyst geodes glistened. Nearby a rangy mutt was barking over a bone.

Merging into the throng of angelic white, we floated past the main café with its irresistible aroma of rich roast coffee, locals taking their seats for strong early morning shots. The road widened as we arrived at the blue and white building and made our way to the main auditorium, where we sat on the second row of benches from the top. In front was a large platform. Paintings of saints and deities from Jesus to Buddha lined the walls along with deceased Brazilian doctors who – it was said –returned in spirit form to assist the Healer. People of all ages and denominations filed into the large blue L-shaped room, some on crutches and in wheelchairs and many with shaved heads, young and old. An overpowering scent filled the air; I could practically taste its oily flavour – a mixture of citronella and neem oil – powerful mosquito repellents.

"I like the music. Very soothing," said Ella. "What do you call it?"

I drew on the information Maria had sent me. "They're known as *bajans*, from the Indian Vedic tradition. The repetition of words in simple soulful songs gives a sense of permanency known as *Shashwat,* which means bringing presence to the now. All the spiritual traditions emphasise being fully alert to our present experience and emotions, no matter what comes up. Living in the now is the path to healing. Only past regrets and future fears unsettle the mind. We need to practice meditation and deep breathing in order to help us stay present and aware of our emotions, even if those emotions are unpleasant."

"I suppose it's great if you can do it," said Ella. The music changed and she jigged excitedly in her seat. "I know this one – I love it! It's *Santiago*, by Loreena McKennitt. It's hardly one of your so-called *bajans,* is it?"

"Not in the traditional sense, but the lyrics are repetitive in the way a mantra is, so it has the same effect …"

All of a sudden, the side door was forcefully thrown open. The Healer burst through – a large, powerfully-built man in a white lab coat. He strode past us and up on to the podium. The many hundreds who filled the room stared at him. His body was trembling as though he were standing on a massive power plate with the volts turned up to maximum. As his head shook uncontrollably, Ella nudged me, sniggering. "He's turning into the incredible hulk …"

"Shh!" I whispered.

Finally, his body quivered one last time and it was obvious a change had taken place as his posture became more erect and he assumed a strong look of intent. I knew from reading Maria's book that he was now 'in entity', taken over by a benign spirit to act as Healer. He called out something in Portuguese and one of the translators announced in English, "Volunteers for visible surgery, please?" Several people put up their hands and were told to step out of the crowd. The first, a young woman in a flowing white dress, was led before the Healer. I stretched my neck to get a better view as he held her hand in his, while placing his other hand on her head. Her body appeared to droop and relax into a semi-trance as he eased her into a chair against the wall. Next he removed her right breast from her dress and held it in his hand, massaging it vigorously before making an incision with a sharp knife. The crowd gasped and there was some muttering as he plunged two fingers into the open wound.

Rooting around, he fished out something round and bloody like a polyp. This he held up for all to see, before placing it in a jar. More gasping and muttering, as Ella nudged me. "The woman beside me says that girl is staying in her *poussada*. She came here with breast cancer. She thinks he's just removed the tumour. Imagine."

I sighed with relief at the thought of my healthy diagnosis. Thank goodness I wasn't desperate enough to undergo something like that. I sincerely doubted that I could have summoned up the same unwavering faith the girl had just exhibited. Years of living with a medic had made me more paranoid about hygiene and germs than I cared to admit. Trevor would have had apoplexy if he were here! And yet, apparently no one had ever contracted an infection after any of the Healer's operations. It was all the more astonishing, when compared to the amount of people contracting super bugs in our sanitised hospitals back home. I remained sceptical however, as I knew everyone who came here was not cured. The ashram warned people not to abandon their regular prescription drugs unless advised to do so by a medical doctor. Conventional medicine has been tried and tested and could never be overlooked on a mere whim in favour of "energy healing". Yet I believed something powerful was going on here – something science could not explain. Whether it was the power of intention, belief or loving energy, nobody could state emphatically. Einstein himself lamented the fact that most of us only use ten percent of our brain capacity, ignoring intuitive and other possible latent talents. Wouldn't it be wonderful to think that at some stage in the near future more of our potential could be tapped into and that we would learn to assist our own healing on both physical and emotional levels?

My thoughts returned to the present as the Healer took a suturing needle from the tray beside him and finished off by very quickly stitching the woman's breast skin back together. Her white dress was barely blood-stained despite the wound having been deep enough to accommodate the Healer's hand.

As she was led away to the infirmary for a period of recovery, a middle-aged woman with grey hair came forward. When the Healer placed his hand on her back, she slid languidly into the chair. Taking a small knife, similar to a tiny penknife, none of which appeared to have been sterilised, the Healer proceeded with his left hand to pull back the skin around her right eye, while he rapidly scrapped the cornea of the eye with the tiny implement. A film of mucous appeared to lift from the eye, which he flicked off before wiping the knife on his white lab coat. He then repeated the same procedure with her left eye. Like the woman before her, she remained relaxed during and after the invasive surgery. An American man behind us was telling his neighbours that the eye operation was great not only for improvements in eyesight but for everything from insomnia to migraine. Having been married to a doctor, I found my scepticism regarding this claim difficult to overcome. "Would you do it?" Ella asked me.

"No. I don't have that kind of faith. I won't go for the visible surgery. I'd prefer an invisible operation."

A man in his late twenties limped towards the podium, struggling on two crutches. Immediately, the Healer walked down to him, and roared something in Portuguese. The translator cried out, "Wake up all of you who do not believe! You need to see something? Then pay attention!" Taking the crutches, the Healer held the man's hands, urging him to walk with him. The man took four steps and then the Healer let go of his hands. "*Vir passear* – come walk!"

The man stumbled forward, one foot entangled in the other, and then like a young gosling found his feet and made two full steps ... then three ... four ... and finally reached the wall. After a long, collective intake of breath from all in the room, Ella and I joined in the resounding applause. "Are you going to join the queue?" I asked Ella. She was always complaining of reflux and digestive upsets.

"Nah, I'll leave it a few days in case he forces those awful herbs on me. I don't want to take them just yet because you can't drink with them. I'm going outside for air. Are you all right here by yourself?" She disappeared in the direction of the door while I joined the queue behind a woman pushing her young son in a wheelchair.

As I got closer to the Healer, I was gripped by a sudden terror. I expected that most sinister version of Mozart's *Dies Irae*, the theme music from *The Shining*, to start up any minute. My hands were sweaty and shaking. In my head, I silently called on the Holy Spirit to protect me in case Aunt Marge's superstitions proved true. Once I felt that connection to a source I trusted and believed in, I relaxed. The Holy Spirit had always been my number one when I needed a bit of help from the other side.

When I arrived in front of the Healer, he took my hand in his, eyes piercing me with a warm intensity. I sensed a sudden change come over me – a lightness I hadn't felt in years. My fears were evaporating and time was standing still. Tears ran down my cheeks as a huge surge of compassion and unconditional love – and something much, much greater – emanated from the man in front of me. Everything was happening in slow motion. I knew I was I experiencing something out of the ordinary – something which would be belittled by an effort to describe it or touch it in any tangible form. I would have difficulty explaining this to Ella, whereas I knew instinctively that James would understand.

The Healer spoke to the translator, who told me that he had prescribed herbs along with three sessions on a crystal bed. My elated mood sank a little as I had been hoping for an invisible operation which supposedly has all the benefits of surgery without the trauma. Resigned, I went outside and made my way to the booking office to arrange appointments for crystal bed sessions in the days ahead.

Chapter Fifteen

*A*fter booking the crystal bed sessions, I went in search of the pharmacy which I discovered was a hatch on the side of an adjacent ashram building. Queuing behind nine other pilgrims, I quickly arrived to face the blue-clad attendants who worked swiftly in dispensing prescription herbs in capsule form. Just as I was leaving, I saw Ella cross the wide open space from the main building where she'd obviously been hanging around near the soup hatch.

"Don't take any of those herbs yet, Kate. We've been invited to a party this evening and they clash with alcohol."

"Where's the party?" I asked suspiciously.

"I have the address here." She showed me a business card.

"Adolfo Gomez. Who is he? Where did you meet him? You can't possibly know anything about him."

"I met him while I was enjoying a bowl of soup at the café. He's perfectly respectable! C'mon, let's get some lunch and decide what we're going to wear – we need to do something light-hearted."

There was no dissuading Ella from going to the party. Only she could find some frivolous diversion in a place of pilgrimage, whereas I wished to experience the possibility of a miracle or at the very least some inner transformation. After lunch I returned to the ashram and tried what they call "sitting in current", the name given to meditating in the healer's presence in any of three adjoining "current rooms". I assumed that since I had been meditating regularly, it should be easy for me to do it here.

Apparently not! The packed room, aired by just a couple of fans, was humid and sticky and I found it difficult to calm my thoughts and stay present. Beads of sweat formed on my brow and I shifted my posture in an effort to get comfortable on the hard wooden bench. My body still ached from the long plane and coach journey and the prospect of sitting still for two full hours was a daunting one. I was in mid-yawn when an angry mosquito began buzzing around my head. Unconsciously, I opened my eyes and waved my hands in an effort to shoo away the pest. *"Keep your eyes closed and your hands on your lap."* A blue-coated assistant was addressing the crowd, but she had her eyes on me. In an effort to conform, I lasted fifteen minutes longer before gathering up my belongings to leave for the *poussada*. I vowed to try harder tomorrow.

It was with great reluctance that I got ready to go out that evening, since I would have preferred to spend time writing in my journal before taking an early night. But there was no dissuading Ella, who called for me at eight to tell me our black cab was waiting. The driver took off at speed up the main street before turning down a side road with high white walls on either side.

"It seems very quiet for a party. Are you sure you have

the right night?" I asked as Ella paid the taxi driver and we got out on the silent street in front of what appeared to be a plain pebble-dash house. With its continuous high wall running along the side, it was difficult to make out its exact size or shape.

"I fibbed. It's a double date. Oh don't be mad, Kate. Nothing serious – just a bit of male company. They're fine. Virtual monks, if you ask me. Hey, you can even team up with the good-looking guy."

"Are you mad? They could be crazies!" I was about to turn away when the wrought-iron door opened wide.

"Hello, ladies," said one of the most fascinating-looking men I had ever met. Of indeterminable age, anywhere between thirty-five and fifty, his facial features were so strong and outrageously unusual, he qualified as both ugly and beautiful. Ebony black skin, wide nose, wide lips, cheekbones so sharp they could slice cheese. With huge expressive eyes and a charming smile, the effect was totally disarming. "We've been expecting you. Adolfo's inside. I'm Nat."

Ella smiled at me and I felt as if I was compelled by a supernatural force to go along with whatever was about to unfold, despite wondering had I taken leave of my senses. As we followed Nat through the house, Ella nudged me, nodding at his trim torso visible through a black t-shirt over denim-clad snake hips. With his graceful, animal-like stride, he led us down the cool white stucco-plastered corridor into a large villa-style living room. There he introduced me to Adolfo, a short, stocky man in his early fifties with an air of business and a whiff of Cuban cigars about him. Ella had told me on the way there that Adolfo was originally from Rio de Janeiro, but she hadn't told me anything about this other man.

"Where are you from Nat?" I asked, after we got over the initial pleasantries.

"I grew up in LA with a Jamaican mother and a father who was half-Brazilian and half-American."

"And where did you two meet each other?"

"I worked in LA for a while," said Adolfo. "Our wives became best friends. I'm divorced now and back in Rio, and Nat's lovely wife passed on two years ago. But we still get together, and I keep this place here for whenever I come to see the Healer, maybe twice a year. Would you like some wine, ladies, or something non-alcoholic?"

Judging by the elaborate mosaic tiles on the floor, I guessed Adolfo was wealthy to afford a place like this merely for the odd visit. Not having started my herbs yet, I agreed to one glass of wine as I sank into the squishy tan leather sofa beside Nat. I wished Ella would stop winking. It was becoming very obvious. Soon the conversation was flowing along with the wine. I was on my second glass. The two men were interesting, both mellow and gentle in the way people who meditate regularly appear to be. Adolfo said he had become less hung up on making lots of money after he underwent a two-year battle with cancer, which had now been in remission for over seven years. Nat's wife had been diagnosed with ovarian cancer and Adolfo had suggested she visit the Healer, and stay in his house.

Nat took up the story: "Lexie didn't recover but she lived a year longer than any doctor predicted and she gained a great acceptance of death, for which we were both grateful. While she was ill, we visited the Healer four times and Lexie found an inner peace she'd never had in her life before. She was so devoted to him, she used to kiss his feet each time she came. She really loved the energy in the ashram and the village."

"This place is very peaceful and so is this house. The view is amazing." Outside the window, a gentle breeze nudged graceful hibiscus trees to salsa in and out towards each other while displaying their dark green leaves and trumpet-shaped pink and purple flowers, as if intentionally attracting the large bumble bees that clustered around them.

"You need to see the view from the balcony upstairs," Nat said.

"I'd love to. I could do with a bit of air." Following Nat upstairs, I wondered why Ella and Adolfo hadn't joined us. At the top of the stairs, Nat turned right into an open space, at the end of which stood a set of double French doors. These he slid sideways, before waving his hand for me to step through before him. I gasped as the most spectacular view stretched before my eyes. The chirping of crickets filled the air, scented with bougainvillea and pine. Tall trees forested the slopes of the untamed valley, while yuccas, cacti and vines flooded the garden below. As we stood there a flock of yellow butterflies fluttered within arm's reach. "It's wonderful," I said. There was a long silence. Eventually, I dared ask, "Why do you come back here, now that your wife has passed on?"

He said, picking a leaf from a mint plant on a tall wrought iron stand, "I have problems with addiction. That's why I've come to see the Healer."

"Addiction to what?" It just slipped out before I realised how intrusive the question was. "I'm sorry, if you don't want to tell me ..." Hiding my confusion, I raised my glass to my mouth.

Nat didn't look like I was intruding. He turned, smiling softly. "I am a sex addict."

I swallowed my wine in a gulp, hastily averting my eyes

to study a nearby jacaranda blossom. I could feel a hot blush turning my face bright red.

He said, "It sounds worse than it is, Kate. I'm not a sexual deviant. I became very promiscuous after Lexie died and I used sex as a drug. Believe me, a lot of people have this addiction and will never own up to it. Someone addicted to porn, even if he or she has never had sex, could be classified as a sex addict. If you understand the nature of addiction you will know that addicts cannot bear to feel their feelings, finding emotions too raw, their wounds too deep to touch. Instead they act out with inappropriate behaviour to dull the pain, but their lives eventually spiral out of control."

"Sorry. It sounds so ..." I couldn't finish the sentence. I wanted to say perverted and realised how judgemental that would sound. After all, I didn't really know anything about the nature of addictions.

"Dangerous? No don't worry. I assure you I'm not a rapist. And I try hard to practice celibacy because it's essential for me. I've started a new relationship with a lovely girl. We've been dating for three months now and our relationship is celibate because I know now that if a relationship starts out being sexual, then my judgement gets clouded. I need it to work on the friendship and trust level first, which is difficult."

I was humbled by Nat's frank admission and felt a surge of admiration for him as I watched him pick another leaf from the mint plant to chew in absent-minded fashion. "That's what I always thought, partly because I was brought up as a Catholic, but also because it felt safe. Then what do I do? At an age when I should know better, I go to bed with a bollocks on the second date." I winced. "Excuse me, that's my new word for someone despicable."

"We all have to learn our own way of being in the world,

Kate, and sometimes it's through our mistakes we learn most of all."

"So … Meeting me tonight? Why did you agree to it?"

"I love the company of women. That doesn't mean I need to seduce every woman I meet. Don't get me wrong. I'd still like to, but I'm learning restraint."

Listening to him talk like that, I was reminded of being told inappropriately at fourteen years of age by a woman I baby-sat for, that the reason she had had five children in six years was because "My husband, like all men, is sex mad." Since then, throughout my teens, I'd feared the sexual urge was similar to the opening of Pandora's box. It was easier for a virgin to be chaste but once tasted, sexual desire would be more difficult for either gender to control. "Good for you, Nat. I think I may be addicted to sleeping pills. I've been taking one every night for almost eighteen years. It doesn't always manage to conk me out, but I haven't been able to give them up." I fell silent, taken aback at my own admission, then turned to look at his face for a reaction.

"Balancing your chakras is important for handling addictions. You can meditate better once your chakras are open." His tone was soft, the expression on his face kind.

"How does that work?"

"I can show you how, if you'd like to sit with me in the meditation room next door."

Glancing at my watch, I asked "How long will it take?"

"Oh, just fifteen minutes." He walked across the landing towards a door on the left and opened it, gesturing for me to enter. It was an unfurnished room, oak floor covered with two large intarsia patterned rugs and a scattering of large square cushions in shades of orange and green. Unlit candles were placed at intervals in front of the skirting board. Nat walked over to a docking system and turned on some relaxing music. Next I joined him in sitting down as he demonstrated the correct posture for sitting in half lotus with the help of a tiny cushion called a *zafu*. I copied his posture, sitting with my spine straight.

"Now, relax your shoulders. Inhale slowly and deeply. Visualise a white light coming through your crown chakra. Relax and exhale."

After a few breaths I could feel myself melting into an easy peaceful bliss. Then Nat spoke softly. "Kate, your heart chakra is very blocked. May I adjust it for you? Just nod if you agree." I nodded. Then I felt Nat's firm hand resting flat on my upper back while his other hand seemed to make a small clockwise motion between my breasts. I told myself not to react even though my personal space was now being invaded and I could feel and smell Nat's warm minted breath on my face. I'd read about healers and gurus adjusting people's chakras, especially the heart chakra which is supposedly concerned with allowing in the emotions of love, forgiveness and compassion. Then a flush of heat swept over me and I gasped in horror. Nat had begun massaging my left breast in a manner more octopus than spiritual. Opening my mouth to protest, I was suddenly silenced by Nat's mouth on top of mine as he tried thrusting his tongue between my teeth. I bit hard. He gasped. Shoving him away, I jumped up. "Some reformed sex addict you are!"

"I'm sorry, Kate. I truly am. Please forgive me."

"Save your wretched apologies. They're wasted on me." I ran out of the room and down the stairs. I stormed into the open-plan living area where Ella and Adolfo were deep in discussion, examining packets of coffee spread out on the table in front of them. "C'mon Ella! I need to get out of here as fast as possible."

"What happened?" Adolfo took in my shocked expression, then clapped his two hands over his head in exasperation. "Don't tell me Nat lost control. Oh my dear Kate, I have to tell you he has been so good for so long but this new girlfriend is driving him crazy. Celibacy has never been more difficult for him. Let me call you a taxi."

"It had better come quickly," I said breathlessly.

"Five minutes, ladies! You have to understand that celibacy is much more difficult for a man. I too practice. But Nat has a girlfriend he loves yet she keeps him waiting. FBS is a terrible affliction!"

"Irritable Bowel Syndrome?" asked Ella, confused.

"FBS! Full Balls Syndrome. It drives a man wild. We feel better with EBS; Empty Balls Syndrome. Nat is so desperate from waiting, he would nearly ride a sheep!"

"Great, that's really great!" I stormed. "I'm practically assaulted and now you tell me he's so desperate I could have been a sheep. That's just lovely."

Adolfo looked pleadingly at Ella. "I'm sorry I said the wrong thing to your friend ... sometimes things get lost in translation. Really, Nat is not a bad guy and he will beat up on himself so much for this. We are all here for healing. Nat is here to cure his sex addiction."

Nat was creeping down the stairs, shoulders hunched, his hands together in a pleading manner. I wasn't going to hang around to absolve him for his wrong doings. "Ella, I'm waiting outside. I don't want to hear anymore."

Ella kissed Adolfo on the cheek and they muttered something about meeting again to discuss importing coffee. I hardly heard, I was already on my way to the front door.

After waiting a few minutes in the chilly night air, the taxi arrived, bringing us back to our accommodation. "Are you really mad with me?" Ella inquired sheepishly after we'd sat into the taxi.

"No I'm not, Ella. Funny thing is, I find myself believing Adolfo, despite the bull – or the sheep, for that matter. I don't think Nat's a bad guy and he probably is trying hard to battle an addiction. On the other hand, he could be a pure chancer." I laughed. "But now I'm more damaged than ever. Apparently I'm as sexy as any old sheep. I mean seriously how do I recover from that bitter blow to my ego?"

Chapter Sixteen

"Are you all right, Ella? I'm off for my final crystal bed session."

Ella had endured a bad bout of vomiting after absentmindedly downing a miniature bottle of gin she'd found in her suitcase two days after she began taking herbs. The retching went on so long, I worried her oesophagus would turn inside out. Being a hypochondriac ex-doctor's wife had its advantages at times – I permanently carried a portable pharmacy with me. I had motillium to quell the nausea and buscopan to stop the spasm in her gut. Soon I had her back on her feet but I thought she still looked a little shook. "Perfect. I'm going for a massage." A smirk formed at the edge of her mouth. "How are you after your invisible operation?"

I shrugged, "I didn't feel or notice anything – we had to keep our eyes closed. I wasn't even sure when the Healer came in to say prayers over us, since a couple of attendants were already praying in Portuguese before he arrived. And I haven't felt any different since."

"Do you think it is for real? And what about the crystal bed thing … I found it a bit disappointing. Thought I'd be stretched out on a giant slab of crystal instead of lying on an ordinary therapy bed with a row of crystals glaring down on top of me. Now how could that possibly do you any good, Kate? I mean this thing about crystals having power?" Ella gathered up her purse and phone from her bed, slipping them into her bag.

"I used to think so too, Ella, but I've researched it on-line and discovered that all rocks have vibrations. You know how we've such problems with limestone in Ireland in the foundation of houses and the radon gases emitted from it?"

"Mm... I remember when I got that last x-ray for my back, I told the radiologist I hated the idea of radiation. She assured me that sitting on a stone wall in some areas of County Clare would do more harm. So tell me what's so good about these crystals."

"Do you remember the watches we had as kids? In those days the status of your watch wasn't determined by which designer brand it was. We all checked to see how many jewels they contained and you'd find the number written in tiny letters on the face. Well apparently those little jewels or crystals helped to power the mechanism. Same thing with radios."

"You're right! I remember gran called the radio a 'crystal set'. Is that the reason?"

"Yes, and the crystals on the arm above the so-called crystal bed are designed by the famous IBM scientist Marcel Vogel, who designed the coating for IBM's hard disk drive. His research proved that all quartz crystals, cut to a set of exact specifications, produce a specific laser-like energy. He did experiments proving crystals were both filled with energy and could act as conduits of energy which is why they are used in watches, radios and modern medical devices."

"God, Kate you sound like Spock. So, what about the chakra thing?"

"I read about that in Maria's book. Apparently the light beams from the seven crystals down on your seven chakras or energy centres. They supposedly help balance our bodies. The word *chakra* means 'wheel of light'. Each of the chakras corresponds to seven different areas of the body which affect the health of the organs in that band." As I spoke I touched my throat, heart and stomach as an example of some of the areas I could remember. "Emotions are stored in each centre, which may block the flow of energy and cause disease. So theoretically ... working on balancing your chakras will help release emotions, get your energy flowing and aid the body's ability to fight disease."

Ella rubbed her tummy with one hand and touched her back with the other. "So I have a lower back problem and digestive upsets happening in the same area. What does that mean?"

"It means your creative and sexual chakra need clearing," I winked.

"Ha ... So the answer is to find a man and get my new career up and running."

I headed out the door laughing.

Having walked to the long low building in front of the ashram gardens, I was met by an attendant who led me into one of the small dark rooms where relaxation music played. I took off my shoes and she handed me an eye mask to wear over my eyes. "Lie down on the therapy bed and make yourself comfortable." She placed a light cotton blanket over me and aligned each crystal over the relevant areas of my body before switching on the lights overhead. In the background, music played, similar to the soothing *bajans* played in the ashram. I lay there breathing deeply, anticipating once more being swept away by a peaceful bliss. Instead images arose in my mind, beyond my control.

I suddenly found myself transported back eighteen years to the most awful morning of my life. My stomach knotted and twisted as pain pierced my chest to the point I couldn't breathe. Beads of sweat formed on my brow and my back felt as though I was lying on a bed of hot coals. My chest constricted, I panted in an effort to breathe but the dull ache I'd lived with every day started to become so acute I felt I'd been stabbed. "No!" I stifled my cry, a creature-like shriek of torment that came from somewhere deep ... outside and inside me, both at the same time. My arms wrapped around my body, I dug my nails deep into my bare arms. I felt bound, straight-jacketed by my own embrace, yet I wanted to run or at the very least tear tormented flesh from my bones – inflict physical pain in order not to feel the real pain. "*Why?*" My voice echoed in a plaintive cry from the bowels of some unearthly place. Thoughts tumbled inside my head – why had my baby David been taken from me? Did God want to punish me for some cruel reason? I'd been tormented by it every single day of my life. Rarely a day had passed when I hadn't thought of David and what he would be doing. Learning to swim or ride a bicycle, swotting for exams, getting ready to join Julie in college. David in love for the first time.

I thought I'd learnt to live with the grief and be philosophical, grateful that at least I had Julie. But now the entire episode was being replayed again. It started with the joy of holding my beautiful baby son, so perfect in every way. God ... I'd sell my soul to step back in time to smell David's baby smell, to touch his soft skin and hold him close. I knew I'd die aching for one last moment with him – begging for a single moment. Why were the feelings so raw now – as raw as though it had just happened yesterday? If there was a God, how could he be so cruel – so vindictive?

All of a sudden I let go, exhausted from my own intensity, no longer able to fight the torrent. Sharp aches cracked through my chest, my abdomen and my head, and just as it seemed it would finally break me, an image arose of me as a warrior breaking the rock of pain with a sledge hammer. Sighing, surrendering to deep breaths as though I were being breathed into by a bellows operated by a winged angel. Tears flowing … now tears of love, intense love, radiant as the Healer's that day in the Casa. David's essence emerging, all around me as I sink into an awareness of having been blessed to borrow him from heaven – for he was never Earth's nor mine to own.

The handle turned and the door creaked open, just as I pictured my hand reaching out to David's tiny index finger. Regretful the session had ended, I put on my sandals and quietly gathered my things to stumble outside in the direction of the garden overlooking a wild meadow of tumbling hills and forest beyond. Aromas of warm soup made with onions and root vegetables wafted on the breeze as I passed near the soup hatch. Pilgrims congregated outside at wooden tables, eating and chatting in competing dialects. But I was lost in my thoughts. I took my seat on a deserted bench on the wooden veranda where pilgrims sometimes went for private meditation and reflection. As I inhaled scents of lavender and jasmine, it struck me as strange that I was supposed to be living in the present moment and yet I had been forcibly sent back to face the past. Then I remembered what Aidan Whyte said on one occasion: *If you have not dealt with past issues they will continuously come up for healing. You drugged yourself with Prozac to deaden the pain. Let go of the fear and allow yourself to feel every emotion and you may find you can handle it. Walk right into the pain – remember, you are bigger than any one emotion."* What he had said seemed abstract at the time and I hadn't understood it, as though emotion was a foreign language I couldn't or didn't wish to grasp.

Opening my satchel, I took out a pen and the floppy A4 pad I'd brought as a temporary "feelings journal", intending to enter into what Whyte called a stream of consciousness – allowing words to appear without thinking. My eye followed my hand scribbling random words around the page: *God and punishment ... Mother's story ... Grim reaper ... The Prophet ... Snow Queen ... Thaw.* I felt I'd entered a vortex with my memory acting as a time machine spiralling backwards.

Trevor had been so happy as the locals in Kiltilough had congratulated us. "You've one of each, a boy and a girl, the perfect gentleman's family." I'd never heard the phrase before and have rarely heard it since. It seemed to imply we had pulled off some mighty stroke, favoured by the Gods smiling down upon us. David had been a quiet baby from the start, only crying if he needed feeding or a nappy change – unlike Julie, who had been very difficult to get to sleep. Initially it made me nervous and I often held a mirror close to his face to check he was still breathing.

Then it seemed, when I'd finally begun to relax, I awoke one morning with an eerie sense of heightened perception ... a sense of time no longer existing. Accompanied by a gnawing emptiness in my chest, I walked towards the nursery and remained for what seemed an eternity rooted to the outer threshold, unable to enter the room. "Don't look up," said the voice in my head. I stared at swirling shadows towards the edge of the carpet, cast from a colourful fish mobile attached to the lampshade and blown by a mocking breeze from the slightly open window. Standing there in the middle of the room was Trevor wearing burgundy-striped pyjamas. Stared at by a huge smiling Eeyore on one shelf and Winnie the Pooh on the other, he held our adorable baby boy in his arms as tears flowed down his ashen cheeks. I knew before I walked over to touch David's alabaster skin and cradle his doll-like remains, clad in a lemon velvet baby-gro. It seemed like I'd known upon waking that he was taken from me. But I could do nothing, not even scream or cry for a very long time afterwards.

The days and months that followed seemed to go by in some sort of haze. The Sudden Infant Death Association put us in touch with other couples who had suffered the same experience. It was good to talk to people who had been through the same awful ordeal, but I couldn't break the endless cycle of self-blame. I knew the starting point of my anxiety had really come into play when I had begun to lean on Trevor for support and direction. I had become another person – the bohemian, enquiring bubbly girl I had once been had died with my baby. Died with David.

Liz came to visit and offer her support in those early days. I told her over and over again in the week that followed, "I was his mother. I should have been better tuned into him. I should have known something was wrong."

"Kate, you did everything right. These things cannot be prevented. You breast fed him for three months ... no, don't tell me you should have done longer. Stop being so hard on yourself. Do you remember the story of a mother, by Hans Christian Anderson, that Dad read to us as children? It suggests that a child's hour of death is decided before birth and nobody should interfere in that."

I had momentarily stopped sobbing as I remembered the story of how the mother tried to bargain with the Grim Reaper until he explained that one of two plants in his garden represented her baby son's soul. The first was capable of spreading happiness and healing to everyone he met whereas the second would only bring evil and destruction. When asked did she still want to interfere in God's plan, the woman declined. I said angrily, "Well if God knew everything in advance, couldn't he have ensured David had the good genes?"

Liz didn't give up so easily. "We only ever have our children on loan – they are never ours to own." She continued her theme of parables in hopes of calming me, paraphrasing a section from Kahlil Gibran's *The Prophet* – a book I had given her one Christmas and had thought she was dismissive of at the time. Obviously, she had found it meaningful even if she couldn't remember the exact words to quote. It felt strangely more comforting to believe that David had been like an angel, merely visiting me for a brief time. This perception cracked through the endless "if onlys" and spoke to a deeper part of me where the need for analysis wasn't necessary. Yes, Liz had been a torrent of strength and wisdom and that had helped me in the early days

The overhead cries of a white-crested eagle awakened me from my reverie, bringing me back to Brazil and the present moment. I turned the page in my journal to write:

I'd become so adrift from my feelings. I'd become a bit like the Snow Queen, freezing my heart in ice to protect it. It finally broke again when my marriage ended. But the value of a broken heart is that it can be put back together and made whole. The real thaw and healing began today on the crystal bed.

I was astounded when I glanced over the last two lines of what I had written. It was through identifying with characters in stories, no matter how childish, that I could begin to accept and trust in a divine plan. I thought back to my experience on the crystal bed and was comforted that in some strange way my connection to the divine had grown and suddenly I had a renewed faith in the words my mother had uttered about David: "He's an angel now and will always be with you."

Chapter Seventeen

We arrived at the airport after sharing a taxi with two American sisters we'd met in our *poussada*. Ella had booked a flight to Rio and rescheduled her flights home for a later date, claiming it would be a mortal sin not to take in Rio after coming this far. And since she had come on a pilgrimage it would be better not to commit such a grave sin. On the lookout for a good business opportunity, she was determined to investigate products in Rio, having discussed importing coffee with Adolfo.

After check-in we met for a browse around the shops in the small airport terminal before entering duty free, stopping suddenly outside a lingerie shop with the most stunning negligee in the window. More like a very sexy evening gown, it really had the "wow" factor, with a silk satin skirt flowing from an uplift lace bra bodice, encrusted with black bugle beads. "Oh Ella, isn't that amazing?" I remembered how Trevor used to buy me nice lingerie. Despite my pilgrimage, I still found it difficult to be a woman alone. I regularly received emails from *"luvpicasso"* aka Geoff, but he was my only contact and we remained platonic friends. It would most likely continue in that vein, as he'd told me in the last one that he had met a girl from the site and had been dating her for the past three weeks. It was just as well I hadn't wanted anything to develop with him; I needed time to continue the healing which had so recently begun.

We went into the shop and checked the back of the gown. Its lace panel tapered to a V at the centre back below the bodice, through which a matching lace thong could be seen. The doll-like Brazilian shop assistant smiled and purred in response to our interest. "It's magnificent, no?" Her doe eyes lit up as she daintily turned the price tag to show us. "Not expensive for you – no? You American?"

"No, Irish." Ella nudged me. "That's an outfit to drive a man out of his mind. It's a Goddess gown. And not that expensive – if it had an Italian label it would cost three times that."

"It's still expensive for a negligee." I considered. "Unless you converted it to evening wear by adding a silk slip underneath."

"Creative as ever, Kate. How are you so brilliant? An evening gown for one hundred and fifty dollars …" She whispered into my ear. "You try it on for size and if it looks well on you I'm going to buy it and try to get it copied. Maybe I'll see if I can prise any information out of the sales girl about the designer."

Five minutes later I emerged from behind the curtains of the tiny fitting room to call Ella over and at the same time have a look in the nearby mirror. "Oh my God!" It was my face, but it didn't look remotely like my body with the clever corsetry uplifting my very average breasts to display a magnificent cleavage.

"Gorgeous, Kate. You look like you could go to the Oscars in that gown," Ella said, and the assistant murmured in agreement.

"Well, if it had an under slip …" I returned to the

changing room to put my own clothes on.

"This designer is a friend of mine. I met her when I was modelling," I could hear the girl telling Ella as they waited for me to get dressed. "What about you? Can I help you pick something special?"

"You can wrap up the gown and I'll pay for it. But do you mind me asking where your designer friend lives?"

"Are you going to Sao Paulo?"

"No, Rio, but I'm interested in looking at importing a variety of products."

"Then my friend may very well meet you in Rio. Here is her business card." The young woman handed Ella a gold-embossed card, just as I emerged from the fitting room. With forty minutes to spare before I was due to board my plane to Lima, we sat drinking coffee from paper cups on a plastic bench in the duty free area, as busy commuters passed by.

"That was a stroke of luck you managed to get the contact details from her," I said.

Ella nodded seriously. "It seems like that was good advice I got from Naomi, the American girl we met that first night, telling me to put in a request for help with starting a business. It certainly appears to be paying dividends. I told you I felt I was being called to Brazil for a reason, Kate. Adolfo gave me a list of export agents representing everything from chocolate-covered almonds to gem-stone jewellery and fashion. I'm over the moon. I think you and I benefited in very different ways from our trip." She paused to study my face. "You look much more relaxed, lovey, and I'm delighted you had a healing experience. I always thought it was unnatural that you spoke so little of David and to be quite honest with you I often had to hold back from talking to you about babies. Afraid I'd upset you. Strange because you were always so open about everything else."

"Trevor practically made discussing David a taboo subject. It all began when people started suggesting I should think about having another baby. First a psychologist mooted it, then Trevor's family and finally my mother. It was always said in the same coaxing manner, head cocked to the side, soft tone of voice as though they were talking to a half wit in need of sound advice. It was hurtful. Trevor and I were in agreement. David could never be replaced by another baby." The tears were coming, and Ella pulled a tissue from her bag and offered it to me while placing her hand reassuringly over mine. I wiped my eyes, before continuing: "I became so sick of the endless coaxing, I felt something had to be done. Since David's birthday occurred four months after his death, I decided to have a mass said in the house, inviting all the family. Trevor and I agreed we would make a speech, thanking everyone for their support, adding that while we knew everyone meant well, the suggestion that we should have another baby was a painful one, that we needed a certain degree of privacy in dealing with our grief. Then for some reason, I didn't understand, Trevor baulked just before everyone arrived and told me he would not stand for me making a speech. Imagine!"

"What did he say?"

"He spoke to me as if he were scolding a bold child, telling me he forbade me from raising the issue. It was the first time I saw a side to Trevor I had never seen before. The Mr Hyde to his Dr Jekyll, capable of frightening me into total submission. Perhaps it was irrational on my behalf for I knew he would never harm me, but his tone was that of a maniac. It shook me to my very core, as it would on later occasions, if ever he felt I might challenge him."

"Poor you! Obviously the grief hardened him. But what happened anyway?" Ella asked.

"After the mass we thanked everyone for their support. In many ways the whole event passed as a cynical exercise since I had given up on God. I saw him as the cruel authoritarian figure of the Bible, whose rules I had obeyed as a good little Catholic since the day I made my first holy communion, but who had punished me by taking my most precious son away."

Ella patted my back as she tut-tutted. "It was so tough for you. Did you both not get proper counselling at the time?"

"We saw the most moronic psychologist. An eejit if ever there was one, full of grandiosity. Lots of chat and back slapping about golf went on as the pompous fool sat back, him smoking Hamlet cigars while he dribbled compliments all over Trevor. He never once suggested we could do with working a grief recovery programme or talk openly about our feelings over David's death. 'You'll both be fine, you're two intelligent people who will cope in whatever way you see fit,' he said, placing an arm around Trevor's shoulder, before we left him after our final session."

"That's disgraceful. What has IQ ever had to do with emotional intelligence? You know I'm not as into all this as you are, Kate, but I was grateful to find a good therapist to help me through my divorce. I've heard some terrible stories of shrinks trained at every level, from having done only a three-month course right up to senior psychiatrists, some of them should simply not be practicing. If you attend one, he or she has to be able to help you work though your emotional stuff."

"Looking back, I don't believe we were ever fine together afterwards," I sighed. "Trevor never wanted to talk about David. He told me: 'I can't revisit the whole thing. It just makes me feel too sad and I can't cope with falling to bits like that.' Crying and feeling vulnerable made Trevor feel like he could be losing his sanity. He liked everything to be neat and tidy in his life and that included packaging up emotions in little boxes. It wasn't until I started having more persistent anxiety three years ago that I became aware of really needing proper therapy for unresolved issues. That's when I began attending Aidan Whyte on and off whenever issues arose."

"I've heard from different people that he's good."

"Yes, he challenged me to peel back my protective outer coating like the layer of an onion; told me that I had shut down emotionally as a result of David's death. That it was made worse by taking Prozac and sleepers over many years. In fact, he said it wasn't much different to having had a pre-frontal lobotomy, I'd become so adrift from my feelings."

"I'll tell you now as your friend, Kate, I didn't recognise you for years. You tried to become a Stepford wife to please Trevor." I must have looked horrified because she laughed good humouredly, hugging me as she continued. "Ah, but you could never put a good thing down for too long and now I can see the old Kate coming back stronger than ever." Taking my arm she raised it and punched the air saying, "Watch out world, here we come!"

"Agreed. Pity we're on herbs. It seems like an occasion for a celebratory drink."

"Are you excited about your trip to Peru?"

"Really looking forward to it and meeting up with James again. The shaman is quite renowned … supposedly very gifted."

"How did you hear about him? What kind of special powers is he supposed to have?" Ella examined an angry looking insect bite on her arm, then rummaged in her bag for a tube of anti-histamine cream.

"James had the contacts through a UK-based tour operator. Our shaman is featured on several websites. Even some movie stars have gone to meet him. A shaman is the South America equivalent of a guru. They supposedly contact spirits so I presume the Healer we just left is also a shaman of sorts." Ella was now rubbing cream into her arm. I thought I heard my plane being announced for boarding but kept talking. "Anyway they believe sickness of the body or mind really starts with a spiritual sickness and our loss of connection to nature. They use various tricks to challenge you to think differently and help you reconnect with nature and honour a deeper part of yourself. Some even say our DNA can re-arrange itself but that sounds farfetched to me. Anyway, shamanism is a method of integrative or energy medicine."

"Well, I'm glad you'll be with James because I'd worry about you going there to meet up with a strange shaman. They sound a bit like witch doctors."

This time I was sure it was my gate being called for boarding. Standing up, I slung my satchel over my shoulder. We hugged and Ella rubbed my back before I ran towards gate number seven. "Mind yourself, lovey," she called after me.

Chapter Eighteen

 *W*ispy cirrus clouds floated past like shredded cotton wool in a clear blue sky, too small in number to obscure the view below. Matchbox houses littered the valley and trucks crawled like caterpillars through mountain passes, cars moving like tiny ants. Normally I hated flying and securing a window seat never held much charm for me, but on this occasion my heart fluttered in excitement to be finally looking at the snow-capped Andes, land of the Incas and older long-lost civilizations. Like a child, spellbound for a full hour by the most spectacular view in the world, I recalled the stories my father had told me of noble Incan warriors many years ago. I was excited and felt liberated to finally arrive in Cusco after connecting from Lima. My first time travelling alone in almost twenty-four years, and I'd arrived without a kerfuffle.

After disembarking, I went to collect my baggage. A curious tingling had begun in my legs and I tripped over my feet as I pulled my bag from the carousel. Feeling drunk, I wondered was this a side effect of high altitude or the pills I'd taken to combat it. I knew Cusco was ten thousand feet above sea level and James's email had warned that it took some adjusting.

As I hauled my bag towards the door of the tiny rural

airport, my phone beeped to tell me I had a message. I presumed it would be from James. Instead it was a text from Ella: "Arr in Rio. Eat yr heart out. Fab place & gorgeous men. Enjoy Peru. Ella x"

In vain, I scanned the small terminal for James. Everyone had cautioned me about Peru being dangerous and I didn't fancy the prospect of going it alone here. I was suddenly worried and my heart began a loud thudding as I started to sweat profusely. Feeling a tap on my shoulder, I swung around to see a smiling James panting slightly. "Oh thank heavens you're here, James. I was just beginning to get worried – I didn't get a text from you. I thought you'd forgotten about me." It was so great to see him, I felt a rush of emotion – I had so much to tell him about Brazil and the trip so far. I'd missed being able to chat to him since he'd been away. No matter how many emails we sent, it was never the same as talking face to face

Now he placed one arm round my back and kissed my cheek. "Sorry Kate, arrived in Cusco yesterday but only just got here and my message sending failed three times. You look great! How are you?" He took my large wheelie bag and pulled it behind him as we exited the terminal in the direction of the car park.

"I'm good. I feel healthy and strong."

"Great, because you need to be fit for hiking. Are you up to a short trek today for our initiation ceremony, up to visit a power place?"

"I think so. My energy levels have soared after Brazil. How was Mexico?" I pulled my sunglasses over my eyes to deflect the glare of the midday sun.

"Loved it. Club Med was a great experience. There were a good few Asian chefs there, so I have an amazing selection of recipes. Took photographs of all the dishes and food displays for you too. They should blow your mind." He stopped before a big black van, a cross between a people wagon and a minibus. "This is it. Maria can't wait to meet you." James gestured for me to climb on board. The vehicle gleamed in the sunlight, polished to salon perfection with three rows of seats and loads of space to stretch out. There was no sign of a driver and the bus was empty save for a pretty blond woman in her early forties. "Meet my cousin Maria," James called, while depositing my bag in the boot.

I slid onto the seat in the second row, and turned to Maria in the seat behind. She offered me her delicate hand as we exchanged pleasantries. I noted a slight resemblance to James in the shape of her oval face and regular features, except her eyes were grey blue under arched brows on either side of a straight slim nose. Petite and small-boned, she had a neat blond bob and an ample figure. The overall effect was of a plain prim woman, much as I'd expected from our telephone conversations, when I found her English accent soft yet precise in tone. However, as she smiled her face lit up with a pretty femininity. "How did you get on with the Brazilian healer, Kate?"

"It was great. He's quite special isn't he? And the atmosphere among the people there is something else. Everyone goes around smiling. We had a lovely time. Thanks for all the information you sent me."

"There's a great mix of people there, definitely an advert for meditation. Some of them look fifteen years younger than their age."

"Absolutely, a great side effect of de-stressing. But tell me, you've been on the spiritual path for some time, haven't you?"

To my surprise Maria threw her head back, laughing. "James calls me a spiritual junkie, I've been on so many spiritual trips and travelled to listen to tons of gurus speak. My brush with cancer started it, but it's definitely become a passion." She sighed as she flicked a strand of pale blonde hair from the side of her mouth. "But to be honest with you, Kate, the real challenge lies in keeping a balance from day to day with the stresses and strain of everyday living."

"Absolutely," James and I chimed in unison.

"You are like other shamanic tourists who come here. You all have such stress back home because you have forgotten what is important."

I turned to see who had spoken.

"Kate, yes?" A man with hawk-like features and a Mohican hairstyle addressed me.

"Yes, I'm Kate and you must be..?" I offered the new arrival my hand and took in his appearance. He was tall, taller than average for a Peruvian man, his muscular frame well-dressed in co-ordinating cream shirt over smart khaki utility trousers. In my skinny black jeans, t-shirt layers and a black goretex jacket, I felt grubby in comparison. His bone-crushing handshake was so firm I had to shake my hand afterwards.

"I am Hakalan, your tour guide and shaman," he announced in heavily accented yet clear English, handing each of us a bottle of cool water before sitting into the driver's seat and starting up the van.

As the van pulled smoothly away, I turned to James. "In your emails you referred to visiting the famous Mayan sites. How was that?"

"Fantastic. I only had one day off per week but I managed to pack a lot in. Eco Coba, Ek Balam, Tulum and of course Chichen Itza."

"I've seen pictures of them and Chichen Itza has some special significance, hasn't it. Something to do with the Mayan calendar?"

"Yes, the Mayan calendar is incorporated into the design of the pyramid. It has ninety-one steps on each of the four sides which adds up to three hundred and sixty-four Also, on the spring and autumn equinoxes, and the summer and winter solstices, the edge of the shadow from the sun falls exactly on the corner of the pyramid, leaving one side in total sunlight and the other in total shadow. Quite amazing. Ouch!" James winced as we hit a huge bump in the road and grabbed the hand grip above his window. I grabbed the grip on my side in order to steady myself.

"Tell Kate about the trick with sound in the pyramid, James," Maria said.

"If you stand in a specific area in front of the pyramid and clap, your clap will be converted to a chirp, resembling the call of the Quetzal bird closely followed by the faint tinkle of a rattle snake. It's very realistic and comes from some echo. Both the bird and the snake were sacred to the Mayan people."

"Wow." For a moment I was speechless, wondering how an ancient civilization had managed such a feat. But I had something else I wanted to ask. "What really was the significance of the Mayans finishing their calendar on the twenty-first of December 2012?"

"Nobody can say for sure, but the general consensus is that it signified the ending of one era and the gradual beginning of another. That we're moving into the possibility of a more spiritual era where everyone will have an opportunity to attain enlightenment."

"I don't know if that could ever happen! It's fine when

you're on a spiritual journey, but as Maria said the real challenge is when we're under pressure coping with everyday life." I looked at Maria, and she nodded quietly in agreement.

"I will be talking to you about all of this during your trip." Hakalan had obviously been listening to our conversation and joined in from the front seat. I nudged James. I was suddenly sure this trip had been the right decision.

The views out of my window were captivating. Nature became art; the ravines, valleys and passes exploded with colour, from the steel grey of mountain rock to the purples and corn gold of crops covering the land. I envied James snapping happily away with his professional Nikon. Neither my camera nor iPhone were up to the job of capturing such beauty, but I knew James would share his pictures when we got home.

"Now we drive uphill, but we cannot go the whole way," Hakalan called back to us from the front. "So we will walk the last part. It's not very high but you need to hold on to your seats because it's bumpy." The bus started to ascend a steep pass. My skeleton felt discommoded from my skin as I bounced up and down in the seat. By the time we stopped it was a welcome relief to have to walk the remainder. Hakalan led the way, through a gate to a rocky pass which veered left and then took an extreme right turn up the top of a small hill, the path sparsely edged with woody shrubs and wild cacti. I found myself walking side by side with the shaman as James and Maria lagged behind chatting.

"Do you mind me asking how you became a shaman?" I asked.

"My father was a shaman before me – there's a lineage in my family. When I was a teenager he introduced me to the shamanic path. Long before that I heard Pachamama calling me to her." He pulled up his floppy wide-brimmed hat which had been hanging from a string around his neck – the sun was beaming strongly down on top of us. "I was naturally attracted to power places even when I was a little boy. The shamanic way is a calling from the place of the heart to tap into an inner wisdom where decisions can be made, not from the rational mind which is related to the ego ...." Here he paused for emphasis before continuing, "but from the heart," while tapping his chest.

"That sounds fascinating." God, I was beginning to sound and feel like a groupie. I'd even begun twirling my hair in a flirtatious manner whenever he looked sideways at me. What had gotten into me? He had a strange animal magnetism, almost panther-like. We'd stopped at the remains of some old stone dwellings and stood waiting for the others to catch up.

"What about you, Kate? Why are you on this journey?" he asked while we waited.

"To heal my broken heart," I said.

"Your heart will heal if you keep it open. Do not allow bitterness in. Have forgiveness," Hakalan said softly. As the others arrived, he announced, "We will have our ceremony here. Would you like to sit down? You can grab one of those big stones to make a seat." Seated in a half lotus position, he asked us to sit with him in a circle. He took several items from his rucksack, including a bottle of yellow-coloured liquid, Peruvian floral water, which he stood up to sprinkle over each of us in turn. The citrusy scent was pleasant and invigorating. "That will help cleanse your aura." He sat down again to cradle a metal bowl containing dried herbs. Striking a match, he proceeded to light them and place the vessel at the centre of our circle. "Now we will have our initiation ceremony to welcome you to Pachamama, our great mother earth," he said, tapping the ground, "This place is what is known as a power place. Can you tell me what you understand a power place to be?"

"A vortex. It has special energy," James offered.

"A place where ancient people came to worship," I said.

"Or give offerings," Maria volunteered.

"Yes, you are all right in some respects." Hakalan's dark eyes widened as he continued. "A line running around the centre of the Earth aligns Machu Picchu with the Great Pyramid of Egypt, the Nazca lines and Easter Island. Electromagnetic underground currents known as ley lines run through these vortexes. Machu Picchu is a primary energy vortex, which like the sun radiates rays to other places such as this place. The ancients understood sacred geometry and how these places were connected to each other along vertical lines. The energy is strong here. Do you feel it?"

James and Maria nodded. I wasn't sure since I'd had a tingling in my legs since my arrival. Hakalan continued, "I want you to close your eyes and breathe deeply. Let go of your thoughts and connect to Pachamama, our great mother earth. What do you want from this, your sacred journey? Go deep and see what it is you need. Then open your eyes."

We did as he suggested and after a few minutes opened our eyes. Hakalan was seated again and he began unfolding a scarlet cloth to reveal an elaborately embellished short Incan sword in an engraved silver scabbard. He kissed the sword and passed it to James sitting beside him. "I will pass this around to you and as you take it, hold it to your heart. Each of you say what you want to receive from Pachamama while you are here."

"I want peace of mind," James said, holding the sword

close to his chest. He then passed it to Maria.

"I want love, also to love myself." After embracing the sword, Maria passed it to me.

It took me a moment to think of exactly what I wanted. Then I held it to my chest saying, "I want to learn forgiveness." I had been planning to ask for the same as Maria, but in truth, I found forgiveness difficult and despite my best intentions seemed to hold grudges as I had done with my sister Liz. Some days I felt as if I could forgive Trevor, since it seemed we were equally responsible for our dying marriage. Then the next day I'd wake up lonely and want to blame him for rejecting me. These opposing sets of thoughts came in and out of my mind like waves in an ocean. After embracing the sword, I passed it back to Hakalan.

"All right, close your eyes again and let us meditate on that for a few moments. We call on the spirit of Pachamama to bring love into our hearts, to love ourselves and one another with great compassion and kindness. We ask that we may integrate the male and female energies in ourselves and in the planet for harmony and peace between all the races of this earth." Hakalan broke into a chant, like a drumming sound interspersed with crying, "Pach … a … mam … a." I flicked my eyes open momentarily and saw him stand up to blow wafting smoke from the incense over each of our heads, before sitting down again. I felt self-conscious as I briefly wondered what Julie and Trevor would think if they saw me. Then, just as quickly, I shrugged away the thought and relaxed. "Now, you finish by putting your right hand over your heart and your left hand over your centre, which is called your dantean. In this way you give yourself a loving hug. We all need to have forgiveness for ourselves and for anything we feel we have failed at, before we can forgive anyone else.

And we need to love ourselves first. Now breathe deeply as you sit there. Know that Pachamama holds you close."

We each followed his instructions. It was very peaceful sitting in the warmth of the afternoon sun, while birds sang in the nearby bushes. Time lost all meaning until eventually Hakalan told us to slowly come out of our trance. As James and Maria got up, Hakalan offered me his hand, a strong muscular grip pulling me to stand up. As our eyes met, a shiver ran through me.

Making our way back, Hakalan walked a few paces ahead of us. I felt a little insecure and wasn't sure why. The shaman had an unsettling effect on me and I felt I was a little on the fringe of James's relationship with his cousin. She was so quiet and serene that I found it difficult to strike up a conversation with her. I knew, as his only relative living in Ireland, she had been good to James when he hit rock bottom and finally admitted he was an alcoholic in need of help. They were deep in the midst of a conversation about family when Hakalan stopped, letting us pass through a gate ahead of him. On the other side he turned around to face us, a glint in his dark eyes as he spoke, "You know that here in Peru we worship the Goddess energy?"

"Yes," James said. "Tell us more about that. I've just come from Mexico and I'm trying to figure out the common denominator between these ancient belief systems."

"Your priests came here and killed my people." Hakalan spoke as though he were expecting a reaction. "They said the Incas were stupid because they were dark-skinned and did not speak their language or worship your God. They destroyed my people. The same thing happened in Mexico." He looked from me to Maria.

"I agree with you," I said. "It was terrible, but the same

thing happened to the Irish. We were invaded and conquered by the Vikings and then by the British. Our land was pillaged and taken from us and then we were left to starve during the famine only one hundred and sixty years ago. Around five million people died. Like your people here, we have a very wounded past."

Hakalan looked decidedly disinterested in what I'd said. "The Conquistadores and the church were all one. The Christian religion is corrupt. It has always been about power not love." He led the way to the van. Opening the door for us, he added, "Now you have all the scandals of priests molesting young men."

"Come on now," said James. "What has happened is terrible but that was not what Jesus stood for. I'm not a Catholic but I do know Jesus was an enlightened master. He didn't endorse the Conquistadores or the issues we have now with Catholic priests. He sacrificed his own life in the hope of saving humanity."

Taking her seat in the van, Maria said, "I was brought up Protestant and even though I no longer practice I believe our religion can be the gateway to our spirituality."

"All Christian religions along with Judaism and Islam insist God is male. All other religions acknowledge the divine feminine. Protestantism even went so far as to abolish the mother of Christ." Hakalan's words landed with a deafening thud. He turned his head away and started up the van.

After a few moments, silence save for the engine and the evocative Peruvian music from the audio system, I murmured, "I'd never thought of that."

James was not amused. "Religious doctrine is different to spirituality. That's why we're here on this trip - to try to unlearn some of the stuff that was drummed into us as children and instead learn some truths." He looked as if he was about to say more but decided not to finish. James was articulate and I knew he would be well capable of entering into debate with Hakalan but for some reason he was restraining himself.

"Me too," Maria said. "All the gurus I've attended have spoken of the need to unlearn before finding truth."

Hakalan said, "Good. In Peru we believe in the divine feminine, the divinity of Pachamama. We have respect for the earth. Christian religions never speak of caring for the planet that is being rapidly destroyed by human beings. Do you know we are the most destructive species to ever walk the earth? We pillage and rob from it, yet give nothing back. Bacteria give more back than we do, because they can recycle waste."

I finally twigged what the shaman was up to. He was provoking us to think differently. I knew that was supposed to be an aspect of the shamanic way of learning, yet I was beginning to find him arrogant. Exhausted, I drifted off to sleep, only awakening an hour later when Hakalan announced, "Now we are approaching Ollyantaytambo in the sacred valley."

We drove into a town nestled at the foot of the mountains, with a river running through it. As we bumped over a bridge, Hakalan said, "That is the Urubamba river. Every year it floods in the rainy season, threatening to wash away the houses and crops of the people who live here. This year was especially bad."

James nodded, "It was on the news. The floods were so bad Machu Picchu was closed down for a few months."

"It must have been awful for the poor people whose houses were swept away," I said.

"These people are stupid. *Stupid*. Why they build houses here?" Hakalan asked indignantly, looking at us in the rear view mirror as he crinkled his face, and shrugged his shoulders. "The Incas were not so stupid. They knew you cannot build houses at the river. They built in the mountains. They were master engineers."

I could feel myself redden from the neck up, dumbstruck by his obvious vitriol. It seemed very out of character with what he had been saying previously, not at all balanced. All spiritual traditions emphasized compassion for others, yet this man was being disdainful of his compatriots. This really was not how I expected an enlightened person to act.

Chapter Nineteen

The sky had darkened to a pre-dusk deep blue by the time we approached the Terra Toscana, a four-storey hotel with a simple entrance on a busy street in Cusco. After we booked in at reception, Hakalan announced he would show us to our rooms. "Leave your bags here and they will bring them up for you. We take the stairs, it is quicker." He smiled like an impish schoolboy and raced upstairs ahead of us.

It was a test of physical endurance after the day we'd put in travelling. Maria and I were both panting as we reached the third floor. After showing James and Maria to their rooms, Hakalan asked me to follow him down the corridor. He opened a door and ushered me inside. "You see what I get for you?" he said, as I stared in astonishment around the lamp-lit, Spanish-style bedroom, and took in the enormous bed, covered with a beautiful intarsia throw. "I get you this special room. It is the honeymoon suite. If they ask you must say your husband is in the mountains and he will join you."

Why was he saying this? "But he isn't with me and he won't be joining me." My voice came out squeaky with alarm.

"But I had to tell them he was coming, in order to get you this special big bed. A big bed is more comfortable for you to sleep in, yes?" This time, there was no doubting his knowing tone and the seductive way he was looking me up and down.

I was shocked – had I unintentionally flirted with him? Yet I wouldn't do that – I knew he was married; I had seen pictures of his wife on the website. "I don't need a big double bed …"

"Why not? You could take a lover while you are here in Cusco. Peruvian men are excellent lovers – they know about the Tantra."

In an effort to buy time and hopefully think on my feet, I crossed the room, opened the window and gazed out as if transfixed by something in the street below. This man was to be our guide for the next seven days. How on earth could I get out of this one without causing offence? Turning to face him, I steadied myself before saying, "No, I don't think so. You see after my marriage broke up I realised I preferred women to men. My lover is a woman, a beautiful woman, and I miss her."

His hawk eyes stretched wide with incredulity; his mouth dropped open. "Oh *qué lástima* … What a pity!" He shrugged his shoulders, and turned to leave. As soon as the door closed behind him, I locked it and breathed a sigh of relief. I'd been a coward making up a silly excuse, but I felt it would have been too uncomfortable to fall out with our guide right at the start of the holiday. I called down to reception, requesting a single room. Delighted to accommodate me, the porter arrived within minutes and showed me to a smaller, duller room with a queen-sized bed, hardly any floor space and badly-hung red curtains. I lay down for a few minutes to catch my breath and recover. It had been a long and emotional day. Then I unpacked, showered and went to visit James. Maria was already in his room, sitting on the edge of one of the two single beds that filled his room

"What do you think of Hakalan?" James asked, standing in the bathroom doorway with his toothbrush in one hand and a tube of toothpaste in the other.

I said cautiously, "I'm not sure. Is he trying to test us? They say gurus do that to push their apprentices or whatever we're called into more conscious awareness. Or is he just arrogant …?"

"Arrogant," said Maria. "I couldn't believe his contempt for the poor victims of the flooding."

I was relieved that her opinion chimed with mine. "You'll never believe what just happened …" I told them about Hakalan booking me the honeymoon suite, and my pretending to be a lesbian. "I don't know why I felt I had to make up an excuse not to sleep with him. I'm so sick of men thinking they can pick me up just because I'm vulnerable after a break-up."

Maria said, her brows knitted, "I had the same problem after my marriage broke down. I think in the early stages you give off this helpless vibe which appeals to men. And you know, a lot of these gurus are sex mad because *kundalini* – which is linked with sexual energy – gets activated through spiritual practice. When I was in India, women would queue up to sleep with gurus who hadn't washed for half a century. Hakalan must have expected you to fawn all over him."

James was disgusted. "This trip is too expensive to be ruined by a lunatic tour guide. When I was booking it, I asked the travel agent if I could contact anyone who had come on this tour previously and she gave me a couple of email addresses. I'm going to run down to the business centre and check them out right away. I should have done it before. You guys can get a taxi to that restaurant we booked and I'll follow on as soon as I'm finished. Okay?"

The taxi ride took us through the town's central plaza. I was enchanted by the prettiness of the place. The central area, dotted with flower beds and exotic palm trees, was lit with old-fashioned street lamps. Swarms of tourists sat on park benches or browsed the well-lit windows of the quaint indigenous shops that lined the streets on each of the square's four sides. Our restaurant, *La Taberna del León*, was rustic with wooden benches and red gingham tablecloths. James arrived as we were ordering, and told the waitress he would have the same as us. As soon as she'd disappeared with our orders, he leant forward across the table: "Girls, I got the guy from Illinois on Google instant messenger. He warned me not to expect anything great. Hakalan looks after Hakalan, he said. He thought him a sharp businessman, not an enlightened master. He was there with a big group, maybe thirty people, and apparently some of the women thought it was desirable to have sex with the shaman. They thought they'd receive the seeds of enlightenment, so to speak."

"They would be more likely to get seeds of STDs if he's that popular," I said, throwing my eyes heavenwards.

Maria sighed, "I expected to learn a lot from this man. I'm very disappointed."

"But maybe our journey is to learn from each other," I suggested. "After all, we've all had different learning experiences prior to coming here. And I did learn something today about the feminine aspect of God, even if Hakalan is a pain."

"You could be right, Kate," Maria said, as our tomato soup arrived. "When I was in India I met a wise woman who told me no guru or teacher can solve your problems because what another tells you is not your life."

"Indeed. There are no gurus apart from the one within,"

said James. "The problem is we paid to come on this journey and none of us are happy with this shaman. So I sent an email to the tour operator telling her just that. I've asked her to see if she can she get us Raúl. He's the shaman on the website, the one we were initially expecting. When she said we'd be getting Hakalan instead, I didn't question it because he supposedly has a good reputation. But I really don't think we should put up with him."

Just then the scent of tarragon in steamy chicken stock heralded the arrival of our main course. It was *Aji de Gallina* – a delicious chicken stew, served with slivers of hard-boiled egg with rice and garnished with olives. Very simple, yet different from any other chicken dish I'd come across. I made a note to remember it for my ever-expanding recipe collection. James drew my attention to a dessert called *Suspiro de Limeña,* a local speciality made with eggs and condensed milk. The friendly proprietor, a stocky woman with crooked teeth in a weather-beaten face, was pleased to tell us it meant "Sigh of a woman from Lima". She hovered beside our table for a few minutes, explaining: "According to legend, this was given its name by the famous poet José Galvéz, who said it was 'as sweet and soft as the sigh of a young woman from Lima.'" As we finished, she reappeared with a piece of paper in her hand. "Here, my dear, is the recipe for you."

Arriving back at the hotel, I felt strangely energised to be in Peru. Saying goodnight to the others in the lobby, I decided to visit the small room which housed two computers – the "business centre", as it was called. I had short emails from Julie and Liz and there was a nice email from Geoff the artist telling me his exhibition went well and he hoped I was enjoying myself. His email made me think about the dating site again. There had been a lot of talk of goddesses in the past twenty-four hours – the Divine Feminine and Pachamama. It made me think about the username I had given myself. The myth of Persephone was a metaphor for depression, a descent into the underworld of darkness. Though a goddess, Persephone was very much a victim, having been abducted by Hades, king of the underworld. She was childlike and frail, an archetype I'd always felt was personified by women like Marilyn Monroe, a baby-woman whom men liked because of her vulnerability. After the run in with Hakalan and the comment from Maria about sending out vulnerable vibes, I knew I no longer wanted to identify with that aspect of womanhood.

I logged on to the dating site. Though I had not used it for quite some time, my profile was still active. I knew as soon as the page appeared that I wasn't at all comfortable with being registered as Persephone. A warning message came up asking me did I really want to deactivate, since I had several unread messages. I did. I wanted to leave Persephone behind forever and I determined that no matter what happened I would no longer see myself as a victim.

A moment later it was done and I sighed in relief at how cathartic it felt. Maybe Pachamama was working through me. Whatever it was, I'd suddenly begun to feel how powerful it was to be a woman with the ability to give life. Hakalan was definitely a pain in the butt, yet he had provoked me to ponder certain questions. I was beginning to feel how genuinely like a mother this great planet Earth was in her indiscriminate support of all life. That potent creativity and the ability to give unconditional love is where our power lies as women. Why had I not considered using the name Demeter, Goddess of the harvest and Mother Earth archetype?

Chapter Twenty

A most unlikely shaman, Raúl turned out to be a slightly plump character with a jovial face that remained boyish despite his fifty-odd years on the planet. The tour guide had told James he was a Kung Fu master. I'd envisioned meeting up with a benevolent and swarthy Omak the knife, or at the very least a rugged brigadier, not a comical character who swaggered as he walked and occasionally referred to Maria and I as "my sisters", James as "my brother". Still he was a welcome change from Hakalan and certainly would be easier company during our time spent trekking to sacred sites for ceremonies and meditation.

Raúl forewarned us that our first trek, to Machu Picchu, would be a spiritual trial, testing us physically and mentally. The plan was to walk in the Incas' footsteps one way along the trail, before taking the train back to Cusco. Even though we had porters to carry our tents and belongings, and even with the help of sticks for support and balance, it was tough going. The sun belted down on top of us as we scaled mountain after mountain. My hiking boots dug into my ankles, and when we stopped for refreshments I had to spend most of my time re-bandaging them. I had not anticipated the extent to which my bones and muscles would ache, or that I would find the night cold and terrifying, staying in tents at campsites along the trail.

That said, my resolve to go on strengthened when I looked at the hard-working peasants in traditional dress, herding flocks of llamas through jungle passes near Incan ruins. The deep lines on the women's weather-beaten faces told of hard lives toiling for very little gain.

"One of the sole comforts they have is their cup of coca tea," Maria volunteered, as we climbed another steep hill. "*Mate de cacao* works like an anti-depressant for them." I'd become fond of the tea as a substitute for my familiar Lapsang souchong and knew it was good for altitude sickness, but I doubted Maria's claim. Too exhausted to chat, I made a mental note to ask about it later.

On the second day of the trek, my body weakened despite my will to plough on. "I think I'm getting a heart attack." I had my hand pressed to my thumping chest, and was leaning on my stick for support. "I don't think I can go on any longer. No wonder they call it 'Dead Woman's Pass'."

"This is one of the steepest inclines. Once we make it up here you'll be fine. Come on, you can lean on me," drawled Raúl, offering me his arm.

"I'm finding it hard to hike up another mountain having just scaled and descended the last one," said Maria. "I worked out in the gym for this trek but boy, it's hard going."

"You're both doing great, girls," James said encouragingly. "Not much further to go and ... Just look at the view!" Suddenly, it seemed as if we had entered a scene from a magical animated film. The misty clouds had parted to reveal ancient moss-strung trees on paths edged with exquisite wild orchids and giant cacti, the meandering Urubamba river far below us. We had arrived at Phuyupatamarca, and our spirits lifted.

Phuyupatamarca was an archaeological centre famous for its waters and springs. The Incas worshipped water, seeing it as sacred because it was vital to life. Raúl conducted a simple cleansing ceremony with us, in preparation for entering Machu Picchu the following day. Immediately afterwards we continued our descent to Wina Wayna, the final campsite on the trail.

"Let's look around, shall we?" James said to Maria and me, after we'd eaten a meal prepared for us by the porters who accompanied us on our trek. The campsite was teeming with tourists, excitement palpable as different groups celebrated arriving so close to their destination. As we walked through the crowds towards the bar, I caught the odd snatch of conversations in Spanish, French, Japanese, German and English.

"What are you drinking, ladies?" James asked.

"Beer, please," said Maria.

"Water for me, James. I need to keep hydrated."

"I recognise that voice," boomed a voice behind me. "Kate Tynan."

Amazed to hear my maiden name spoken on a Peruvian mountain, I swung around to find a man not much taller than myself, smiling broadly, blue eyes dancing in an impish face. "Billy Bunter! I mean, Billy Costello!" He was no longer as chubby as he had been when I'd last seen him, at his parents' thirtieth wedding anniversary, although he still had a cherubic face for a middle-aged man.

"Pippi Longstocking!" He grabbed my hand and shook it wildly. He'd obviously been out walking like we had – his bald head had received a fair burning from the sun. "How are you? Fancy meeting you here on the other side of the world and we haven't met up in Dublin for yonks."

"But what are you doing here?"

"Imports and exports. I come to Peru all the time, but this is my first time on the trail!"

I introduced him to James and Maria: "This is Billy Costello, my old neighbour. We grew up together, always teased each other mercilessly. Billy meet James and Maria."

After exchanging pleasantries the two cousins left us to catch up on old times. As we walked away from the crowds in search of a quiet place to chat, Billy said, "Sorry about your marriage, Kate. Your mother told my mum. Divorce is a nasty thing. I've been through it myself. But there is life after it." We found a wooden table beside cactus bushes displaying prickly fruits. I sat on one side and he took the bench facing me.

"So I'm beginning to believe," I said. "But tell me about you. You're the one who surprised us all. Lazy Billy Bunter who just wanted to eat chocolate and cake suddenly became the success story of the century."

"Yeah, I was as lazy as sin at school. But when I lived in the UK I set up a haulage company and then a food processing plant. I came back after my divorce five years ago – I'm living in Wicklow now."

Billy was the nearest I'd ever had to a brother and I wondered how we'd ever managed to lose touch. When we were teenagers, I knew he had developed a crush on me, mainly because I was always baking cakes. I never took him seriously as he had posters of Farrah Fawcett on his bedroom wall and I suspected he had a bigger crush on my sister Liz who was blond and toothy with big hair like Farrah, while I was tubby like him from eating too much cake. Yet I loved him and enjoyed the platonic relationship we had – in many ways I was afraid of the whole idea of having a boyfriend.

Afraid of what that might entail. Afraid of getting my heart broken. Afraid of sex and getting pregnant. Afraid of being on the pill and being considered a slut. I thought I was clever avoiding all that, but now it seemed as if I had missed out on learning some valuable lesson. I'd definitely had grass growing out both ears when I met Trevor. And the lessons arrived later in life, despite my caution. "Food processing? We always had food in common," I said laughing.

"Good job we never married or we would both be obese with a gaggle of roly-poly kids. Is your marriage definitely over, Kate?"

"Yes, definitely. This trip is helping me accept the finality of it. How about you?"

"Believe it or not Kate, I was a workaholic so we didn't see a lot of each other. My son and daughter are both in college in Dublin. It's great since I moved back – I see them often. The ex lives in London with her new partner. Hey, remember how I used to tell you about the house near my grandparents' in Wicklow?"

"The old house with stables and its own lake? You used to say you'd own it when you grew up and we laughed at you."

"That's it. Well, I bought it four months ago."

"I don't believe you. Seriously?"

"Cross my heart and hope to die. Isn't that what you always made me say if you doubted me?" He mockingly made a gesture of blessing himself, the way he used to do as a boy, and we both giggled. The gesture evoked warm memories of the fun we'd had together and I realised how much I'd missed my dear friend over the years. "Anyway, I got it at half the price it sold for six years ago. It's a bit of an old auntie that needs a hell of a makeover, but I've got great plans."

"Wow, that's what they call the law of attraction. You

seem to be good at manifestation, Billy."

He nodded. "I read one of the early books on the law of attraction – Napoleon King's book 'Think and Grow Rich' when I was nineteen, and it spurred me on to buy a truck and start that haulage company. But you know something? When it comes to my love life, I've been a disaster. I've attracted one drama queen after another. The wife was addicted to drama – she's a functioning alcoholic. Then I had a glamorous girlfriend, a total prima donna! I'm telling you, one after another. I could write a book on them but no-one would believe it."

I shook my head. "Nobody has it all, Billy. That's for sure."

"What about you? Are you still teaching?"

"For my sins, yes."

"Is it that bad, Kate? God, you were the most talented person I ever met when it came to food."

"Teaching can be a thankless job."

Billy went quiet for a moment, looking at me thoughtfully. "Well if you ever fancy a change of scene I'm opening a private cookery school on the estate in Wicklow. I'm not just saying this out of the blue. I'd intended contacting you anyway. It's just a major coincidence we met here."

"Are you serious?"

"Deadly serious. Cross my heart and hope to die!" Our laughter splurted into large adolescent guffaws, drawing the attention of four Italian tourists at a nearby bench. It was as if we were once again teenagers.

We chatted on, but my eyelids grew droopy and I yawned. "I better go Billy. I need to be up early for the final hike tomorrow."

"Me too. Give me your number and email and please

think about my offer."

"I will think about it." Running a private cookery school was certainly enticing, but I knew it would not provide the security my college job offered. I leant towards him for a hug. Gripping me firmly, Billy drew me into a close embrace with his right arm while tickling me lightly under my ribs with his left. He always tickled me when we were younger, enjoying the fact that I was especially sensitive. Things hadn't changed and I could feel the giggles bursting from me.

We arose at three in the morning for breakfast. We needed to arrive at Machu Picchu early, as only so many people were allowed through at any given time. An orchestra of hummingbirds added to the pre-dawn chorus as the pitch of night changed to a lighter blue, with streaks of orange, reds and purples spreading out along the horizon awaiting the sunrise. As Maria, James, Raúl and I walked through a mystical cloud forest it was easy to imagine the spirit of the Incas lingering. A flock of wild parrots flew over my right shoulder.

"The Sun Gate is here," Raul finally announced, his toothy smile lighting up his face. And there we were, standing facing what the Quechua people called *Intipunku* – the Sun Gate. We were about to witness another world.

And what a world that was.

It was so indescribably beautiful, no words or picture could ever do it justice. There in the distance, set atop two mountains, was the ancient city of Machu Picchu, built in the shape of a condor eagle spreading her wings. The early morning climb had been worth the effort after all.

"Incredible!" was all I could say, before falling silent, taking in the majesty of the fabled citadel, the sun rising behind us to light it up.

"I've heard it said that God has words you have never heard, places you have never been, and joys you have never experienced. Looking at this, I can begin to understand what that means," said Maria.

I wanted to stand there all day but with tourists arriving constantly it was necessary to move on and begin our descent into the city, exploring the ruins, with their intricately carved steps, altars, walls, houses, portals and terraces. "Look at how the huge stones fit together so perfectly, in all sorts of jigsaw shapes, without the use of cement," said James.

"And built to withstand centuries of earthquakes. The Incas had incredible knowledge of architecture and engineering," Raúl informed us, as we made our way to the bus which would bring us down to the village below.

"Isn't it incredible that the Incas managed to transport such big rocks to such a remote place?" Maria ran her hand over the side of a huge boulder. "No wonder legends abound about them being a race of super humans."

The bus took us the primitive yet bustling little village of Aquas Calientes and we went in search of a restaurant. "I have never seen so many pizzerias in my life!" I exclaimed in horror as we passed one after another set between shops selling souvenirs and handcrafts.

"That's because it's difficult to transport fresh food here," explained James. "Flour, cheese and tomatoes are less perishable than meat or fish."

"This is the best place to eat." Raúl paused in front of a French restaurant and bowed, with his hand out, to Maria and me. "Ladies first."

I gasped as I walked in the door of the pretty ranch-style restaurant with wooden floors, oak-beamed ceilings and ornately carved furniture. The tables were set with yellow tablecloths and blue serviettes to complement the yellow and green stained-glass doors and green carved wine racks. We climbed curved stairs to an outdoor seating area with a view over the town. After perusing the menu and making our choice, Raúl resumed telling us the history of Machu Picchu. "As well as an administrative centre, it was most likely a place of pilgrimage for noble men and women, a secret citadel unknown to lower classes. This is the very reason why the Spanish never found it, since its existence was not widely known."

"Was there a Goddess connection?" I asked.

"Ah my sister, some say that Machu Picchu was home to priestesses called 'Mama Cunas', the sacred virgins, who worshipped the sun and moon. This made Machu Picchu an important ceremonial or Goddess site, since it was also an observatory. The Incas were advanced in acknowledging women, yes? While in Europe, women who were healers were burned for being witches."

Our main course arrived. Maria and I had ordered ginger chicken, which arrived coated in a brown sauce. "Delicious." I purred with satisfaction at the taste of ginger in red wine sauce and Maria nodded as she savoured a mouthful of hers. Raúl had opted for a vegetarian dish consisting of potatoes, corn on the cob and French beans.

"Try this and tell me what you think," said James, placing some of his mango and chicken dish on my side plate. "See if your educated palate can decipher the ingredients and we can make a note of it." He placed a forkful in my mouth.

"Hmm ... Much sweeter than mine. Mango salsa with ...

lemon juice, sugar and garlic. They've then added roasted red peppers and almonds. The chicken may have been marinated overnight, it's very tender and bursting with flavour. What do you think?"

"I believe you're right, but with the addition of cilantro." Noticing Maria's raised eyebrows, he elaborated: "A herb similar to coriander."

Maria laughed. "You are both amazing with food."

"Not me. Kate is the one who can produce it better than anyone," said James, waving his hand in my direction.

"You are the Food Goddess," Raúl joked.

"Can you tell us more about what the Goddess means in spirituality?" I asked him. He had told us on the way here that he had spent time in the east studying the Kabbala, Buddhism and the Tao.

"I will tell you everything I know when we get to Amantani Island. That is the place to learn of the Goddess," Raúl answered with his trademark toothy grin.

Chapter Twenty-one

The evening we arrived in Puno before our visit to the island, Raúl delivered us to our hotel in the city centre opposite the plaza. After we'd booked into our rooms, he told us he would collect us the following morning, saying in his Peruvian drawl, "Okey dokey ... Six thirty, I am here waiting for you. Yes?"

James, Maria and I met for breakfast at six, just as the dining room was opening. Since most of the kitchen staff hadn't yet arrived, a continental breakfast of tea, toast and orange juice was the only choice. Forty-five minutes later we were standing outside our hotel, and still there was still no sign of our shaman.

"Where is he?" I asked impatiently.

"If we knew he wasn't going to be on time we could have had a lie-in after the journey yesterday," said Maria indignantly. "What's the point in getting us up so early?"

Only James remained unperturbed, busying himself with his camera as he adjusted the lens. Holding it at different angles he experimented with shots of the plaza across the street, now bathed in early morning light. Three young boys arrived, dressed in black jeans and t-shirts. Two of them had a wooden shoe-shine box swinging between them. "You want your shoes polished?" the first one asked in broken English.

"How much?" James asked.

"Ten dollars."

"Too expensive."

"I do yours five dollars," another said to me.

Though I'd made an effort at washing off the mud from the trek, my shoes were still in a bad state after our hike. I rooted around my small rucksack where I kept a little coin purse with just enough money to see me through the day, and took out a five dollar bill. Immediately, the youth argued with me that he would need ten dollars to polish both my boots. I presumed he was going to barter so I told him I would pay six dollars maximum. To our surprise they appeared to suddenly lose interest, picked up their shoe-shine box and ran away. Just then Raúl arrived, all friendly smiles.

"We've been waiting here since six thirty," I said, pointing to my watch.

His face turned crimson. "I'm so very sorry. I should have said seven thirty. A problem with translation. But listen, I make it up to you by getting you nice food for a picnic. What do you want? Fresh bread, cheese, plum tomatoes, ham, olives?" He looked at us expectantly. It was hard to be angry for any length of time with this good-humoured man. "You eat all this? Yes, with some fresh herbs and pastries? Yes?"

"Hey, I'm coming with you." James stuffed his camera into a rucksack and handed it to me. "Mind this, Kate – a camera's a liability in a market. I want to pick up some of that wonderful dried oregano. I'll get you both some."

They disappeared like a puff of wind into the van. Since it was such a beautiful morning, Maria and I decided to cross the street to the town plaza and pass the time sitting on one of the wooden benches watching the world go by. Puno definitely couldn't compare with the colonial splendour of

Cusco, but the plaza was pretty on a sunny morning. We sat back to witness preparations getting under way to celebrate a local fiesta, the place gradually getting busier as women in traditional costume passed by. The cooing of pigeons filled the air as a few men erected a stage several feet away, behind some trees. We paid no more attention to the numerous boys hanging around with their shoe-shine boxes.

"Aagh!" Maria screeched as something landed on her face. Large white daubs were hitting us both, spattering my pink cotton cardigan. "Damn pigeon poo." But it was far too plentiful to be pigeon poo. Two boys with spray-paint guns were aiming straight at us. Suddenly, another boy grabbed James's rucksack from beside me and ran. Leaping to my feet, I chased down a side-avenue after the boy, wiping the paint out of my eyes with my cardigan as I ran. Fired on adrenalin, I screamed "Stop thief!" to the almost deserted street. The boy, probably aged around fourteen, rounded a corner and I followed, finding myself out of breath in a shadowy alley with four youths walking menacingly towards me. I froze, aware that I could not escape as they circled me like vultures.

The tallest of them came closer to me, brandishing a flick knife. He was probably no more than fifteen but when someone holds a knife that close, they've all of a sudden become very powerful, no matter what their age. My Taekwondo skills were not up to scratch. Where was Raúl now that I needed him? He was supposed to be a Kung Fu master. The boy spoke – first in Spanish and then in accented English. "Empty your pockets, lady. Give me your watch and ring."

Trembling and sick with fear, not knowing what else to do, I emptied my pockets which contained several crumpled tissues and a stick of chewing gum.

"Your watch and ring," he ordered again. Seeing me hesitate, he repeated himself and came closer, seizing my hand roughly. My heart raced as terror coursed through my veins. I attempted to buy time – someone must have seen me chasing them, would come to help.

"They're both fakes. Give me time. I've got a credit card back at the hotel. I can get some money for you at an ATM machine."

"You think we fools, lady? Last time I ask. Give them to me."

"Okay, okay!" Terrified for my life, I slid the watch off, followed by the ring.

"Leave her alone." It was James's voice, and in an instant they had pushed past me and then him, fleeing like a pack of hyenas. "Are you all right?" James was panting, concern in his eyes.

"They've taken your camera, I'm so sorry." I was shaking. "And my watch. And my ring."

He put his arm around me. "It's me that should be sorry. Christ, I feel guilty for not being around."

"No. Really, it's fine." Tears stung my eyes. "This would never have happened if Raúl had kept to his word. First he doesn't show up, then after he arrives he disappears. Well, he'd better use all his tricks to find my jewellery …"

"What possessed you to run after the boy?"

"I don't know, I just thought he'd panic and drop the bag. Really, I don't know, James. These guys looked so innocent in the square – only children, really. A different story when you meet them in a deserted alley …"

"Your watch and ring were insured, right?"

"But they can never be replaced – especially David's ring."

"David's ring?"

As we walked back in to the plaza, I spilled out my rambling thoughts between stifling sobs. "Trevor gave me the Rolex when Julie was born and the ring was to celebrate David's birth." I wept as James squeezed my hand in sympathy. "On my first Sunday home from hospital, Trevor called me after my mid-afternoon nap. I'll never forget, he was holding David and had Julie by his side. She was so excited, she said, 'Mummy the baby has a pressie for you in his handie.' And then she jumped on to the bed beside me and opened David's little fist to reveal the ring." I drew in a shaky breath. "The gesture was so cute and so imaginative for Trevor. It was one of my most treasured possessions. How ironic that I should come on a spiritual journey and be robbed of the one possession I vowed I would be buried wearing. I regret coming to Peru now."

"Kate, you don't mean that. Maybe this is your personal challenge to overcome."

"James, I've had enough personal challenges over the past couple of months to last me a lifetime." As we rounded the corner, we found Maria and Raúl talking to two policemen, their postures erect in smartly-tailored dark uniforms. We could hear Raúl's voice, "Ah … is terrible." I was furious with him.

Maria, suddenly spotting me leaning on James's shoulder for support, came running towards us. "Are you all right, Kate? I was so worried."

"My watch and ring were taken along with James's camera," I announced loud enough for all to hear.

"Now we must all to go to the police to file a complaint," Raúl said, leading us across the plaza towards the police station. Once there, a plump woman in police uniform handed us paper cups with coca tea, which I drunk gratefully –I had come to love the drink. Raúl translated questions between us and the police in the tiny grey-walled office. We were shown a series of mug shots, all young offenders. It was almost impossible to identify any of them for certain, since people of a different ethnic background tend to look alike in the eyes of tourists, unaccustomed to the subtle nuances we spot in our own race. Children's faces are even more difficult since time has not yet weathered differences in their features. I could only be certain of the eldest one, as he had come close enough to threaten my very existence. I could never forget his menacing stare. But I certainly didn't want to point the finger at an innocent boy. James and Maria said they recognised two of the shoe-shine boys, but I wasn't sure about identifying them either as the ones with the plastic guns or as members of the gang in the alley. Raúl explained that the policeman was certain they were part of a group from Juliaca, a nearby town. From what they were saying, I realised that there was very little hope of retrieving either the camera or my watch and ring as all stolen goods were quickly passed on for sale on the black market. Most likely they would be sold over the border, into Bolivia. A black cloud enveloped me as I realised I might never again wear the ring that connected me to David. The thought of it being roughly passed around and ending up in the hands of someone oblivious to its sentimental value was soul-destroying.

"These boys were obviously watching you for a while to see what each one of you had in your bags. They knew exactly which bag to steal," Raúl translated after one of the policemen spoke in Spanish to us.

"That makes sense – my rucksack was very shabby in

comparison to either of yours," said James.

We left the police station and made our way slowly back to the hotel. The overcast sky now appeared menacing, the heat more humid and clingy than I'd previously found it in Peru. My mouth was dry and I felt quite nauseous. I felt driven to explore every avenue in the hope of getting back my ring. I would go to all the markets, bribe anyone in the hope of getting it back. I called Raúl over. "I've seen how people acknowledge you here on the street. You must have contacts. Surely you can ask around. I'll even offer a reward. A finder's fee to get my ring back."

"It doesn't work like this, my sister." He squeezed his hands together, as if pleading with me to understand. "This older boy is from Juliaca, part of a gang like a local mafioso. They are not trusting of anyone. They will not take a reward. But I can bring you to the black market to buy a very good fake Rolex for thirty dollars."

"Are you mad?" I stared at him in disbelief. "That won't solve anything."

"I can only tell you how sorry I am."

"How do you know they won't take a finder's fee? If I offer five hundred dollars as a reward, that's much more than they could make selling my watch and ring on the black market, right?"

Raúl alternated between screwing up his face and stretching his eyes open wide as if he was searching for the right words to convince me. "It does not work this way, my dear Kate. You have insurance, yes?"

"But the sentimental value …"

He placed an arm around my back. "I understand this is upsetting for you but James has also has lost something, his camera, and he accepts it."

Immediately, I felt the tears flowing. "Oh James, I'm sorry, all your lovely Mayan photographs and all the food pictures…"

"Kate, don't worry about that. It would be much worse if they'd cut your finger off to get the ring, because that can happen…"

"You're right, I'm sorry, but I can't help grieving… It was my precious link to David…"

As we arrived in the door of our hotel, Raúl said, "Why don't we go on the journey we had planned for earlier today? It's just one hour away. We can meditate and have a ceremony. Maybe something will happen during this time." I didn't know what he meant by this, but James and Maria agreed and so I reluctantly accepted the idea, despite feeling I'd rather storm the whole of Puno looking for my ring.

The three of us boarded the black van, and the shaman drove in silence. I was reminded of the Healer's ashram as Loreena McKennitt's soothing music played on the stereo – the Canadian singer was popular with "spiritual folk". We passed men and women herding llamas, sheep and goats against a backdrop of mountains, some of which were curiously flat-topped. Finally, after driving up a steep pass, we got out to hike the remainder. It was an easy climb as the mountain was paved with wide evenly-paced steps.

"We are ascending." Raúl was walking ahead of us, but half turned towards us, taking sideways steps, motioning his hands in the manner of an orchestra conductor. "As we ascend physically, our spirits find it easier to ascend."

On the top of the mountain were pre-Incan burial chambers called *chulpas*. Made from large rocks like those we had previously seen in Machu Picchu, the stones once again slotted together without the use of mortar to form a cylindrical funerary tower on one side and a rectangular tower on the other. Each had an opening at ground level. All the openings faced east, Raúl told us, due to the belief that the sun is reborn by Mother Earth each day.

Raúl had spent some time in Asia studying martial arts and the Tao. He explained to us that by practicing very simple Qui Gong, we could channel energy and improve our health. I was familiar with this idea from attending Taekwondo classes where the instructor taught us a little about Qui Gong. As we stood on the top of the mountain, Raúl led us through some very basic exercises, while we breathed deeply and stood in an open stance with our weight evenly distributed on both legs. It was strangely relaxing yet empowering to do this on the top of a mountain. "These exercises will help you clear away all the negative energy of the day. Help to free you up and to allow great spirit work through you," Raúl said.

Afterwards, he invited us to sit on one of the many large rocks littered around as he shook scented Peruvian flower water over each of us. Next, he talked us through a visualisation for meditation. Sitting there, with my eyes closed, simultaneously aware of the stunning view, I felt totally enraptured by nature. The warm breeze caressed my cheek, like a tender embrace from Pachamama herself. My upturned palms began to quiver, as though they were powered into a gentle current sending soothing waves throughout my body. Though I couldn't understand what was happening, I relaxed into that lovely feeling. My heart was opening as though my chest was expanding – there was a sudden feeling of surrendering to a power so much greater than anything I'd ever dared imagine, let alone believe existed. I knew there and then that my capacity for love had no boundaries, that I was loved unconditionally, and that my spirit understood love. I was simultaneously the lover, the beloved and love itself. And I wanted everyone in the world to have the gift of feeling as I did in that moment.

When Raúl told us to start coming out from meditation, I didn't want to. I wished to remain in that blissful state forever, there on that mountain forever. Of course that wasn't possible. Looking across at James and Maria stretching their arms like newborn infants, it seemed they too had experienced what I had felt. Afterwards we picked cocoa leaves and as we blew on one each, we made an intention, like a wish, before placing it in the opening at the base of the circular burial chamber called a *chulpa*. My intention was that I would again experience that same sense of serenity whenever I most needed it.

We walked back to where the bus was and the shaman lifted our picnic basket out of the van, bringing it over to us as we sat on one of the wide steps nearby. Despite the trauma and gloom of the morning the atmosphere had changed between us to that of light gaiety. In the warm sunshine, as the basket was opened, the scents of home-grown oregano along with nectarines and mangoes filled our nostrils.

"Here you go. You must only eat peeled fruit in Peru." Raúl placed an enormous peeled tomato on top of tin foil and began splitting an avocado. "You can spread this on your bread, then sprinkle herbs before adding some delicious tomato." He was smacking his lips. We did just what he suggested, beginning with lashings of avocado, followed by fragrant oregano and succulent tomato. It tasted like the best recipe Larousse Gastronomique could ever produce. I felt that if I could condense the taste of Peru, I would bottle this simple combination.

"Kate, thanks for trying to save my camera. I feel guilty

about what ended up happening to you," said James, as we sat on a step near the bus enjoying the remainder of our picnic.

"Oh God, don't feel guilty. I was the one who ran after the boy. I don't know what madness came over me."

"When you come on a journey like this, whatever happens, be it good or bad, it's teaching you some lesson you need to learn," Raúl said, between mouthfuls. "Do you think you can accept this?" He glanced from me to James and back again.

James said, "What happens if you don't accept the lesson?"

"Then life will teach you the same lesson over and over again until you finally learn it."

"And what is the lesson?" I asked, knowing what the answer would be.

James answered for the shaman: "Not to be too attached to anything," and Raúl nodded in agreement as Maria also murmured: "Yes, non attachment."

"Oh look, I was mad as hell but I don't want it to ruin my time here," I said. "I'm certainly willing to chalk it up to having learnt a lesson. It would have been so much worse if any of us had been stabbed by those boys. And I still have my memories. I came here to heal and that's more important than worrying about possessions."

Maria touched my arm gently as she looked at me saying, "Kate, that is what my mother would call 'grace'."

Chapter Twenty-two

*O*ur next stop was for two days on Amantani or "Love Island". We stayed in a mountain-side guest house, and every morning and evening we scaled the path to the summit to meditate on love and compassion. Raúl had suggested that I should try sending love and light to Trevor as an exercise in forgiveness. He said, "Where there is a loving intention, un-forgiveness cannot exist. You will eventually feel gratitude for the lessons learnt and your heart will mend." I focused on this exercise whenever I visualised love and light at the start of a meditation. Bit by bit I began to find it easier than I would have thought possible. It made me feel light-hearted, as though I were being released from shackles.

As we headed down to the guesthouse after yet another ceremony, Raúl told us: "I am taking each of you in turn for a tarot reading in my room and afterwards we can have a discussion on the boat back to Puno. First I see Kate, while the rest of you do whatever packing you need."

There's always that strange sensation, entering a man's room, knowing he has slept there. I knew I need not fear Raúl making any untoward advances – in fact, he had an asexual vibe. Yet as I walked in, I was immediately hit by a very strong male odour, like testosterone mixed with smelly socks. I found him sitting at a small table with two decks of cards piled on either side. He indicated for me to take the chair opposite him, and I sat down feeling somewhat apprehensive. What was he going to tell me? He asked me to shuffle the first deck and then cut it into bundles of three, which I did. Then he asked me to choose one bundle. After I chose the middle section, he proceeded to lay out the cards on the table.

"Oh, you're reading my fortune – I hope it's good."

"Ah no, my sister!" He threw his hands in the air – I was surprised by his evident frustration with me. "The tarot is a tool for revealing your subconscious. The past is irreversible but things must be learned from it. The future can never be foretold, unless you give someone that power over you and you make it a self-fulfilling prophecy. The power, *your* power, is in the present moment and that is what you need to learn. If you do not realise your true power by the time you leave here, then your journey will not have been completed."

"Do you mean I manifest my own future from the thoughts and intentions I have today?"

"Yes indeed. Good, you are getting it. You need to have right thoughts, rights words and right actions in the present, then your future will be as bright as possible." He grinned at me before returning to examine the cards. "You have been accustomed to luxury and now you feel insecure, yes?" When I nodded, he continued, "A new phase of your life is beginning yet you are resisting change, afraid to trust?"

"No, I have improved. I am more accepting of change now. I accept that my marriage is over. That was hard in the beginning."

"Ah, but opportunities are being presented yet you want to stay as you are for the sake of security." Raúl glanced up at my face, before spreading the cards around and continuing: "Seven of cups says you must decide to use your talents. There are other cards to suggest new talents. Page of swords: a new creative talent. Ace of pentacles: a new venture could bring financial reward. 'Whatever you sow, you shall reap tenfold.' Kate ..." Here he looked up, his eyes intent, "You have always tried to be in control but this has not worked for you. Why not let go and trust – you see? – like this card." He pointed to the 'fool'.

"Because that's exactly what a fool does. Doesn't make plans and just saunters along through life." I fired back. The card depicted the fool ready to walk off a precipice with merely a knapsack on his back, apparently whistling as he went. Ridiculous.

"No," he answered me, although I had not spoken. "No. You are wrong. The fool is also wise, and trusting like a child. He knows that when you trust in life and you stop trying to control everything, the universe and the divine work with you. They cannot work with you if you push them away through doubt and blame. Then you are making yourself a victim as if you are at the mercy of cosmic forces. You need to see yourself as a co-creator of your life."

"Are you saying I should simply sit back, do nothing and everything in my life will work out fine?"

"No, I am suggesting you start being true to yourself and follow your heart's desire rather than force yourself to fit, like – how you say? – a square peg in a round hole, because this is what you did in the past when you wanted to please people, maybe your parents and your husband. Yes?"

"Oh I get you. Yes, marrying Trevor impressed my parents and offered me financial security."

"Ah, finally you are beginning to understand. You did not

listen to your heart. Me too. I was afraid to trust in my work as a shaman and I spent ten years working in business making a lot of money. I married a woman because she was pretty and respectable – the wrong reasons to marry. Then one day, she disappeared to Mexico with my child leaving me broke." He placed his two hands on his head as though squeezing his skull. "Ah … I had an ulcer and had to start from scratch again. Funny thing, when she was gone I realised I was happy although I had lost everything. I hope I never do such a thing again."

"What do these cards mean?" I asked, pointing at four cards to the left.

"Here you have the card of the queen of cups, which means you are a woman men find alluring and mysterious, like a goddess. And because you have had a lot of pain and you have embarked on healing, others will be aware of your healing energy. Not consciously, but they will be attracted to you for healing. For this reason, you could attract many men but they would be wrong for you."

"They all seem to be wrong for me," I sighed.

"Again you must first follow your gut instinct and then listen to your heart. Next you have the card of the devil which says you must break a dependency before it becomes an addiction. You are a very driven person, very creative, but this can lead to compulsive behaviour. I have seen you carry around a little black bag with medicines for headaches and all sorts of sickness. Do you think you have a problem with needing pills?"

I felt my heart pounding as I looked at the image of the devil with horns, cloven feet and a tail. I could barely focus on the image as Raúl's words sounded like a distant echo. I rushed to defend my position. "I take a sleeping tablet at night, but not more than one even if it doesn't work. I can't sleep without it."

"You should stop all dependencies as soon as possible. When you are dependent on someone or something you cut yourself off from your own power. Imagine a powerful woman like you enslaved to a little pill! The problem is that your dependency could increase, so you must conquer this. Yes?" Raúl's eyes locked with mine. "You know the Qui Gong exercise we did on the mountain. I want you to do this every night, bringing down the energy from your head to your feet, so that your thoughts slow down. Then you can lie down and do deep breathing. Believe in this and it will work."

"Ok, I'll do that," I told him earnestly. He had voiced my own fears concerning the sleeping tablets. I had never taken a second one, even when I hadn't slept for several consecutive nights, because I knew that could lead down the slippery slope of addiction.

"Now before I tell you the last cards I want you to pull one card from the other pack. These are power animal cards." He fanned out the other blue pack of cards and I picked one. "Ah … Like me you are a wolf." He beamed as he showed me the card with a wolf baying at the moon. "My name means 'Wolf, the fearless adviser'. I think you were a shamanic medicine woman in a past life. Maybe this is the reason you like medicines." He laughed and I joined in. "You see your last cards in the tarot are the moon and the high priestess, symbols of the Goddess Hekate, the moon goddess. The wolf is associated with the moon and learns a lot of lessons in this life; she in turn can teach others. The wolf can adapt to new circumstances and outwit her enemies. Is good. But you must remember to stop the blame. You must accept life as it is right now and then you will come into your power."

"Oh but Hekate is a terrible goddess." I knew from Greek mythology she was the patroness of witches. Bad enough that my birthday fell on Halloween and I'd been teased for being a witch, as I was growing up. Yuck! Hekate was even called the crone … an old witch. This is not what I wanted to hear.

"No, she is wonderful. The most integrated goddess, full of wisdom. You will learn Kate. " He stood up. "But now I must see the others. Tell Maria to come for her reading."

I went downstairs to the kitchen where I found James and Maria drinking tea, their overnight back packs stacked against the wall.

"Maria, Raúl wants to see you now." I walked over to switch on the kettle and throw a bag of coca tea into a cup. I noticed James watching me curiously.

"How was it, Kate?" Maria inquired.

"Interesting and quite empowering. He doesn't really tell you anything specific because he says the future depends on our own intentions and decisions."

"He's most insistent that you realise your own power as a human being. He feels we lose our power when we depend on anything or anyone to fix us," James said. "I know that from past experience. By the way, Kate, do you know that coca tea comes from the same leaf as cocaine?"

"Yes, but it doesn't go through the same chemical process as cocaine, so it's not addictive."

"Hmm … It gives a bit of a kick all the same. How many are you drinking a day?"

"Anything up to eight cups with camomile, it's been brilliant for combating altitude sicknessm…" I suddenly understood what he was saying. "Christ, you're a bit late warning me against it now, we're going home in four days' time."

"Just start cutting back to gradually wean off. We won't be this high up when we go to Arequipa or the Colca Canyon."

Maria sighed. "I wish I was coming with you. I can't believe I'm going home tomorrow. I'll miss you both."

"I'll miss you too," I said. "It's such a pity you can't stay the extra few days. But we'll meet up again in Ireland."

Back in my room, packing for the next leg of our trip, I fell into deep thought about what the shaman had said. There was no doubt he had been very intuitive and I could finally understand what he meant about being open to change. I was excited about the prospect that perhaps I would learn to trust and follow my heart's desire but I knew this was a process, not something which would happen overnight, since I'd always needed security.

I unzipped my wash bag to take a look at my sleeping tablets. As James had suggested I do with the coca tea, I knew I had to wean myself off the pills. But I felt I couldn't just stop them overnight. After all, I had been taking them for the best part of seventeen years, since David's death. But I'd needed someone to speak firmly to me about them and Raúl had done a good job of convincing me to stop. Each pill had a little line down the middle so I could cut it in half with a sharp knife. I decided I would alternate between taking a full tablet and a half tablet every other night. Then after two weeks I would cut down to a half tablet every night and eventually stop altogether. That way, I would be off them completely in six weeks' time and I'd probably feel a lot better as a result.

When Raúl had finished all our readings, we walked downhill to the pier. The blue and white speed boat in which we had arrived was there waiting for us. The driver started the engine as soon as we were all on deck, seated under the canopy. Raúl threw open a picnic basket, for each of us to help ourselves. We were ravenous, as we had long worked off our breakfast with all the walking. The boat sped along over the calm waters of the lake, sparkling iridescent under a clear blue sky.

Between eating, our conversation turned to James's excursions to Mayan sites. "Raúl, what do you believe the end of the Mayan calendar meant?" James asked.

"Ah that is a good question!" he said, holding up his right index finger and pursing his lips. "It was not about the end of time, rather a new time for humanity. A time of awakening to our true life purpose. I call it the Goddess power because it is the Divine Feminine … a moving away from the love of power to embracing the power of love and caring for our planet. Yes?"

"So are you suggesting that all of humanity will be swept up by this urge to change?" Maria asked.

"No. Not everyone will want to change, but in time when they have suffered enough pain and sickness, those who are wise will see the old ways are not working. It will also become apparent that we must care for our planet."

"Can you explain how that could become a new order? I don't understand how?" Maria asked.

"Oh, many times before we have had new orders. Just think of the ancient Egyptian empire, the Incas and the Mayans," Raúl said.

"Or the Enlightenment in Europe," James suggested.

"Yes, it was a similar energy in some ways – yet this time, it is not the preserve of an elite group. I need to draw a diagram for you to explain." Raúl rooted out a hard-cover notebook from his overnight bag. In the centre of a page, he drew a vertical line, with an S-shape replete with curvy tail going though the centre.

"That's like a dollar sign but with more curves," Maria said.

"Yes, the dollar has been the most recognisable currency – a powerful yet one-sided symbol representing economic systems along with a love of money and power. Now look how this symbol can change." Raúl beckoned us in closer as he drew a backwards-tailed S intertwining the first one. "Look, now do you see how it becomes more balanced, changing into a symbol of integration?"

"It's the symbol of the medical profession – the *caduceus* from Greek mythology," I answered, proud to give a well-informed answer.

"It's also used in the East," Maria offered. "I was in India and did some Kundalini yoga. It's the symbol of Kundalini energy. But that's an ancient symbol."

Raúl grinned. "Yes, we are now looking to the wisdom of the ancients. In Kundalini the staff represents the spine in the body and one snake is ascending while the other is descending through the body's energy centres. Kundalini is known as the integration of opposites – the unity of male and female energies within all of us. The Goddess energy moves up and down in a wavy motion along the spine, raising consciousness."

"So what has the Goddess to do with this?" I asked.

"The Goddess is the feminine aspect of God or the cosmic breath of the universe. It is present everywhere, all around you and because it is pure spirit, you can access it so easily. You may know it as the Holy Spirit, for the Chinese it is Chi and in India it is Prana, the breath of life. All you have to do is spend time each day concentrating on your breath, breathing deeply and bringing yourself into the present moment. This is the way to banish fear from our lives and come into our hearts." Raúl breathed in slowly then exhaled, placing both hands over his heart. "The world can be very different if more and more people take the short drop from their minds to dwell in their hearts. This way you learn to become an observer of your mind rather than take every thought seriously. When you become an observer of your monkey-mind, you learn to master it. You learn you are more than your mind, and you can live in the present moment."

"Are you saying the Holy Spirit is the feminine aspect of God?" I asked.

"Yes, definitely. The Kabbalah refers to it as the Shekinah and in Buddhism it is the Goddess Quan Yin. They all mean exactly the same – the Divine Feminine."

"I can't believe what you're telling me. I have always had a problem with God as a patriarchal figure and I have been drawn to the softer energy of the Holy Spirit. It makes sense to me now."

"Is it easier for women to attain enlightenment?" Maria asked.

"Yes, because more women are in touch with their emotions and all women have the innate capacity to love unconditionally as a mother loves her child. However the Divine Feminine can work through men just as easily as women. And for you, my brother, is not a problem," he said, smiling at James as we all laughed. "But remember enlightenment is about integration or the end of polarity, so we must see the bigger picture of God as both masculine and feminine."

I was enraptured by the thought that the Goddess was making herself known to me in a variety of different ways.

It seemed as if I had always felt her presence, yet she had remained in the fantasy land of my childhood books. Now I was beginning to feel her essence whenever I meditated and connected with love within myself. Maybe my ultimate healing would come about if I managed to oust the inner critic which had stemmed from the image of a judgemental, frightening God who was solely masculine.

Once back in Puno, I finished my packing for the following day's flight to Arequipa. Afterwards, I headed down to the business centre to check my emails. It hadn't been possible to do so, on the island, and it might not be possible for some time again. "Any news from home?" James asked, startling me as he popped his head round the door.

"Julie's job finished in Boston and she's back in Dublin in great form. Ella arrived home from Rio. Have you looked at your emails yet?"

"Yep, I looked earlier when we came in and guess what? I had an email from my ex, Alex, saying he missed me … So who knows, we may get back together. He says the weather's awful though, so another few days here will help us face the winter. I'll see you later for dinner then. Ciao!" He disappeared from sight. I felt a little tug at my heart, thinking how I'd miss James if he became part of a couple once again. Then I scolded myself for being so selfish. "Think 'right' thoughts," I reminded myself as I shut down the computer.

Later that evening James, Raúl, Maria and I had our last meal together in Puno. Since Maria would be leaving the next day, we reminisced over the high points of our travels – the trek to Machu Picchu, meditating in the mountains and Amantani island. We shed a few tears, agreeing that we had learnt a lot from each other and promising to keep in touch. As we walked back to the hotel from the nearby restaurant,

Maria turned to Raúl. "We enjoyed our time with you so much. You know we didn't find Hakalan very spiritual."

"Ah my brother, Hakalan. He has not right thoughts, right words or right actions. I am afraid life will teach him some difficult lessons," he said, with a mischievous glint.

"We learned from your company, Raúl," I said.

"My prayer for each of you is that you will find your own inner guru or goddess."

Back in the hotel, we were all reluctant to say goodnight and decided to continue our chat, sitting in the foyer. Raúl ordered a pot of camomile tea as a night cap. I went to the bathroom. It must have been a good area for mobile reception, because my phone instantly started beeping. I had five texts. Two were from my sister Liz and three from Julie, all sent hours ago. What had I missed? I read the first text from Liz, and my heart leapt into my mouth. "Kate, Dad's had an accident. Come straight to St Vincent's hospital as soon as you arrive." I felt sick and dizzy, the words blurring before my eyes. Back in the foyer, James stood up to meet me, alarmed and puzzled. "What is it, Kate? You look as though you've seen a ghost."

"It's my father! He's had an accident, he's critical!"

"What happened? Who told you?"

"Liz and Julie sent texts, but they've only just arrived. They're all beside themselves with worry. He mixed up his tablets and crashed the car. God, my poor mother … I need to phone home straight away. I'm going to have to leave tomorrow. As soon as possible. Can we see if I can get on Maria's flight?"

Chapter Twenty-three

The sky was overcast and Dublin looked like a concrete jungle after having spent so much time outdoors in rural Peru. We'd arrived at the hospital and James, who had insisted on coming home with me, was driving around in circles looking for a parking space.

"Do you want to hop out while I park? I don't mind waiting until you're ready to leave. Then we can transfer your luggage into Liz's car."

"I really appreciate this, James. Just knowing you're here is such a support." I scrambled out of the car and ran towards the hospital entrance.

It was now over forty-eight hours since my father's car crash. Julie had been in regular contact by text and we'd talked on the phone as soon as I'd arrived in Dublin.

"He's out of the woods now, Mum. They were worried about him because he'd blacked out. They kept him under observation in case he had a brain hemorrhage. Apparently, he accidentally took an extra anti-depressant, then went off to the pub intending to have a glass of non-alcoholic beer but one of his friends insisted on him having an Irish whiskey. The alcohol clashed with the drug, and when he was parking the car he hit the accelerator rather than the brake and ran into the big oak tree in the garden. Pure misfortune, as Nanna said."

"God, you mean to say he'd arrived in his own gate when it happened?"

"Yes. Anyway, they have him under psychiatric observation because of his blood toxicity levels. Nanna is up the wall over that. She thinks there's a terrible stigma to it."

Now I had arrived at the hospital and the nurse was holding open the door of room twenty-seven. "Another visitor for you, Mr Tynan." My mother, Liz and Julie were sitting around his bed.

"Oh Mum, it's great to have you home." Julie came over to embrace me. It was wonderful to be finally holding her after missing her for so long. My coming home ought to have been a happy occasion – I'd imagined arriving back in Ireland in a state of enlightenment, having become a beacon of light and wisdom like a female Dali Lama of sorts. Instead I was inwardly a wreck, yet I had to appear calm rather than fall to pieces.

"Hi, Dad. How are you?"

He was sitting up in the bed, ashen apart from the scuffs and bruises around his face. I'd expected him to be bandaged but it looked as though he'd got off lightly. I leaned over to hug him, his body feeling frail and bony as though he'd lost a lot of weight. It can't have happened over night, but I hadn't noticed it since he always wore tailored jackets with loose fitting shirts underneath. It was strange seeing him look so helpless, lying there hooked up to a drip.

"I'm fine, Kate. They shouldn't have been worrying you. It was a very minor accident. As you can see I've no injuries apart from this." He pointed to the small bandage on his right temple.

My mother linked my elbow. "Listen to him. We were

very concerned, weren't we, Liz? Your father was under surveillance in case he had internal bleeding. The car took a fair wallop and the air bag didn't open. But he's fine now."

"Great to have you home, Kate. Mam's right you know, but thankfully the worst's over now and Daddy should be out of here in no time." They both seemed determined to tell me he was fine.

"I heard something about psychiatric observation. Is that to do with your anti-depressants, Dad?"

"Don't mind them. Your father doesn't need a psychiatrist. Who told you that?"

"How was your trip, sweetheart?" my father inquired, in his eagerness to change the subject. He had never called me sweetheart in his life before. They all seemed to be putting on some kind of act here. My mother noticed my concern, and rushed to distract me: "You've got a great tan, Kate."

It maddened me when she said silly things to distract from the real issues, but I humoured her. "I had a great break – the weather was lovely. How do you feel now, Dad?"

He opened his mouth, but this time it was Liz who jumped in. "Daddy's great! He'll be out of here as soon as we can get him discharged. It's home he needs, not an institution like this."

Julie stood behind the two of them, shaking her head and pointing from one to the other, before placing a finger to her temple and alternating it clockwise and anti-clockwise. I said, "Can I have fifteen minutes alone with Dad?" Both my mother and Liz reddened and got ready to protest, but my father spoke up.

"That's a good idea. I'd like that."

Liz threw me a dirty look and my mother assumed the evicted martyr's posture of slouched shoulders as they left, shepherded out by Julie. "Oh, Julie." I called her back. "Take my phone and ring James. He's in the car park with my luggage. Maybe you could get him to put it in Liz's car?" That would ensure I had plenty of time. As soon as they'd left, I turned my attention to my father. It pained me to see him look so haunted, hunched there in the bed. He'd always been independent and aloof and though that meant I'd found it hard to ever truly connect with him, at least there was something solid about him, something predictable to depend upon. During my last visit home, he had been forgetful and confused. I shuddered to see him like this – a frightened, crumpled old man letting my mother talk for him. I'd often worried that he might die before we ever truly had a chance to talk. Before I ever had a chance to know who he was. I desperately wanted to grab that opportunity now, before it was too late. "Dad, I'm going to talk straight to you because I'm concerned about you. You seem to have been under huge strain since Uncle Larry died. Mam told me you were taking anti-depressants. You really should have been going to talk to someone rather than relying on the tablets." I sounded a lot surer than I felt. I was taking a chance speaking to him like this. He could clam up but I was hoping to provoke him into straight talking, appeal to the lawyer in him who liked the truth to be known.

"Katey, you could be right. I've been muddled and I could have killed myself or God forbid someone else. My mind is addled." He hadn't called me "Katey" since I was little. It felt strange, like the clock had somehow been turned back.

"Dad, something's been not right for as long as I can remember. Maybe if my marriage hadn't broken down I'd be acting like Mam and Liz, burying my head in the sand. But I'm not prepared to live that way anymore. I think I can be more understanding now of anything you choose to tell me." I paused and looked at him, hoping he would decide to unburden whatever weighed so heavily on him.

"Your mother's a good woman, has been the best wife to me, but you're right – she brushes things under the carpet. That's the way she deals with things. She lives by the three monkey philosophy: hear no evil, see no evil, speak no evil."

He was right. I'd never thought of it before; my mother even had a little brass ornament of three monkeys sitting side by side. The first monkey covering his ears, the second one covering his eyes and the third with his hand over his mouth. I'd loved it as a child and had asked my mother if I could play with it. She'd told me it was a paperweight and had been a gift from her sister. I'd never imagined it had any deeper significance. "What has she brushed under the carpet, Dad?" I asked, perplexed by his ready admission that all was not well.

"There's been a lot going on." He faltered as the blood rose to his face. I knew the mood had suddenly changed, that he had quickly reflected on what he was about to say and baulked. "Since the economy collapsed and the property market slumped we're doing a lot less conveyance work. The practice has suffered, yet I still have eight members of staff to pay. It's very difficult."

"Dad, that's only material things. You still have a fine practice and you don't have any residual debt. I'm sure you're not as profitable, but you're silly if you're letting that get you down at your age." I stopped for him to answer, but he remained tight lipped. "You say Mother doesn't deal well with things. Neither of you were ever great with emotions, Dad. I think it's a family problem." I suddenly noticed I was fiddling with my left ring finger, perturbed by something.

Then it dawned on me that I had expected my emerald ring would be there.

"Katey, you've always said what was on your mind. I've always admired that. In fact it reminds me of …" He couldn't finish, as my mother had knocked then stuck her head around the door, asking if we were finished yet.

"The nurse says visiting time is over now. We have to go." She came over to fix the bedclothes around my father's bed. She was all bustle, like a clucking hen as she quickly re-arranged the items on his bedside locker and hurried us into saying goodbye before rushing us out of the building. When I was younger I used to object to my mother stage-managing situations this way, but now I knew that was the way both she and Liz coped with things.

Liz deposited the three of us off at my parents' house before heading home to her husband and children. She had been uptight in the car, barely speaking apart from snapping out the odd comment like, "All this fussing over Dad needing psychiatric attention is just another way for the hospital to take in funds." She glared at me in the rear view mirror as she spoke.

Once inside the house, my mother seemed to relax. "Would you like something to eat, Kate? You must be hungry."

"Whatever's handy will do fine. Some brown bread and ham or cheese." I opened the fridge door for a look. "How are you coping, Mam?"

She looked exhausted, slumped in an armchair. "Ah, I'm fine. I don't like this needless fussing over your father having taken an extra anti-depressant. The silly psychiatrist even went so far as to ask me did I think Jim was suicidal. Imagine that!"

"Well, you told me yourself that his doctor recommended

that he see a psychologist or therapist when he gave him the prescription for Prozac. The drug is not supposed to be used alone, Mam. It's advisable to accompany it with cognitive behavioural therapy in order to address the real situation."

"Ah Kate, you're a right therapy junkie. You go from one quack to another in search of cures."

Julie had been engrossed in the latest edition of Elle magazine, but now she looked up laughing in surprise at my mother's choice of words.

I was trying to hold my temper. "Therapy junkie? That's not a term I've ever heard you use before, Mam."

"When I told Aunt Marge you'd gone to that healer she said only therapy junkies went to see him."

I could feel my blood boil at the mention of her sister's name. "Mam, I don't know why you ever listen to Aunt Marge. She's the last person I'd tell anything to."

Julie was still laughing. "Gran, mum is right about Aunt Marge. She's a sanctimonious holy roller, always finding fault with others. I mean she lives in Chicago and we haven't seen her for four years, yet she thinks she can dictate to all of us every time you have a telephone conversation."

"Julie's right, Mam. You allow that silly woman too much power in our lives. Stop telling her our business."

"Ah no, she's got a good heart and she's a very prayerful person, she will be on her knees for your grandfather. Well, I'll take my leave of the two of you and head off to bed. Goodnight."

When she'd gone, Julie sat down opposite me at the kitchen table while I drank my tea and had a sandwich. It struck me that my daughter had lost weight. I knew women controlled their food intake as a way of controlling their inner world; compensation for their outer world falling into chaos.

And boy, hadn't Julie and I had plenty of chaos during the last few months. "Julie, aren't you going to eat something?"

"No Mum, I'm never hungry late in the evening." As she talked about her time in Boston, I noted how pretty she looked. She had Trevor's eyes and nose; my mouth and cheekbones. She was the best thing to come out of our marriage, proving we had worked well on some level. She had obviously enjoyed working for the law firm, though the hours were long. She was fascinated by my stories of Peru. "You know most of my class in college listed either Peru or Australia as the place they most wanted to visit. It sounds really cool. But I'm shocked by you losing your ring and watch. I'd warned you not to bring them, Mum. It was silly."

"It was very upsetting, love. But I can't waste time crying over them. Even your grandfather's accident proves how we shouldn't cling to material possessions."

"I know, mum, it's just … If only you'd left them at home or at least in the hotel safe."

Changing the subject, I asked her what had happened since her grandfather had been admitted to hospital.

"After the initial scare passed they wanted to move him to the psychiatric unit but Gran and Liz wouldn't hear of it, so a Doctor Waldron visits him twice daily. He says Granddad is depressed and needs treatment."

"I thought so. Mam gets bad advice from Liz and that weasel Marge. It frustrates me that they have so much influence over her."

"I think you underestimate the influence you can exert, Mum. Gran thinks very highly of you. She constantly says how good you are with people, that you have a gift for helping people. All the neighbours around here think you're special. They all want me to visit them because I'm your daughter.

They all have lovely stories about you."

"Are you serious? I always thought Liz was the golden girl." I perked up for the first time since I'd landed back in Ireland.

"No, Mum. She may be closer to Gran in lots of ways because they seem to have a common understanding. You're different, but Gran can see you're very well intentioned."

I suddenly felt a ray of hope. Maybe I really could help them to be proactive in my father's recovery. I had to believe I really could help heal others by healing myself, just as Raúl had suggested. "I think I'll visit Dad alone tomorrow," I said. "By the way, are you dieting?" I had always worried for her about anorexia, having had a brush with it myself in my teens.

"No, Mum. I guess I'm like you – fast metabolism. I just lost weight from working hard and being under a bit of stress in the job. I'm sure I'll put all back on now I'm home with two weeks to spare before college starts."

Chapter Twenty-four

I awoke early the following morning to a text from Geoff, aka *"luvpicasso"*, the artist I had met on the dating site. I'd told him I was going to Peru and I had emailed him my phone number before I'd heard of my father's accident, saying it might be possible to meet up in Dublin on my return. Then I'd texted him to tell him about my father and he'd replied to say if I fancied a break he would be happy to meet me for a chat. A bit of diversion sounded good, so I agreed to meet for coffee not too far from the hospital.

As I approached the café, I spotted a man with curly fair hair wearing a blue check shirt seated at one of the tables outside in the sunshine. I wondered was it Geoff, but his hair looked blonder than in photographs. As I came closer he stood up to his full height of five feet eleven, and smiled at me. "Kate, great to finally meet up with you." He offered me his hand, his grip firm and reassuring.

"You too, though I'm not the best company you could have right now." I sat down opposite him. I was conscious of not having been in the mood to make much of an effort. My hair needed a wash and I felt scruffy wearing denims with trainers, even though I'd topped them with a nice linen jacket belonging to Julie.

"I don't expect you to be. Relax." He spoke calmly, his

smile spreading all the way up to his amber-flecked blue eyes, soft lines etched at their corners. A waitress came and took our order.

I told Geoff the details of my father's accident and finished by saying, "I don't know why I told you all that. I'm sorry – I guess I'm just preoccupied and can think of nothing else right now." I was fidgeting compulsively, pushing my hair back behind my ears and fiddling with the ring that wasn't there.

"Stop apologising, Kate. You're concerned for your dad and it was obviously stressful for you to hear about his accident when you were so far away. I'm a good listener. Now just relax." He smiled then exhaled slowly while moving his hands downwards as if deflating a balloon. He radiated an inner peace which made life seem easy, as though the pulse of the city was calming down around us. I knew that was the sort of peace I wanted in my life. I sighed and sat back more comfortably in my chair as the waitress placed our coffees in front of us.

"You seem very calm, Geoff. Do you work at it? I mean, meditate?"

"I'm just naturally very chilled out. Always have been a bit of a dreamer. Some people might see that as a fault – a lack of ambition. My ex told me if I was any more chilled I'd be in a coma and maybe she was right." He laughed. "But you know something, one of my close friends died recently and I thought life's too short to live it in a stressed-out state."

"I'm sorry to hear that. Was it a sudden death?"

"Cancer – only discovered last year. It spread quickly. Only the same age as myself ... It shows how quickly you can be snuffed out." He clicked his fingers in the air, regretfully.

"You're right, and we tend to forget that too easily.

Only last week I was in Peru promising myself I would stop worrying and now here I am in a state over my father." I shrugged my shoulders as if to shake off concern. "Anyway, tell me about your exhibition."

"I can't believe the response. It was a joint exhibition with three other artists but I was singled out for some amazing reviews in the papers. Mind you there's not much money out there right now. I keep prices low so I'm trekkin' along. Did you see my website?"

"Oh God, I didn't get a chance to look." I could feel myself blushing. "I was in Brazil when you sent me the link." I picked up my coffee to hide my embarrassment. Damn, I'd made a note to have a quick look before meeting him but I'd found it hard to organise myself this morning.

"I'd love you to have a look because I think you might like it. Tell me what you think. Will you?"

"I will of course. Are you still on the dating site?"

"Not that one. I moved to another one. If you're on it too long you just keep seeing the same old faces scroll across the top all the time. I told you I met someone?"

"It seemed to go well for you?"

"Right, for four weeks. History now." He smiled, his eyes sparkling with a mischievous glint.

My heart fluttered as I smiled in response. But time was passing. I glanced at my watch. "I'm sorry I have to go, I need to see my father. It's been really nice to talk to you at last." I drained the last of my coffee, before standing.

"Me too, Kate. You're a lovely woman and easy company." He stood up to plant a kiss on my cheek. As I walked away, I half turned, glancing back. Catching my eye, he smiled and waved goodbye. For some strange reason, I suddenly felt lonely, disappointed that he hadn't asked to see me again.

I hate hospitals with their smooth easy-clean surfaces and lack of texture, the clatter of nurses' shoes and over-sanitised smells. No matter how many plants or designer chairs they place in the foyer, the corridors and rooms remain soulless, demoralising places. My father looked vulnerable as a newborn, propped up on puffy pillows in a yellow-painted, metal-framed bed. He had been surprised to see me arrive alone and I could sense his apprehension as I sat in the chair close to his bed. I was usually the one who had felt ill at ease in his company. "Dad, I want you to know something I never told you or Mam." At this, he raised his eyebrows. "I've suffered from anxiety ever since David died. At times it's been very acute with my thoughts racing – terrible reprimanding thoughts that nearly drive me crazy. I've had feelings of guilt and remorse that made my life a living hell." I rubbed my hands across my face. "I just want you to know that I understand what anxiety is. I'm telling you this because I know you haven't been yourself lately. I know you've been depressed since Harry's death."

"My poor little Katey." He put his hand out to me. I took it in both of mine and, looking up, saw his eyes well with tears.

"No, Dad. I don't need sympathy. I'm fine. I cope better lately. It's you I'm concerned about. I want you to feel you can share your thoughts with me."

Just then a knock at the door signalled the arrival of a nurse and a tall bespectacled man in a grey suit. "This is Mr Tynan's psychiatrist, Doctor Waldron. Would you mind waiting outside for a few minutes?" asked the nurse.

Damn it, I thought, *just when I was getting somewhere.*

"No problem," I said aloud, stepping outside. After waiting several minutes, walking up and down the corridor, the door opened and Doctor Waldron stepped out. I introduced myself: "I'm Kate Canavan, Jim Tynan's daughter."

"I'm glad to meet you. Your father seems to think you have a better understanding of mental health issues than your mother or your sister. It's good he has someone he can talk to. I believe I was in college with your husband, Trevor."

"Yes. My ex-husband now."

"I didn't know. I'm sorry."

"Don't worry. I'd like to help my father, Doctor Waldron. It seems strange that he was on anti-depressants and yet wasn't advised to see a psychologist or indeed yourself. What's bothering him?"

"Doctor-patient confidentiality, Mrs Canavan. I can't tell you myself, but I do believe your father is ready to talk to you. Regarding him talking to a professional, I'm sure you're aware that was recommended when he was first prescribed Prozac. Now, good day."

"Thanks," I said weakly. Though I'd married a medic, I'd never become accustomed to how cut and dried they were. They had a way of making me feel inferior. I knocked on my father's door before entering.

"Come in," he called.

Taking the chair at his bedside, I said, "I want to tell you that you were always the best, Dad. You've always been so kind to less fortunate people. You are the kindest person I know." I'd remembered all the times he'd brought me with him to visit the homeless, bringing blankets and flasks of soup on Christmas Eve. The countless people he had given free legal aid to. I had always looked up to him, seeing him as a modern day Messiah who never looked for thanks or praise.

"No, Katey, I haven't been. That's the problem." His eyes grew misty as he continued: "I had another brother. He would have been your uncle. Charlie was his name." I was shocked. I had thought my father only had one brother and three sisters. I remained silent, trying to look unperturbed. "He was six years older than me and I looked up to him. He was funny and kind and like you he spoke his mind. Charlie was thirteen when Mamma was confined to a wheelchair. I don't know what happened but he had grown impulsive and a little aggressive. Then six months later, he suddenly disappeared from our lives. I asked about him but was never given a satisfactory answer until one day my father said he would bring me to visit him."

"Where had he gone to?" I asked, the blood draining from my face.

"We drove for what seemed like hours, until we eventually came to a large set of gates leading to a huge grey building. My father was a silent man, believing children should be seen and not heard so I knew it was futile to ask questions. Inside, we were met by a nun who told us she would bring Charlie to see us. After a while she returned with him, except it wasn't the Charlie I knew. It looked like him all right, apart from his slow shuffle and his vacant eyes which seemed unable to even register who we were. The three of us went out for a walk around the hospital grounds and Charlie never spoke a word during our time with him. As we drove back I asked my father, "Dad what happened to Charlie?" to which he replied impassively. 'Charlie had a nervous breakdown. He can't live with us anymore.' I accepted what my father told me, though I was deeply saddened. I didn't know then that Charlie had had several bouts of shock treatment and a prefrontal lobotomy."

"Oh God. But why ...?"

"Oh Katey, it could have been something as simple as autism. I see Liz's youngest little fellah and he reminds me so much of him and he's been diagnosed with ADHD." His voice caught. "It was so cruel! He spent his whole life living in a mental hospital. I should have done more. He died seven years ago but it's only in the last few months when ..." His voice caught in his throat. "When Harry died and I was under stress at work, I began to have a lot of memories. A nurse from the hospital took Charlie out to live with her and her husband during his last three years when the hospital closed down. She contacted me recently when she was visiting Dublin to talk about him and give me his rosary beads. A very simple humble woman. Her kindness towards him made me feel so selfish."

I could feel my father's excruciating pain. The torment he'd felt as a little boy was evident in his shaky voice, as he gasped for breath. I shuddered to think how cruel my grandfather had been; an intolerant army doctor from another era. Squeezing my father's hand, I said, "But they were different times, Dad, and you were too young to be able to help him." This explained my father's strange moods over the years. I'd never understood how he could be so happy one minute, playing with Liz and me on holidays or at Christmas, and then the next moment his joyous face would turn glum and he would wander off to be alone. As a child I used to wonder had I done something to upset him. Later it just angered me, because I didn't understand the reason for such odd behaviour. I came out of my reverie. "Does Mam know?"

"Yes, she came to visit him with me a few times. She baked cup cakes for him. You could see that he liked that."

All of a sudden I felt anger towards my mother for having kept this from us, for having denied us the chance of knowing our uncle.

"Why were we never told about Charlie? I would have liked to have met him." I twiddled my empty ring finger.

"Ah, you know your mother. She was afraid it would upset you and Liz. But it's not her fault. I also was ashamed and worried about the stigma of having a brother who was institutionalised. I hope Charlie forgives me, wherever he is." He glanced heavenwards.

"Of course he does, Dad. He's in a better place now and he's possessed of a higher intelligence than to hold any earthly grudge."

"Thank you, Katey. That's a lovely way of putting it. You're a blessing to me." A knock on the door signalled the return of the nurse, this time to check his blood pressure and change the needle in his hand, which was attached to the drip. I took it as my cue to leave and gave my father a hug, checking to see if there was anything he wanted from the shop downstairs. "No Katey, thanks for everything." He smiled, looking less strained, as though he had unloaded a boulder from his broad shoulders.

I arrived back to my parents' house to find Billy Costello sitting in the kitchen having tea with my mother. Julie had gone to town to catch up with some friends from college. "Goodness, Billy, you appear everywhere. You survived Machu Picchu then?"

"I did, all right – great place. I was just visiting my mam when she told me about your father. Thought I'd drop over and see how he is. It's great to hear he's on the mend."

"I've just been to visit him. He's only got a few scratches, really." His cup was empty. "If you're finished, I'll walk you down as far as your mam's house, Billy."

"Have you thought about my offer to you?" Billy asked, as we walked.

"I'm very flattered. But you know me of old. I'm a bit of a stick in the mud when it comes to relying on the good old permanent pensionable job. No offence to you or anything."

"Is it worth it? I mean you as much as said your present job was a drag. I'll match your salary and set you up with a pension policy."

"No, honestly, Billy. I can only cope with so many changes in my life at one time. I'm too long in the tooth for uprooting myself and starting all over again." As I spoke, my sister Liz's black Mercedes passed us, heading towards my parents' house, Liz waving out the window.

"I think you underestimate yourself, Kate. Give it some thought, will you? Maybe come out to visit me in Wicklow. We could catch up on old times."

"I will do, Billy. I'd better get back to my mam, now." I knew I was distracted, but my father was on my mind and if I'd learned nothing else in Peru, I had to deal with one issue at a time. As I walked back up the drive, I breathed into my belly and visualised my connection to the earth below me, while calling on Spirit to be with me, in an effort to ground and centre myself for what I needed to do.

Liz was just getting out of her car as I arrived and I followed her into the kitchen. "I need to talk to you both." I pulled up a chair to join them around the kitchen table. I told them everything my father had told me and finished by saying, "All this has weighed very heavily on his shoulders over many years. I'm not an expert but it's obvious his recent depression following Harry's death brought back memories. I think he should be encouraged to see a psychiatrist on a weekly basis."

"But your father's not mentally ill." My mother's voice hinted at hysteria.

"Mam, it's time to stop talking like that. There's no stigma any more about depression. It can happen to anyone and Dad had a complicated childhood. I think he could have done with seeing someone a long time ago. His regular disappearances and anti-social behaviour indicated a problem."

"Oh for God's sake!" Liz said. "Daddy was a very good father. You shouldn't criticise him like that."

God she could be exasperating, always shoving accusations down my throat. "Liz, I'm not criticising Dad. No offence, but you've always had your head in the sand. Dad needs help and we have to encourage him to get it."

"Kate's right, Liz," my mum said, as Liz visibly reeled. "Life is short and it's not worth putting on an act for anyone. No more than your Jonathan's ADHD. You want to do the best for him and you don't love him any less because he's finding school more difficult than the other three, do you?" My mother spoke softly. Liz sighed. Mam had hit a nerve by mentioning her youngest child who'd been a worry since the day he started school.

"I've been finding it difficult but I suppose you're right. It's hard when things don't go according to plan," Liz said earnestly and I could feel her letting go.

"The three of us have to do everything we can to support Dad and help him put the past behind him," I said. "That means we have to all sing from the same hymn sheet. If that means encouraging him to get help, are we on?"

"Yes, Kate. He has been acting very confused lately and the hospital suggested he see someone. I suppose I've always had a problem with hearing the word depression and in Daddy's case I just hoped it would go away. But I want him to go privately … I mean I wouldn't want him sharing a waiting room with some psycho."

I smiled inwardly. At least she was coming round even if she wasn't quite willing to let her prejudices go. I leaned over, stretched out both arms, to touch both of them. I remembered Raúl's words about coming into my heart. The past twenty-four hours had been harrowing for me and I felt drained, yet in some strange way I felt a genuine heart connection to Spirit guiding me. I had initiated something positive by addressing an old problem which had affected us as a family. Some good had come out of my father's accident, since I felt closer to them than I had done for a very long time.

Chapter Twenty-five

*I*f August anywhere is a wicked month, August in the west of Ireland is even more so. Clammy weather beloved of fungi, moulds and wild mushrooms, along with congested traffic, made me decidedly uncomfortable. Oh don't get me wrong, I was relieved to have left the madness of Dublin behind, delighted to arrive back to Galway City. My father had come out of hospital and Julie had moved into a new apartment and now I had time to meditate and meet up with friends.

But that's where the problem lay. All my friends were elsewhere. Ella had gone to stay with her daughter in London and James had gotten back with his partner Alex and was driving Alex's band around the country doing various gigs. I obviously hadn't achieved enlightenment. In fact, in my present state I felt as though I'd taken two steps backwards after having taken one forward. I felt very alone, especially since I was acutely aware that Julie would soon be going on a week-long break to the Algarve with her father. I had plenty to do to keep me occupied between catching up on laundry and planning classes for the college year ahead, and I should have been content with peace and quiet but for some reason I was discombobulated. A lovely word that, and you really only know what it means if you feel that way, a bit like an old scarecrow with lots of stuffing hanging out and with a brain that doesn't really work. Except I had no Wizard of Oz to go to, and I had been to enough shamans to last me a lifetime.

I wondered was it the coca tea … Maybe it really had had an effect and I was suffering from withdrawal from that as well as the sleeping pills. I had been meditating twice daily but that too seemed to space me out even more. In fact when I researched it by typing into a search engine "Can meditation space you out?" I got loads of hits confirming that yes, in certain circumstances, too much meditation could make you feel spacey, if not balanced with other more active pursuits. Great! And here I was too woozy for active pursuits, so what was I to do in my solitary state?

I found myself wondering about dating sites. Geoff had said he had moved to a different one and Ella had mentioned trying a selection of sites. Finally, I gave in to curiosity and found Geoff's site. He had a brand-new profile, this time calling himself "*Warholesqe*". I liked him and was disappointed he hadn't found me attractive. But then I had looked like something the cat dragged in on the day we met, and I'm sure he had lots of women running after him.

I decided to put up a new profile under the name Demeter, Goddess of the Harvest; she was the closest any Goddess comes to Mother Earth, since her role as Persephone's mother also meant she was known as the Mother Goddess. In Peru, I'd loved the feeling that Pachamama could work through me. It would be interesting to see what would happen if I invoked her energy so I logged on and started putting my profile together. To find that, damn it, the name was gone. Okay, I'd use a variation of the name. Demetra … no … Demetriana … that's it, the exotic sounding "*Demetriana*".

Next, I uploaded some pictures of myself in Peru; one

of me standing on a mountain on the way to Machu Picchu and another one in national costume on the floating island. I also uploaded a recent photo James had taken of me wearing a navy dress with delicate art deco embroidery around the neckline and just for good measure another of me in a little black number.

It struck me that I looked a lot more confident and happy in these pictures than in the very poised photos I had used as Persephone. Odd, since the previous set had been taken while I was married to Trevor. My shrink was seemingly correct when he said our marriage had been under strain long before we broke up and that I had been in denial. I had obviously been more like my mother and Liz than I cared to admit. But not anymore. Now I believed in tackling issues head on before they spiralled out of control.

Cyber communication was so convenient yet it could be endlessly time consuming as blocks of days passed with me spending hours in front of my laptop. I kept in regular contact with my father through Skype and was delighted to hear about Mam and Liz supporting him in getting therapy. Emails flew back and forth to Julie helping to banish my insecurity about her spending time with her father. This was helped by the fact Martha had chosen not to join them in the Algarve. But the bulk of my time-wasting was spent on the dating site as the romantic in me still hankered after a knight in shining armour. That I couldn't fight this longing was further evidence that I had an addictive personality and found it difficult to break old habits. Living in the now was easier on a mountain top and enlightenment was a slow process. I had however become shrewder in my use of the site, discarding the chancers and charlatans after brief correspondences, and I was no longer interested in empty flattery or a quick fix ego boost.

One guy managed to provoke my interest all the same. His username was *"FordmodelT"*, which was a bit more interesting than *"drightone"* or *"ilovecheese"*. I presumed it referred to an interest in vintage cars, until I saw his picture. Reclining against a wall, in an immaculately cut anthracite sports jacket over an open-neck white shirt, his stance drew attention to a well-honed physique. The dark brown hairline formed an exaggerated widow's peak above a tanned brow. Deep-set brown eyes smouldered at the camera. On first impression I was convinced he had downloaded a photograph of the designer Tom Ford. The similarities were uncanny, right down to the designer stubble looking like a two or three-day shadow. I wondered was the image a composite, perhaps a photo shopped version of Tom Ford superimposed over this guy's photograph – the face shape was squarer and the nose more aquiline. I looked at two other pictures he had posted on his profile and he looked a bit more normal. Less incredible, less like a movie star, less like Tom Ford, yet similar to the main picture.

He sent me a message saying, *"Hi, your profile is really interesting and you look great in your pictures."* No signature.

I read down through his profile. It seemed unassuming enough until I got to "profession", which read "designer". I fired a message straight back saying *"Thanks for the compliments. Are you an interior designer?"* I had previously had emails from an interior designer living in Galway and found him full of affectation. To read his long introductory message, you'd think he was saving lives, he'd banged on so much about his lofty career. As soon as I'd informed him that I lived in Galway I never heard from him again, so I presumed he was married. Male interior designers had been added to my growing blacklist of professions to avoid on the internet. Anyway much to my surprise *"FordmodelT"* sent back an immediate reply:

Hi Kate,

Good to hear from you. I'm actually a structural engineer specialising in sustainable home design. I encourage people to build homes which are virtually self sufficient in power and water. I've just finished a huge project on an eco-friendly factory on Dublin's north side. You may have heard about it on the news.

I've attached the url of my website.

Isaac

Hi Isaac,

Yes, I heard about it and was very impressed. You must be really proud to have been part of the team. I looked at your website and found it fascinating to think houses can now be so much more efficient. Yet they looked stylish and comfortable.

Kate

Contrary to my initial prejudice, my curiosity was now aroused by both the good looks and the altruistic occupation. Isaac's website was incredibly impressive and once again I found myself putting a man on a pedestal as I wondered what on earth someone so talented was doing on a dating site. Was I setting another man up to be my imaginary Prince Charming? I didn't hear back from him but his picture would scroll across the top of my profile on a regular basis, indicating that he had been looking at my profile. I found myself hoping he would make contact, so three days later I sent him a message telling him I could see he had looked at my profile on several occasions and I was wondering had I inadvertently insulted him.

A message came back telling me he was very shy and was intimidated by me because I dressed so well and sounded so accomplished. I was astounded and flattered. How could someone like him lack confidence? I supposed you never knew. Eager to save his pride, I replied in a very reassuring manner that there was nothing to be concerned about as I didn't always dress so well. "I have bad hair days like everyone else," I said.

Mails went to and fro and he seemed very gentle and normal, so we agreed to talk on the phone. He called me at nine o'clock one evening and we chatted as if we'd known each other all our lives. It was not a problem that I was living in Galway and he lived in Cork as he worked here often and was currently overseeing a large project at one of the local factories. In fact, he told me he would be in town in three days' time and would love to bring me out for dinner. I liked his voice and he sounded like the perfect gentleman, although I reminded myself how I'd fallen for that one before with "*Elmtree*". After my spiritual journeys I was supposed to be watching how my monkey-mind worked hand in hand with my ego to construct false beliefs, which would ultimately set me up for a fall. If I met him I'd need to rely on my gut but I wasn't totally sure that would work.

In the meantime, I asked him about his photograph and he told me when he was getting pictures taken for his website, the photographer insisted on making him pose like Tom Ford. "So you get the Tom Ford similarity all the time then?" I asked.

He laughed. "No, not all the time. That was just a bit of fun with the photographer. We had a laugh. You can only see the likeness if I haven't shaved for a few days. I'm generally clean-shaven. What about your photographs? When were they taken?"

"They were all taken in Peru, apart from the one in the black dress. I'm just back from holidays there."

"Do you have any more?"

"Well, yes. But the pictures from Peru are the most recent." I was aware that this line of conversation was all about human ego and what a woman looked like rather than who she was inside.

"Send me any others you have. Would you mind texting back your email?"

"No problem." Maybe I could test myself to find out had I changed since Peru or was I still intent on chasing rainbows. After the phone call, Isaac sent me several emails saying he thought we would be very well suited and for that reason he had decided to deactivate his membership on the site. Since he would be working in Galway the following Tuesday on a new eco-friendly home, he wished to meet me and show me the house afterwards.

I hadn't known what to think since Isaac had bombarded me with emails and texts, ranting about his ex and increasingly suggesting he had high hopes of us having a relationship. I know I'd been out of the dating loop a long time, but this certainly seemed like the height of Walter Mitty fantasy. I suppose I had started off like that too but I was fast becoming disillusioned before I ever met up with him.

However, I was impressed and curious about the work he was doing. Hakalan had been very forceful in making his point about our need to care for the Earth. The Peru experience had raised my awareness of environmental issues, as my time sitting in the mountains seemed to increase my relationship with the earth. I now saw her as Pachamama, a living breathing organism, rather than one great big land mass under my feet. I was very excited about the prospect of seeing the eco-friendly home in west Galway – in fact, I was more interested in seeing the house than Isaac at this stage.

As my interest in Isaac as a man began to diminish, I'd begun thinking about Geoff again. I was disappointed that he hadn't contacted me since we met. I'd thought that perhaps he'd make contact through this site, but no. Maybe it was up to me? But first I would have to look at his art. I took out his business card and typed in the url of his website.

His website appeared and I looked at it in disbelief. As I gazed at his paintings, I was so embarrassed I must have blushed seven shades of red through purple in the privacy of my own home. Geoff had four separate galleries on his website devoted to "myths and legends of the old world". There were stunning paintings in each section – Celtic mythology, Norse mythology, Egyptian mythology and Greek mythology. He must have thought I was heartless not to have contacted him since I was so interested in myths. Hurriedly I set about composing a message:

Hi Geoff,

I hope you're keeping well and happy. Excuse the delay in contacting you.

It was great to meet you. I love your website and can't believe you never told me you were into mythology! The paintings are amazing, so rich and vibrant. I especially love Pandora's Box. The girl is so beautiful and appears so innocent as she lifts the lid to reveal such horrors. Truly you capture the myth very well. I would love to call to see the paintings next week when I visit Dublin. Will you be around?

Kind regards, Kate

Ten minutes later Geoff sent me a message saying he would be in Galway next Tuesday and would love to bring me out for dinner. My heart leapt in my chest with excitement.

Great. I'll look forward to that.

Immediately I began day dreaming about what I would wear and where would be the best place to go… Or should I impress him with my cooking? Holy Moley! Suddenly I remembered Isaac had postponed his visit until Tuesday so now I was officially double-booked. I contacted Isaac to tell him I would be able to meet him for lunch before taking a look at his eco house, but something else had cropped up that evening.

Tuesday morning, I was woken by my phone bleeping. Rubbing the sleep from my eyes, I saw I had received a text from Isaac:

Excited to c u. Please cancel ur evening apt. Spend the day tgethr.

I hadn't yet met him and I was already worn out from answering ridiculous texts and emails as though he were a needy child constantly looking for his mother's attention. Maybe he needed a mother figure and had been attracted to the energy of Demeter? The idea of squeezing two dates into one day was getting stressful, though Ella had told me she did three in one day – morning coffee, lunch and dinner.

Love & the Goddess

I'd arranged to meet Isaac in a Quay Street fish restaurant at twelve thirty. As soon as I entered the room, I could see his gleaming mahogany tan offset by a white clingy t-shirt, all the better to show off his toned torso. Either that or the white was intended to match his glow-in-the-dark polished teeth. As we exchanged pleasantries, he pecked both my cheeks in a very "hello darling" continental manner. I noticed his thick dark-rimmed sun glasses bore the logo "Tom Ford". I grimaced to myself – if the designer resemblance was such a coincidence, he was REALLY going out of his way to avoid it! As I sat down, the waiter handed me a menu which I scanned.

Isaac leaned towards me. "You're lovely, Kate. Just like your pictures. I'm sorry to have asked for extra ones. It's just that I have gone on these dates and the women end up being so much fatter and older than their pictures. One night I met a woman in a pub in Cork and I was terrified someone could walk in and recognise me. I would have been so ashamed to be seen with her." He broke into a laugh.

"But she could have been a very nice person," I said, smiling at him.

He bit his lip. "You're right. But she came under false pretences. She looked nothing like her picture. She was huge."

The waiter came to inquire were we ready to order lunch. I ordered baked salmon, French beans and fries while Isaac ordered grilled lemon sole and a side salad. When the waiter left I took up the conversation where it had left off. "You were talking about someone having weight on. I always think that any one of us could end up overweight at any given time. A hormonal imbalance or a need to go on cortisone tablets can add three to four dress sizes to a slim woman."

He lowered his voice to a whisper. "Can I tell you a secret?"
I murmured that he could.

"I was overweight when I was at school. The guys used to laugh at me for having man boobs. Imagine!"

His confession made me wonder why he didn't have more empathy for others in the same position. "So how did you get rid of them?" There was no sign of excess flesh through his super-tight t-shirt.

"Lipo-suction!" He arched his eyebrows. I felt myself mimic his expression, my eyes widening with incredulity as our steaming hot plates were delivered.

"Did you get anything else done?" I tried to feign indifference, digging a fork into my salmon.

He frowned down at his plate. "Oh, no." Then he smiled. "But my ex got loads of stuff done: breasts, botox, lipo and fillers. I've a client who's a plastic surgeon so instead of him paying me he would do work on the ex. She misses that now, I'll tell you." He shrugged. "Anyway, tell me about yourself, Kate. They say we're not supposed to talk about our exes."

I thought to myself that he was a bit late discovering that pearl of wisdom, after the way he'd already gone on about her in emails and over the phone. I recounted my experiences in Brazil and Peru, and he was an attentive listener, asking pertinent questions every so often. As I spoke, I noticed that the only part of his meal he touched was the fish, ignoring all carbohydrates. He returned to the subject of having deactivated his profile on the website in the hope of us having a relationship and was disappointed when I mumbled that it was a bit early to know if we were suited.

"I suppose you're right, Kate. It's just I've met so many women and you're the first one who has the whole package. I mean, you're so slim."

"Isaac," I said, quite sharply. "I have to say I think you judge women as though you were looking for a mail-order bride. How on earth can you reconcile kindness to the environment with your awful attitude to women?" I hadn't noticed my buttons being pushed until I was truly in mid-flow, my teacher's voice escaping.

He turned crimson. "God, you sound exactly like my wife. This is why I left her. I did nothing to you. It's true what they say about internet dating – you must be the fourth looper I've met on that site!" He stood up and threw a fifty euro note on the table, sneering, "That should cover the bill." As he sashayed out the door, I noticed that the logo on his jeans pocket read "Tom Ford". What a mess of contradictions! As far as I was concerned, he could look elsewhere for a skinny barely-sustained woman to share his sustainable home with. He definitely hadn't posed much of a challenge to my gut instinct – it was a case of instant revulsion.

But would I feel the same way about Geoff when I finally got to spend time with him?

Chapter Twenty-six

*G*eoff had suggested we go out for a meal but I'd quietly decided I'd rather cook. We had been in touch for long enough for me to feel I could trust him. By five o'clock, I had the table set and the food prepared, when my phone beeped with a message saying he was in Galway and was just about to leave the Rehab art exhibition in Dominick Street.

I texted him back saying I hadn't seen the exhibition but I'd love to come in for a look right now since it was only down the road. He sent a message back: *"C u dn."*

I barely understood what he meant. I would never get used to text speak, I thought, as I changed out of my leggings into slim white jeans and a long-sleeved Inca-inspired tunic with a subtle take on the famous intarsia pattern.

Fifteen minutes later, I arrived at the tiny gallery housed in a Georgian town house. A plain room with white walls and uneven oak-stained floorboards, it was unfurnished save for three old pine chairs with basket-weave seats in a far corner. Geoff was in the main gallery area as I walked in, chatting to a group of people who seemed to know each other. My heart skipped a beat as I watched him run his hands through dishevelled curly hair, a cleft in his chin becoming more pronounced as he smiled – something I hadn't previously noticed. After the designer's processed look of mahogany tan and glowing teeth, Geoff was all man, well-built with broad shoulders but not toned to ludicrous perfection. He was wearing indigo jeans with a light blue chambray shirt, relaxed and comfortable. A petite dark-haired girl in her mid thirties was hanging on his every word, her lips parted as though she hoped he'd kiss her.

Three young men and slightly older girl, all of whom had the distinct features of Down syndrome, were also part of the group around Geoff, and after a while I realised they were the artists. The petite dark-haired girl was discussing the paintings on the wall – colourful bold abstract canvases encased in pale wood frames. "For people who were once considered devoid of an inner life, they can be amazingly creative," she warbled in an affected "arty" manner. I thought she sounded very condescending. Just then Geoff caught my eye, smiled and beckoned me over with a wink and a nod of his head.

"Meet a friend of mine from Galway. This is Kate," he said. One of the young men with Down syndrome came over and took my hand in both of his to shake it vigorously. "This is Pete, one of our wonderful artists," said Geoff, before introducing me to each of the group in turn.

An older woman, who seemed to be looking after the artists, explained to me, "Geoff did great work with the group. We're thrilled to have the exhibition travelling around the country. Well, we'd better go. The bus back to Dublin will be waiting for us."

The young man tugged at Geoff's arm. "Come with us!" and the other young artists clustered round, also begging him to join them.

"Sorry, Pete. Not this time." Geoff was laughing heartily; he placed his hands on Pete's shoulders and looked him straight in the eye. "But I want you to promise me you'll finish that great painting you started last Monday."

"I will, I promise. I'll do it for you."

"They love him," the older woman said to me, as she urged the young people towards the door, adding, "Sometimes it's like herding mice at a crossroads!"

Geoff grabbed his jacket from behind a chair and, turning to the petite woman, said, "Myra, I have to go now too." She looked sulky, threw me a dagger's look, then sidled up to him and pecked his cheek. "See you in Dublin then," she called after him as we left together.

Once outside, I said to Geoff, "You never told me you taught art."

"It's just two mornings a week. It's been great. I think I get more out of it than they do. Do you want to get a bite to eat?"

"No, I've actually been cooking so I've plenty of food in my place – I only live a few minutes' drive away. I thought it would be quieter, we can chat better."

"That sounds great. I'll take my car and follow you out. I'm not drinking – early start in the morning. Where are you parked?"

"Here on the street."

"Great! Me too." He pointed to a wreck of a Toyota, two cars up from where my silver Audi was parked. As he followed me home I could see his car in my rear view mirror, choking and coughing. I was sure the emissions in Galway were hitting their highest ever.

Once we got the flat he asked, "Would you mind if I smoked outside?"

"Of course not. I'm not fond of the things, but outdoors is fine."

"I'd given up but reached for them after my friend died. We used to smoke together as students. Silly I know, and I'll chuck them again soon," he explained apologetically.

Opening my back door on to the garden which was shared among all the residents in the building, I put on a CD of the Beatles' greatest hits. Then I busied myself in turning on the oven and tossing the salad of rocket and *lola rosa*. As I glanced at Geoff reclining against the wall, it struck me that he had a way of making smoking look sexy; his long graceful fingers held the cigarette and he languidly drew on it, before puffing out circles of smoke. No wonder they banned adverts for smoking if it could look so provocative. After finishing his cigarette he walked inside and bolted the glazed double doors back into place, then smiled his beguiling smile. He began singing along with the song "Money can't buy you love". He had a great voice. The lyrics suited him, of course, but I had my doubts about their veracity. Being broke and down at heel wouldn't be great for keeping the flames of passion ignited after the initial sparks began to dwindle. There again, I had plenty of money with Trevor and look where that ended. I found myself wondering if my new-found spirituality could obliterate my desperate need for financial security, especially if I met the right person.

"Ready whenever you are." I headed through the archway from my sitting area to the kitchen and pointed to the table which I'd set with a cream linen cloth, the starter of seafood sushi ready to go.

"Christ, Kate! You've gone to a lot of trouble."

"It's just second nature to me - no more than you dabbing a few brush strokes on a canvas," I said, sitting down and helping myself to a piece of sushi with soy sauce and wasabi. I ate as I spoke: "I couldn't believe you were into mythology

– you never mentioned it to me."

"I love it." He buttered a slice of brown bread. "But I think I'm coming from a different angle to you. I love fantasy. Lord of the Rings and all that. I love magical realism where art remains representational, but with dream-like and fantasy elements included. Myths are a great way to incorporate these elements. My interest is not as pure as yours."

"There's no such thing as coming from a purer perspective. My dad read myths and legends to me as a kid, so my interest is quite childish. But tell me more about magical realism. Some of the South American authors like Borges and Gabriel Garcia Márquez use it in their work, don't they?"

"Absolutely… Yep, I love it. Are you familiar with some of the South American poets? Neruda and Salinas?"

"Just Neruda, whom I love, along with the Argentinian poet Borges. Do you know his poem 'You Learn?'"

He said, raising an eyebrow, "*After a while you learn the subtle difference between holding a hand and chaining a soul …*' "

"Yeah, I feel it's about what a loving relationship should be. Each person having independence and yet being part of one loving unit."

"That's it exactly. You'll also like Salinas. I'll read him to you sometime, when… When I'm not getting heated up on wasabi! Whew!" He gasped and groped for a drink of water. "It's just gone shooting up my sinuses!"

"Are you all right?"

"Fine, fine … Great for clearing the head."

"Well if you're okay, I'll put on the steaks." I was laughing as I stood up to prepare the pan and check that the *gratin dauphinois* was not burning in the oven. "Keep talking as I'm cooking, Geoff. I'll keep my concentration on the steaks but you talk away. How do you get that magical realism effect in your paintings?"

"I use photographic images. I'll explain it to you later when I show you images of unfinished canvases. That picture you like, Pandora opening the box, is of my daughter Shannon. She's eighteen now. It's from a photo of her when she was fourteen so she's a little bit childlike in it. She's starting art college next month."

"She's gorgeous. You must be proud of her. She's your only child then?"

"No, I have a sixteen-year-old son, Liam. He's special: he has Down syndrome and he's very loving. He's part of the group you met but he didn't travel today because he had an earache."

"My cousin had Down syndrome. Sadly she's passed on. I found her so funny and lovable when I was a kid. She made us all laugh." I tended to the steak, throwing a tablespoon of brandy on the pan and then lighting it with a match to flambé. Flames burst forth from the pan.

"Christ! It's gone on fire!" Then he laughed helplessly when I told him it was all in aid of a well-flavoured sauce. I mixed in some cream, a handful of peppercorns and stock, whisked up the sauce and turned everything out on to two hot plates. "This is heavenly, Kate. Thanks a mill for cooking for me. I love my food, but I'm more accustomed to bacon and spuds."

"Well, tuck in and help yourself to some salad for a change," I said, handing him the salad bowl. As his hand touched mine, a bolt of electricity surged right through me.

"Ever thought of opening a restaurant?" His eyes met mine for a split second. I looked away, could feel a blush rising as I sat at the side of the table.

"Several times, but I find having a secure pensionable job is one less thing to worry about. There's a lot of extra work to a restaurant between balancing books and getting the customers in."

"You seem wasted in a college. Everything about you is creative and enterprising. You're an innovator and big establishments stamp that out." He was smiling, his amber-flecked blue eyes crinkling softly. I felt a sudden glow around my heart which spread immediately all the way up to my cheeks.

"That's kind – you aren't far wrong, yet you barely know me," I said, puzzled.

"I know that you don't accept the status quo just because everyone else says it's fine. I know you're very imaginative and you have a strong aesthetic. It doesn't take a genius to figure that much out."

"Stop or I'll get a big head," I said, putting my hand to his mouth. It felt warm and moist. Immediately, without thinking, I moved to kiss him, my lips touching his as they parted slightly, our breath mingling. Then I pulled back and sat down like a prim school girl who'd been called back to her senses. "Whoops – excuse me!" Embarrassed at my forwardness, I blurted, "So tell me the bad things you've observed about me?"

He was smiling. "Nothing bad, Kate." He tilted his head sideways while appearing to consider how to phrase what he was about to say. "It's just you're still guarding your heart too much to let anyone in. You haven't fully gotten over your last relationship. Your beautiful green eyes are full of sadness and you're doing your best to push that away rather than deal with it." He half rose and reached across the table, tracing a finger across my cheek. I could feel my eyes fill with tears.

"And what about you, Geoff? Are you over your last relationship?"

"Ah now, that's complicated," he said

"What do you mean?" I asked.

"Just that. It's complicated." As he smiled, his eyes flickered between something akin to melancholy and mischievousness. I couldn't tell whether or not he was teasing me and suddenly felt frustrated. Maybe there was someone else. After all, Myra in the gallery had said she would see him in Dublin and he was still on the dating site. I didn't want to appear over-eager by probing too much. Silence descended, and I knew he was not going to be the one to break it, so I stood up to clear the table and at the same time asked him whether he would like tea or coffee.

I said, "I'd love to see more of your paintings."

"I've some images on my laptop if you have wireless."

"I do." I was relieved to be on safe ground and keen to see them. "Why don't you go out to the living area and set up your laptop while I get coffee ready?"

"Yes, mam." He put on a mid-western American drawl. "And while I'm there I think I'll have another fag. Outdoors of course."

A few minutes later, I arrived out to him with a tray and found him sitting on my sofa, MacBook on his lap. After placing two mugs along with a dish of Pavlova on the coffee table, I sat beside him, curling up. Despite the fact he smoked, it didn't appear to linger on his skin which had a warm woody scent mingled with musky overtones from whatever cologne he used. Dewy perspiration drops caused his wavy blond hair to curl at the temples, like babies' kiss curls. A wave of desire swept over me and I had a sudden mental picture of losing control and throwing myself at him, like a hungry wolf. I fanned myself, afraid he might read my thoughts. He looked at me and smiled, then glanced at the coffee table.

"No dessert for you?"

"No, I'm full ... Oh my goodness, is that your daughter?" A series of beautiful images had just appeared on his screen.

"Yeah, that's Shannon. I took these photos of her in the woods."

"She's like a model and the photos are stunning – like a magazine spread."

"That was the idea, in a way. She wanted to model along with going to college, so we did this thing in the woods with her looking like a wood nymph. She gave them to a Dublin agency and they signed her up."

"I'm not surprised." I gazed at the photographs of the tall willowy girl dressed in white chiffon, her strawberry blond untamed tresses tumbling around her face. In one picture, she wore a coronet of twigs covered in tiny red berries.

"I'm working with one of the photos to turn it into a painting," he said, showing me an image of an unfinished canvas. "I've projected the central image of Shannon on to canvas and then painted over it with oils. Afterwards I worked on the background to add in all manner of fantasy creatures and plants."

"And these men and women," I said, pointing to the subjects of other paintings. "Are they all people you've photographed?" As I spoke, I suddenly recognised one of the models as Myra. So they were old friends and maybe more? I hoped my demeanour didn't betray any feeling of envy.

"In some cases." His eyes lit up. "I see you've your own Goddess picture in pride of place." He pointed to my beloved print. "The triple Goddess, Persephone, Demeter and Hekate the crone."

"Everyone who comes in here comments on it. You're the first one to recognise which myth it represents. But then, you're into this."

"Yes, more and more. Like I said, mythology suits my genre with its mix of realistic Jungian archetypes and fantasy."

"You're a bit of a dark horse, Geoff, if you don't mind me saying so. You never told me you were into any of this. And how can you read me like you did in the kitchen?" I asked.

"I'm really a very simple man, Kate." He closed his laptop and rested it on the table, turning to me, resting his hand on my knee as he spoke. I feared my flesh would burn through my white jeans. It took a huge effort to push away increasingly erotic images as I gazed into his blue eyes. "I was reared on a farm in County Meath and I've been close to nature all my life. I hope I don't sound in any way pretentious when I say that some things are easy to see if you don't allow yourself to be blinkered by the outer stuff in life." I could barely take in anything he said as my eyes were drawn to the sensuous curve of his mouth. "Any possessions I have are necessary for work – like my laptop there. I struggle as an artist to pay my bills but I'm committed to follow wherever my heart leads me." Then he laughed and said, "I'm not 'edumacated' as you are. I'm only a country boy who likes to feel rather than think my way through things. I was slow to talk as a child so the need to define and analyse things has never been for me. To some people that would make me a bit on the thick side. I figure things out through art without the need for endless rumination." He paused, "And on that note I'd better be leaving you." He stood up.

My heart sank – had I just received a brush off? "You're

not thick in any way," I said hurriedly, and was once again disarmed by his enigmatic grin. I didn't know if he was enjoying a private joke at my expense and I found myself fumbling as I handed him his jacket, thrown on the back of the sofa. Maybe he thought I indulged in endless ruminations? "I'll let you out." I led the way upstairs. As I walked ahead of him, self-consciousness overtook me and I tripped on the second step from the top.

"Good job we didn't have the wine," he said, helping me up. Was it my imagination or was his smile more dazzling than ever? I was relieved to reach the front door without faltering for a second time.

"Thanks for a lovely evening, Kate." He kissed me on the mouth as I held the door open. Just as he seemed about to penetrate my lips, he drew back and smiled, saying, "Let's be friends, then. Shall we?"

"Yes, of course."

He turned to walk towards his car.

On my way down to the apartment I wondered had he found me as superficial as I'd found the Tom Ford imitation designer earlier in the day. Maybe he was playing with me? After all, he seemed to be able to converse intelligently and eloquently in between slipping into acting like an "unedumacated thick" as he'd called himself. He was by far the most interesting man I'd met and I was hugely attracted to him but he represented several challenges to me. I didn't know if I was up to facing those sorts of challenges at this late stage of my life. And I didn't have a clue whether he was remotely interested in me. One thing I was pleased about was how quickly I'd seen through Isaac, not allowing his ridiculous flattery to blinker me from the fact he was a moron with an emotional age considerably less than his shoe size. By contrast I could see Geoff's magnanimous spirit as he engaged with the young artists. After Peru, I was definitely better tuned into my gut instinct and had finally started listening to it. In many ways the dating had helped to enliven me, and in the process lift that woozy spaced-out feeling I'd been suffering from. I would return to meditation in an effort to help deal with my issues and keep me balanced in the midst of new romantic stirrings. This time, I didn't want to let things run away with me in the way I had allowed my thoughts to construct the elaborate fantasy I'd entertained for Ray.

Chapter Twenty-seven

The following morning after meditation and breakfast I logged onto my emails and then the dating site. Much to my surprise, Geoff had already contacted me.

Hi Kate,

Glad u left Persephone behind since u make a great Demeter/Demetriana surrounded by nature in ur Peru photos. Whew! A sexy one too in that black dress. Shouldn't be allowed! Though for the life of me I don't know what in Goddess's name u're doing on a site like this?

Geoff

A flush of exhilaration swept over me as I read his message. I'd convinced myself he hadn't found me attractive and that perhaps there was something going on with Myra, what with her antics in the gallery and her presence in his paintings. The one unmistakable fact was that he was still on the website, so that surely indicated he was not in a relationship. It was surprising how much more flirtatious he sounded on the site – maybe being at a distance helped overcome his shyness.

I decided to be bold and try to provoke a reaction:

Hi Geoff,
The Goddess wouldn't be on a site like this if a certain artist had asked her out. But then he has a complicated love life and heaven knows what that means? Too many beautiful women?
Kate

As soon as I'd sent it, I regretted having alluded to his love life and started mentally beating up on my self. Maybe I'd never hear from him again? Would he think I was desperate? Then awareness struck and I decided I was right to clear the air. If he didn't like what I'd said, tough luck – it just meant he wasn't for me. In fact I was beginning to think that my hankering for romance probably brought the craziest highs and lows possible and in many ways interfered with my spiritual progress. I didn't know why internet dating sites were so addictive, and I vowed that I would soon give them up ...

Just then, a message came in from Geoff:

My dearest Demetriana,
No it's not at all complicated that way. I'll tell u when I see u. The silly artist didn't think the Goddess would be interested but now that she's said she is. Well that's different! Can I visit u on Friday and bring u to the woods at Coole Park to take some photographs? Ur long red hair loose around your face is a must! How about finishing with drinks and dinner in a restaurant? Can't have the Goddess cooking again.
Your humble servant, Geoff

I read it and printed it off just to make sure I understood

it correctly. He was inviting me out on a date! And he must like the way I looked since he wanted to photograph me, and drinks surely meant he must intend staying overnight. Did this mean we could finally move from platonic friends to … what? Lovers? My heart started to flutter madly as though it could take flight through my chest and start humming at the same time. Then I reminded myself that it would be wise to hold off after what happened with Ray. The problem was, I found Geoff totally irresistible.

If Friday had been any slower arriving I would have auto-combusted from sheer impatience and excitement, despite my best efforts to stay calm and centred.

Geoff was due to arrive at noon and I'd been up since the crack of dawn, doing everything from plumping cushions to messing with my hair. If I fiddled with my hair one more time it would look contrived, and contrived was the last thing I wanted to look for Geoff. Natural it had to be. But a natural no-makeup look was very difficult to do, as was dressing well for the woods. For the hundredth time, I checked my reflection in my full-length mirror. Was I over-dressed in my kick-flare blue jeans, worn under a light voile mini kaftan in shades of pinks and russets on a cream background? It was certainly a hip look, but did I look too much like a regular at Glastonbury? At least for dinner it would be simply a matter of swapping trainers for heels, and I'd be organised with minimal fuss.

I'd just decided everything was fine when my phone rang. I saw it was Billy, and answered it.

"Hi Kate. I know it's short notice, but I'm in Galway visiting my aunt in hospital. Your mam said you lived in Taylor's Hill. Right?"

"Yes …"

"I'm only five minutes away from you, then. Would you mind if I stopped in for a cup of coffee? Won't stay long as I've to get back to Wicklow this afternoon."

"Of course. I'll text you the address." *Damn!* Geoff was due in an hour's time. And there was no way I could wriggle out of Billy dropping in. He had been sending me texts reminding me that I'd promised to visit his new cookery school. (I had a plan to bring my father with me for the pleasure of a day out, although he had grumpily informed me he was in no mood to travel anywhere at the moment because he was flat out going to see his "bloody psychiatrist". Mam told me that "you'd need a watch tied to his behind" to time my father's mood-swings these days. She blamed it on the therapy, saying it was better not to rake up the past since it was well and truly buried for a good reason. I reasoned with her that sometimes the past had to be dealt with before we could move on and that my father had to face the skeletons that had come back to haunt him. But to be honest, it was a waste of my breath trying to convince her.)

The sound of the bell signalled Billy's arrival, and I buzzed him in. He'd be gone before Geoff arrived, I assured myself, as I opened my apartment door.

"Great place, Kate. You never lost it, did you? The ability to surround yourself with beauty … You have impeccable taste!" He gave me one of his great big bear hugs followed by a smacker on my cheek before he walked into the living room and had a good look around.

"Sorry I didn't get round to visiting your place yet, Billy," I said to his back as he peered up at the Triple Goddess before moving to look out the window.

"Well you know what they say: 'If Mohammed won't come to the mountain then the mountain will have to come to

Mohammed.' So here I am, but thankfully not as mountain-sized as I once was." He patted his quite trim torso. Then he turned to twiddle the leather handcrafted dream catcher hanging by the window, its rainbow coloured net of threads glistening in the sunlight. "Perhaps your dream catcher drew me here today Kate … any chance of a coffee?"

"I'm not a big coffee drinker, so I've only got instant …"

"Oh no! Ah, only kidding, instant's fine. A little milk and no sugar. I want to talk business with you, Kate." Following me into the kitchen, he sat at the table and opened the black leather cover of the iPad he was carrying. I handed him a mug of coffee, and took the chair beside him. He showed me a picture of a one-storey building faced with old stone and beautiful teak barn doors set in a central arch. "This is the outside of the cookery school. We converted one of the outhouses." The next photo showed a very professionally laid-out lecture room, similar to that in third-level colleges. The top table was set on a podium with an overhead mirror, so that students could watch the teacher's technique. Each of the eight units had its own worktable with fitted hob, while the oven and microwaves were wall-mounted. "Now of course we'd get you whatever equipment you needed, Kate – I'm thinking, an interactive display board, an automatic movie camera and a large screen."

I was amazed. "It's state of the art …"

"I've held back on ordering small equipment because I know you'll have your own ideas regarding baking tins, food mixers and so on. You'll also need to hire another cookery teacher or chef to work with you and share hours, and …"

I touched his arm. "Hang on, Billy, you're talking as though I've said 'yes'."

"What's to stop you? I'll add twenty-five per cent to your

present salary and give you one of the cottages on the estate rent free. Look! Isn't that cute?" He brought up four images of a stone-faced cottage with a wild garden.

"Gorgeous. But I have a job here and this is where my friends are."

"Ah, come on Kate. That's just a job, not a career you're passionate about. And you can make friends anywhere. I know you." He was smiling at me intently, as if he couldn't and wouldn't understand a refusal.

I didn't know what to think. "But I'd planned to stay working where I am until retirement … The timing is all wrong … I've just had the greatest upheaval of my life with my marriage break up … Maybe I'd consider it in five years time if you have a vacancy on the team …"

"No. I know you, and if there's one thing I'm certain of it's this: you have to be in charge of this. You won't want to join later, and have to work under someone else. You've always been stubborn and proud, and however they have it organised you'll tell me you would have done it differently. So it's now or never. I need someone to head the school and you're perfect. I'll give you a week to think about it because after that I'm going to have to advertise the post. We're starting a six-month course in January and I need the teacher to work on the syllabus before then. I want brochures printed and a website running for mid-October." Softening his tone, he said, "Please tell me you'll consider it."

"I'll think about it. I promise." But all I could think of was that I needed to get rid of Billy right away, or Geoff might assume he'd spent the night. "I'm a creature of habit in lots of ways, Billy, and this would be a big upheaval, a huge lifestyle change."

"One that would improve your quality of life no end. I'm

telling you, you'll fall in love with the estate. Look at these pictures!" He brought up images of the great house and its sprawling grounds. He turned to face me, his eyes shining: "We've almost finished work converting another outhouse into a lifestyle store to sell crafts, fashion and soft furnishings along with foods and preserves from the cookery school. In one corner, we'll have a little bistro and coffee shop with a garden. Kate, it's made for you. I don't know why you're not jumping in the air over this."

"Billy, I wish you the best of luck with it, really it sounds great." I was a teacher who had spent all my life working from nine to five within certain parameters. Billy's enthusiasm scared the living daylights out of me.

"Don't you see I want you to manage all of this? It's the business opportunity of a lifetime! And I'm solvent, I have the funds to do this properly – I'm not like the rest of the schmucks who flew too close to the sun during the Celtic tiger years."

"I'll give it some thought. I promise." I stood up. I needed him to go, right now.

"Kate, you know something?"

"What?"

"I believe in serendipity and meeting you so near Machu Picchu was the universe's way of re-uniting us. I believe you and I would make a great team, and who knows where that could lead? They say when it comes to choosing a mate we should look to the person who could most easily be our best friend because friendship and loyalty will still be there long after the fireworks have gone out."

"Billy, please …" I could feel myself flushing. Would he ever stop talking and get out? "Listen, we'll talk again, but I have a very important meeting …"

"Ah, she's throwing me out now. Okay, I'm going." He gathered up his iPad, but then stopped at the door. "I'm only going on condition you'll give this serious consideration."

"I promise, I promise." I pecked his cheek and opened the door for him. "The switch at the right of the front door opens it."

What felt like only two minutes later Geoff rang the bell. I grabbed my jacket and ran upstairs to meet him. Scanning the car park, I was relieved to see that Billy had disappeared. "Hi!" I said shyly. "I'm ready to go now unless you want to come in for tea or coffee first?"

"No, I'm ready too."

"I'll drive, since I know the way." I pressed the automatic key to open my silver Audi, and its lights flashed.

He smiled a wry smile. "Okay, I won't refuse a ride in your nice sleek car. I tried to get rid of the smell of cigarette smoke out of mine, but it lingers. Just let me get my camera equipment."

As I led the way to my car, I hoped I hadn't sounded too eager.

The drive to Coole Park in South Galway took longer than usual – the traffic was heavy in Clarinbridge, where the Oyster festival was in full swing. Once there, we walked together through the walled garden and studied the famous autograph tree bearing the carved initials of writers from Yeats to Synge to George Bernard Shaw – all regular visitors to Coole when it had been the private residence of Lady Gregory. Great literary works had been written in her magnificent home surrounded by exotic trees, many of which her husband Sir William had imported from his time as Governor of Ceylon. Now people came from far and wide to walk their dogs, while young families brought children for picnics because the walled garden was an ideal place for kids to run wild under their parents' watchful eyes.

The surrounding woods were quieter than the garden – there was only the shimmying of the wind through the trees, the soft calling of the birds that nested there and the snapping of twigs beneath our feet. Scents of cedar, musk and wild garlic rose up to fill our nostrils. We arrived at a magnificent giant redwood with russet bark so scaly and hairy it resembled a prehistoric mammoth with seven trunks soaring from one root. The higher branches reached out and curled at their ends like tusks. "Feel it!" Geoff said, taking my hand and placing it on the bark. He set his hand above mine and we stroked it together. "It almost feels like a horse!" I said. "So animal-like."

"It's magnificent," he said, and I could feel the warmth of his breath brush my ear. Then he stood back and took the cap off his lens. "Stay where you are and let's try some shots," he said. "Do whatever you feel like doing, just don't pose."

As I stood leaning against the redwood, I could feel the energy pulsating through the tree as though it were travelling rhythmically from her roots.

"That's great, Kate, you're a natural. Now just turn to the left ever so slightly and loosen your shoulders, while elongating your neck." I could hear the shutter clicking.

"Now, shake out your hair, relax your jaw muscles and think of something nice."

Hmm … That wasn't so hard, since I was looking straight at the object of my fantasies.

Afterwards he came over to show me some of the shots

on the camera's digital display unit. Standing that close to me, his thigh touching mine, I was enveloped by his scent. "Wow, they're good, Geoff. Probably the best shots I've ever seen of myself." I tried to keep my voice even. Footsteps and the sound of wheels approached, and Geoff pulled me gently out of the way as a young mother arrived wheeling her toddler in a buggy.

"One last shot, Kate, of you walking down the centre of the path towards me. I want you to think power and grace, as though you're the queen of the forest. Not arrogance, just inner power and self assuredness. Your natural qualities."

But I felt self-conscious. I wasn't used to doing this sort of thing. Standing exposed in the open, I had no prop to hide behind or hold. Suddenly an elderly man came down the path, tugged along by a golden Labrador. "Sorry to interrupt you," he cried. "Great place for photography. I used to take a lot here one time myself."

"Oh, could I borrow your dog for the picture? What do you think, Geoff?"

"Ideal, if he doesn't run away with you!"

"He won't," the man assured me, handing over the dog's lead.

Click … click … click … click … "Great shots." Geoff showed the man the images on the camera and handed him his business card. "If you call me, I'll send you a few. Would you like to have your own picture taken with Kate and the dog?"

"Ah no, sonny. This aul mug's seen better days. She's a gorgeous gal but she looks better with you, mate." And he headed on his way.

We continued on our trail, holding hands while Geoff told me more about his painting and the fact he was planning a big exhibition for early December. "I work fast, so I'm fairly prolific. I just wish they flew out the door as fast as I finished them." We had arrived back at the car park, and he lit up a cigarette as he leaned against the bonnet of my car. He had a habit of knocking back several tic tac mints as soon as he'd finished, which was just as well since I hated the smell and taste of smoke.

We drove back to Galway and carried on our day in a restaurant at the Spanish Arch, a simple rustic place with wooden tables and stone walls hung with fishing pictures. We had pre-ordered the slow-cooked shoulder of lamb for two, and delicious aromas of wild rosemary and thyme floated up around us as the succulent meat fell from the bone.

"So good, so good ..." murmured Geoff between mouthfuls.

I decided to broach the subject of relationships. "Do you mind me asking what you meant last week about your love life being complicated?"

"Not at all. What I meant is that I have a responsibility to Liam, my teenage son with Down syndrome. I and my ex-wife share custody, and he's in residential care during the week, but he often comes to stay with me. I love him to bits and I'm never going to abandon him."

I asked, amazed, "How could anyone expect you to abandon him?"

"The last woman I was involved with found my commitment to him very trying. It's one of those issues that can really test a relationship."

"And how do you see us? Do you think a relationship could work?"

"I know the distance could prove a problem, and I have to stay in Dublin for Liam … But I'm falling hard for you, Kate, despite a voice in my head warning me that I don't have much to offer you."

"All I want is the right person to love me and me to love them. I don't expect anything else. But let's take things slowly."

By the time we arrived back at the apartment it was ten in the evening. I felt safe in Geoff's company and knew I could trust him, so as I parked the car I offered:

"Geoff, it's getting late. Maybe you'd better stay the night. I've a spare bedroom."

"I was hoping you'd invite me." He smiled that wry smile again. "I'll fetch my overnight bag and cancel the guesthouse."

As I turned on the lights in the living room, Geoff handed me a bottle of prosecco. I put it in the freezer to hasten its cooling. "Do you fancy watching a movie?"

"Love to. What have you got?"

"I've a few subtitled French and Spanish movies. Ever seen 'Like Water for Chocolate?'"

"I have, but I'd watch it again. Magical realism, right? But hang on now, it's a bit steamy – I'll have to behave myself while I sit beside you. How about we take a rain check on it for when we get past the taking-it-slowly stage?"

"Okay, what about a vintage Bollywood comedy called 'Chupke Chupke'?"

"Perfect," he said, grinning at my choice. "Do you mind if I use the bathroom first and then make a call to my daughter?"

"Of course not. Bathroom's on the right and your bedroom's on the left if you'd like to call her in there."

As he made the phone call, I found myself hoping this would be about more than just passion because I considered I might be falling in love. Geoff made me feel young and carefree and I loved his wild creativity coupled with his intense love of nature – it appealed to my artistic side. Being in his company was like seeing the world in vivid technicolor after living in a grey place for a long time. When I talked to him, I found I knew things about art I thought I'd long forgotten, and everything took on a magical glow. I liked who I was in his company. I hadn't fully gotten round the issue of him being an impoverished artist but maybe my spirituality would help me evolve on that front.

"A penny for them," he said, coming into the kitchen behind me. I swung round to find him smiling at me.

"I was just reflecting on the nice day we spent together." I pulled the prosecco from the freezer. "Will you try a Bellini cocktail?"

"What's that when it's at home, Kate? You're what my mates'd call a 'posh bird'! I'm not used to such fancy fare!"

"Prosecco with peach snaps and a little peach purée," I said, laughing at the idea of being called a posh bird.

"I'll take your word for it, you being a domestic Goddess and all that!"

"You sit down outside and I'll have it in to you in a jiffy. Just press play and the movie's ready to roll."

"Are you always this hyper-organised? It's a bit scary for the likes of me, I tend to be a bit disorganised."

"God, Geoff, I'm the most angst-ridden creature on the planet. The hyper-organisation is a cover up. Are you the kind of man who can calm an anxious woman?"

"Well, I could try." He came over to me and took the glass out of my hand. "Does this work?" he asked, before embracing me and covering my mouth with his. With his warm deft tongue, he parted my lips and searched my mouth, his hands moving over my waist and buttocks. He drew back. "Well?" His blue eyes were dancing as he looked into mine.

"Hmm … Yes, I think that could help. Not exactly calming, but it could get me through the odd crisis."

"Come on then, let's sit and watch the movie," he said, taking my hand.

My head was spinning and spine tingling as I took my Bellini in my free hand and allowed him to lead me out to the living area to sit on the sofa. As we watched the movie, we cuddled close together – I with my shoes thrown off and my legs curled underneath as he turned in to me and played intermittently with my hair and examined my hand like he had never before seen a hand. And God, it was so sexy when he kissed my ear and proceeded with a trail of kisses down my neck. How could just kissing my earlobe have me wanting to abandon myself to him, to tell him to take me there and then? It took all my resolve not to do so.

When the movie ended and we stood up to go to our separate bedrooms, he placed his mouth over mine and kissed me tenderly yet passionately, circling my tongue with his and sucking it playfully. He was the best kisser I'd ever met and I felt myself soaring with desire as *kundalini* energy rushed up my spine. But we'd promised to behave and behave we did, despite the sizzling electricity we appeared to generate whenever we touched.

Chapter Twenty-eight

The following morning I slowly awoke to the sound of my phone ringing incessantly in the living room. As soon as I opened my eyes, it stopped, but then it started again after about two minutes. Sighing, I hauled myself out of bed and went to find it. Trevor. Wasn't he on holiday with Julie? What on earth did he want? "Hello?"

"Kate, how are you?"

"Never better. You?"

"Look, I know this is unexpected but I'm worried about Julie."

I became fully awake. "What do you mean? Has she been in an accident?"

"No, no, nothing that immediate. It's just her preoccupation with dieting that concerns me."

"I asked her about her weight loss before she went on holiday with you and she flat-out denied she was dieting. How was she with you?"

"I found laxatives in her room in the hotel and she barely touched her food. Whenever she did eat to prove me wrong, she immediately headed for the nearest bathroom. Her weight is dangerously low, Kate. She must be under a hundred pounds."

"Oh my God! At her height that's crazy." I felt as though

I'd been suddenly whipped up by a giant tornado. "You're back on Sunday, right?"

"No, I decided to come back earlier because of Julie. We've just arrived in Dublin airport. I've left her to get the luggage. Can you come up to Dublin and I'll meet you at your parents' house? Both of us need to be singing from the same hymn sheet on this one if we're to nip it in the bud. And we both need to tread carefully with her."

"Yes, yes." I pressed my left hand to my forehead as my thoughts raced; I tried to think logically. "Yes of course. I'll leave right away." If Trevor was this worried, then things were really bad. He clearly thought our daughter was anorexic. Why was life always like this for me? As soon as things started to look up, some disaster struck. It was hard not to wallow in self-pity and feel I was jinxed.

"Geoff, I'm sorry." I stuck my head around his bedroom door. "An emergency's cropped up with my daughter and I have to leave straight away. I've just heard now and I have to rush."

He sat up rubbing his eyes as the early sun streamed in through the curtains. "Sorry to hear that, Kate. What's wrong? Anything I can do to help? I'll be ready to leave in a moment – I'm heading to Dublin myself, to collect my son."

"No rush, take your time, just check all switches are off when you leave and pull the door behind you ..." I headed into my room, pulling off my nightie as I went. I was like Road Runner on speed as I dressed in jeans and a t-shirt. Pulling my overnight bag from the bottom of the wardrobe, I hurled in pyjamas, t-shirts, underwear, socks and a wash bag as fast as I could. No exodus in history, including the flight into Egypt in Herod's time, could have been faster as I dashed for my car.

On the journey up I wondered had the break-up been to blame for Julie's descent into anorexia? Or was it solely my fault? Was I wrong to have brought magazines like Vogue and Elle into the house? That awful "waif" trend would have been around when she was at an impressionable age. And like any woman who wanted to look her best, I'd subscribed to the French adage of "il faut souffrir d'etre belle". I'd stood in skyscraper heels at weddings, only to have to visit the chiropractor the following day and have my vertebrae re-aligned while my screams could be heard by Julie as she sat in the waiting room. Afterwards, she'd commented innocently: "So those shoes are definitely headed for the bin then, Mum?" to which I'd answered: "God no, not after all the compliments I got yesterday!" I knew I'd occasionally gasped in horror when I found I couldn't fit into my favourite pair of jeans, muttering under my breath: "I'm a disgrace!" as I showed Julie my recently acquired midriff bulge which was threatening to grow into a muffin top if I didn't cut out biscuits and chocolate. My years as a very plump teenager who loved making and eating her own cakes were always at the back of my mind. I'd had such a battle to lose the bulge back then. Now I realised I'd been a terrible mother, passing on such superficial values. It was no wonder my life had fallen apart, forcing me to take the more spiritual path to self-awareness. I just hoped it hadn't happened too late.

Driving in the gate to my parents' house, I was seized by a sudden compulsion to shove the car into reverse mode as I caught sight of the number plate on Trevor's silver BMW parked to the left. Just then, I saw Julie appear at the door and I remembered why I was here in the first place. Julie came first in my life before anybody or anything else and she always would.

"Hi, Mum! Do you want any help with bags?" Her tone was buoyant.

"Hi love, great to see you. No, I just have an overnight bag." I embraced her ultra-slim frame. "You've lost more weight." Standing back to look at her, I registered to my relief that though she was slim, she didn't look as thin as Trevor had led me to believe. She was definitely a good twelve pounds over what he had suggested. Still, he had a right to his concerns. She was a young woman, and air-brushed images of stick-thin models graced every magazine and billboard, setting impossible targets of female beauty.

"I'm just eating healthily, Mum, I'm *fine*. You're always worrying about someone." She tossed her head as though I were insane. "Dad's inside with Granddad. He's helping to humour him and Gran's delighted because Granddad's been difficult lately."

I told myself I could handle this as I followed Julie through the front door and into the hallway, where my mother intercepted me. "Great to see you, Kate. Trevor and your dad are in the living room – I'll get you a cup of tea." This was followed by a whisper into my ear: "Dad's delighted Trevor's called. They've had a great chat. He has nothing but praise for you. I think he still loves you."

Holy Moley and Saint Joseph – would somebody tell the ground to open right now, please. Aware that Julie was watching me intently, I held my tongue, gathered myself together and even managed a smile as I entered the living room. Julie walked towards the kitchen.

For some strange reason, when I saw the two men who had played such a big role in my life sitting there together, a warm feeling of familiarity and security seemed to wash over me. It was just like old times, but it didn't make sense in light of new developments in my life. Maybe the whole business with Julie was confusing me.

"Kate, you look amazing." Trevor got up from his chair to put an arm around my shoulder.

My body stiffened as he kissed my cheek. "You look well too," I muttered and then went over to give my father a hug. "How's Dad keeping?"

"Sick of going for bloody therapy and the cost of it. I was asking Trevor's opinion of all this twice-weekly malarkey going to shrinks."

Oh no, I thought, Trevor would have undoubtedly said my father was fine with just Prozac. I'd kill him.

"I told Jim that therapy is exactly what he needs. As time goes by, he won't need it so often. Jim, you've got the best psychiatrist in the country. Forget about silly taboos regarding depression and see this as physiotherapy for the mind."

Who was this enlightened person who resembled my ex-husband? Could an alien have abducted him, and was maybe now inhabiting his body? This from the man who thought all manner of shrinks were charlatans and would never be caught dead going for counselling? Were his concerns for his daughter making him see things differently?

"Physiotherapy for the mind! Well that's a good analogy. I like that …" My father smiled, as he got up to leave the room. "I'll leave you two to catch up, then."

My mother arrived with a tray bearing two mugs of tea and a plate of assorted biscuits, which she laid on the coffee table. "Thanks, Mam." I sat down, conscious of Trevor taking in my every movement. At least the mug gave me something to play with as I sneaked a look at him, while pretending to decide which biscuit to choose. He was tanned from his holiday and as usual neat as a new pin with his pepper-and-salt hair coiffed like an Italian's, pomade ensuring no wave or curl strayed out of place. He was handsome, no doubt, but he looked older and drawn.

He said, "I was sorry to hear about Jim. I wanted to come as soon as I'd heard but I didn't think it was my place."

"I appreciate you considering my feelings and keeping healthy boundaries. Mind you, I couldn't get over what you just said to him about therapy. You, who never agreed with counselling."

"People can change, Kate. I've been doing a lot of soul searching recently and it's made me think about things differently." He threw his hands out, palms turned upwards, shrugging his shoulders, then paused before linking his fingers and leaning forward in his chair to look closely at me. "So how have you been?"

"Does it really matter to you, how I've been? You couldn't wait to get rid of me."

"I made a big mistake, Kate. I realise that now. And after having Julie on holidays with me I realised how important family is. The three of us together were great. Julie has suffered through this."

"Well, you've realised that too late, Trevor."

"Is it too late, Kate? I'm willing to give it another try if you are."

You could have knocked the socks off me. I hadn't seen that one coming. What had happened to him? "What about Martha?"

"She's gone, Kate. I told her to pack her bags and get out."

I couldn't help laughing. "You're making quite a habit of throwing women out, Trevor!"

"Kate, I'm serious. I love you and I want you back. Can you forgive me and give me a second chance?"

"I don't know, Trevor. It would be hard to trust again. But tell me … Were you really concerned for Julie or was this all a ruse to get me here and ask me back?"

"God no, Kate, I'm genuinely concerned for her. I feel the best thing for her is for us to be a family together again. Hell, I'll even go to counselling with you. Give up golf and help you write your book. I'd just love you to give us another chance."

There were tears in his eyes as he leaned over to hug me. He clung to me in the way a small child would cling to its mother. Having been without me, he must have finally realised how much I had filled his life. I'd arrange everything perfectly for him, from laundry to beautiful meals. I'd always facilitated him, no matter where he wanted to go and I'd been affectionate to him in a way I couldn't imagine Martha capable of. I felt sorry for him and I knew he really needed me – but he didn't deserve me. Yet he was right about Julie needing her family.

Then I thought of Geoff, with whom I'd just shared the best day of my life. If there was such a thing as soul mates, then I was pretty damn sure I'd found mine. Not long ago my life had seemed lacking in options and now all sorts of choices had to be made. I was well and truly torn.

Chapter Twenty-nine

$\mathscr{I}$ now had two issues which needed addressing: to choose between Trevor and Geoff and to decide between my present job and Billy's offer.

Not for the first time I realised what a difference one day can make.

Though I'd become better at meditating and catching my thoughts, I still felt my life was being ripped apart by chaotic outside events. Memories of good times with Trevor came rolling into my mind as though I were watching one movie reel after another with all but the best of times edited out. A simple naive girl when we'd first met, I'd grown up with him and in lots of ways we'd been great together.

Trevor and my job in the college represented the tried and tested parts of my life whereas Geoff along with Billy's job offer represented a walk into the unknown. Geoff was four years younger than me and I'd only met him three times so I knew it would be silly to throw everything away for him. I knew too that I'd grown to love Galway and I didn't want to leave my friends. As well as that, Trevor was asking me to come back to the home I had spent the last twenty-two years putting together – a home that was also Julie's home.

My most immediate concern, however, was my daughter's welfare. Trevor left and I persuaded Julie to stay overnight in her grandparents' home with me. It gave me an opportunity to observe her eating habits and at the same time inspect the toilet after both lunch and dinner, since she ate as heartily as she'd always eaten.

When I looked, I couldn't see any signs of regurgitated broccoli or spaghetti bolognese or any other meal she'd eaten, so I came to the conclusion Trevor had exaggerated. The term "drama queen" is always attributed to women. In my experience men are just, if not more, as capable of creating unnecessary drama, since they are often driven by unconscious fears and urges. Trevor had regularly been prone to wild exaggerations especially when he had concerns about Julie. If he'd had his way he'd have hired a nanny to accompany her to university. No wonder I'd been full of angst living with him. He had a knack of exacerbating my already inflated fears to such an extent that my anxiety would run off the Richter scale.

Since Julie was anxious to return to her new flat early Sunday morning, I delivered her there en route back to Galway. Geoff had sent me several texts the day before telling me his thoughts were with me. I'd promised to call him on Saturday night. But in many ways I didn't want to talk to him right now – I felt I wouldn't want to talk to him for quite some time, I was so confused.

Since meeting Trevor, I'd started to get Catholic flashbacks. And when I examined the feelings coming from the knot in my gut and tight shoulders, I realised I really felt as though I was cheating on the man I had spent most of my life with. It takes four years to get a divorce in Ireland and at least a year to get a legal separation. I was still well and truly married. And that awful word "adultery" was sitting before me, floating in a speech bubble from somewhere near my right temple. I'd felt a tinge of it with Ray but I'd reassured myself Trevor and I were definitely over, and that had assuaged my guilt.

I really thought I'd transcended all this, especially in light of my trip to Brazil and Peru. But whenever I was exhausted, archaic beliefs ingrained in me from childhood by a vicious nun wielding a sally rod returned to haunt me with images of a cloven-hoofed demon. As James had suggested in Peru, it was not so easy to "unlearn" the old stuff.

Nonetheless, I needed to phone Geoff and early morning was as good a time as ever. I pulled in off the motorway and rang his number. He sounded groggy as though the phone ringing had just woken him up. The fact that I hadn't rung the night before contributed to a sense of awkwardness between us, as we exchanged initial pleasantries. Then Geoff asked me about Julie.

"She's lost weight but I think she's probably like me and has a fast metabolism," I said. "She's been under stress from us splitting up but she'll be fine."

"That's such a relief."

"Yes, her father is prone to over-worry where she's concerned. You know the way with an only child."

"Will I see you at the weekend then?"

"No, I don't think so. I have to get ready for going back to school." I sighed then blurted out, "Geoff, I really like you and I had the best day of my life with you but I've just realised I need more time and space. Right now, I'm confused."

"It's because you met your ex, isn't it, Kate?"

"No … Yes … I don't know." I sounded distant even to my own ears.

"Really, Kate, I do understand. The timing's not right is it?"

"Apparently not." I choked back the tears, sniffing, "I'm sorry."

"Don't worry. I'd better let you go. Goodbye, Kate."

I arrived back in Galway at noon, in time to meet James for lunch an hour later in a café in Salthill. We'd just finished eating when a text came in from Ella. She was back in Ireland, but we hadn't yet found a suitable time to meet up. *"Are you around? Call over. I'd love to see you. Ella x."*

I texted back: *"With James in Salthill & about to order coffee."*

"Better coffee in my place. Bring James with you. Ella x"

I said to James, "That was Ella. Fancy calling round with me?"

He laughed. "You know me. I never refuse an opportunity to hear the latest girly gossip."

In the car on the way over, I asked James how he was getting on with Alex. Their relationship had been on and off over the past two years. Sometimes they were close and sometimes, like this summer, they had taken breaks from each other before re-uniting once more. "You won't believe it, Kate. Just when everything seemed dandy after me missing him so much in South America, Alex tells me he wants us to get married and have a child by surrogacy."

"Are you serious?" I glanced at him briefly as I drove. "That was the last thing I'd expect from him."

"Deadly serious and you're right, I didn't expect it either. I don't think he has it well thought out but he's carried away on some fantasy notion of playing with a kid and teaching him or her drums and guitar. I've tried explaining to him that there's a lot more to rearing kids than dressing them cute, and teaching them stuff. He's eight years younger than me though, and he's not mature even for his age."

"Maybe it's just a notion that'll pass. After all he spends most weekends doing gigs with that band. Does he realise he'd have to give that up? I can't imagine you stuck in all weekend playing wifey." I was laughing but James was not amused.

"It's not funny, Kate. I love kids but I'm happy to be a doting uncle rather than have my own. I'm annoyed because we discussed it two years ago when we first became a couple and he told me he'd no interest in kids."

We had arrived outside Ella's house, and she greeted us at the door in her customary cheerful manner. "Hi, you two – you're both looking great after your odyssey. Come in." She ushered us both inside. "You have to try my coffee." She held up a bag with the 'BlendElla' brand name. "It's fabulous if I may say so and you get to try it before it hits the supermarket shelves!"

"Congratulations, Ella!" James and I chimed simultaneously. It was at times like this that I most envied Ella's unbridled energy and enthusiasm.

"It's only the beginning. I've lots more ideas from my trip spinning around in here," she said, tapping her head. Lifting the coffee pot, she poured us a mug each. "I'm getting gorgeous mugs designed to go with it for initial promotions. Brazil was a good experience for me, I'm telling you." She wriggled her hips and gave a self-satisfied wink. I smiled as I considered how incorrigible she could be. When Ella set out to achieve something, she never let anything hold her back. In comparison to her I was positively a shrinking violet.

James was breathing in the aroma from his mug. "It's heavenly, Ella. Best of luck with it, darling."

"It's fabulous and I'm not even an avid coffee drinker," I agreed.

"What about you, Kate – tell me all the news? You were too busy to meet us last week and you said you'd tell us everything when we met up?" This was the moment I'd been dreading but maybe they could provide an outsider's perspective on my situation. I pulled at my ring finger to twiddle my ring, missing it once again.

Placing my two palms over my eyes, I groaned, "Oh God, I'm totally befuddled. Where do I begin to tell you everything that has happened?" I described my meetings with Geoff, Billy's offer and Trevor's invitation that we get back together.

"I don't know what your problem is, lovey. The answer's very simple from where I'm looking at it. You've just met Mr Wonderful and you've been offered the dream job. Take them both with open arms and forget about Trevor." Ella shook her head in disbelief at my indecision. "Wicklow isn't Timbuktu. We'd always visit you."

"It's not that simple, darling," James said, looking at Ella and then back to me. "Kate and I are creatures of habit. I know exactly how she feels because I'd find it hard to leave my pensionable job for something which required me to suddenly think totally outside the box. Institutions do that to you – they provide you with a funny sense of security. It's different when you're under thirty-five and you're not so set in your ways."

"Exactly my sentiments!" I said, patting his arm. "Unfortunately not everyone's like you, Ella."

"But surely you're not seriously considering going back to Trevor?" she asked, staring at me in horror.

"I'm not sure how I feel anymore. You see when Billy sprung all this on me it made me aware that I'm quite timid really. I'll be forty-five next month and that's like half my life over if I live to be ninety. I mean it could be downhill all the way from here and I've always needed to feel secure. Also I miss being part of my little family with Julie."

Ella pounded the wooden table with her fist. "Would somebody please tell me where our friend Kate has disappeared to because I haven't seen her for quite some time? James, are you sure that shaman didn't steal her spirit in Peru?"

"No, she was in fine fettle but in all honesty she's had a fair bit of trauma between the robbery and her dad." Turning to me, he placed his two hands on my shoulders. "Kate, I think you're just overwhelmed. You need a good rest to clear your head."

Ella put up her hand. "Can I please ask just one question?"

"Sure, what is it?"

"What have you said to Geoff?"

"When he rang I told him more or less what James just said. That I was overwhelmed by events and confused. And even though I cared for him I needed space and time to think."

"Kate, that's called using your head where matters of the heart are concerned."

"Exactly." I nodded, glad she understood.

"No, no. I didn't mean that was *right*. You can't let your head decide what's right for your heart."

"Since when did you become the Dali Lama?" I asked her cynically. "It turns out I still care for Trevor. Now, that doesn't mean I'll definitely go back. But when I thought about moving east side I realised it's not for me. And if I'm not prepared to move then my heart obviously isn't totally convinced about Geoff either. I had concerns about him being involved with a woman called Myra who was in the Dominic Street art gallery with him that day. Either of you know her?"

In turn, they shook their heads. "I'll make inquiries with my sister Lorna. If there's a story, she'll know it," said Ella.

"I've one piece of advice from my twelve-step meetings," said James, "H.A.L.T. What it means is never act or make a decision if you're H for hungry, A for angry, L for lonely and T for tired, because if you do then it's usually a reaction rather than a positive action."

"That makes sense, James," I said. "I'm going to try to remember that one because right now I'm in total deadlock."

Ella had asked us to stay for lunch and a viewing of her new *'Allo, 'Allo* boxset. Unable to rise to their level of enthusiasm, I left them to it in favour of a walk on the prom before returning home. At around four in the afternoon, in the privacy of my own apartment, the L word struck and I felt lonely. I was restless and craved diversion – something to lift the feelings of uncertainty and loneliness. Geoff had mentioned trying a different dating site and I'd started wondering if I could find it. I was in no mood for dating, so had no intention of putting up a proper profile with pictures. I'd only recently deactivated my profile as Demeter on the last site, having decided she wasn't such a powerful Goddess archetype after all; she was a mother who spent half the year in mourning for her daughter and her story seemed to be as heart-wrenching as my present dilemma. I reckoned I would be better off without Demeter's energy in my life just as I had previously discarded Persephone.

Since it's not possible to look at members without signing up, I made a spur of the moment decision to use 'Hekate' as my user name. I'd read up on her recently and no longer found her as scarily intimidating as I'd initially thought her to be. The blurb on one website said she was Goddess of the crossroads and she helped people make decisions when they came to a fork in the road of their lives. I knew it was only silly but any psychological tool that helped me, from prayer to meditation, to a strong Goddess energy, was welcome right now. In the Greek myth, it was Hekate who eventually helped Demeter rescue her daughter Persephone. Perhaps it would do me no harm to have the powerful Moon Goddess in my court at the minute. I could do with resurrecting my inner bitch, especially if that meant becoming more decisive about what was best for me, Kate.

To all the questions on the dating site, I merely ticked the box saying "will answer later". So the only information my profile gave was my age, star sign and user name. From my experience nobody would bother to give such an anonymous profile a second glance as it would get lost among a sea of more interesting profiles with photographs.

Before I'd deactivated my profile on the previous site, I'd noticed Geoff had deactivated his. Of course that had thrilled me at the time, as I felt it showed a commitment to me. But if he were to move to this website what would he call himself? Picasso and Dali were both Spanish. There was a third artist... What on earth was the name? Miro, that was it. I'll just type *"luvmiro"* into "search username". No, Nothing there. I tried *"Miroesque"*. My heart fell down to the pit of my stomach when Geoff's picture and profile came up. He'd obviously given up on me and wanted to move on. Well, I supposed I couldn't blame him. I took another look at it and printed it off. This site gave information regarding the time each user had last been online, indicating Geoff had logged off within the last hour. I couldn't help thinking that he wouldn't be on this if I had agreed to meet him this weekend. Maybe I should call him? Was it too late?

Just as I was wondering where my phone was, it began ringing and I followed the sound to the kitchen. "Kate, after you left, James and I thought about going out to Clarinbridge. Will you come?" Ella asked.

"But it's the end of the Oyster festival."

"I know. But my sister Lorna rang. She's there with a gang of women and says there's a bit of craic going on. Today's a more casual day and you don't need a ticket for the marquee. She said there's a good band playing. We were thinking of getting a taxi and having a few drinks."

"No, don't bother getting a taxi. I'm not in the mood for booze so I'll drive. I'll collect you both in fifteen minutes. Okay?"

The only time I wear black from head to toe is if I'm having a fat day or I feel insecure and wish to appear almost invisible. Today I was definitely the latter. I ripped off the multicoloured t-shirt I was wearing and swapped it for a fitted black shirt, teamed with black scarf with white skulls. In my three-inch wedge soled boots I looked a bit like the grim reaper as I set out to collect Ella and James.

"Hey, for someone who likes colour you're very black today," Ella said when she saw me.

The festival car park was thronged but I was lucky enough to get a parking space just as another car was pulling out. As we walked towards the entrance, I spotted a wreck of a red Toyota in the distance and thought it looked similar to Geoff's. As soon as we entered the marquee, the music seemed to go up several decibels, making it hard for us to hear each other speak. The dance floor was palpitating, children and pensioners alike, flapping to the cheesy seventies hit "the birdie song". Several young women looked very drunk as they attempted to jive in skyscraper-high heels. Some of their partners looked as though they'd slept in dinner suits from yesterday's oyster-opening event, which would have been the festival highlight. In the far corner of the marquee, two clowns sat painting children's faces. It was an odd mix of family day for some, hangover heaven for others.

Surveying the single men, I felt depressed to think this was the best on offer. None of them could hold a candle to Geoff. For the second time that day I thought about calling him. Later maybe I would ... when I returned home.

Ella was texting her sister Lorna in an effort to locate her. "She says she's at the left side of the bar in the other room. Follow me." We pushed through the crowd to find the infamous Lorna perched at the bar surrounded by a coterie of gossipy women. Thank heaven it was a little bit less noisy here, because Lorna spoke faster than Speedy Gonzales. The eyes in her round jolly face lit up when she spotted me, which meant she was either eager for gossip or would have something juicy to impart to me. After introducing her three friends, one of whom was the famous Jennie whom Ella had told me dated Ray, Lorna turned her attention to me. "Well, Kate, you're looking very rock n' roll, I have to say. I believe it's all off between Trevor and Martha?"

Here we go, I thought as Ella handed me a glass of soda water. "Yes, apparently."

"Everyone said he would want you back. That tramp was never in your league but I believe she was screwing him ... oops, sorry." She clapped her hand to her mouth.

"Unfortunate choice of words. So, I hear she was two-timing Trevor with a younger man? I suppose what goes around comes around." Taking in my shocked expression, she added cheerfully, "Didn't you know?"

"No, I didn't." I knew one thing though: Lorna was a dangerous gossip and was obviously fishing for a quote from me to pass by bush telegraph to all her friends all the way out to Kiltilough in north Galway. "Excuse me, Lorna, I need to talk to James. I'll catch you later." Just as I turned, I spotted someone who looked like Geoff across the room. I had to do a double take. It *was* Geoff. Then my jaw fell to the floor as I spotted Myra approaching him, curling her arm around his waist as she whispered in his ear. I blinked to make sure I wasn't seeing things. No. It was definitely him. My stomach lurched and I suddenly felt wobbly on my high-soled boots.

"Kate, are you all right?" James asked, breaking from his conversation with Jennie. "You look as if you've just seen a ghost."

"I've just spotted Geoff with that Myra from the gallery. He was supposed to go back to Dublin yesterday morning. He said he had to pick up his son."

"Who? Where is he?" James asked, as Jennie listened.

"Blond guy over there with the dark-haired girl."

"Oh, I know her to see," Jennie offered. "As far as I know they have a son together. Her parents weren't pleased when she took up with an artist. She used to be a dentist and has gone all bohemian in the last few years."

"No, you're wrong. His fifteen-year-old son has Down syndrome and lives in Dublin."

"Not him, I'm talking about the little lad with them," Jennie said. I turned back and saw a little boy, now perched on Geoff's shoulders. For a brief moment, our eyes met across the room. Handing James my soda water, I said, "I have to go." Suddenly my energy returned as rage ripped through me at the thought of having been deceived.

"No, wait, Kate. Do you want me to say anything to him for you?"

"No, it's like what you said, James – when you're hungry, angry, lonely or tired it's better to do and say nothing. Just tell Ella I decided to leave. You two intended getting a taxi anyway."

"Hang on. I'm coming with you. I'll tell Ella."

"Okay, I'll be in the car." I could see Geoff attempting to weave through the crowd in my direction, after having handed the boy to Myra. I elbowed my way quickly in the opposite direction and ran to my car, starting it up immediately and driving it around to the front of Paddy Burke's pub on the main street. I was in no mood to listen to any excuses from Geoff. I sent a text to James telling him where to find me and as soon as he arrived I took off like a supersonic jet. "Ella's hanging on because she spotted a couple of good-looking men. I told her we'd phone her later to explain our departure. Are you all right, Kate?"

"Mad as hell," I fumed, as my foot pounded the accelerator.

"Look, you had the good sense not to sleep with him. Don't be hard on yourself. You're better off without him."

"You're right, I'm better off without him. He told me a load of lies and I thought he was so sincere.".

"If you ask me, he probably thought you'd have plenty of money between your job and your split with Trevor. You've to be very careful with some of these guys."

"I'd hate to think he could be so mercenary but you never know." I gritted my teeth. "Anyway, another one bites

the dust. At least I won't be wondering about him any longer. God, it seems like I wouldn't recognise a decent man if he knocked me down on the street."

"Don't be hard on yourself," said James. "It's early days yet."

After getting home, I printed off Geoff's profile page, tore it up and danced a jig on it before binning it. A text from him appeared on my mobile, saying, *"Kate I can explain. Please call me."* Two more came in shortly afterwards but I deleted them without looking at them – I was certain it was more lies. God, he could put on a very convincing act. All that chat about being a devoted father to his Down syndrome child, and he had a younger son he hadn't even bothered telling me about! That's what he'd meant about his love life being complicated – why couldn't he have told me when I asked? I briefly wondered was Myra in on some plan to scam me but dismissed the idea as old-fashioned paranoia. He'd probably treated her as badly if not worse than every other woman he met. At least two questions had been answered tonight. Geoff was ruled out and I would definitely be saying no to Billy's offer.

Trevor had hurt me by betraying me, yet he now sought my forgiveness. Over a twenty-three year period, he had certainly treated me better than any of the men I'd met in the last three months, although if Lorna was right and he'd only got rid of Martha because she'd had an affair, it put a different slant on things. Sitting on my sofa with a cup of Lapsang souchong, I looked at the image of the Triple Goddess and I thought of James's advice. For some strange reason this painting always soothed me, as though the three Goddesses were enveloping me in a tranquil mist, wispy as the clouds over the Andes.

I wrote H.A.L.T. on a piece of yellow card and wove it into the net of the dream catcher, which I had moved to dangle from beneath the painting. This would be my new mantra. I prayed to the Holy Spirit to please help me find the patience to hold back and wait for the answers to come rather than feel I had to rush headlong into things.

Chapter Thirty

My return to work in mid September coincided with the arrival of an Indian summer. The sun shone high in an azure-blue sky while a cool autumn breeze nudged early fallen leaves into a light-hearted dance. I thought I'd dread the start of term but instead I found myself looking forward to the structure that work would bring to my life. There were many different careers I'd imagined pursuing from anthropology to writing children's stories, but ultimately there was something about teaching that suited me. I liked interacting with young people and helping them. Like coaxing fledglings to fly the nest, I was always proud to meet past students and see how they'd blossomed.

Trevor had sent me several texts asking me to come back to see the house. He knew I was sentimental by nature and would have missed the house that I had spent so much of my life living in. I had always loved returning to it after holidays abroad and would tell him no five-star hotel ever compared to it.

But I told him I needed time; that right now I was busy getting back into the swing of things. I always found the first two weeks back at college draining as my job demanded long hours standing on my feet. Along with that, classes had to be planned, lecture notes needed updating and ingredients had to be bought for demonstrations.

As I stood at the top of my classroom giving the new first years an introductory talk, I was struck (not for the first time, if I'm honest) by how repetitive this had become after twenty-three years. Almost boring. But who was I to complain? After all the upheaval I'd had, boring was good in my book. I thought of an old Chinese proverb I'd heard that said "Pray for an uneventful life!" I used to think that was the most absurd saying I'd ever heard but now I understood too well the wisdom behind it.

My thoughts were interrupted by the bell signalling the end of the lecture as students gathered up their bits and pieces, shoving pencils, pens, spectacles and jotters into satchels and rucksacks.

"Ms Canavan. Can I have a few minutes?" came a familiar voice as Mike Darcey, head of my department, hovered near the door. Wearing a fawn jacket over a white shirt and with his hands behind his back he looked every inch the weasel I'd always considered him to be.

"Of course."

As the last student left the room, Darcey pulled the door closed behind him. "And how are you keeping after your holidays, Kate?"

"Very well, thank you. And you?" I needed to appear composed and capable and not let him think I could be vulnerable after the creepy way he'd come on to me after hearing of my separation from Trevor.

"I'm very well, thank you. However it appears we have a problem with a certain Mr Clarke's result in his final cookery examination."

"Oh? And what's the problem?"

"He was very dissatisfied with not having received a

distinction from you and he's appealing it. I'm afraid you're going to have to re-examine him, Kate."

"I expected something like this would happen with all these cutbacks. Leaving teachers to examine their own students without the assistance of an outside examiner is fundamentally flawed." And it would be just like Ron Clarke, of all last year's students, to be the one to test it.

"Can you set a practical examination for him for sometime next week, Kate?"

"No problem. He certainly didn't deserve a distinction and I can't imagine him having risen to that standard. He falls down on procedures and hygiene practice."

Darcey edged closer to me to the point we were sharing the same air space. The man had no sense of personal boundaries and his breath stank to high heaven. "Kate, if I were you I'd simply give him what he wants." He lowered his voice, though we were alone. "We don't need any unpleasantness here. We don't want him kicking up a fuss. And you know he's well capable of so doing."

I pulled back, overwhelmed not only by his breath but by his attitude. "I understand. I'll brief him well in advance. That's the best I can do. Now if you'll excuse me, Mike, I have a meeting with a colleague before my next lecture period."

As I passed him, I could feel his eyes appraising my legs. I'd chosen to wear a knee-length skirt, but sometimes I felt like wearing a nun's habit when I saw the lecherous way Darcey looked at women. I made my way to the staffroom to find James. He was sitting at a window table in a quiet corner, assiduously checking his diary against a sheet of printed paper. In another corner, three teachers congregated around a kettle, mugs in their hands. Elsewhere, people checked timetables, some looking happy as they discovered a block of free time, others dismayed by how scattered their hours were. It was always the luck of the draw what you ended up with. I was happy with mine since I'd a few decent free blocks throughout the week.

"You won't believe what happened?" I said, as I took the chair opposite James.

"Darcey told me Kate. That little brat Ron Clarke. I had him for first and second year. Remember? He was always trouble but nobody says anything because his father's a local politician and holds sway with some of the department's associates."

"Did Darcey tell you he expects me to automatically give him a distinction this time around?"

"Not in so many words but it was implied. That's why I got a copy of your timetable to check when we both have free periods. I don't want you leaving yourself wide open to controversy so I'll examine him with you."

"God thanks a million for that, James. You're a brick."

"How about we schedule it for the second Friday in October at nine thirty? First hour is prep and then put him straight into a two-hour exam. Technically I'm not free for the full three hours but I'll get someone to cover my classes."

"Sounds good."

After I had left James, I headed for my triple cookery period with the third years, an amicable crowd unlike the nasty shower who had recently graduated. I'd ordered in the ingredients for them to make a variety of pastries from choux to filo and puff pastry. The kitchen had a lot of windows and with temperatures outside higher than they had been all through the summer months, the room was like a hot house. This made it tricky, even with air conditioning, for the students to keep everything from ingredients to utensils and their hands as cold as possible. "That's one of the principal rules of pastry making. Keep everything cold," I said as I wrote on the board after they'd finished clearing up. "What's next?"

"Ingredients must be weighed precisely," called Lucy at the back.

"Why is that so important?" I asked, and lanky Bill put his hand up. "Yes, Bill?"

"Because something like choux pastry won't be successful unless the ingredients are in the precise ratio. There's no room for error."

"Exactly," I said, as the bell rang. "Now please do out your time plans for Thursday's class and have all ingredients in. And don't forget to bring enough jars. You'll want to pot your lovely jams and chutneys."

"Thanks, Ms Canavan. Would you like a profiterole?" A blonde girl held a lunchbox open for me to take one.

"No thanks, Sharon. Not today." Some classes left me inwardly grinning, despite the jokes remaining the same, with girls teasing the boys by asking them did they fancy me. You'd think that would have subsided at my age but my newly single status seemed to have re-ignited curiosity. At the beginning of class, I'd noticed them look at my hands as they took in the lack of rings, followed by whispering and elbowing each other in the ribs, yet the atmosphere was playful and good-humoured. A class like this gelled well; they were part of the reason I loved the job. I suddenly gasped aloud – I'd forgotten to ring Billy to tell him I definitely wasn't interested in his offer. I owed him that much.

That evening after dinner, I called him. We exchanged the usual pleasantries and then got to the crux of the matter. "But I thought you didn't like your job very much, Kate?"

"Truth is, I'm glad to be back, Billy. I like being part of a team. That's what I am really – a team player rather than someone who would flourish independently."

"I don't believe that for a minute, but I have to accept that you're saying no and move on. I'm gutted though."

"Don't be. Things'll work out for the best. You'll get someone who's just perfect for the job. I know it!"

"I've had lots of interest in it already, and I haven't even advertised the post – but it's you I wanted. Anyway, no point in going on about that anymore! I was thinking about having a party here on Halloween? As it's your birthday and mine is two days before we can celebrate together. What do you think?"

"Sounds good. Can I bring a friend?"

"Bring as many friends as you like. I've a few of my own pals staying but I can sleep an extra five or six. Even more, if they're happy to sleep on a sofa or in a sleeping bag on the floor."

"Great. I'll let you know nearer the time how many are coming. It'll be like the old days with you boasting about being a year and two days older than me."

"Not a boast any longer, Kate. It's good to be the younger one at this age. We'll have good craic at the party. Fancy dress, remember!"

It could be fun, I thought as I made a note in my diary to tell Ella and James. I hadn't been looking forward to hitting forty-five and becoming well and truly middle-aged but now I had something to look forward to.

Chapter Thirty-one

The next two weeks were spent getting back into my old routine of planning my classes and going for a daily half-hour walk along the prom or occasionally in Barna woods where I would find a space to sit in quiet meditation. I'd become strangely fond of the woods since that day spent with Geoff and I thought about him often. I had to keep reminding myself that I'd built up a fantasy in my head of who I thought he was, since the reality was obviously so different. He'd sent texts and emails which I'd chosen to delete in case I was tempted to read them and fall for whatever line he was choosing to spin. I was curious and it killed me to block him. But I had to stand firm after his obvious deception. I was still beating up on myself for having been such a romantic fool.

Time passed and the second Friday in October arrived. This was the day of Ron Clarke's repeat cookery exam. I'd met with him on Wednesday to give him a choice of two briefs, allowing him sufficient time to ensure all the necessary ingredients were ordered in for Friday. I hadn't liked his attitude but I'd kept my mouth zipped as I knew he was just looking for a chance to say I'd marked him unfairly.

"I spent two months working in a French Michelin restaurant and they couldn't understand how I didn't get top marks in my exam," he'd sneered. "And do you know that mark militates against me when applying for a full-time position?"

"I'd have thought if you'd gotten on so well in the Michelin restaurant they'd have given you a glowing reference to counteract any exam mark," I said, smiling at him, but he'd merely tut-tutted in his customary off-hand manner. I knew from experience that Michelin restaurants often disregarded professional qualifications and only took on young chefs as gofers. Then, if the gofer earned his stripes by starting at the bottom, he could work through the ranks, but it required exceptional talent, stamina and patience along with a "yes sir" attitude and a "how high do you want me to jump?" willingness. I couldn't see Ron Clarke fitting in there. I offered to help him in his choice of menu and he immediately rebuffed me.

"I have my own ideas after being in France. I'll make my own choices. If you don't mind … *teacher.*"

James briefed him on matters of hygiene but he was equally dismissive, telling him we were both "hygiene freaks" since they didn't bother with all that nonsense in France.

Friday morning he arrived dressed in full chef's regalia, an enormous chef's hat on his head with the words "cordon bleu" embroidered in royal blue. Much sharpening of knives started up as he looked at me threateningly, his eyes narrowing. Then, pointing a filleting knife at James, he said, "What's he doing here?"

"Mr Mitchell is co-examining with me to ensure you are happy with your result this time around."

"No way, I'm not having it. Every other student had only one examiner and you think it's fine to bring your best friend in here to support you." He was about to rip off his apron when James asked, "Well, what about Miss McGrory?

I happen to know she's free at the minute."

"Oh, the new one. That's all right. I'll put up with her but not with you."

"I'll relieve Miss McGrory then."

As James headed out of the door, I thought I detected a hint of a smile from Clarke. I realised I was dealing with someone who didn't believe in playing straight. I should have guessed, since his politician father was renowned for double-crossing people while smiling sweetly at them and promising the sun, moon and stars if he got their vote. Still it wasn't fair to assume the son was cut from the same cloth. "Carry on with your preparation while we're waiting for Miss McGrory, then."

Helen McGrory had joined the staff last year as a part-time teacher. She had earned a good reputation in the Dublin college where she had full-time hours, but had given that up to move back in with her aging mother who suffered from Alzheimer's. Fifteen minutes later she arrived, similarly attired to me with a white butcher's apron tied over a lab coat and her hair secured in a net. Smiling a greeting, she went to the nearest sink to scrub her hands before coming back up to the podium where I stood with my paperwork spread out on the table. I handed her two A4 sheets, a breakdown of the marking scheme with blank areas to fill in comments and marks, and Ron Clarke's cookery brief.

"I've only one copy of the menu he's chosen but I can get you another."

"No. I have it. James gave me his copy. An interesting and extremely challenging choice, I have to say." Her eyes were wide as she glanced over the elaborate menu. "I'm dying to see his pressed duck. I believe the restaurant he worked for in Paris is famous for it." Now how on earth did she know anything about him working in a French restaurant, never mind what it was renowned for? I felt a shiver of apprehension run down my spine.

He was certainly a student with unbridled enthusiasm, but he was sloppy. He fought with the duck as he tried to bone it, turning the leg inside out as he yanked and pulled on the bone until it flew out of his hand. He slipped over backwards and the duck hit the window, leaving skid marks down the glass as it plonked into the sink. I almost laughed out loud before my mirth turned to compassion. After all, he was around the same age as Julie and I knew how conflicted she was in trying to assert herself. I walked over to him as he was pulling himself up, all red-faced and flustered.

"Are you okay, Ron? At least your duck hit the sink rather than the floor. Let me give you a hand."

"No thanks," he snarled at me like a rabid dog. He had serious anger issues.

I had regularly helped students during exams and not docked marks from them, but this boy was determined to go it alone. Watching him was agony as he thumped pasta around with a rolling pin and horsed it through a ravioli cutter. I had to intervene in his treatment of the lobster as the poor creature kept climbing out of the pot of boiling water, one side of it partially cooked as it fought for survival. I told him, "Please kill the lobsters humanely by piercing the head, between the eyes, with a sharp knife or skewer. It's cruel to cook them alive and the endorphins produced by their fear will toughen the meat and ruin the flavour."

With the continuous clatter of pots and pans, he was a one-man symphony, producing only cacophony and chaos. His wash-up now filled five sinks. I looked at Helen and we rolled up our sleeves to tackle the colossal mountain of dirty plates. As we cleared it, the pile never seemed to diminish, with Clarke feeding in more pots, pans, crockery, cutlery and equipment.

By twelve thirty he had his table set with a white damask tablecloth, a beautiful printed menu standing at the top beside a silver stem vase holding one red rose and a sprig of gypsophila. All the wash-up was done and put away and each of his dishes was well presented as he placed them on the table. I was about to tell him he could leave when he produced a very professional-looking camera from a bag under the table and started taking photographs of the dishes and table layout from various angles. When he'd finished, he looked at me with a steely glint in his eyes, his jaw puckered. He'd managed to make things look a lot better than they were by adding clever garnishes he'd prepared the night before.

"Very good, Ron. You may go now," I said. "How do you feel that went?"

"I think I did brilliantly. What time can I come back to collect all this?"

"Exactly one hour."

As soon as he left, Helen McGrory said to me, "That was definitely overly ambitious for his standard."

What a relief. At least we were singing from the same hymn sheet. I'd sent James a text to come over and join us in case there was any discrepancy in the marking. After he arrived, the three of us tasted the food. "Ravioli's like shoe leather. Duck's okay, but it's not what you'd call pressed duck," James said.

"No, you'd need to press it overnight. I had to stop him from stacking a tower of your precious cookery books on top of the bird this morning." I laughed at the look of horror on his face.

"You mean he didn't have the proper equipment to do it?" James's eyebrows had almost taken flight.

"Since I saw him stick his fingers in the ice-cream after handling raw duck, I'm afraid to taste it in case of salmonella," said Helen.

When the hour had passed, Ron Clarke arrived as Helen left for lunch. "So did I get my distinction?"

"I haven't totted up your marks yet. I'll let you know on Monday."

"Well, I won't stand for him having any say in my results." He pointed at James.

"There's no need for such antagonistic remarks, Clarke."

"I'd say plenty more to the two of you if I didn't have to hold with political correctness." Ron returned to the business of packing his dishes into a large cardboard box.

I was about to say something firm when James put his finger over his own mouth, signalling me to keep quiet. As soon as Ron had gone, I spluttered, "He still thinks he deserves a distinction!"

"No way. You heard Helen. We're all of like mind."

"God, I'm tight as a spring." I tried to swivel my head, while massaging my vertebrae with my right hand. "I've had a very stiff neck recently. Maybe it's because I find this business with Ron Clarke such a pain in the neck."

"Kate, forget about him. It's over. Do your meditation and the Qui Gong Raúl taught us," James advised me.

Monday morning arrived and I was in the middle of collecting books from my locker in the staff room when Helen McGrory handed me a copy of her exam report on Rob Clarke. At sixty-nine per cent, her mark was slightly more generous than mine but it wasn't going to bring him close to a distinction. Ten minutes later, as I was speaking to James, Mike Darcey's secretary came up to me, asking me to call into the head's office. James winked as he stood up to follow me.

Darcey was sitting at his desk, peering out over his glasses. "Well, have we a result?"

"It's not as good as his summer result but we can allow his previously higher mark of seventy-two per cent to stand," I said.

"And I'll stand by Kate on that one. I saw the finished exam," James offered.

"With due respect James, it has nothing to do with you since Helen McGrory was co-examiner."

"There's no disagreement between me and Helen," I insisted.

"I've just spoken to Helen and she's willing to up her mark to a distinction for the sake of peace."

"What? There must be some misunderstanding!"

"I'm merely saying, we need to find the marks somewhere." He began nervously scattering papers about in front of him.

"I have principles and I'm not going to be blackmailed by one student who'd enjoy telling everyone it's possible to intimidate Ms Canavan into giving you a higher mark. It's an insult to the other students who work very hard to achieve their mark in an honest manner. The result stands."

"Well I'm not interested in your principles, Kate. The student has a clear case of you discriminating against him. His father rang me Friday afternoon and he said if there were any discrepancies in his son's marks, he'd bring this department to court. I have to answer to the college authorities and nobody wants negative publicity. I'll ask you firmly one more time to concede on this occasion, please."

"No." I was about to turn my back when he called my name.

"Ms Canavan, I insist, and if you go against me I'll have to discipline you."

I looked from his face to James, who had turned a deadly pallor. I began to shake with anger. "How dare you! I haven't a notion of falsifying a mark to suit a local politician."

"Well if you don't, I'm going to suspend you."

"On what grounds?" I asked furiously.

"Discrimination against a student."

"But you can't do that!" James said.

"If you value your job, I'd advise you to keep your mouth in check, James."

"Don't worry about me, James," I said, suddenly fired up. "I'll walk out of here with my integrity intact and my head held high and as for you ..." I threw Darcey a filthy look. "You can stuff your suspension and your job." With that I boldly walked out of the door, relief flooding over me.

Maybe I was prone to the odd bout of mania whenever things seemed to fall totally and irretrievably apart, like when I thought I would lose my breast soon after my marriage broke up. Or was it that when things seemed so utterly hopeless, the need to control and manipulate vanished and in the process I lightened up and started living in the present moment? In some strange way, I always felt I could totally surrender to Spirit when there was nowhere else to go.

James was concerned that I had made a rash decision and he asked Ella to meet us at the Gourmet Tart coffee shop in Salthill.

"I think you have a clear legal case for suing Darcey," Ella said.

"No Ella, I'm very clear in my mind. I don't want to go back. I'm not interested in a legal battle. Maybe this is the incentive I need to finally write my book."

"Helen will be delighted," said James gloomily. "I don't mean in a malicious way, but she hadn't a hope of getting a full-time position due to cutbacks. Now she'll walk straight into your job – a permanent, pensionable job. That's like gold dust in the present climate. Are you sure you're not self-sabotaging by leaving like this?"

"No, I'm very clear. It just seems like fate."

"So I presume you'll take Billy's offer?" Ella inquired.

"No. Unfortunately it's gone. I rang Billy straight away and his voicemail said he was in Paris. Afterwards I got on to his manager who told me the contracts have been signed with a French woman. He told me Billy will be upset but they couldn't go back on it at this stage."

"Oh no ..." James was even more horrified.

"Look for some reason, I'm cool with all this. I've been head-hunted by restaurants offering me jobs over the years but I never took the bait. Now I think I'll be open to anything and I'm going to trust something will crop up. When I walked out the college door, I felt a great weight lift off my shoulders. I hadn't realised that maybe I was burnt out from the tedium of doing the same job for almost a quarter of a century. This need to hang on to security has haunted me all my life. It's time I worked at letting that attachment go."

"You're right, Kate," Ella said. "I'll have my company up and running by January and I'd love you to join me. I need a sales rep and it would be great if you could demonstrate coffee-making in some of the bigger supermarkets. And I'll be travelling back to Brazil to sort out lingerie and evening wear imports, along with costume jewellery. So there'll be loads to do if you want to come on board as manager or business partner. Choose your own role, lovey."

"Thanks, Ella. That definitely sounds like we could work something out." I smiled at James. "Now there you go – a job offer already."

I could see James was not convinced; he threw Ella a suspicious look. Behind her back, he often said she could be opportunistic and selfish, though he also acknowledged she had a heart of gold. Whatever it was, I felt just like the fool in the tarot card – walking over the precipice with nothing but my knapsack on my back, whistling as I went. All my worst fears had come to pass and there was nothing left to fear. I was exhausted from trying to make myself conform to something which worked for others but no longer seemed to work for me. Somehow I felt everything in my life was pushing me in a different direction to that which I had originally planned, and I had to go with it, whatever that was.

Chapter Thirty-two

As I drove out towards Kiltilough I felt as though I were acting out a re-run of a scene in my life; going through the motions in something which was predestined. Hadn't Shakespeare said "All the world's a stage" and something to the effect that we were all "only players"? But this was no time for sleep walking, since a serious decision had to be made. I reminded myself that I needed to have my wits about me and stopped for coffee at a service station in the vague hope that caffeine might keep me alert to my innermost feelings.

The voice in my head was telling me to take the easy option and go back to Trevor. I would get my beautiful home back along with security and social status. And were they not the very things which compensated for an aging face and body? One day soon I'd wake up a wrinkled hag with breasts resembling a marble at the end of a sock. Fine for tribal women in Papa New Guinea, who tossed them over their shoulders, but it wasn't acceptable in twenty-first century western society.

On the other hand, if I listened to my gut and my heart I might be guided by what was really best for my spirit. And I might possibly connect with the strength and ability to ignore superficial values which never brought true happiness. I hadn't told Julie about losing my job as she would have told her father and I didn't want Trevor thinking I was vulnerable or compromised. If he had that kind of information he would know how to manipulate my tendency towards anxiety and need for security.

He was there waiting at the front door as I pulled up. Immaculate as ever, dressed in a white shirt and beige chinos with a crease down the middle, he came over to open my car door like a hotel valet. "Good to see you looking so well, Kate. Can I take in your bag?"

"It's in the boot." I'd decided to spend the night in the spare room in order to be sure whether I did or didn't want to go back to my old life.

Carrying my bag, he gestured for me to walk through the door ahead of him, in keeping with his customary manner of never walking in front of a woman. My nostrils twitched from the overpowering scent of a thousand household cleaning agents, from Windowlene to furniture polish. Slippers had been laid out for me by the front door and I changed into them as Trevor bent down to retrieve my shoes and place them in the cloakroom cupboard to the right of the door. You could have taken up skating on the marble floor tiles, they were so highly polished. He beamed at me. "I've found a great housekeeper and she's cooked a delicious pot roast using your recipe."

I'd forgotten about the old folder of typed-up recipes I'd left behind. There was no doubt about it; Trevor knew how to spoil a woman. But my stomach was too tense for food. "I couldn't possibly eat anything."

"Will you have a glass of wine, then?"

"Thanks. Do you mind if I look around? It's just I haven't been here for so long."

"You don't need to make any excuses to me. This is still your home. Go right ahead and I'll get you a glass of white."

As I walked upstairs, the old memory reel was playing several images all at once. I could see myself harnessing a gate to the bottom of the stairs to prevent Julie crawling up as a determined toddler. Then Julie at seventeen, dressed in a long damson silk gown for her debs as she stood on the fifth step with her proud parents looking on. My mind filled with vivid images, and I recalled tender moments along with many years of feeling lost and lonely amidst these high walls. And then I remembered the arguments – not least the night when Trevor announced he wanted a divorce.

My mood lifted when I entered Julie's room and the evening light flooded in. Everything was as it always had been, with her collection of porcelain dolls occupying the top of the book case and her soft toys covering the bed. I checked the spare bedroom where I would sleep tonight – the room that had been David's nursery. I'd kept it as a shrine to him to begin with, but dismantled it three years after his passing in order to move on and give the furniture to a young couple who couldn't afford a cot and wardrobe. There was nothing of David here now, but I knew I carried him forever in my heart. I could still become tearful but since my time in Brazil my heart was no longer heavy. Though I shed a tear now, it was not for self pity – rather, a type of sweet sorrow moved through me.

Next, I walked into the master bedroom and my nostrils filled with an indefinable odour that both repelled and puzzled me. Of my five senses, smell is my most heightened. I'd often thought I could have been a "nose" or, as the French call it, "Le Nez", meaning a person who blends perfumes and has very high olfactory recognition. I could almost taste the essence of any scents that lingered in my nostril hairs – a terrible affliction when odours were less than pleasant. My former bedroom had never smelt so foul before; the air seemed dank and heavy. As with any room where two adults compete for oxygen during sleep, it had often needed a good airing – but this was something vile.

Hang on … I'd somehow forgotten that Martha had slept here as mistress of the manor during my absence. I went to my half of the wardrobe and slid the central panel to the left. The force of sliding the doors open caused the empty wire hangers to rattle. But there was still a cream jacket hanging there, which I'd left behind. As I pulled the jacket close to my nose, the blood rushed to my head in anger. I knew without a doubt that Martha had worn it. The collar was make-up stained and the mix of odours conjured up an image of sweaty nylon stockings, mould spores, stale perfume and body odour. I'd felt repelled by her the very first time we'd met; her personal scent had been hard to decipher, made up of a heavy dose of hairspray, synthetic cologne and a weird medical smell. Maybe my nose was the key to my gut instinct, which in her case had tried to warn me of a threat to come. Whatever it was, I now knew this room would have to be fumigated and purged if I were ever to sleep here again. Martha's energy clung to the bedclothes, the headboard and the curtains just as if she'd left a slime trail in her wake. I gagged and ran into the en suite to retch over the toilet; nothing came up. Minutes later, when I'd regained my composure, I went downstairs.

"Everything okay?" Trevor was waiting for me at the bottom of the stairs. His jugular nerve pulsated visibly to the left of his neck and I realised he was more nervous than I.

"Yes, everything's fine."

"Would you like to go for a walk outside?"

"No, thanks. Let's just talk. I'm a little cold this evening." I wrapped my long black cardigan around me as I walked ahead of him into the living room where a very inviting log fire blazed in the hearth. I sat down on the sofa, and he took the armchair bedside me.

"How do you like being back at college?"

"It's fine, but I'm considering other options. Ella's starting a new business and I may join her in that." Here I was, lying to a man I was considering spending the rest of my life with. It didn't augur well if I didn't trust him not to take advantage of the truth.

"Good for you. You know you'll have my support in whatever you choose to do, whether we get back together or not." He sounded optimistic.

"Thanks, Trevor. I can't make that decision lightly. I can't just come back and pretend nothing's happened." I needed to be truthful or I'd end up deluding myself.

"But we would have to start afresh. I'd need you to forgive and forget. I mean you're into this spiritual stuff – you were always more spiritual than me. Forgiveness is a big part of that surely?" His tone was demanding as his eyes held mine. I felt a shiver of apprehension as I remembered how easily he could dominate me.

"Yes, I try to walk a spiritual path and you're right – having forgiveness is important and it is my intention to constantly remind myself to let go. But it's a gradual process and I slip up at times. What about you also forgiving me?"

"For what, Kate?" A puzzled expression crossed his face.

"I think husbands and wives need to constantly forgive each other for even the smallest transgressions. And they need to respect each others' differences."

A steely look briefly hardened his face, a look I knew only too well. It was usually followed by a lecture on the need for me to see and do things his way.

I said, "If you'd loved me despite my failings, wouldn't we still be together?"

"But I can't have you constantly reminding me of my mistake, Kate."

"Trevor, if there's one thing I've learnt it's this – memories can be triggered easily, bringing up all manner of unexpected emotions. I now try my best to live in the present but I can't offer you absolutes. Even the Dali Lama has to work at remaining conscious by meditating and praying up to four hours a day. You said you'd go for counselling. Have you done anything about that yet?" Even to my own ears, my tone was more forceful than I'd intended. I realised suddenly that the dynamic of our relationship was based on a power struggle, and I was as much to blame as him.

"No, but I will if it's what you want. I need you in my life, Kate. How about we travel out to Connemara tomorrow, just like we used to do? We could get a spot of lunch in one of the hotels?"

The kitchen was bathed in soft yellow light the following morning, the air crisp with the dew frosted on the grass outside. A yellow finch tapped his beak on the window, confused by his reflection in the double glazing. Maybe his family had forgotten him as they headed south for winter. Poor little thing, I thought, as I watched him.

"Nice morning isn't it?"

I jumped when Trevor spoke, as I hadn't heard him come

in. I'd been lost in a world of my own. "Yes, great day for Connemara," I said, swinging round and stretching a smile.

"Yes. About that Kate. I just had a text from John Murphy reminding me of a golf game he'd arranged with two visiting doctor buddies. I promise I'll get back here by twelve thirty and then we can go. You don't mind, do you?"

I couldn't believe it – after a text from him earlier in the week, begging me to stay the night! So much for his pledge to give up golf for me. Not that I'd expected him to, but neither did I want to always play second fiddle to his number one obsession. "For God's sake, Trevor, you knew for the past five days I was coming here today."

"Have a bit of tolerance, Kate. You're the one who said we needed to respect each other's differences."

"That's twisting what I said. We've been estranged and today was supposed to be like a date. At least that's how I saw it." Exasperation had crept into my voice.

"Well I didn't know that. You should have told me. I'll try harder next time."

God, I hated when he said something like that – deferring to me as if I was his mother. "Trevor, there won't be a next time. Love isn't about trying hard, the way you have to think about making moves in a chess game. It's a lot simpler than that. A loving relationship should not be complicated."

"Look who's talking. You started getting hysterical as soon as I mentioned golf."

Here goes the shame button, I thought, remembering how he could make me feel less than human. "Don't be ridiculous!" I knew I was beginning to sound hysterical.

"As for you spending the night, you went off to bed rather than spend time with me. I need the comfort of your touch Kate, not the sight of your back retreating to the spare bedroom. When we called it a truce I didn't expect I'd have to endure a cold war."

I stared at him as he spoke and realised that I could never imagine us making love again. It struck me as very strange because he had been a good lover, presenting me with the Kama Sutra early on in our marriage, when we couldn't figure out the half of it. Part of me instead longed for him to take care of me in that gentlemanly way he had always done. I quickly dismissed the thought, however, as I realised I'd learnt to do a pretty good job of taking care of myself. He had become like a father to me and perhaps that's where everything had gone wrong. And when he asked for my softness, it was the softness of a mother he longed for, since he always said his own mother was cold and emotionally unavailable.

"Trevor, this isn't going to work. Whatever we once had ended a long time ago, before either of us was willing to admit it was over." As I spoke, he reddened with anger, as if he was about to explode. But by the time I finished the sentence, his shoulders slumped and he paled, as if the reality of what I'd said had struck him a heavy blow.

"Kate, I'm so sorry. Don't go …" He came closer to me, pressing his hands together. "I'm begging you … and, you know me, I never beg."

I felt sorry for him but I knew this was how our relationship always used play out, based as it was on co-dependency. We had developed a pattern of him pushing my buttons and me reacting. A row would follow and it would finally end in guilt, shame and promises of increased mutual understanding. Ultimately it never changed.

"No, Trevor. It's over. We're not capable of spending twenty-four hours in each other's company without having a disagreement. If we're to live each day as if it were our last then it should be lived with grace. You and I do not afford each other that luxury. Goodbye, Trevor."

As I drove home I felt light and free. On an ego level, perhaps a sneaking feeling of triumph lurked there among all my other emotions, since Trevor had been the one to dump me. On a deeper level, I knew I was being true to myself and true to Trevor and that felt very genuine. There and then, I visualised sending him a laser beam of light, full of forgiveness and blessings. I needed to wish him well in order to release us both from the ties that bound us together.

As a child I'd been told divorce was a mortal sin. My grandmother had a massive crush on Dean Martin and used to look forward to the Dean Martin season of movies, screened on consecutive Sunday nights. When she suddenly heard he had divorced his first wife, she swore she'd never look at or listen to him again. She even went so far as to smash two of his vinyl records. I'd shuddered at the intensity of her disgust and thought divorce would be the worst evil that could ever befall me. I'd also cried for poor Dean Martin who, on my grandmother's say so, was sure to end up in hell for his wicked deeds. Now, I thought, perhaps divorce can sometimes be a spiritual choice, based on compassion and authenticity. And I hoped in my heart of hearts that eventually Trevor and I would become good friends.

Chapter Thirty-three

I was busy looking at an employment agency website one evening, when the phone rang. Seeing it was from my sister, I answered.

"Something terrible has happened, Kate."

My heart sank to the ground on hearing Liz's panicked voice on the other end of the phone. "Is it Dad?" I asked, voice shaking

"No, he's fine. It's Alan. He's just told me he's gay." Alan was her eldest son and my godson, an absolutely gorgeous young man with the most gentle, loving nature. I'd often suspected he could be gay but never said anything. Liz had always pushed her children to be high achievers and had drilled it into them that they needed to marry well. "Can you talk to him and try to convince him he's not? I mean it's totally unacceptable for a doctor and he's in final year medicine. Imagine getting this far and he decides to turn gay."

"Liz, this isn't a terrible thing. And he didn't just decide to turn gay. He was born that way and he needs you as his mother to accept that. He's still the same wonderful young man. What he needs is your unconditional love."

"What about his career? Nobody'll want a gay doctor coming near them and he still wants to do surgery."

"Liz, wake up, we're living in the twenty-first century. Lots of gay men are more responsible than straight men when it comes to sexual practices. Employers can't discriminate on grounds of sexual orientation. Why don't you come to Billy's party – well, it's my party too? You'll meet James and he'll set your mind to rest."

"Oh God, I'm in no mood for a party, Kate."

"All the more reason you should come! When is the last time you let your hair down? Leave hubby at home baby-sitting the younger two. We'll make sure you enjoy yourself!"

"I'll think about it. Is there no way you'll come up to talk Alan round?"

My doorbell rang. I walked over to peer at the pin-hole camera. It was James. "No, Liz. Alan's business is none of my business. Now I'm sorry, but I have to go." I pressed the button, opening the front door and waited for him to come down the stairs. "C'mon in," I said, pecking his cheek and helping him remove his coat. He followed me through to the kitchen where he spotted my laptop on the kitchen table, open at the employment website and with print-outs of restaurants scattered all over the table. "Would you like tea?"

"No. I came to tell you something."

"What is it?" I noted his serious expression with alarm.

"I was in Mayo on a visit to Maria and she was asking for you. She mentioned how gorgeous you were; she said you must have men chasing after you."

"Ah, that was sweet of her. I must call her. Though she couldn't be more wrong about the men bit," I said, rolling my eyes.

"Anyway, I hope you don't mind but I told her the story about you being soft on an artist who was involved with someone called Myra."

"James, I don't mind what you tell Maria. She's not a gossipy type."

"Well, it happens she knows Myra."

"Really?"

"Yes and the story we heard is totally wrong. She knows Myra's sister and it turns out Jennie had her story all wrong. Myra's artist husband died recently, leaving her with a three-year-old son." James paused for emphasis. "Geoff was a very good friend of her late husband's and he's been very supportive to her since he's also the child's godfather. Repeat ... *godfather,* not father. I knew I should have made an effort to speak to him on your behalf."

I could feel myself redden with mortification at having swallowed idle gossip. Why hadn't I given Geoff a chance to explain? Yet I had caught him with Myra, when he'd claimed to be in Dublin. "Well, it's a bit late now, James – I just want to forget about him."

"Are you sure, Kate? I mean, you were very keen."

"I'm sure, James. That opportunity came and went," I said adamantly. "Now I'm looking at employment websites."

"Is there anything worthwhile on offer?"

"Lots of relief work for one and two week periods. I figure I'm a free agent so I can live like a nomad spending two weeks in Dublin followed by a week in London or Cork. The pay is good as they find it hard to get a decent chef to cover the absence of a head chef."

"When does the first one start?"

"After Billy's party, on the twentieth of November. You're coming to that, aren't you?"

"Definitely, darling. And without Alex, so tell Billy to invite some nice gay guys will you?"

"So you're definitely not getting back with Alex this

time then? And what about your own advice to abstain from relationships after a break-up?"

"I know, darling, it's the right thing to do and I did before but when I'm lonely I can't help but wish for Mr Right to come along. That need has to burn itself out, the way it did with you. You're so much less needy now, Kate."

"I'd still like to meet someone but I'm less hung up on meeting a knight in shining white armour. I just wouldn't mind an occasional date even if it went nowhere. I'd quite like a platonic relationship, like I have with you."

"Hmm ... you know that's difficult between a man and a woman except if one is gay. Have you gone back on the dreaded dating sites?"

"Not actively, even though I registered on that site Ella's on. Didn't put up a profile. I was only thinking about it last night that it could be fun to line up the odd date to coincide with working in different locations." Then, wrinkling my nose, I added, "But I've arrived at the stage where I'm not really pushed if I ever have a man in my life again."

"Then you've arrived at a good place, Kate. Why don't you put up a whacky profile for the fun of it? I could do with a laugh. I want to see how you do it."

"Right so ... Pull your chair in closer, and we'll see can we manage to generate a few laughs. Now have a look at these photos and tell me which to use for my profile." I opened a folder on my laptop.

"I like that one." James pointed to an image of me wearing false eyelashes. "You look like Julianne Moore in it. What name are you using?"

"Hekate. What do you think?"

"Appropriate for Halloween. You're getting in touch with your wild side, Kate. I like it – Goddess of the dark side of the Moon and patroness of witches. Didn't you tell me Raúl suggested you had an affiliation with her?"

"Yes and I nearly went ballistic when he first mooted that. I always thought she was an evil old crone, ugly and gnarled. Everything I would wish to be the opposite of."

"So you see when we try to deny any aspect of ourselves it can take on a power of its own. I know that from trying to repress my homosexuality and how it tormented me. When I came out it was no big deal. Hekate represents not only acceptance of getting older but also the gifts that come with age."

"You're fierce philosophical, James." I attempted an old crone's voice: "And pray tell me, what gifts can I expect?"

"Wisdom and increased creativity wouldn't be bad for starters, would it?"

"Not bad. Now let's get cracking here with Hekate's profile. I'll keep this simple yet quirky ..." I wrote:

"I am a woman of contrasts; one who likes to run through the woods at dawn and twilight, yet also enjoys dressing up for an evening at the theatre. I would like to meet a man to read Borges, Salinas and Neruda to, watch several film versions of Anna Karenina with, meditate on a mountain top with and explore the Amazon jungle with.

Difficult to meet the right man but if you are reasonably chilled out with a sense of humour and an optimistic nature then drop me a line."

"Good grief Kate, anyone who understands that will know you're a passionate woman, but I'd be surprised if they get it. Now fill in the next part."

"No, I couldn't be bothered. I'll tick a few boxes like 'attractive' rather than 'very attractive', but I'm not serious about this so I'll leave the rest blank the way a lot of people do."

"Right, let's have a cup of tea and we'll see if anyone gets back to you."

As I made tea, we got chatting about preparations for Billy's party and what we would wear. But James was soon curious to see if any messages had come in for Hekate, and made me look. There were already several responses,.

I was puzzled. "James, two of them start with '*Hey Kate*'. Do they know me from a previous site? One says: '*Hey Kate, How's it going?*'"

"Read it out."

I recited: "*Hey Kate, Do you know Hekate is the Goddess of witches? Why use this name when you could have chosen Aphrodite or Venus? Is it because it's so close to Halloween? I can only presume your name must be Kate! You say you find it difficult to meet the right man. I think you must be hard to please but I like a good challenge and would like to put myself forward. John.*"

"So there's your answer. They think it's a take on your name. Yer man John looks all right. Will you write back? You could say 'Aphrodite or Venus, when it's all about your penis.' It kind of rhymes. When they want you to be Aphrodite it's definitely part of a sexual fantasy."

"James, I'm shocked by you. You were the one telling me to forget about men. I'm definitely not writing back anything so provocative. In fact, I'm in no mood to write back, full stop. Oh God look at this. It's totally weird. I knew I'd get some weird stuff."

The message read:

My Dear Hekate

While I do not fit the description of your 'date', I'm afraid that there is no way I can NOT send you this message!! You correctly describe yourself as attractive, but the left hand section on 'more about me' is quite irresistible!

Running through the woods, eccentric or not, hints at a primal awareness. As for me, well ... if I alluded to the Wolf – not to the 'Jack Nicholson' portrayed version, all predatory and selfish – but to a deeper awareness and energy, would that make sense to you? I am deep, a diver, not shallow, a surfer. I am aware, but have my blind spots!!

I can talk and discuss anything you wish, and would love so to do

Jake

"Christ, Kate, does he think he's a werewolf or something? You have to write to him. Go on!" James was splitting his sides laughing. I wrote a few lines thanking Jake for this most unusual mail and within ten minutes he had sent another more lengthy reply about *"Hekate and the power of the crone"*. "He says 'us spiritual types find it hard to accept our psychopathic tendencies but Hekate is about the total illumination of every area of yourself'," James read out loud in alarm.

"And he finishes by asking can he have my telephone number! Says here that he's a psychiatric nurse. He sounds intelligent, but the stuff about psychopaths is really scary."

"A lot of psychopaths are above average intelligence. I'd drop him before he scares you senseless. He's a potential stalker and you don't want that. Look, I'd better go. See you before going to Billy's on Saturday night. You could write back to the first guy though. He wasn't bad."

After James left, I realised that internet dating no longer held any fascination for me. It required a lot of effort to separate the wheat from the chaff and I constantly doubted my ability to discern which was which since it was so easy to build up a rosy picture from a picture and profile. I was beginning to realise that when we met someone in the flesh for the first time, our five senses informed our gut about the suitability of that person. I was only just learning to listen to my gut, after ignoring it for so long.

Maybe someone like Jake really was genuine person but in the real world it was unlikely our paths would ever cross. Looking at pictures of these men, I felt dizzy as they all appeared to morph into one generic prototype. Maybe it was because it felt like so many of them thought they were "shopping" for a mate. There and then, I deleted my profile as Hekate. In the past few months, several people had advised me to stop trying so hard to control my life and instead, just let it happen. I thought I could meet the perfect man through spreading my net wide as Ella had suggested but it hadn't happened. I now reverted to my original belief that there had to be an element of serendipity in meeting the love of one's life.

As I prepared to turn off the lights, I glanced towards my painting and the dream catcher, I suddenly remembered Louis Pasteur's famous words: "Chance favours the prepared mind." Well, I would prepare my mind by connecting it to an open heart in case the possibility of love should come my way. If it happened, I'd be happier than if I'd won the lottery, but if it didn't I wouldn't spend my life in mourning. I now knew the difference between loneliness and being alone and I was becoming increasingly contented in my own company.

Chapter Thirty-four

Ella, James and I arrived early on the Saturday evening at Billy's Victorian pile set among spectacular gardens. "Nice knockers!" James said, admiring the elaborate brassware on the large front door. "Why, thank you," said Ella, cupping her ample breasts as she jiggled one in each hand. We were all in high spirits anticipating the party. Seconds later the door flew open with Billy standing there to greet us, his eyes drawn to Ella's impressive cleavage.

"Great to meet your gang, Kate. Come on in. Are you all set for the party tonight then?" Billy said, giving me a hug before telling the others to join my sister Liz in the drawing room. Gripping my elbow, he said, "I'm still cut up over my cookery job being gone when you finally rang to say you'd take it. Talk about bad timing. Mind you, that vacancy for lifestyle store manager remains open if you're interested?"

"I'm game for anything at the moment, Billy. Though I don't have experience in buying and merchandising."

"We can talk about it by and by. The shop won't be up and running until April." He led me in to join the others who were having coffee and tea in the drawing room. I kissed Liz who was poised on a chaise longue, her elegant legs to one side like a Victorian lady. I was pleased to see her looking reasonably relaxed after her hysterical phone call but I knew it wouldn't be that easy getting our Liz to thaw out since she was always conscious of keeping up appearances and "behaving in a dignified manner", as she would say. At least she hadn't chickened out and seemed at ease as she chatted with Ella.

"Everyone got their costume in order?" Ella asked, looking around.

"Kate, you never told me it was fancy dress?" Liz squealed in horror.

"Never thought to mention it. But don't worry, we'll improvise, put something together between us."

Liz didn't look convinced; she shifted uncomfortably, and glanced towards the door like she might flee at any minute.

"How about I show you all to your rooms and you can get ready?" Billy offered as people finished their coffees.

Obediently we trooped out of the living room and followed him up the cantilevered stairway. Billy opened the door to a large room with gold-flocked wallpaper and dark walnut floorboards. "This is yours, Ella."

Ella chirped for joy as her eyes fell upon the white four-poster bed with matching white dressing table and antique oriental screen. "Oh my God ... this is fit for a queen."

On the next floor, James was given a room decorated in shades of cream and chocolate with a mahogany sleigh bed. Liz's room was pretty and feminine in shades of topaz and light turquoise with a gorgeous central chandelier cascading from a purple satin shade.

"Now, I thought you'd like this one," Billy said, opening the door to the left of Liz's to reveal an all-white room with long voile curtains draped on either side of the window and lining the opposite wall. The wardrobes were flush with a third wall, making it seem that there was no furniture apart from the bed, two side lockers and a large cream Buddha sitting on the window ledge. "Oh, it'll be like sleeping in angels' wings." I dropped my bags on the floor and walked towards the large bay window to soak in the panoramic view of the gardens and lake. The sun was slowly sinking behind a curtain of gold, the distant hills mysterious as an undulating serpent. Like liquid mercury the water in the lake pooled in shades of evanescent silver and blue while the moon had already appeared like one large pewter disc. "Look at the sunset, Billy."

"It's a special harvest moon this evening, Kate. Supposed to be bigger than usual. What's sometimes known as a blue moon."

"The sun and the moon together." I marvelled at the sight before my eyes. "Thank you, Billy!" I blew him a kiss.

He laughed on his way out of the door. "I arranged it especially for you – special cosmic order."

No sooner had he gone when Liz came in, a stricken look on her face. "Kate, I could kill you for not warning me about the fancy dress."

"Calm down! You can take my costume if you like."

"What is it?"

"A vampire."

"I suppose … But what will you wear? You can't not dress up!" She still seemed very up-tight.

"One black maxi skirt coming up along with an old black wig Julie had for a costume party," I said, pulling both items out of my bag. It was by pure chance I'd put my hand on the wig and decided to bring it. "And Ella's sure to have a black top I can borrow. I've a couple of black bin bags in the car to make a cloak, and after that it's just a matter of a little face painting. Here, relax …" I handed her the vampire costume, still in its suit cover. Forty minutes later I knocked on her door, a generous wine glass filled to the brim with champagne in my hand and a bag of face paints tucked under my elbow. I'd brought two bottles to the party – one for Billy and a spare for Liz, and I'd slipped down to the kitchen to find some glasses. "For you, your favourite champagne, Veuve Cliquot," I said, handing Liz the glass.

"Oh fabulous, sis! You are so good." There was nothing like a bit of bubbly to thaw her out. She stood sipping the champagne. "Your makeup is amazing, Kate. You look more like an enchantress than a witch."

I'd backcombed the wig, then spread out the strands before settling them into flowing tresses, tamed with the help of hairspray. Pencil and shadows around my eyes gave them a winged effect, while a large black mole sat to the left of my mouth, which was painted green. Wearing a long black duster coat Ella had lent me in lieu of a bin liner, I suddenly felt strong, stronger than I'd felt for a long time, and strangely hopeful that the coming years would teach me the wisdom of the crone Goddess Hekate – she whom I had feared so intensely.

"Right Liz, your turn now. Sit down and I'll make you look as if you've just bitten someone's neck."

"As long as it's subtle, please not overly dramatic. Oh dear, maybe I should have gone for your option …"

"Too late now!" Wielding the face paints and a fine brush, I set to work darkening her brows.

By eight thirty the house was abuzz with activity as Liz and I arrived downstairs. Aromas of wild game with garlic and herbs wafted by as Billy offered us a glass of spicy mulled wine. "Happy birthday, Kate." He pecked my cheek. "I'm withholding your present until tomorrow morning."

"But this party is your gift to me, Billy. It's fabulous to be here among my best friends."

James circled his arm into my elbow and steered me into the drawing room, saying, "C'mon, Liz, it's time for Kate's presents."

"I left mine in the car. Back in two secs." Liz sashayed awkwardly towards the front door.

"Liz looks like she's a little behind the eight ball?" Billy mused, quizzically.

It had been worth plying her as I definitely preferred her this way, all dreamy and floaty and not giving two hoots what she looked like. "Why wouldn't she be after drinking half a magnum of champagne? I brought another one as your gift, Billy."

"Gosh Kate, that's some trick to get Liz langers. If she's not careful she could end up enjoying herself," he said chuckling.

"Here's the birthday girl," announced James, guiding me into the living room. Everyone started singing Happy Birthday, culminating in mad clapping as a magnificent pumpkin-shaped cake was wheeled in on a trolley with one huge candle sitting in the centre.

"Don't forget to make a wish when you blow out the candle," shouted Ella, who was dressed as Lady Gaga replete with blonde wig. As soon as the words tripped off her tongue I thought of Geoff. Now why on earth did he have to enter my head at a time like this?

"Glass of champagne for the party girl," Billy cried, interrupting my thoughts as he handed me a glass of pink bubbly. I'd just sat down on the sofa between James and Ella when Liz came stumbling in like an overeager teenager, thrusting her gift into my arms.

"Think you'll like it 'cos the shop assistant said the print is all the rage this season and I know you don't like the classic type I wear." I opened the silver wrapping paper to reveal a gossamer-light python print scarf, wide and long when unfolded. "I adore it. It's beautiful." I kissed her fondly.

"Our gifts all go together." cried James, throwing his arms around my sister and Ella. "You're in tune with our vibrations, Liz!" Liz looked startled and perplexed, as if she found my friends a little overbearing – she'd never quite got used to the way we gelled and laughed between us.

"Sounds intriguing – I like it," I said, as three small gifts were piled on my lap. Eagerly I tore the paper off the first to reveal a padded white box with the name "Thomas Sabo" written on it. Inside sat a slim black rope chain with a crown pendant. I'd once admired something similar on Ella. "Oh Ella, it's beautiful!"

"See the loop at the bottom of the crown? You can attach your other pressies on to that. Quick open them." James was nearly dancing with impatience. Dutifully I tore open the other packages – two similar white boxes, smaller in size. In the first was a red apple charm and in the second a glittering silver and marcasite snake charm. Each charm had a hook which James secured on to the crown, as proudly as though he'd personally designed them. "We know you love myths and you see the deeper symbolic meaning in stories, so we felt it was appropriate to give you the apple as the symbol of love and the snake for universal knowlege or *kundalini shakti*."

"I love it. It's stunning." I jumped up to kiss each of my friends in turn. "You're right that I don't accept the orthodox meaning of Eve having precipitated the downfall of man. I believe in … What's she called, James?"

"Mito …? Mitochondrial Eve," James remembered.

"Yes, the mother that unites the human race, the woman we all descended from somewhere in east Africa, regardless of colour or race." Then, lifting my glass, I cried, "Eve rocks!" and everyone clapped. Maybe the champagne was getting to me already.

"I didn't know your birthday was themed when I bought you the scarf!" Liz was still bewildered. "But I'm glad I got it right, even if I'm not into all this pagan stuff." She was biting her upper lip, but thankfully the champagne had mellowed her enough to stop her scuttling away in the usual panic.

"Yes, great coincidence that Liz, and I love it. And it's not pagan to question the validity of what you were told as a child or to investigate other beliefs which may hold some truth. But forget that now – it's party time."

"C'mon!" Billy clapped his hands. "Help yourselves to food in the kitchen! There's more people coming later and next door's cleared for a disco. Have you all got your dancing shoes on?" He led the way downstairs to a huge old-fashioned kitchen similar to that on Victorian period dramas. Billy's housekeeper, a broad-shouldered countrywoman with a ruddy complexion, had prepared a choice of venison stew and glazed salmon along with a variety of salads and rice dishes, all laid out on a huge central oak table. I chose a small piece of salmon to nibble, and stacked the rest of my plate with brown rice, salads and vegetables. I needed to keep an eye on Liz, ensuring she ate enough food to soak up the alcohol or she'd end up sloshed in no time as the champers flowed and we were offered Kir Royals and Bellinis. Come to think of it, I realised I'd better keep count of my own alcohol intake since my tolerance wasn't much higher than Liz's.

Billy's friends began arriving, among them his sister

Louise and her husband, two other couples and three single men varying in ages from forty to fifty. I didn't think any of the men attractive, which was just as well because I would have had to compete with Ella who was charming the pants off them. "Is Ella a bit … *racy*?" Liz whispered, watching the three men roaring with laughter for the umpteenth time at another of Ella's jokes.

"Not in the slightest, but she has PhD in flirting. Something you and I were never very adept at," I replied.

Billy approached with two Bellinis in hand. "We need to get a bit of atmosphere going, girls. Upstairs to the dance room!"

"Have you had a chance to chat to James, yet?" I asked Liz, in the hallway.

"Not really … He's very camp, isn't he?" She was obviously worried by his Hamlet costume replete with tights and pointy shoes.

"Only when he's out enjoying himself. You'd never think he was gay if you met him in college." As he came up the stairs, I called him over to join us. "James, Liz is afraid her son is going to become very camp now that he's come out of the closet."

James laughed. "Not necessarily. There are all types of gay men just like there are all types of straight guys. They're not all camp. In fact, they're often very 'manly'. And most don't go in for cross-dressing." My sister had lived a very cosseted life, unaware of what goes on in the wider world, but as James chatted openly to her about gay men, she began to visibly relax.

The hall was filling as everyone drifted up from downstairs. Billy arrived at my side, collapsing on one knee, his two arms outspread in a dramatic gesture: "Kate, my dearest witch, will you join me in leading everyone on to the dance floor, please?"

"Of course, my dear warlock," I said, giving him my hand. As we entered the dining room, converted to look like a club with black and silver balloons, Lady Gaga's "Poker Face" started playing. Ella went into high performance mode, pretending to be the singer. Her youngest hanger-on looked on admiringly as she threw theatrical shapes on the dance floor. Out of the corner of my eye, I noticed Liz had unwittingly attracted the attention of the older one and James was chatting with the third guy who was by far the best looking.

Within minutes, the dance floor was full as everyone joined us for a good old fashioned boogey. Liz bumped hips with me, like we used to do as teenagers in Wesley when up-and-coming bands played the odd gig. I remembered seeing four very young men bursting with confidence and with strange names like The Edge and Bono. They weren't bad, I'd thought, as I sat out one song beside a stocky youth who turned to me saying: "U2 are gonna be big." I thought his grammar was appalling as he repeated the sentence three times, until he explained the band's name was U2. "A mate of mine is in the band," he enthused. "They're gonna be big."

Billy said something as we danced but I couldn't hear him over the music. I moved closer for him to whisper in my ear, "You were always a great mover, Kate, but I never saw Liz let it all hang out before."

And why not? I thought, throwing myself more fully into the moment and dancing with wild abandon. So much, that I didn't notice Billy had swapped over to dance with Ella, until the man opposite me took my hand and swung me around to a Beyoncé track. He was a brilliant dancer and much to my surprise, I found myself moving easily as he twirled me around, drawing me in and out. He tried chatting in between but as always it was difficult to compete with the noise. I had no interest in hanging around with him after the dancing in case he misunderstood my intentions, so I was glad when James joined me during a break in the music. I sneaked a look around the room to check Liz wasn't yet falling down but I couldn't see any sign of her. Ella and Billy seemed to be getting on like a house on fire as I overheard Ella mention coffee imports.

"Oh yes," James informed me. "Billy has promised to use Ella as one of his suppliers for this shop of his."

"Looking at the body language between the two of them, I think there could be a bit of chemistry there," I said, observing their legs crossed towards each other and Billy's hand on Ella's knee as they sat side by side.

"Nobody here that interests you?" James asked, throwing a glance at the man I'd been dancing with.

"No, he's a nice guy but I feel all the men I meet seem to meld into one another. They're all so eager to tell me how eligible they are. I find it boring at this stage." Suddenly my attention was drawn to a figure standing on a makeshift podium beside the DJ. I hadn't previously noticed the little stage but there was no missing it now that a spotlight had been trained on it. The DJ was handing Liz a microphone.

"Oh no! I have to stop her from making a fool of herself!" Sober, my sister would never sing karaoke – she would be furious with me in the morning for letting this happen.

"Leave her alone. You need to stop worrying about other people, Kate. It's not good for you." James pulled me back as Liz started singing Blondie's seventies hit "One way or another". All eyes were on her as she shimmied and gyrated, all the while retaining her elegance. I used to envy her when she sang this so well as a teenager. I'd never been a songstress. Catching my eye, she suddenly beckoned me to join her. When I shook my head, she persisted until the DJ held up a second microphone. Everyone stamped their feet and clapped incessantly, shouting "Kate! Kate! Kate!" until I relented and joined her on the podium. At first I croaked out the words in a hoarse whisper. This was my worst nightmare, ever since a nun had told me as a five year old never to sing in public because I was a crow. But buoyed on by the crowd's enthusiasm, I eventually started singing along and enjoying myself. Afterwards the DJ ran straight into "Sisters are doing it for themselves" and much to my surprise we remembered all of Annie Lennox's dramatic hand gestures and dance moves. Towards the end, we looked at each other and began laughing convulsively in between words. That was it. We couldn't attempt another song, which was just as well since there was a queue waiting to take their turn.

We had a blast, with the action carrying on until five in the morning, when we finally crawled upstairs barefoot, with pinched toes and aching pelvises, exhausted but happy. It was the first time I had really managed to let my hair down since Trevor dumped me. It was easier to remain balanced and enjoy myself when I didn't have to worry about a partner. If I was with a man I would have spent most of the evening worried about him being happy. Alone, I felt carefree.

Chapter Thirty-five

Floorboards creaked and pipes rattled in the ancient plumbing system as the house came to life the next morning. Billy was right about one thing – period houses are like old aunties. I might add that they are like old aunties with digestive problems. The banging and clattering of the central heating sounded like a steam locomotive gathering speed as the old pipes expanded and contracted. After waking Liz around noon, I headed down to the kitchen. Soon Billy and James descended for brunch. Ella arrived in some time later with Liz on her heels.

"I have a splitting headache," Liz whispered as she sat beside me. "What happened last night?"

"You had the time of your life." I said, laughing. "Never knew you were such a party girl."

"I'm not, Kate, and you know it. I hope I didn't make a fool of myself?" She anxiously searched our faces.

"No, you were very sensible," James assured her. "Apart from the strip tease to entertain the men …"

"*Kate, please tell me I didn't?*"

"Don't worry, it was very tasteful and you have a great body," Billy chimed in.

I knew by her face that she was about to burst out crying and make a run for the door so I had no choice but to tell her we were just messing. She sighed with relief. "I could kill the lot of you for making me sweat that one."

As everyone finished laughing, Billy placed a large flat box on the table in front of me. "Happy birthday, Kate." He put his arm around my shoulder and kissed my cheek.

"And I could kill you for embarrassing me by buying me a present after throwing me such a wonderful party," I said, pulling open the purple ribbon. It was a beautiful decorative box that could be reused for storing clothing on an open shelf. Lifting the flap-over lid, I peeked inside to see copious layers of white tissue paper. I tore open the sticky paper seal on the tissue to reveal an envelope. I shook it and something rattled inside.

"What's this?" I pulled out a large heavy key. "I thought keys were for twenty-first birthday parties?" Was I missing out on some joke that everyone else was in on?

"It's the key to your new work place," Billy whooped.

I was still not getting the joke; I felt myself blushing.

"Kate. The job is yours. You're my new cookery school teacher. The French woman couldn't take it after all."

"Are you serious?"

"Absolutely. And I hope that's a yes this time."

"Yes … Oh definitely, yes!" I was hugging him and jumping up and down for joy as everyone cheered. I felt a weight lift off my shoulders and my heart sung at the prospect of coming to work in this beautiful place. It was a wish come true for me. A sign from the universe that my life was finally coming together.

It had seemed a waste, Ella, James and I driving in tandem,

rather than travelling in one car. Yet we had discussed it and felt it afforded each of us a better choice of when to depart and which route to chose. As it turned out, I stayed an extra couple of hours at Billy's in order to see the cookery school and discuss plans. James headed straight back to Galway and Ella was planning a circuitous route around Wicklow in the hope of finding fresh outlets to sell her coffee.

As I was passing through the picturesque village of Enniskerry on my way home, I spotted her coming out of a supermarket. A few seconds later my phone beeped. She wanted me to meet her for coffee in a nearby café. As I parked my car, a heavy shower started up. I sprinted across the village square to Poppies café. Inside, Ella was installed at a table earnestly studying her small red diary, pen in hand. "I've just been out to Avoca in Powersourt, Kate," she said excitedly as I joined her. "And they're willing to stock my coffee. It's a really important deal – they may also be willing to sell some of the costume jewellery I've sourced!"

"Congratulations, Ella. That's brilliant news. I'm delighted for you."

"Great news for you too, Kate. You must be thrilled."

"What would you like, ladies?" asked a foreign girl with blonde hair, holding up a notepad and pencil.

Ella ordered an Americano and I ordered a soya decaf latte. "Have you gone vegetarian?" Ella asked, scrunching up her nose.

"Not really. Just a phase." As I spoke I ran my fingers through my hair and shook my head to distribute the wetness more evenly through my curls. Just as I was about to turn back to focus on Ella, a poster on the opposite wall caught my eye. "I don't believe it."

"What?"

"Back in a minute," I said, getting up from my chair to walk over to the poster. Two women nearby stared at me, then started whispering to each other. I couldn't believe my eyes. I felt my cheeks flushing with embarrassment as I tried to make sense of what I was looking at. The poster featured a painting by Geoff, advertising his new art exhibition "The Goddess" to be held on the twenty-second of November in a Dun Laoghaire art gallery. The painting depicted the Goddess Hekate strolling through a forest at moonlight. It was based on the photograph he had taken of me that day in Coole Park – though with a magnificent wolf-like husky on her lead rather than the labrador dog I'd held. The Goddess Hekate was unmistakably me.

"What is it, Kate?" Ella had come over for a look. "Oh my God, it's by that artist fellah, isn't it? James told me that Lorna's friend Jennie had been wrong about him being the father."

"Come on, we better sit back down. Everyone's looking at us." I hurried back across the room to our table.

"There you go. One Americano and one soya decaf latte." The waitress placed our coffees on the table in front of us.

"I don't understand it, Ella. Why would he use my image to advertise his exhibition?"

"Well, he must be mad about you, lovey. Damn my sister Lorna and her friends. I'm sorry you had to hear that gossip."

"Still, he looked pretty cosy with Myra."

"I think you should meet him and talk it out, Kate. If you want, I'll make contact. I feel responsible for the misunderstanding."

"No, don't, Ella. I shouldn't have blocked his emails and deleted texts without reading them. But I still don't understand what he was doing with her since he was supposed to have gone back to Dublin the day before." I was muddled and embarrassed as I'd convinced myself that Geoff was as bad as Trevor. I felt guilty about having cut him off at the knees before he'd had a chance to explain.

"Well if I were you, I'd start by unblocking his emails," suggested Ella.

I'd promised to call to my parents and stay the night since they wanted to wish me happy birthday. As I drove there, I thought about Geoff and felt flattered by his beautiful painting and quite chuffed that he had chosen my image to advertise his new exhibition on "The Goddess". Once again, those warm feelings I'd had for him resurfaced yet they were tinged with confusion and a fear that I could possibly lose myself.

When I arrived at my parents' house, I found my father alone in the house in pretty good spirits as he watched rugby on television. "Didn't get a chance to see Saturday's game, Kate, but got the recording from next door. Some great tries," he said, excusing himself from any attempt at conversation. I'd just sat down to read a magazine when my mother and Liz arrived in the door, laden down with bags. Liz had left Billy's a few hours earlier than me and had obviously come straight here to collect my mother for a shopping trip. I followed them into the kitchen.

"Just back from Dundrum shopping centre, Kate. It was relatively quiet so we had a quick whiz around." My mother was beaming at me as she set about unpacking her shopping. "Dad and I are delighted with your news. It'll be great to have you live so close to us. A chocolate cake for you there."

She plonked a pre-packed birthday cake on the table. "Did you find the card Dad and I left for you up there?"

"No, but thanks." I took the envelope off the kitchen windowsill – a card and a voucher for a fashion store. "Thanks, Mam. I'll have no problem getting something nice with that."

"And I bought you a couple of little trinkets as an extra memento." She handed me a distinctive black and white bag with the name "Thomas Sabo" written on it. I glanced at Liz who winked surreptitiously. In a round jewellery box sat two charms. I held up the first one: two silver doves on either side of a glossy red heart dangled on a silver chain. "I knew you'd like it because of your devotion to the Holy Spirit," my mother said confidently as Liz grimaced behind her back.

"And I also love the angel. Thanks, Mam. That's so sweet!" I said, hugging her.

When my mother had gone to check on my father, Liz said apologetically, "I told her to buy you the silver chain as a choice for your other charms but she insisted on buying you what she regarded as 'Christian symbols'. I'm sure you can change them."

"I wouldn't dream of it, Liz. I may not be the most conventional Catholic but Christianity is still the gateway to my spirituality even though I respect other belief systems equally."

She looked surprised, then said, "You've coped really well with your break-up, Kate. I'm finding this thing about Alan being gay very difficult. What works for you as a coping mechanism?" I detected a hint of desperation – I knew she was cynical of what she presumed were my whacky beliefs.

"I've learnt several things, Liz. The first is to live in the now, because the past is irreversible and the future depends on decisions we make in the present. Secondly, I try to meditate every day. It helps me to remain calm, no matter what happens. And the third thing I've learnt is that everything happens for a reason and every person we meet has something to teach us, even if we don't like it." She was listening eagerly as if trying to memorise what I was saying. "In South America they have a saying 'In Lak'ech'. It means 'I am another you'. When I find someone difficult or don't like them, instead of getting annoyed I now ask myself what part of me I see in them. It's helped me to have more understanding for others, and for myself."

"I find I'm questioning everything lately because we were brought up to believe being gay was a sin and Alan is such a good son. I wish I could be like you. But are you lonely?"

"It hasn't been easy. But having time alone has given me the space to learn lots of things. I worry that being in a relationship would send me right back to where I started – that even minor conflicts would unhinge me. I have peace now, Liz, and I don't want to lose that." I ran my finger through my hair. "Lonely? Yes, I'm lonely sometimes but I think everyone is, even in a crowd. I'm learning to feel my emotions and not push them away. When I accept that I'll occasionally feel lonely, it's no longer so frightening."

"I can see how well you cope on your own. You never look sad or pathetic in the way I fear I would. Relationships are difficult and marriage needs constant work to keep it on track. Do you still believe in God?"

"Yes but I no longer see him or her as the old man sitting in judgement. My connection is better through meditation and I no longer want to define God as solely masculine or feminine, because I believe any definition is too narrow." I stood up to knock the kettle on and throw two teabags into the pot. "You know, I've always loved myths. You do too. It's not that I believe them. Rather they add to my enjoyment of life and speak to my soul. Walking in nature does the same for me." I'd taken a risk in being so open to Liz, knowing she was more interested in materialism and status than I was. But I felt she had changed a little over the last few months and she had a great capacity for kindness.

"Yes, Kate, Daddy really gave us a great gift by reading stories, myths and legends to us. But you definitely have a greater passion for them than me. And I can see how you'd have trouble remaining as you are now if you got involved with a man. Men are so insistent on exact logical definitions. Sometimes they don't see there are two ways of looking at things."

Hmm, I thought, Liz could do with expanding her own horizons. Amazing how much more creative she was after a few drinks – dancing like a dervish and acting out Debbie Harry's moves while singing. "That's why the energy of the Goddess is right-brained, involving intuition, empathy and creativity rather than squeezing your brain too hard for a solution. It's about living in the now and accepting what is. And it's not exclusive to women. Anyone can tap into it and enjoy life more fully." I paused before adding, "And Liz, I'm far from perfect. I don't get it right all the time. It's a continuous process that requires constant awareness so I don't fall back into old conditioned habits of thinking."

Later that night in the privacy of my bedroom, I opened my laptop and logged on to my emails, asking myself out loud, "Will I, won't I, unblock Geoff?" Pride urged me to forget him, yet my heart told me to be open, so I unblocked him and did a mail search. In came an invite to his exhibition in the Holland Art Gallery in Dun Laoghaire. I felt a shiver of terror course through my veins as I stared at the image of Hekate with my face peering off the screen. I was astounded by the pull of its magnetism and needed to summon up all my reserves in order to resist the urge to phone Geoff.

I had lost myself once in a relationship and only recently managed to find all my missing pieces and glue them back together again. I feared that I could once again become disintegrated, since it was easier to remain conscious and live in the present as a single person. And I now had the prospect of a new career with a new life in Wicklow. I really didn't want to push my luck too far. I was determined to hold off and let destiny help me decide.

Chapter Thirty-six

Leaves danced in shades of copper, gold and russet reds before being whipped away by the wind, the trees now barren, stripped of their former glory. Their fate comforted me as I made several journeys back and forth to Wicklow, feeling my life was mirroring nature as I prepared to allow the old vestiges fade away. I had learnt that it was never easy to leave the past behind, no matter how exciting present and future prospects seemed. Despite my excitement, everyday things took on a slight air of melancholy. I feared I would miss my friends and my life in Galway. I'd miss the smell of seaweed and the taste of salty sea air while walking the prom in Salthill. I'd miss the shop assistants who knew me by name and the hairdresser I'd been going to for the past twenty years. Heck, I'd even miss my dentist!

My biggest wrench, however, came with the need to shed some of my possessions. Several cardboard boxes remained unpacked from my move to the apartment five months earlier, making it time to finally part with excess clothing and all manner of "things" I'd collected. I had always been a hoarder, holding on to clothes in case they came back into fashion or could be respectably regarded as "vintage pieces'". After several failed attempts to part with anything apart from the worn and torn, I asked Julie to come and help.

That way, she wouldn't be able to say something like, "Oh no, you should never have given that away!"

Soon after she arrived, we started sorting the clothes into three lots: the ones I would keep; the "vintage type" clothes Julie would take; and the remainder, which would go to the charity shop or be auctioned on ebay. The process was slow and painful as the first lot grew to three boxes, then four, and I was unexpectedly resistant about the "giveaway lot".

"I'd forgotten about this, Mum." Julie held up a very theatrical coat made with several different fabrics in hues of peacock green, teal, gold and brown. "It's like an emperor's coat," she said, trying it on. "But what on earth would you wear it to?"

"I think it's one of those aspirational purchases, Julie. Something I bought after watching Sex and the City. I'd let my imagination run wild, thinking something like that would fit in with my lifestyle and make me feel fabulous. It's the same with those towering heels I never wear. Anything over three inches really should go."

"Yeah, definitely not your sanest moments! But maybe someone else would love them."

"Do you know, that's the best thing you could have said to me, Julie? I can give things away more easily if I feel they might light up someone else's life." We both laughed and the sorting gathered speed as we ruthlessly denigrated clothes to the "aspirational but not practical" section and I finally whittled the "keep" pile down to more manageable proportions.

"You know something, Mum, when you first told me about moving to Wicklow, I found it very hard as it finally dawned on me that you and Dad were never getting back together. But now I think maybe that's a good thing to help me finally accept it. You're each so different, I don't know how you ever got together in the first place."

As she spoke I felt a wave of relief sweep over me, and my shoulders noticeably relaxed. I hadn't realised how ashamed I'd felt for letting her down by ending the marriage. I'd done her a grave disservice by fretting over her inability to cope.

She went on, "If I don't end up going abroad to get a job I may decide to live in Dublin. I like the life there. I'm young, I'm open to anything. It'll be good to have you nearby and I can still go home to Dad for the odd weekend."

Listening to her, I realised for the first time how independent she was, a young woman on the threshold of starting her own life. At her age I was planning my forthcoming wedding, thinking I had all the answers. Julie was less sure about where life would lead her and it struck me that the ability to remain open-minded was essential to following the route of the human heart. After all the excessive angst concerning her weight, she was looking healthy and vibrant. She'll be fine, I thought. After all, she's my daughter.

While I prepared to leave Galway I didn't see much of Ella since she was on the road a lot, acting as sales representative for her company. James, however, had taken to calling most evenings after he finished work. One particular evening he seemed unusually pensive and subdued.

I said, "Hey, you know I'm not suddenly going to disappear. I'm leaving my furniture here until the end of December, so I'll be back and forth. And you said you'd visit regularly. Now that you're single again you've no excuse. So no need for the long face."

"I know that, Kate, and of course I'll visit. That's not the issue."

"Well, then …?"

"Ella and I were wondering had you thought about attending Geoff's exhibition?"

"As a matter of fact, I have."

"And?"

"I can't make up my mind. One minute I say 'yes, I'll go' and the next I say 'no'. I don't need complications in my life. I've been hoping for divine guidance, a sign, but it hasn't come."

"For God's sake, what are you waiting for? Do you want Tinkerbell to tap your thick skull with her wand, or a hammer more like it? The sign came a fortnight ago when you spotted the poster in a café. What were the chances of that happening? That's what Carl Jung would call synchronicity."

"Strange all right." I pretended nonchalance. "Being in the right place at the right time sort of a thing, I suppose."

James practically wrung his hands. "You have to go, Kate. Don't you see, you travelled thousands of miles on a personal quest? And yet you're prepared to leave this question unanswered? Maybe he's the one."

"Hey, you warned me not to rush into a relationship after I left Trevor."

"That was then and this is now." James's eyes were pleading. "Maybe you'll just spend a few months dating. So what, if that's all it is – it could be good for you. It's just that we all think he sounds like a nice guy who needs you to give him a chance."

"Okay, okay! I'll go. But I might still decide to chicken out at the last minute."

As I drove through Dun Laoghaire, I was amazed to see my face staring back at me from posters in every shop window. The invite said seven, so I deliberately waited until after seven thirty to arrive at the Holland Gallery, in the hope I might remain unnoticed in the crowd. As I approached the door I could hear excited chatter rise above Enya's mystical music. Expensive perfumes mingled with the smell of oil paints, as the aroma of canapés and champagne tickled my nostrils. A middle-aged man of small build, salt-and-pepper hair and a neat moustache greeted me, dressed in a dinner suit. Judging by his demeanour, I assumed he must be the gallery manager.

"Ah, you're the famous Hekate! No need for you to show your invite," he chuckled, handing me a brochure with my picture on the cover. I sighed, accepting that there wasn't much hope of going unrecognised in this place since my image was plastered everywhere. Maybe I should have dyed my hair brown before coming?

I swept my eyes over the small crowd gathered in the outer room. Through an archway, I could see a large press of people thronging the main gallery where I presumed most of the paintings were hanging. I noticed Myra at the edge of the inner room, speaking to two well-dressed men. In an attempt to look goddessy, she'd donned a cream Grecian-style toga with a burnished torc around her neck and matching slave bracelet on her upper arm.

Thank heavens, there was no sign of Geoff. And Myra hadn't spotted me. A sign to the Ladies pointed up a narrow stairway on my left; even though I was only in the door, I was already in need of some respite.

Much to my relief there was nobody in the bathroom. I leaned against a sink and drew in a few deep, slow breaths. I hadn't expected to feel this nervous. Eager to look at the brochure, I flicked past the introduction to the paintings. I recognised Geoff's daughter Shannon, who was depicted as Persephone. And Aphrodite also looked like her, but was painted as more mature with chiselled cheekbones. I noticed Artemis's resemblance to Myra and on closer inspection I spotted that she was also the Hindu Goddess, Tara. Suddenly I felt a twinge of envy and immediately reprimanded myself for being ridiculous. Turning the page I studied Demeter, resplendent in golden robes amidst a fertile field of corn. I had to blink a few times before I realised she was me, with brown hair, fuller cheeks and a considerably larger bosom. So dying my hair wouldn't have worked after all, I thought, laughing out loud.

"It's the first sign of madness, you know, laughing or talking to yourself."

I jerked up my head – I'd been lost in a world of my own when the door opened. I blushed when I recognised the blonde teenager as Geoff's daughter.

She cracked a warm smile. "I'm Shannon, by the way." We simultaneously extended our hands for a handshake. Hers was firm and warm despite how fine boned she was.

"Hi Shannon, I'm Kate."

"I know. I wondered what you'd be like. Do you like your picture?"

"It's gorgeous. Very flattering."

"Come downstairs. I know Dad's looking forward to seeing you." My face must have betrayed my shock at her willingness to share her father with me, because she leaned forward as though sharing a secret. "To be honest, I hope you'll save him from the black widow's clutches!"

"Black widow?" I wondered was she referring to Myra.

"Never mind. She's no competition as Dad's already said he likes you. Come on down with me or you'll miss the party. Everyone wants to meet you." She placed her hands on my shoulders and turned me towards the door. As teenagers go, she was certainly a tour de force – tall and blonde as a Valkyrie with an attitude I'd never before encountered in all my years teaching her age group. As I descended the stairs, I caught sight of a young man with a magnificent dog standing near the door. With an immaculate white coat, shaded dove grey and anthracite in spots, it gave off the air of nobility which Geoff had captured so well in the painting. I went over to them.

"Hi ... I'm Kate. I love your dog." I bent to stroke the animal. From the corner of my eye, I was relieved to see Shannon disappear without me into the inner room.

"I'm Liam." The boy had slanted eyes in a flat face; he extended his hand for me to shake. "And this is Koda, the Indian name for wolf."

"Ah! You're Geoff's son."

"I paint too," Liam stammered shyly. "Do you?"

"I used to. Haven't done for a long time and certainly not as well as your dad does." Suddenly I was conscious of somebody standing behind me. I could smell his musky scent and my heart skipped a beat before I swung around to see Geoff's blue eyes looking intently into mine. A smiling Shannon stood nearby, after having obviously directed her father my way.

"Kate. I see you've met my family before we've had a chance to talk. Will you take a short walk with me?"

"Okay, but will your guests not miss you?"

"Just fifteen minutes to talk outside," he said to me, while simultaneously throwing a nod at Liam. "Back soon." The strong father-son bond was immediately obvious in the way they understood each other's glances.

Outside the air was chilly and I hadn't worn a coat over my favourite dress – an art deco patterned silk jersey number in swirly shades of teal, burnt orange and cream. Seeing me shiver, Geoff removed his tan suede jacket and placed it on my shoulders. "No, really, I don't need it." I handed it back to him; I didn't want him having any advantage over me given our previous misunderstanding.

"I'm so glad you came, Kate. You've no idea how much it means to me."

"You're right. I don't. I'm completely perplexed as to why you chose me to be one of your main subjects." I sounded unintentionally abrasive, yet I needed to hear his explanation.

"Kate, I haven't been able to get you out of my head since that day we spent together. That's what artists do. We convert our obsessions into art to try and make sense of them."

"But you told me you were heading back to Dublin to collect Liam that Saturday. Then I saw you with Myra on Sunday. What was I to think?"

"I know. That's why I sent you emails trying to explain but they all bounced back. And I tried calling you, to no avail. You've no idea what I've been through." He rubbed the back of his neck in an agitated manner. I resisted a strong urge to console him by wrapping my arms around him. No molly-coddling a man this time around, I reminded myself. The mothering thing doesn't work long term.

"Well, if you had been where you told me you'd be, the misunderstanding wouldn't have happened in the first place. And I found it very odd that you didn't tell me you were in

Galway when I rang on Sunday morning. Surely, I thought, if he's interested in me he'd have asked to meet me when I told him I was confused?"

"It all happened unexpectedly," he said. "My ex rang on Saturday morning to tell me she was taking Liam to see her parents in Drogheda, so there was no need for me to collect him. Then I got a text from Myra telling me she wanted to give me her late husband Joe's unused canvases, so I thought it was as good a time as ever to call and collect them since I was in Galway." He stopped to turn and face me. I also halted, expecting him to light a cigarette, but he didn't. "Myra was supposed to be on her way to the Oyster festival – she's been a committee member for the past two years. But when I called to her house, I found her in a state of shock, crying her eyes out. She's not normally like that, but she'd never gotten on with her husband's family and her mother-in-law had just been on the phone and said something nasty to her about not insisting Joe give up cigarettes after his diagnosis of lung cancer. Myra was inconsolable. He's only dead four months so it's still raw for her." Geoff glanced at me. "I've given the cigarettes up by the way." He waited, looking at me for a reaction before returning to the subject of his late friend. "Joe and I go way back as childhood friends, so I told her I'd stick around and go with her to the festival that day and the next."

"And there's nothing between you and her?" I asked. "I mean you've painted her quite a bit." I realised the ironic nature of my question given that he had painted me and put me on the cover of his brochure.

"Kate, I only know so many pretty women who carry themselves well. Myra happens to be one of them. I've advertised for sitters in the past, but the women who turn up are more suited to page three than art." He was smiling now and we both laughed. "As well as that, Myra is brilliant at public relations. She knows everyone in the art world and she kindly agreed to help me with this exhibition. But as for fancying her? No. She's not my type. Too poised and detached for me."

"Well, she seemed very possessive of you the day we met in the gallery and you looked very close to her that Sunday. And Shannon suggested something to me about her having you in her clutches."

His face flushed crimson and he stopped dead in his tracks. "You met Shannon for just a few minutes and she said all that? Well, why am I surprised? She can be just like her mother." He spat the words. "Sees and hears the grass growing and thinks she knows what's best for everyone. God, I'm sorry she said that Kate. I'll kill her."

"Please, Geoff, just tell me the truth. There is something going on between you and Myra, isn't there?"

"It was only a snog. I told you the truth about why I went to see her. Then you rang on Sunday morning to say you were confused after meeting your ex and I felt let down. It's not just women who get hurt when it comes to matters of the heart, Kate." His eyes were teary as he gave me a pleading look. I never knew what that word "snog" meant. Was it a kiss or was it much more?

"So the black widow welcomed you into her bed, no doubt?" I threw the bait out to see what he'd say.

"More like she tried to climb into mine – but that was after you rang, and it was over before it started with her." He added: "Her husband was my best friend."

I felt a flush of anger sweep over me to think how quickly he'd run to her after engaging with me on such a deep emotional level. "Oh my God. I knew it when I saw the two of you together." I started walking fast with the intention of crossing the street in the direction of the car park, but the traffic whizzed by without a break.

"Kate ... Kate." He grabbed my arm. "Please give me a chance. There's nothing between us apart from her setting up the exhibition. Joe asked me to mind her. That's why I stayed with her when she was upset." Breaking free of his grip at just the right moment, I made a quick sprint across the street. He followed and once again clamped my arm, tighter this time so I couldn't move. "Kate, it's all in her head. I care about you. Please come back to the exhibition with me."

I hesitated. "If you let go of my arm ... But don't think it means anything."

We walked another few yards before finding ourselves opposite the gallery. I thought about heading for my car but spotted Shannon waving across to us. If he was worth fighting for, then I had a powerful ally on my side. Geoff looked at me, an endearing smile on his face as he held his hand out to me. "Have I told you how much I love holding your hand?"

"No." I huffed, refusing to give him mine.

So instead, he placed his hand gently behind my back as we walked across the street towards the gallery where more guests were arriving. Red stickers had already appeared on nearly all of the paintings, denoting a reserve, and the gallery manager hurried over to us. "It's a sell out ... Unbelievable! I've never known this gallery get a crowd like it." Myra was also coming towards us, a disapproving look on her face. Geoff once again placed his hand on my back, this time as a gesture of reassurance. Throwing me a look of utter contempt, Myra linked her arm in his, trying to drag him away.

"Geoff, it's time we opened. People were starting to miss you." The manner in which she accented her vowels gave the impression she was a member of the Anglo-Irish ascendancy class. The posh accent was perfect for waxing eloquent on matters of art. I found her intimidating.

"No problem. We can start now," he said, bringing me through the crowd to the top of the main room.

"Kate!"

I swung around to see Ella and Billy. "What are you two doing here?"

"James rang me a few days ago to tell me you were coming and …" Ella started.

"… And I wanted to see Geoff's work so I contacted him through his website and wangled an invite. Aren't you pleased to see us?" Billy said, finishing her sentence as if they were an old married couple.

"The two of you?" I said, looking from one to the other.

Ella laughed and kissed me. "We've been going out since your party and we're getting on pretty fine so far. Happy days."

"How're you getting on with the artist?" Billy asked.

"So-so." I said, balancing my hand like a scales.

"Kate, he's mad about you," Ella gushed.

"How would you know?"

"We had coffee with him earlier today. Don't give me that look, Kate. Billy wanted first look at the paintings 'cos he needs some art for the café in the shop. When Geoff heard you were moving to Wicklow he started jumping for joy."

I shrugged. "The Myra situation is complicated."

"Oh, I know she's all over him like a bad rash, but it's obvious he can't stand her. He's too polite to tell her where to go." Then, wrapping a reassuring arm around my shoulders, she continued, "Ignore her, lovey – she's irrelevant!"

I was about to answer when Myra began hitting a gong to get the crowd's attention. I could understand Shannon's dislike of her now that I saw the possessive way she looked at Geoff. Her condescending attitude was at odds with the bohemian air she worked so hard to affect and the hardness of her jaw hinted at a ruthless streak.

When the room finally fell quiet, she spoke: "Ladies and gentlemen. You're all very welcome to Geoff Kelly's much anticipated exhibition on 'The Goddess'. This is his first major solo show and judging by the reaction here tonight it certainly won't be the last. Now please put your hands together to welcome the artist."

"Thank you, Myra. Ladies and gentlemen, you're all extremely welcome. I'm most grateful to you for leaving the warmth of your firesides to face the elements on a cold November night." He was obviously nervous, his shy blushes endearing, but the gentle laughter that ran around the room seemed to relax him. "Firstly, I want to thank all my Goddesses, some of whom were unwitting models." Yes, me, I thought, wondering what he would have done if I'd objected. He'd certainly taken a huge risk. "Thanks for being the women you are. I have to posthumously thank my late friend Joe Riordan for all his support. And a special thanks to his wife Myra for organising this. We miss you, Joe, but you're here in our hearts." The clapping that followed was controlled, reverential in its deliberate rhythm as Geoff wiped away a tear. He went on, "I'm going to talk to you about my fascination with contradictions or opposites and how they exist side by side like male and female. It's one of the reasons I love magical realism as an artistic genre, allowing me to combine the ordinary with the extraordinary.

"I chose Hekate as my poster girl." He smiled fleetingly at me. "Hekate has learned the gift of alchemy, whereby she can transform her life experience into the gold of wisdom. She knows that a life which has been truly lived is like a multi-coloured tapestry; its inherent flaws adding to its overall beauty. And that brings me back to contradictions; the Goddess is seen as an extraordinary woman, yet she is everywoman. Take Kate here!" He swept his hand over to where I was standing. Oh no! I hadn't expected to be singled out. "A beautiful woman who embodies the very essence of femininity and creativity while remaining grounded in reality." Clapping erupted with the odd suggestive whistle. He winked at me, setting my heart fluttering like a hummingbird. I blushed as I became conscious of several people throwing surreptitious glances in my direction. I was mortified by the attention and wished I'd stayed near the back of the room. "Kate is the person who inspired this exhibition. From our first encounter it was obvious that we shared a love of mythology but never before had I met someone who understood the significance of Goddess archetypes in the modern world. Kate was able to bring the myths to life for me, allowing me to see their rich symbolic meaning. As soon as that clicked with me, my art took on a new, more vibrant energy. That's the reason why I'm suddenly getting reviews like I never got before. To you, Kate, I owe my heartfelt gratitude."

Somebody started to clap, then a few more and soon a mad clatter of clapping threatened to lift the roof off the building. I just couldn't stop myself from smiling and laughing. I'm sure I must have looked like the cheesiest cat that ever got the cream. Well it's not every day a girl meets a gorgeous man who makes her the star of his show.

Epilogue

One year later ...

"*M*am, stop fussing and leave the food alone. It looks amazing, but you don't. You need to go upstairs and get ready right now."

"Okay, okay. As soon as I finish touching up the desserts." I was just about to refill the piping bag when she snatched it out of my hand.

"So much for your suggestion that we'd do a twenty-minute meditation before everyone arrived for the book launch. Not a hope in hell." Julie's tone was authoritative. "Get out and get ready now or you'll regret it when it comes to getting photographs taken."

"She's right, you know," Shannon chuckled from the doorway.

It was bad enough being bossed around by Julie, never mind Shannon chiming in. It was all very well for the pair of them, having had nothing else to do all day apart from dolling themselves up like super models. They had a point though. The press would be arriving soon and I'd be disgraced if they caught me looking like the wreck of the Hesperus while sneaking into the big house. It was great to have the use of a room here, so near the cookery school. Billy was magnanimous in opening his home to the world. Strange, I thought, for someone who was reared an only child. Personally, I was glad of the solitude the cottage afforded me.

As I showered, the plumbing choked and rattled from the amount of water used throughout the day. Floor boards groaned and creaked as everyone ran around pulling on their glad rags. I needed to keep an eye on the clock in order to get back downstairs ahead of time. After drying I pulled on my smalls. Well, no longer so small, after all the experimentation and food tasting. I looked in the full-length mirror at my more voluptuous figure encased in a vintage bias-cut dress in shades of copper and gold. Next I back-combed and tweaked my hair in different directions. On appraisal, I was pleased that my hair looked great, more natural than salon perfect. I was in the process of sliding into embroidered copper mules, when I heard a light tap on the door. "Come in."

The door opened. He locked it behind him and walked towards me.

"You look and smell good enough to eat." Geoff planted a kiss on my neck. "I've an idea?"

"What?"

"We keep the door locked. Then pretend there's no one here when they come looking for us. We can surely keep ourselves amused – right?" He traced his fingers along my neck as he spoke softly. The mere suggestion of intimacy with him caused desire to flush through every cell in my body, such was the delicious yet authentic nature of our love-making which could go on for hours on end. "Then when they're all getting sloshed because you've stood them up, we sneak down the fire escape and head for Dublin airport."

I laughed as he tickled my imagination with his zany

humour. Even when I was stressed he could make me loosen up and feel suddenly carefree, like we had a choice every minute of our lives either to conform or just go off like Percy and Mary Shelley had in the eighteen hundreds. At times we were like two naughty children, yet our love allowed us to respect each other as two separate selves coming together as one.

"How about heading for Buenos Aires and you read Borges to me each evening?" I said, before changing my tone to mock concern "But what if my publishers sue me for failing to turn up at my own launch?" Taking my hand and holding me at the waist, he leaned me backwards into a tango pose.

"We'll phone them after three weeks and tell them we've spent the advance so they'd better send us more money to get you home. What do you think?" he whispered in my ear as he brought me back up towards him.

"I think you're gorgeous and irresistible but we'd better be nice to everyone who's coming to meet us." I kissed him on the lips. "Later my love."

"Is that a promise?" Teasing me, he waved the key in front of me, alternating with hiding it behind his back.

"Yes, a promise. Now, please open the door."

"Here she is!" Ella announced as we came downstairs. The crowd clapped and cheered. After we'd greeted everyone fleetingly, Ella ushered us into the drawing room to have photographs taken. Some of the furniture had been removed to make the room more spacious. A display stand stood to the right of the baby grand piano, filled with several copies of my new cookery book.

Ella decided the order in which photographs were taken, telling each press photographer to take one of every frame as individual shots were set up. It was hard to believe how much had happened in the last year. I'd thought Ella was really tempting fate when she accepted Billy's offer of a management job while also dating him, but six months later she'd moved lock stock and barrel to live with him.

They were both incredibly gregarious and together they were a formidable team, bouncing business ideas off each other the way Geoff and I did with more dreamy creative stuff. Billy said we were like Yin and Yang; Geoff and I had the moon's Yin energy while he and Ella channelled the fiery Yang of the sun. Maybe he was right, because Geoff and I had taken things a bit slower, still living separately though we spent most of the week together.

Once the official photographs were over, it was time for more informal shots with friends and family. It had felt right standing with Geoff, Julie, Shannon, Liam and his dog Koda. My new family. Yet I had a twinge of regret for Trevor since he had been part of my life for so long and I occasionally worried about him being lonely. I'd invited him along but he'd said it wouldn't be his thing. No, that's how we'd always differed, each unable to find joy in the other's interests. It was right that we had gone our separate ways.

"Geoff," I said as our family photograph finished. "Tell everyone to start helping themselves to food from the trolley, will you?"

He clapped his hands above his head, announcing, "Right everyone. Food's here." Then he placed an arm around my mother as he led her over and started to serve her and my father. There was no doubt about it – he was a natural, the way he fitted so effortlessly in with my friends and family, getting everyone to relax and enjoy themselves.

James's cousin Maria came up to me. "Congratulations, Kate, you must be so proud of what you've accomplished."

"Yes, I'm thrilled. Thanks for coming, Maria – it means a lot to me to have you here." I placed my arm around her shoulder. It felt wonderful to have so many people I knew circulating and chatting with each other in this room. This was the key to my remaining calm – I was always relaxed with friends and family around.

"Kate, I've rounded up the journalists to chat and share a glass of wine with you." Ella steered me over to the seating area near the bay window. The book had already garnered great enthusiasm when early editions were sent out to food critics, so in effect the main bulk of the publicity work was already done, but Ella always wanted more.

"*Kate Bakes: Cooking with Love and Style.* Explain the title of your book," said a male journalist.

"The most important ingredient in cooking is to add a sprinkling of love. The nurturing instinct drives us, along with the desire to make our friends and family happy by cooking mouth-watering food. You know the way a mother wants to give her baby the most nourishing food because she loves her and she wants to see her thrive? And the way a woman seduces her lover with delicious, sensual food?" Geoff was across the room with Liam and I'd presumed he wasn't listening as the chatter level was high. On hearing my last sentence, however, he turned and flashed me a smile. I blushed and hurried on, "My book is not only full of gorgeous easy-to-follow recipes for all occasions, you'll also find simple prayers for blessing food, all from different spiritual traditions. Along with that, there are mantras for transmitting the energy of love to food. Remember Socrates said 'Let food be your medicine'. I believe food can heal us physically, emotionally and spiritually. The sharing of food can strengthen bonds between friends and families."

"There's a Buddhist or Hindu image on the back of the book," the youngest journalist butted in. "What's the significance of that?"

"She's called Quan Yin - the Buddhist Goddess of compassion. As a symbol she represents divine loving energy."

"Do you see yourself as the Food Goddess then?" a female journalist asked.

I laughed. "Thankfully, I've no such delusions. However, I believe the Goddess energy is alive and well in every woman and man who believes in love. Cooking with love is a good way to channel her." And, laughing again, I held my book up to the side of my face. "In other words buy *Kate Bakes* and do some cooking!"

"I love the stories and illustrations about Goddesses and food. What inspired that?" the second female journalist asked. Geoff arrived over to sit beside me, wrapping one arm around my waist. After a year, it still triggered the same tingling up my spine. I asked him to tell the reporter about the Goddess sketches and how we worked on creating food stories for each of the Goddesses mentioned in the book. The two female journalists were transfixed by him as he spoke. Geoff had an incredible effect on women. Quite simply, every female from two years of age to ninety was putty in his hands. Initially it made me feel very insecure to be with a man who had that kind of magnetism until I realised he was quite oblivious to it. Well maybe not totally oblivious, as he was well able to turn it on when he wanted to sell a painting. But in reality he regarded unsolicited female attention as quite annoying, knowing there was nothing deep or meaningful to it.

My eye was drawn to movement outside the window. I asked to be briefly excused, leaving Geoff to keep the journalists entertained as I headed outside in search of James, who was walking Liam's husky. "Koda's a stunning animal, isn't he?" I said, bending down to stroke the dog's luxuriant mane.

"He seems really fond of you," said James, as Koda nuzzled close to me.

"He's like family since Geoff has him so often," I said, caressing the dog. Then standing up to my full height, I asked, "What do I and Billy have to do, to persuade you to join us here? I've told you how much I need you."

"I've already told you – get me a man, darling."

"You'd be spoilt for choice if you worked here. I mean anyone can turn up at the Lifestyle store … Sorry, emporium." I'd forgotten it had been re-christened the "Heritage Emporium". "James, the café is more like a restaurant. It's so popular at weekends. Not to mention some of the gorgeous men who come on our shorter cookery courses. Did you meet the Italian guy, Lorenzo?"

"No good, he's straight."

"You're joking me! I must be losing my gaydar."

"A sure sign you're no longer looking at men. You've got it bad, Kate."

"You know, I think you're right. I miss Geoff when I'm not with him and it's like everything that happens, I can't wait to share with him. I don't think I've ever felt like this before."

"Will you still say that once you're famous?" I felt Geoff's arm around my waist. I hadn't heard him creep up from behind – I'd been watching Ella steering the journalists out to see the Heritage Emporium.

"Of course I will." Was it possible he felt insecure? "You know when we were joking earlier about going away? Well I hadn't time to tell you but my agent is planning an international tour for early next year." His face fell but he made an effort to smile for my benefit. I asked softly. "So are you coming with me as my partner?"

His eyes widened. "Is that a proposal of some sort?"

"Yes, I suppose it is. Heck we are partners. Why not formalise it and move in with me?"

"I thought you'd never ask," he said, sweeping me off my feet to twirl me around and plant a kiss on my lips. I hadn't anticipated how great the idea of him as my partner would feel. I wanted to smother him in kisses but we had to settle for mutual grinning and giggling instead as our eyes conveyed the intensity of our heartfelt feelings.

"Well, if that's the case you're going to need a really good cookery teacher to take your place while you tour the world," James said, interrupting our lovers' gaze.

"Oh James – really? You mean it?"

"Yes, Kate. I'll join you after Christmas."

"You two. Sometimes, I don't know who I love more," I cried, wrapping my arms around both of them. I could have included all my family and friends in that statement, such was my intense feeling of joy. I would never have dreamed life could be as wonderful with family and friends as it had been that day on the mountain. The level of contentment I now enjoyed was beyond my wildest dreams – so far from where I had been when I had first set out on my journey. I hadn't discovered the Holy Grail and nothing had happened instantaneously. Rather it was the slow realisation that only *I* had the answers to what made me happy and once I'd begun to tap into that, everything else followed.

Acknowledgements

$\mathcal{I}$ am most grateful to all who encouraged and supported me during the writing of this book.

Thank you to my wonderful children, Mark, Janet and Emily for brightening up my life, always loving my stories and making allowances for me throughout the writing process.

Thank you Ferdia Mac Anna for patiently mentoring me and telling me I had a gift for writing comedy. That was the best thing you could have told me: - Ferdia you are a gem. Much thanks to Vanessa O'Loughlin at Inkwell Writers Group who guided me every step of the way. Thanks to my copy editor Helen Falconer – there would be no book had you not been so encouraging at that crucial end stage.

Thanks to my parents Joe and Breedge Mc Farland who gave me loving support and provided me with a retreat whenever I was exhausted from long hours of writing. I am also grateful for the encouragement received from my sisters Paula and Lynda Mc Farland.

Thanks to former politician Mary O'Rourke for entering me in an essay competition while she was my history teacher. Seeing my winning essay in print gave me the first seed of hope that I could one day be a writer. Many years later, a novel writing course facilitated by the beautiful and talented Valerie Blumenthal gave me the confidence to pursue that dream.

I am blessed to have many wonderful Goddess friends:
First and foremost I have to thank Mary F, for being my rock of support – Mary you are the Goddess I aspire to be.

Thanks to my college pal Carolyn O'Louglin who is a wizard at working the law of attraction to benefit others in the most generous way possible. Constance Harris for her insight and encouragement every step of the way; you truly are as nurturing as the Goddess Demeter. Shelley Murphy for her support, humour and optimism.

Friends and neighbours Mary O'Halloran and Elizabeth O'Halloran for providing much needed artistic encouragement. To my loyal and trusted friend Pauline Grenham, who always offers practical advice. To Carmel Foley who embodies the Goddess in her wisdom and humour.

Thanks to Mary Mc Cann and Denise Mc Cann for being unconventional women in the manner Clarissa Pinkola Estes urges us to be. To Selina Brennan who loves the Goddess principle as much as I do.

Thanks to Ann Farrell and Cathy Hughes for Goddess fun and Kathleen O'Donnell for your prayers and good wishes.

Thank you Debbie Williams for walking so gracefully into my life one day in Coole Park accompanied by your gorgeous dog Koda – your image inspired the latter part of my book and I simply had to give Koda a starring role. Thank you to the women and men who accompanied me on my travels through South America. And special thanks to the wonderful and generous Healer and all at the ashram in Brazil – your work continues to benefit me in so many ways.

Thanks also to the women who provided me with stories of internet dating, but for obvious reasons do not wish to be named.

Thank you to the men who believed in me, the Goddess and this book;

My good friend Inigo Batterham along with Val O'Halloran and Fergal Geraghty who each told me I was a writer long before I believed it myself. Thank you Jason O'Shaughnessy for sharing your extraordinary story of healing and allowing me believe that miracles do happen.

Thanks to all my Twitter and Facebook friends for your words of encouragement. And finally, a special and sincere thanks to my ex husband for the love and the lessons we shared. We remain united in loving our children.

In lak'ech,

Mary Elizabeth

Supportive website: - www.goddessmeca.com

Mary Elizabeth Coen assists the Goddess through sharing my love of cookery, fashion, mythology and blogs.

My website was set up to complement this book. Since my main character is a cookery teacher there are a lot of food references throughout the novel. You can find all of these recipes on my website to download free of charge.